I0725194

Return Engagement

Return Engagement

**A Serialized Novel by
Wesley Adams and Daphne McGee**

Book 10 of the Soap Opera Inspired Story Collection
Series Created by Gary Brin

Episodes 1-14

Series Finale

Standish Press

The serialized story in this novel is fiction. Real persons, geographical locations, books, television shows, films, music, and specific events mentioned or which appears as part of the multi-character ensemble in this story were dramatized for entertainment purposes only and have no actual connection to fictional characters and created storylines in this book or reflects upon actual reality of things that may have happened previously or of which seems somewhat similar to real-life situations.

Names of real people mentioned in this book are in bold letters.

Select comments by fictional characters in this novel about historical figures, true crime cases, and, or pop culture icons are based on fact and additional information can be found online in reputable sites as well as numerous published books.

This book features a character from the 1912 novel *The Lost World* by Arthur Conan Doyle. This alternative storyline exists only within the pages of *Return Engagement* and shouldn't be considered a sequel to the 1912 novel.

Several characters from the novels *Glass Owl*, *Desperate Lives*, *Thomas Nix*, *Ocean Landing*, *Games People Play*, *Ocean Landing Dangerous Games*, *Marble Hills* and *Virgin Islands* appear in this book as part of the continuing storyline. The serialized novels stated above are original publications from Standish Press and are part of the Soap Opera Inspired Story Collection Series.

Cover photograph courtesy of Pexels Stock Images.
Cover photograph was digitally enhanced and visually altered for this edition.
Cover design and book layout © 2025 by Standish Press

FIRST EDITION

Copyright © 2025 by Standish Press

All rights reserved. No part of this book may be reproduced by any means whatsoever without written permission from the publisher.

For more information about reprint rights please visit
www.standishpress.com

ISBN—978-1-945510-18-2

MANUFACTURED IN THE UNITED STATES OF AMERICA

This serialized novel mentions a well-known former child star named Bobby Driscoll several times throughout the book as part of the storyline in the conclusion of the *Soap Opera Inspired Story Collection Series*. Driscoll had a promising future as an actor until it was taken from him by horrible people who cared more about making money than being decent human beings. Although the storyline about a film being made about his life is fictional—the details mentioned in this novel about what happened to him in the years leading up to his death in 1968 are factual. It should be noted that Driscoll's story is just one of hundreds about child actors from Hollywood's golden age and the abuse they suffered at the hands of cruel industry executives who saw children only as employees to be repeatedly exploited without concern for the damage inflicted upon those they depended to turn a profit.

A real friend is someone who stands by you in both good times and bad—not just when it benefits them.

Contents

Intro

The series finale for the Soap Opera Inspired Story Collection Series is titled *Return Engagement*. The story is featured in multiple geographic locations—many of which have been used as a backdrop for earlier novels in the series. Like previous novels in the collection—the story exists only in the pages of the series—not reality. But like earlier novels in this series many of the locations mentioned do exist. With the exception of certain fictional names used—all other geographic locations stated as backdrops for the story are real and can be found by using Google. As with other published titles in the Soap Opera Inspired Story Collection Series—characters from other books will make appearances as part of the concluding storyline to resolve plotlines that were left unresolved previously.

In creating the final book for the Soap Opera Inspired Story Collection Series—the idea was to follow several storylines from previous books in the series with the intent to wrap up some select events that were left incomplete. Nevertheless *Return Engagement* was specifically written to resemble traditional classic soap operas of the past to a certain extent—and was written with the intention that it's playing to a visual audience and therefore will emulate a scripted format used primarily for television—rather than the usual storytelling methods displayed in popular full-length episodic crime novels such as *Black Widow* by Christina Crawford and *Against the Law* by Michael Eberhardt. It should also be noted that each episode of this series were written in a brief span of 6-12 days or less and therefore shouldn't be confused with being great literature. The goal of this serialized series of books was simply to mimic episodes of prime time soaps of years past—by creating visual entertainment on a printed page—and not to create a masterpiece of great literature.

The present storyline in *Return Engagement* takes place about a year after the events in *Virgin Islands* and *Marble Hills* concluded. Several of the characters from previous novels in the Soap Opera Inspired Story Collection Series are featured in this story in order that unresolved storylines from the previous nine novels in the series could be concluded in a satisfactory way.

Gary Brin
Series Creator

In an effort to have an accurate portrayal of the dialogue used for the *Soap Opera Inspired Story Collection Series* people were anonymously observed in shopping malls, schools, places of employment, and on public streets in order to capture a definitive portrayal of how people of various ages and cultures interacted and talked to each other when they thought no one was listening. While some select dialogue was exaggerated for dramatic purposes when needed—the manner and tone of which people were observed speaking to each other in casual and private conversations is accurate. Exact wording was not copied verbatim for the most part, but the way certain types of topics and conversations are addressed by characters in this serialized series is based on actual situations that were observed over a period of several dozen years.

Prologue

1
Three Years Before

A man plows through thick smoke blanketing a hallway on an expensive yacht. As he runs through the smoke his rage gets the better of him while he appears to be looking for someone. He stops several times as he seems unsure of where to go. He calls out again but hears nothing. He curses loudly as he begins running along a hallway while flames leap out at him from the paneling on the walls. Several pieces fall in front of him as the fire continues to spread—but he continues calling out to someone he can't see. As he runs further he sees someone coming toward him and seems poised to shoot—until he realizes it is someone he knows—a member of his crew. Someone he can trust.

2

"I want him dead. Do you hear me? I want that wretched excuse for a human being dead. He must pay for what he did."

The man standing before him shakes his head and seems to agree. He looks at the gun being pointed at him and sighs.

"Give me the gun. I'll take care of it. I know where that weasel is hiding. Saw him a few seconds ago. I'll even the score for you. Just give me the gun—leave it up to me. Trust me."

They look at each other for a few seconds.

"No—I want to take him out myself. I want to see the look on his face as I point my gun at his temple and let loose."

There is an uneasy silence between them that seems to last for hours—but in reality takes place less than one minute.

"He has a gun—he showed it to me."

He watches as the old man reacts to what was just said.

"He has a gun? He told me he didn't like guns."

His hand seems to tremble. The younger man notices and waves his hand in the air. He seems pleased for some reason.

"He lied. He has several awards for marksmanship."

The old man looks at the gun in his hand again.

"He has to die—no one insults me and gets away with it especially after he was warned to be on his best behavior."

He watches as the man standing in front of him reaches for the gun. He reluctantly lets go of it. He sighs loudly. As the gun changes hands he notices the odd smile on the other man's face as the gun is handed over. They look at each other again.

3

"Uh-huh—just as I said. He's by the stairwell. He's an absolute mess. He will be taken out with his own gun."

He listens as laughter echoes from his cell phone.

"Where is his wife? How should I know? She's probably servicing her latest thrill. They've been hitting the sheets plenty. I got pictures—pretty explicit. I sent you some earlier."

He laughs slyly and gestures.

"Uh-huh—that's right. Look in your folder. That chick sure knows how to please a man—keep his penis doing back flips."

He laughs again and glances at the hallway.

"I've got to go—got to find our stalwart assassin—seems she's taken a fancy to her target's teenage son—playing him."

He rolls his eyes as he hears loud yells coming from his phone and turns away. He seems annoyed and sighs loudly.

"She's an adult. It's not my job to keep tabs on who she's playing house with. She has a penchant for college guys."

He runs his fingers through his hair.

"Don't worry. She'll take the old man out as planned. No one will be the wiser after the fact. It'll look like an accident."

He grimaces as loud yells come through his cell phone again. Flames can be seen in a distance. He seems nervous.

"I've got to go. I'll call you later."

He nods a few times and looks at the hallway as flames seem to be growing. He begins running toward a stairwell a few feet ahead and sees two people coming toward him in a panic.

4

He looks at the thick smoke permeating the hallway as he reaches the far end of the yacht. As he turns to look at the huge blaze engulfing the front end of the yacht two people run toward him in a panic as several collapsing beams fall around them.

"What happened?"

"How the hell should I know?"

"What's with the attitude buddy?"

Smoke seems to permeate the area as silence engulfs the couple standing by the stairwell. The other man is gone.

"Where did that jerk go?"

The woman shrugs and peers through the thick smoke as screams are heard in a distance. They quickly make their way down a narrow stairwell as smoke seems to be everywhere.

A Brief Look at the First Episode

Unrelated events occur in the lives of several people in multiple locations while two unrelated situations in San Francisco threaten a powerful family as secrets from the past begin unraveling.

Homecoming

1
Pacific Coast Highway
Present Day

"I thought I made it clear earlier. It's over."

Roland O'Brien seems irritated as he stares at his cell phone. He watches as Marianne Singleton starts to cry.

"I said I was sorry."

Roland seems about to explode.

"So you say."

"It just happened. It meant nothing to me."

"Did it? You and that lowlife played house for several weeks before I caught you coming out of a motel on Second."

Roland shakes his fist at the cell phone.

"I thought we had something. You knew how seriously I take relationships. I never strayed—never even attempted."

Roland runs his fingers through his hair.

"You played me—made me look like a fool to the entire town. Everyone knew but me—people gossiped for weeks."

Marianne shakes her head knowingly and sighs.

"It wasn't my fault Roland—I'm sorry."

Roland runs his fingers through his hair again.

"You're sorry you got caught—you're not sorry you spread your legs for that miserable excuse of a human being."

He shuts his cell phone off and sighs.

2
Santa Barbara

"Did that shameless coward say why—or give a reason?"

Marlisa Vigaro seems irritated as she turns to look at the beach a few hundred yards away. She stifles a brittle laugh.

"I'm sure you're right—must be something else in it for him other than money if he was willing to throw everything I offered away. I certainly hope what they offered was worth it."

Marlisa angrily clenches her fist.

"Loren Fawcett is going to pay. I assure you."

She seems upset and sighs loudly.

"He'll pay dearly for costing me this deal. He and his father both. They think they've won but I'm not going to let it go."

She glances at a copy of a recent newspaper lying on top of a coffee table several feet away. She gestures briefly.

"Uh-huh—exactly. Loren Fawcett. He played me for a fool for months until he got what he wanted. But the end to that story is still in play I assure you. I've got something really nasty planned for dear Loren. Something that lousy bastard won't forget."

She begins giggling as she looks at her cell phone while she pulls the sliding glass door to the balcony shut. She stops.

"I think I'm gonna start with his people. See who he considers most valuable. Once I know I'll act—retaliate."

Marlisa shakes her head and grimaces.

"He will be in for a rude awakening shortly. His nightmare is just starting—guaranteed to be terribly unpleasant."

She glances at the newspaper once more.

"This was just one of many chess pieces in my quest to destroy Loren Fawcett's life—I won't stop until I get even."

She looks at the woman on the video screen.

"Uh-huh—nothing will stop me from getting revenge on that cruel bastard—I'll destroy anyone who gets in my way."

She glances at the newspaper again.

3
Honolulu

Carmen Pendleton looks at the paperwork in front of her and seems irritated. She turns around to face Natalie Abdul.

"I'm going to crucify that miserable slut."

Natalie looks at the paperwork again and shrugs.

"She played her role well."

"That worthless piece of Texas white trash is gonna regret tangling with me. I'm *so* going to enjoy making her pay."

Natalie reaches for a cell phone on her desk. She faces Carmen and sighs. They look at each other for a few seconds.

"I checked her phone records earlier—seems she placed numerous calls to someone in San Francisco—Loren Fawcett."

Carmen reacts to the name.

"Get Randolph Gregory on the line."

Natalie nods in agreement.

4
Orchid Bay
Wolper Beach Condo

"Forget your father—he's a selfish brute."

Sarina Wolper pulls Jason Shappe toward her and smiles as his erection brushes against her naked waist. He laughs.

"You'd think I killed someone the way he's been treating me. So what if I slept with his girlfriend. What's the big deal?"

Sarina slides her finger across Jason's erection and pulls him toward her again. She giggles as he winks at her and kisses her neck. They look at each other for a few seconds. He sighs.

"Maybe we should just move to Santa Barbara."

Sarina gives Jason a knowing look and watches as his fingers glide across her breasts. He looks at her and winks.

"I hear Santa Barbara is nice this time of year."

Seconds later he aggressively penetrates Sarina.

"I'll think about it."

She strokes his hair as he continues to ram her.

"In the meantime I think you should consider getting a place of your own—probably a studio apartment or loft."

Jason looks at Sarina curiously.

"How would I pay for it?"

Sarina pulls away from Jason.

"I'll pay for it—at least until you figure things out."

Jason seems upset and shrugs.

"Is this your way of saying you're tired of me?"

Sarina wags he finger at Jason.

"What would ever give you that idea?"

She watches his reaction.

"I just think it would be better if you had a place of your own. I'm fully aware you're a sexually active young man—I'm not stupid—I know your rep in this town—people talk plenty."

Jason grins slyly.

"I offer no apologies for my actions."

Sarina licks her lips.

"I would never want you to apologize. But nevertheless I think it would be easier if you had a place to bring the latest flavor that catches your attention—starting with Mara Steffington."

Jason stifles a laugh.

"She made a pass at me at the mall—made me an offer I couldn't refuse—left no doubt she knows her way around men."

Sarina rolls her eyes in disgust.

"That bitch is shameless. She probably took lessons from Vina Phamler—those two are one in the same—*ugh*—gross."

Jason looks at his exposed penis.

"Her tongue is a weapon—made me weak."

Sarina seems disgusted and climbs out of the bed. She turns to face Jason with a warning look. She gestures briefly.

"That's exactly why I think it would be best if you had your own place—I haven't and wouldn't think of dictating who you should or shouldn't get friendly with. You're a grown man and can make your own decisions concerning sexual activity."

Jason climbs out of bed.

"I see your point."

They look at each other.

5
Orchid Bay
Spring Street Diner

"Have you spoken to Vera Holliday today?"

Daniel Brandt seems confused as he looks at Zarina Fuertes sitting across from him inside a diner facing a garden.

"I spoke with her last night. She said Warren Copley has been really helpful in getting her access to her father's estate."

"Is she planning to move to Los Angeles?"

"She didn't say. I assume."

Zarina seems upset.

"Everyone knows about her sordid history with men—that woman has no fans in Orchid Bay. She's made plenty people angry—wrecked her ex-husband's life—slept with a killer."

Zarina gives Daniel a sharp look.

"I haven't forgotten what happened a month ago with you and Loretta Osborne either. She knows I know her deal."

She pulls a strand of hair away from her face.

"Loretta Osborne is even more trouble than Vera Holliday ever could be. That said I'd prefer you stay away from Vera. Let some other guy deal with her problems—someone gay."

Daniel glances at his cell phone.

"You know I can't do that. It's part of my job."

Zarina takes a sip of tea and grimaces.

"I know it's your job to represent her—know you need to have clients—but I just wish it wasn't Vera. I don't like her."

Zarina sighs and gives Daniel a warning look.

Page **21**

"If you stray again—we're through. No more chances Daniel. I won't be in a forgiving mood like I was with Loretta."

Daniel reacts and turns away.

6
Orchid Bay
Clerke Apartment

"I don't like you talking to that woman. She's still after you—wants you back in her bed—keeping her company."

Kayla Larsen jabs Patrick Clerke several times. He shuts off his cell phone. He wags his finger at her and laughs.

"Vina Phamler isn't trying to get into my pants—she knows my deal—I'm with you—end of story. She just wanted my advice on something—knew I wouldn't lie to her. That's all."

"Uh-huh—and I was born yesterday. I know her deal—she wants to break us up—said as much to Jan McDaly yesterday."

Patrick laughs again and pulls Kayla toward him.

"I'm yours—yours only."

Kayla reaches out to stroke Patrick's hair.

"Please don't cheat on me Patrick—I couldn't handle knowing that you bedded someone else. It would destroy me."

"I've always been true to you Kayla—never even thought of skipping around since we officially became a couple."

Kayla wipes a tear from her eye.

"I can't help how I feel Patrick—I love you."

Patrick gently reaches out to hold Kayla's hand.

"I know you love me—said as much when you stood up to your father and told him if he ever hurt me you'd never speak to him again—made it clear that day—left no doubt whatsoever."

Kayla wipes another tear from her eye.

"My dad likes you—a little anyway."

Patrick laughs loudly.

"Well, that's a start. I guess I don't have to buy a plot at Falling Pines at the moment—at least not for another month."

Kayla jabs Patrick and stifles a laugh.

Page **22**

"I told you, you've got nothing to worry about concerning my dad wanting to cemetery you—he's all bark and no bite."

Patrick looks at his cell phone again and sighs.

"I've got to call Vina."

Kayla shoots him a warning look.

"Can't she ask someone else for advice?"

Patrick shakes his head.

"All her friends are lairs."

Kayla rolls her eyes knowingly.

7

San Francisco

"Who the hell is Trevor Boleyn? How rich is he?"

Houghton Fawcett turns to look at his son and seems irritated. He clenches and unclenches his fist several times.

"How come I never heard of that fucker before?"

Loren Fawcett shakes his head.

"I have no idea. He apparently just showed up on our radar two days ago. Made a play for our stock—bought a huge chunk of it from what it looks like—probably European is my guess."

Houghton seems about to explode.

"I don't give a fuck about where's he's from. I want him dealt with immediately. I won't tolerate his antics—won't allow him to buy one more piece of stock. I want him dead."

Loren stands and faces his father.

"Where would we start? He's everywhere and nowhere at the same time. No one has anything—knows even less."

Houghton slams his fist on top of his desk.

"I didn't get where I am by waiting for things to happen. Have you forgotten what befell the Whitney brothers? Had one rubbed out and imprisoned the other—destroyed them."

He begins laughing hysterically.

"How is dear old Todd doing anyway? Is he enjoying his accommodations? How about his sweet young daughter—Anton has been relentless—made her his prized personal whore."

Page 23

Loren makes a lewd gesture with his hand.

"Todd Whitney is a shell of his former self. He knows his days are numbered the minute you give the word—fears it."

Houghton burst out laughing and stands. He grins.

"He made threats—I had to act. Had to make sure he knew I'm not the kind of man he should casually threaten."

Houghton points at Loren and smirks.

"Upon realizing I ordered his brother and his family killed in the Bahamas—Whitney's spirit was broken beyond repair."

He waves his hand in the air.

"Of course there's that issue with his precious daughter being repeatedly raped by Anton. From what Lizette said when Todd was told his daughter and Anton had become sexually involved he had a meltdown. Lost it—made a lot of threats."

Houghton seems amused and stifles a smirk.

"Lizette said she had to remind Whitney making threats against me was a mistake since I controlled whether he lived or died. She went as far as to suggest he beg me for mercy—pledge his loyalty to yours truly or suffer the same fate his bother did in the Bahamas. Said he told her to fuck off and continued to make vile threats against me despite the precarious situation of him being in a locked room with no means of escape—*idiot*."

Loren runs his fingers through his hair.

"Whitney's daughter has been dutifully servicing Anton quite nicely. He has an insatiable sexual appetite where that girl is concerned—shown no mercy. Uses her like a cheap prostitute."

Houghton laughs loudly again.

"I always liked that boy. He stops at nothing to get what he wants. He made it clear to me several years ago he wanted to get between that girl's legs—said he'd get her—achieved his goal no doubt. I assume when he tires of her he'll put a bullet in her head and toss her corpse into San Francisco Bay. Certainly wouldn't be the first time he's discarded one of his conquests by throwing their lifeless body into the ocean—to each his own I guess. Maybe I'll have her father watch her bon voyage."

Loren seems upset about something. He gestures.

Page **24**

"Why is Todd Whitney still alive? It's no secret that Anton wants to kill him with his bare hands. Said as much for over a year now—wants revenge for a past slight—of which I understand."

Houghton seems irritated and shrugs.

"I have my reasons for keeping Whitney alive. He's my captive and he knows it. I enjoy the power I have over his life. But that said I'm aware of Anton's desire to kill Whitney. I assure you when I decide Whitney's fate Anton will have his revenge."

He laughs and seems pleased.

"You can tell him that if you feel like it."

Loren glances at his cell phone.

"Anton's anger toward Whitney has been getting the best of him in the last few months. He's been taking his frustrations out on Bridget Whitney daily. According to our security tapes he's raped her multiple times this week already. I assume he intends to kill her shortly. I've seen this pattern with him in the past."

"She's Anton's girl—his alone—he can do with her what he chooses to. If he kills her in a fit of rage after fucking her—so what? Last time I checked she's just a whore—worth nothing."

Loren runs his fingers through his hair once more.

<h1 style="text-align:center">8</h1>

Orchid Bay
Pioneer Trail Mall

"I'm *so* tired of that man stealer. Ever since she came back from Europe she's been causing trouble everywhere she goes."

Vina Phamler turns around to face Tim Bergman as he opens the door to his car. She appears visibly annoyed.

"Did you hear what I said about that woman? She's been a serious thorn in my side ever since she came back last year."

Tim waves his hand in the air. He seems upset.

"How about we talk about something else?"

Vina becomes enraged and grabs Tim's arm.

"She needs to know her place."

Tim jerks free of Vina's menacing grip.

Page 25

"What are you going to do about it Vina? Shame her for catching Patrick in her web? Face it—she bested you royally."

"That wretched slut didn't best me."

"Kayla Larsen is not a slut. Patrick is the only guy she's ever slept with. I made a play for her as you recall—on your orders. She rejected me—said she had a guy—didn't want me."

Vina makes a gagging gesture with her finger and grabs her cell phone. She turns to face Tim again and smirks.

"According to my cousin, Kayla isn't as innocent as she claimed. I have it good authority she danced between the sheets with a rich French guy she met when she was in Europe."

"Are you seriously taking cues from your cousin? Have you forgotten what she did to you last year? Embarrassed you in front of everyone at the beach by telling anyone who would listen to her that you went down on Tara Charney's uncle—seriously that guy is like a hundred—*ugh*—old—insulted you publicly."

"Steve Charney isn't a hundred—he's forty-three."

"I thought you said your cousin lied about you and that old man? You said she made the whole thing up to spite you."

Vina gives Tim a knowing look and smirks.

9
San Francisco

Houghton seems pleased with himself as he leans back in his chair. He looks out the window at San Francisco Bay when a slight movement catches in his eye. Seconds later he sees a reflection of a teenage girl staring back at him from a mirror.

"Storm clouds are forming."

Less than a second later Tiffany Johnson stands a few feet away. She takes a step forward. Houghton backs away. As Tiffany slowly approaches he seems panicked. She grins broadly.

"You and I have unfinished work to attend to."

He glances at his cell phone.

"I'm not in the mood to play games."

"Who said you had a choice."

Page **26**

He reaches for the cell phone. Without warning it bursts into flames seconds later. He turns to face her in shock.

"That phone cost me two thousand dollars."

Tiffany takes another step ignoring his comment.

"As I was saying before I was rudely interrupted. We have unfinished work that needs addressing—starting with Ralph."

Houghton reacts to his son's name.

"Ralph? What about him?"

"It seems not everything was what it seemed concerning how he met his demise—plenty of unanswered questions."

They stare at each other.

10
Boston

"I'll call you tomorrow or I'll have my assistant call before ten-thirty or eleven. It's the best I can do at the moment."

Trevor Boleyn nods and stands up.

"I appreciate it. Thanks for listening to me."

Jeremy Winterfield watches Trevor walk to the door. As the door opens he sees Jessica Monet standing in the doorway.

"I came as soon as I could—terrible traffic. Sorry if I inconvenienced you in any way this morning. I'm really sorry."

Jessica and Trevor smile at each other and then Jessica walks toward Jeremy. They look at each other. Jessica sighs.

"Was I interrupting anything?"

Jeremy gestures with his hand several times.

"No—he was hoping I could help out with something he's been dealing with lately—reclaiming business assets."

He seems amused as Jessica glances out at the Boston skyline and takes in the view for a few seconds. He smiles.

"Hard to believe this was once a quaint little town with only a few houses—maybe a few ships in the harbor as well."

"I didn't know you were such a history buff—never even thought for a second you might be into New England history."

Jeremy grins broadly and gestures.

"Read every book I could if you must know."

Jessica comes toward his desk. He glances at a folder in his hand. He smiles and hands it to her. She takes the folder.

11
Orchid Bay
Pioneer Trail Mall

"What does he have that I don't?"

Adam Mills glares angrily at Tabitha Bairstow.

"He's nice to me. Something you're not."

"He's using you."

"So says you."

He watches as she glances at her cell phone.

"It's over between us. Deal already."

Tabitha continues looking at her cell phone as Adam watches her go. He pounds his fist against the fender of his car.

"I'm gonna teach that lousy girlfriend-stealing punk what happens when someone crosses me. He's gonna get it."

He turns around and grins.

"Kyle Derringer is gonna regret messing with me."

Adam laughs and then stops suddenly.

"Once I fix Kyle I'll have Tabitha."

He looks at his erection straining against his faded Levi's and looks at Tabitha again as she stops to talk to a few friends.

"I have no intention of letting Derringer make a fool of me by flaunting his charming college-graduate good-guy image."

He clenches his fist again and sighs loudly.

12
Orchid Bay
Cane Bridge Park

Denise Stone seems pleased as she pays a taxi driver and faces the park. She grins broadly as she notices a young man looking out to sea. Denise licks her lips and walks toward him.

Page **28**

"Excuse me—can you tell me where I can find."

The young man turns around and Denise seems surprised to see Ryan Pena staring back at her. She sighs loudly.

"The years have certainly been good to you Ryan."

Ryan reacts with a sly grin.

"Denise Stone?"

She nods and acknowledges him.

"How have you been doing?"

Ryan gestures with his hand and grimaces.

"Erica Gersh and I just split."

Denise reaches out to touch his arm.

"You're too good for her. You deserve better."

Ryan seems upset and turns away.

"She caught me in bed with her best friend."

Denise seems about to laugh.

"Is that all?"

"That's what I said. It happened."

Denise takes a step forward.

"It's her loss—not yours—forget her."

Ryan shoots Denise a curious look. She reaches out to stroke his arm. He notices. She winks slyly at him and laughs.

"I recall you telling me back in the day you didn't want to get married on account you wanted to move to Seattle and focus on college. I assumed you would've left town already."

Ryan grimaces as he wrings his hands.

"I got Alicia Virella pregnant. It happened right after I became unemployed on account of that nutjob Harley Steyton killing Brent Noguchi and burning his diner down. We started seeing each other and one thing led to another and we made a baby girl together. I wanted her to abort it but she refused."

Denise strokes Ryan's arm again.

"Harley Steyton made a mess of things in Morro Bay too. I heard he took a leap off the cliff at Banning Point last year."

Ryan waves his hand in the air.

"It served him right after what he did."

Denise leans closer to Ryan.

"What happens now?"

Ryan runs his fingers through his hair.

"I got an apartment this morning. I'm so screwed at the moment with Erica. She's not in a good mood—pissed."

Denise stifles a laugh.

"What about her friend?"

"They're not talking right now from what I know. Erica is on the warpath. Janet Virella had better watch her back."

Denise seems surprised and laughs.

"You banged Mark Virella's other daughter?"

Ryan gestures with his hand once more.

"It was a one night stand sort of deal—no strings."

Denise rolls her eyes.

"Sort of the deal we had."

Ryan laughs loudly.

"Uh-huh—exactly like what happened to us in the parking lot of Brent's Diner. We met—we fucked. No strings."

Ryan gives Denise a curious look.

"I heard you were in prison for breaking into your ex's house if I recall. People talked for weeks about what you did."

Denise seems upset and gestures.

"I'll just bet they did."

She licks her lips and sighs.

"I just got out. I'm all alone. I've got nothing—no one."

Ryan glances at Denise curiously.

13
San Francisco

A photo of Ralph Fawcett lies on top of a mahogany desk as a hand suddenly reaches out to grab a glass of wine lying near a stack of printed material. Houghton seems upset as he turns around. He waits a few seconds and takes a sip. He sighs.

"I miss that boy so much. I wonder what that damn girl meant by stating not everything was what it appeared to be."

Seconds later he throws the glass against the wall.

14
Santa Barbara

A woman appears enraged as she walks back and forth several times in a rush. She sighs loudly and stops suddenly.

"I don't care what you have to do. Get him on the phone this instant. No more excuses—none. Is that clear?"

Marlisa turns around and seems out of breath as she glances at the sun-drenched hills in a distance. She reacts.

"That's right. Tell him if he doesn't pick up the line I'm going to have a long talk with his wife—an x-rated talk."

She smiles broadly as she realizes the person staring back at her seems unsure what to do. She snaps her fingers.

"I'm gonna count to ten."

Wynette McClendon reacts and turns to look at the old man sitting on the sofa a few feet away. Marlisa smirks.

"Uh-huh—I see you Kirk. There's no place left to hide. I want answers or else. Don't make me come over there."

Kirk Berfield seems upset.

"It just didn't work out as we planned."

"What happened?"

Kirk glances at Wynette and shrugs.

"I don't know. Yesterday he said he was going to sell his vineyard—but I think he found someone else—said no."

"Did he? Who is it?"

Kirk shakes his head. He seems unsure.

"He said he was expecting important visitors shortly."

Marlisa gives Kirk a knowing look and sighs.

15
Pacific Coast Highway

"How did you get this number?"

Erica Gersh stares angrily at Janet Virella from her cell phone. She seems really irritated and sighs loudly.

"Your sister gave it to me."

Erica stares at Janet for a few seconds.

"What do you want?"

Janet gives Erica an odd look and shrugs.

"We need to talk about Ryan. You've treated him so badly—and for what—like seriously—it meant nothing."

"Some friend you turned out to be."

Erica watches as Janet licks her lips and makes a lewd gesture with her finger. She sighs loudly and laughs.

"He wanted to fuck—so we did."

"You *bitch*."

Janet licks her lips again. She makes a lewd gesture with her finger once more. She seems pleased as she stifles a smirk.

"He was like a wild animal."

Erica grimaces and glares at Janet angrily.

"Lose my number."

The image on Janet's phone goes blank.

"She's got some nerve—especially given her behavior with every straight guy in this town. She even slept with a priest."

Janet looks at her cell phone and stifles a laugh.

16
Orchid Bay
Corrington Home

"I thought you said you were on the pill?"

Mark Corrington slowly runs his fingers through his hair as he reaches for his boxer briefs. He turns around to face Dana Mills and shakes his head. She climbs out of bed and faces him.

"I'm sorry—so shoot me already."

Mark grabs his jeans from the chair.

"What did the doctor say?"

Dana turns around to face Mark.

"I took one of those pregnancy tests you get at Target. I couldn't risk going to my doctor—he'd tell my mother."

Mark runs his fingers through his hair again.

"I thought doctors can't talk about their patients to anyone—not even parents. It's a rule—against the law."

"Have you met my mother?"

Mark winces.

17

San Francisco

"Look—I already told you not to take my father's damn calls. Who the hell thought it was a good idea to give him a cell phone anyway? He's where he is for a reason. Ignore him."

Vladimir Orlov angrily slams the phone down and turns around to face Loren. He seems frustrated and sighs loudly.

"I should've disconnected his fucking phone weeks ago."

Loren grins slyly.

"Your old man is a handful no doubt."

He shoots Loren a dirty look and clenches his fist. They share a knowing look as Vladimir seems to become agitated.

"It's his fault he's in that place—his fault alone."

Loren shakes his head as he walks over to where his cousin in standing. He gives Vladimir a knowing look.

"You had no choice—he was losing it. Talking endlessly about conspiracy theories—it was lunacy—bonkers."

Loren grins broadly and gestures.

"Uh-huh—seems this all worked out for you perfectly. Got the old man out of the way—made a daring move—sneaky."

Vladimir shakes his fist at Loren.

"It was gonna be mine anyway. Who else was he gonna leave it to—Helen—my illegitimate half-sister? She's a slut."

Loren smirks and shoots Vladimir a knowing look. They share a grin and laugh. Vladimir makes a lewd gesture with his finger and points at his sister's picture among several family photos. He runs his fingers through his hair and shrugs.

"I think I should take a page out of your book. Your brother's death was a sweet deal for you a few years back."

Vladimir laughs loudly and points at Loren.

"You put a bullet in Ralph's head. Bold move cousin—you took your own brother out and blamed it on an old man that went nuts in the Caribbean—you dad is none the wiser. It's been years and he's never suspected his son's killer was his other son. Like a frigging plot right out of a true crime drama—scene by scene."

Loren waves his hand in the air and grins.

"It is what it is. Tristan Montgomery Bell intended to make dear Ralph's death look accidental after he found out my brother had slept with his trophy wife. I simply took advantage of the situation and made it look like Bell's scheme worked."

He turns to look out the window.

"I waited until my brother was alone in his cabin as a blizzard blanketed the mountain with snow. Then I paid Ralph a visit and shot him as he peacefully slept. It was the perfect crime if there ever was one. No one suspected I took him out. It was assumed he died in the blizzard—and Bell got blamed for it. My old man never even thought it was me who took Ralph out."

Vladimir walks over to Loren.

"What about the autopsy?"

Loren wags his finger at Vladimir and grins.

"There was no autopsy—paid everyone off and they looked the other way. My father was never told the truth."

Vladimir laughs loudly as he points at Loren.

"I got to hand it to you cousin—you're a piece of work no doubt. A cold-blooded killer you are—no guilt whatsoever."

Loren clasps his hands together.

"Like you're one to talk? Last time I checked you killed more people than I care to remember. Started with that twerp from high school—poor dude got run over on prom night."

Vladimir begins laughing.

"Jude Vanov."

Loren gives Vladimir a curious look.

"His only crime was making a play for your girl."

Vladimir clenches his fist.

"He disrespected me. I had to act."

He looks out the window.

"I waited until after the prom was over and plowed into him with my car as he walked home alone. Heard his bones crack under the wheels of my car. Ran him over twice to make sure he was dead—then went home and waited. The press was all over it for weeks afterwards—but the case quickly ran ice cold."

Vladimir faces Loren again.

"That wretched bastard has been dead for almost twenty years—lying up in Colma under some pathetic shrubs."

"Didn't you fuck his sister that night?"

"Uh-huh—I fucked her on the day Jude was laid to rest too. Played her royally for weeks afterwards—that dumb bitch never figured out it was me that iced her saintly twin brother."

He watches Loren's reaction.

"What should I do about my half-sister? As long as she's alive she's a loose end. I think decisions should be made."

Loren nods in agreement and shrugs. He points toward a glass cabinet with several small caliber handguns and grins.

"I think your sister's fate has been decided. Suicides happen every day in California. Unhappy young woman falls to her death from her pricey condo—couldn't face life anymore."

Vladimir nods as Loren smiles slyly.

18
Orchid Bay
Cotler Apartment

"I thought I told you I wasn't interested."

Tammy Cotler seems annoyed as she stares at Jason standing in the doorway of her apartment. She shrugs.

"Avery is due back any moment."

"That dude is not good enough for you. He's got no game. Nothing to offer you—other than endless bad experiences in your bed pretending he knows what to do with a woman."

"You of all people shouldn't throw stones about people. Last time I checked you didn't have a job—just sponging off those rich older women who think you care about them—disgusting."

Page **35**

Jason aggressively grabs Tammy's arm in a rage.

"How dare you speak to me like that? This isn't about me—*this* is about *you*. Show me some respect you *cunt*."

He pulls her toward him. She tries to pull away. She looks down to see his erection straining under his jeans as it presses against her thigh. He grins and tightens his grip. He sighs.

"I'm not gonna let you make a mistake with that pathetic dweeb. You and I have an understanding in case you forgot."

He pushes her into the apartment and shuts the door.

"I'm through playing games with a mouthy bitch."

He forces her toward the bedroom.

19
Honolulu

Carmen walks back and forth as she stares at her cell phone. She stops suddenly and sighs loudly before dialing.

"Texas white trash—damn her."

She sighs again and curses loudly.

"I warned you about her."

She looks at Randolph Gregory.

"Is that all you can say?"

"I told you Shirley Beecroft was not to be trusted after you found out she bedded your son the same day they met."

Randolph points at Carmen.

"Women like her always have agendas."

Carmen angrily throws her cell phone on the floor.

20
Orchid Bay
Phamler Garden Condo

"I'm all alone. I have no one—no one except you."

Patrick watches as Vina slowly wipes a tear from her eye.

"What about your folks?"

Vina rolls her eyes knowingly.

Page **36**

"They're not talking to me at the moment."
Patrick shoots Vina a cautious look.
"Why not—what happened?"
Vina gives Patrick a knowing look.
"They think I lowered myself living with Jason Shappe a while back. Said he was just using me. Said he was nothing but a player and that people were talking about me—saying I was a slut just like my trashy cousin. They were both pretty brutal."
Patrick runs his fingers through his hair.
"I'm no saint but Jason gives new meaning to the word slug. Of course he was using you—he plays women for fools."
Vina seems insulted and reacts.
"You sound like my folks."
Patrick shakes his head several times.
"Jason Shappe is a rape case waiting to happen."
Vina walks over to Patrick and looks at him silently for a few seconds. She reaches out to tug at the buttons on his Levi's. He pulls away. She seems upset and begins to cry softly.
"It was so good between us. You never treated me like Jason did—what exactly went wrong between us again?"
Patrick seems upset and turns away suddenly.
"You slept with Tim Bergman's brother."
Vina reaches out to touch Patrick's hand.
"That's old news Patrick. He and I are just friends."
Patrick runs his fingers through his hair again as Vina licks her lips seductively. She comes toward Patrick once more.
"I've got to go Vina—it was nice talking to you."
She begins to unbutton her blouse.
"Wait."
He stops.
"What is it now?"
She pulls out a cell phone and grins.
"If Kayla saw this video of you and me at the beach last year she'd be done with you—see you for what you really are."
Patrick glances at the video playing on Vina's cell phone and rolls his eyes. He seems bored and yawns several times.

"Kayla knows all about my past before she met me. Face it you've got nothing Vina—I told her all about us weeks ago."

Vina seems upset and grabs Patrick's arm. He watches as she slides her fingers over the buttons on his jeans. She sighs.

"It's not over between us."

Patrick pulls away from Vina.

"Uh-huh—it is. There's nothing left to say. Everyone was right about who you really are. I've got to go. Bye Vina."

He leaves. She watches him go and grimaces.

"You'll pay for this Patrick Clerke. I swear I'll make you pay for choosing that bitch over me. I'm gonna destroy you."

She begins to laugh as she looks at her cell phone for a few seconds before she begins dialing. She grins broadly.

21
Orchid Bay
Bairstow Apartment

"He said that about me—with his record?"

Kyle Derringer seems annoyed as he watches Tabitha closing the door behind her. She sighs loudly and stops.

"It really doesn't matter. He's just angry."

Kyle walks over to where Tabitha is standing.

"At least I have a job—what does he have? Not a damn thing. Dude lives in a frigging studio. Mooches off everyone he knows. Seriously, that fucker has some nerve—jerk."

"I told him I was with you."

"I bet that really went over well with Mills. He thinks he's all that. Thinks women find him charming—*ugh*—freak."

He shakes his fist in the air.

"I'm surprised he didn't try to say he beat me up last year at Perfection Beach. I broke his nose if you recall after he talked trash about my mother—said she was a husband-stealing whore who chased his no-account father for years—lied about her."

Tabitha slides her fingers along Kyle's bulging biceps and giggles as she looks at him. She seductively licks her lips.

"Everyone knows you flattened him at Perfection on the Fourth of July. No one blamed you afterwards either. He got what he deserved—held a grudge ever since—he hates to lose."

Kyle makes a gesture with his finger.

"My mother is happy with Lionel Black Feather. They've been together for seven years now—couldn't be happier."

"Adam Mills was just blowing off steam on account I threw him over for you. That man hates to lose—hates rejection."

Kyle looks at Tabitha for a few seconds and kisses her. They share a second kiss. He turns to look at the bedroom.

22
Orchid Bay
Studio Apartment

"Oh, I could come to like this deal no doubt. You certainly know your way around my dick—no secrets to wonder about."

Ryan glances over at Denise as he sighs loudly. She reaches out to stroke his sweaty forehead. She smirks.

"I was inspired. You played really hard."

Ryan sits up in bed and looks at the stained sheets. He grins broadly and looks at Denise again. He laughs slyly.

"I guess you know I'm leaning toward having you hanging with me a while. This could work out quite nicely for both of us over the next few weeks until you can find a place to live."

"I accept your offer."

They look at each other again as Ryan notices Denise's attention seems to be focused on his erect penis. Denise smiles as Ryan aggressively pulls her toward him. He begins kissing her.

23
Orchid Bay
Mills Family Home

"I thought we talked about that boy already. He's not good enough for you. His father slept with that Osborne girl."

"You don't know that mother—that's just what your friend says—and what does she know anyway? She never leaves that house of hers. Claims she has some sort of phobia. Uh-huh—like really—I bet the real reason is she knows what she looks like."

Daphne Mills grabs her daughter's arm.

"It's not nice to make fun of how someone looks."

Dana angrily jerks free of her mother's grip and faces her again as she puts her hands on her hips. She sighs loudly.

"Uh huh—and it's not nice to spread vicious rumors about someone you don't know either. Why don't you just face it mother—Lacey Vanwick is a troll—a horrible troll. I'm surprised she lives in a house—and not under a bridge. I hate her."

Daphne reacts to her daughter's behavior.

"I won't tolerate you talking about Lacey Vanwick like that again. Nevertheless I don't want you seeing that piece of trash."

"You can't stop me. He and I like each other."

Daphne gives her daughter a sharp look and faces the kitchen window for a second. She clenches her fist angrily.

"Are you sleeping with that boy?"

"Ask Lacey Vanwick. I'm sure she knows. Bet she knows if he uses a condom—if he has other girlfriends on the side."

Daphne seems stung by her daughter's words as Dana leaves the room. Daphne glances at her cell phone. She picks it up and stands frozen for a few seconds. She begins dialing.

"That boy is going to regret messing with my daughter and turning her against me. He needs to see the light."

She smiles as the phone is picked up.

24
Santa Barbara

"I had no choice. Fawcett demanded I go along with his offer. They had the papers with them. It's done—over."

Marlisa glares coldly at Steve Syverman as he wipes sweat from his brow. He cautiously watches her reaction as she realizes the truth. Suddenly she grabs the paperwork on the table.

"This isn't over yet. We had a deal."

Steve shrugs as he watches Marlisa slam the front door to his house shut. He sighs loudly and looks out at the beach just a few yards from the house. He seems upset and sighs again.

"She better stay away from Fawcett—his guys don't play fair. Made it clear to me what they do to people who get in their way—what they liked doing when things don't go their way."

He looks at the beach again and grimaces.

25
Orchid Bay
Studio Apartment

Erica waits patiently as she knocks on the door of a studio apartment. She looks at her watch as she notices the stained carpeting in the hallway. She rolls her eyes in disgust.

"Ugh—is this all he could afford?"

She knocks on the door again just as it opens. She stares at Ryan. He's naked except for a towel around his waist.

"I came here to talk."

Ryan looks at her with a confused look. Before he can answer Erica notices him looking at the bedroom door.

"Who the hell is she?"

"What's it to you?"

Erica seems about to explode in rage.

"I came to see if we can work things out—but I see you've already moved on with some skank—I'm *so* out of here."

Erica storms down the hallway as Ryan looks at her with a look of amusement on his face. He closes the door.

TO BE CONTINUED

A Brief Look at the Second Episode

Several couples dance carelessly around the issue of infidelity while past secrets haunt others in the present as an unscrupulous woman preys on the weaknesses of a man with a tortured past in order to exact harsh revenge for a business deal gone wrong.

Out of the Past

1
Orchid Bay
Cotler Apartment

"This was a long time coming, *cunt*. You provoked me with your behavior—but enough is enough. It is what it is."

Jason Shappe grins as he zips up his jeans and looks at Tammy Cotler lying on a bed several feet away. He laughs.

"I assume you learned your lesson."

"I'm going to report you."

He laughs loudly.

"Go ahead. No one will believe you. It's your word against mine and everyone knows you're a slut. You're a regular Kelley Hampshire no doubt. That bitch is no better than you—cut from the same cloth—always teasing us men with her behavior."

He grabs his jacket and smirks.

"You needed to know your place for a while now and today you learned plenty—learned not to play me ever again."

He walks to the door and stops. He points at her.

"If you tell anyone I swear I'll kill you."

He begins whistling as he walks down the hallway.

"Did this really just happen to me?"

Tammy nervously glances around the room for a while still seemingly in shock as she suddenly reaches for her cell phone.

"He's not going to get away with it—I can't let—I won't let him treat me like that—no. Roland O'Brien will believe me."

She looks at the cell phone and sighs.

2

San Francisco

"Oh-oh—it seems that you've made someone else angry other than you dear old dad. This bitch is really mad too."

Vladimir Orlov laughs as he points at Loren Fawcett when he enters Loren's office and closes the door. Loren smirks.

"Marlisa Vigaro is no doubt the bitch you're referring to from the looks of it. She and I have a history—unpleasant."

Vladimir makes a lewd gesture with his finger as he walks over to where Loren is sitting. They share a look and a laugh.

"She and I soiled plenty of designer sheets for months—of course that was until she found out I was just using her."

Loren gestures wildly and smirks.

"Her father owned a huge amount of stock in a company I had my eye on—so I did what any guy would do to get what he felt was his regardless. I fucked her plenty until she signed over the stocks and then I cut her loose telling her my wife wasn't the forgiving type—made it clear she and I were finished."

Vladimir licks his lips several times.

"What about Lenore? Can I assume she has no idea her beloved hubby has strayed—playing the field as if marriage vows mean nothing—except to dear, precious Lenore of course."

Loren rolls his eyes and grins broadly.

"She wanted to get married—so we did. That's the deal between us. She thinks we're exclusive—I say differently."

They share another laugh.

"What happens when she finds out?"

Page **44**

Loren gives Vladimir a sharp look and sighs.

"What can she do? Lenore came into this marriage with nothing. If she chooses to leave—she leaves with nothing."

Vladimir gestures with his hand.

"What about Corinne and Bradley?"

Loren clenches his fist.

"Like I said earlier she leaves with nothing. No way will my children go anywhere I don't approve of—and I certainly won't allow Lenore to insult me by taking my children away."

Vladimir shakes his head.

"You're definitely your father's son."

Loren stands and slowly walks toward a huge window overlooking San Francisco Bay. He turns to face Vladimir.

"I'll take that as a compliment."

At that moment his cell phone rings.

3
Orchid Bay
Falling Pines Memorial Park

"I still can't believe it ended the way it did."

Kevin Alsten turns to face Lauren Corrington as they look down at a faded marble headstone under a large tree.

"He brought it upon himself. He caused his own death. No one blames you. There was no other way it could've gone. He had so much anger—so much rage. Everyone knew it—saw it."

Kevin nods and glances at the grave again.

"I know. I just wish what happened could've been avoided before so many lives were changed. His parents tried to sue."

"They were just overcome with grief—wanted revenge for what happened to Judd. The judge didn't see it their way."

"It seems like it happened twenty years ago instead of just four. His brother threatened to end me—made vile threats."

Lauren slides her arms around Kevin's waist as they begin walking out of the cemetery. She reaches out to kiss him.

Page **45**

"Forget about her—she doesn't deserve you."

Denise Stone looks at Ryan Pena slyly as she lets her finger slide across Ryan's erect penis. He grins broadly.

"I'm just not in the mood for her theatrics. She's not exactly the picture of perfection—spent plenty of time pining for Riley Wickerson after he threw her over without so much as a real explanation. Tried everything to get him back in her bed even on the day of his wedding—it was so sad actually. Seriously, what was she thinking, he was marrying his pregnant girlfriend. It was quite a sight as the bride, in her last months of pregnancy, and her future husband about to take their vows—and Erica."

Ryan makes a lewd gesture with his finger.

"There she was in the middle of the ceremony begging him to come back to her—saying she loved him and couldn't live without him lying next to her in bed. People in this town talked for weeks afterwards—caused her quite a bit of shame."

Denise looks at Ryan's erect penis again.

"This kind of drama would've worked so well on an old series I saw on cable recently called *The Colbys*. Everyone had secrets and none of them good. Quite a lot of fun—but it didn't last long—got cancelled after two seasons—terrible ratings."

He laughs as she points to his bedroom. He grins.

"I'm game—fully charged no doubt."

Denise gently takes Ryan by the hand and stops suddenly.

"What happened to Riley Wickerson and his bride?"

Ryan rolls his eyes and gestures briefly.

"Last I heard was that he and Evelyn Templeton moved to Montecito. They just had to get away from freak show Erica."

"I'll never be like Erica Gersh. She's pathetic. You can fuck whomever you want. There are no rules between us—none."

Ryan laughs loudly and glances at the bedroom door as his cell phone begins to ring. He sees a name blinking.

Orchid Bay
Rose Lane Parking Lot

"I have no idea where you heard that I threatened you. Get your facts checked before you come at me with a mountain of lies—seems to me you should stop listening to idle gossip."

Kyle Derringer glares at Adam Mills for a few seconds. He seems about to explode. Adam attempts to walk away.

"I'm not done with you yet. Seems we have to get a few things straight right now—or next time I'll repeat what happened at Perfection Beach—but this time I'll break a few bones."

"I was drunk that day—otherwise I would have wiped the beach with you face. Face it, you just got lucky. End of story."

Kyle flexes his muscular arms.

"How about now hot shot—want to test your theory? I'll make you beg for mercy once I start hitting you—you're nothing but a sad pussy—a nobody who thinks they're somebody."

Adam takes a swing at Kyle. He dodges Adam's swing and lands his fist on Adam's jaw. Adam staggers a bit and collapses.

"I guess you're drunk now too?"

He brings his boot down on Adam's chest.

"If you so much as come near Tabitha again I swear I'll finish you off for good. Send you straight to Falling Pines."

He clenches his fists and smirks.

"Do you hear me?"

Adam looks up at him and nods.

"You come near my girl one more time and I'll make sure you never do it again. I'm sick of you talking trash about me all over town—sick of listening to people telling me what you said. Most importantly—my girl is off limits to you. She doesn't want you in her life. *I* don't want you in her life. This is your final warning. I hope I'm making myself clear. If I hear anyone tell me you said anything I'm coming for you—and I assure you no one and nothing will stop me from breaking your fucking neck."

Kyle glares at Adam for a few seconds and takes his boot off his chest. He gives him a sharp look and walks away.

"That fucker is gonna pay—he's *dead*."

Adam stands up and looks around. A few people look at him amusingly and begin laughing. He seems annoyed.

6

Pacific Coast Highway

"Uh-huh—exactly. Work him over quite a bit. Teach him a lesson he won't forget—just enough to inflict serious pain."

Daphne Mills nods several times as she looks at Sergei Lycov staring back at her. He grins broadly and sighs.

"You and Adam are like family to me. Don't worry I'll work this teen dream over a bit—broke a few bones if necessary."

Daphne smirks slyly and nods in agreement.

"Is tomorrow too soon for a visit?"

Sergei gestures with his hand and laughs.

"Tell Adam I said hi—tell him to look me up when I come by tomorrow. He and I have a history of being naughty."

"Uh-huh—I know."

She sighs as she watches the screen goes blank.

"My former brother-in-law might be a wretched creep but he has useful friends. Dana will certainly be surprised when she finds out what I've got planned—and not in a good way. I've just got to make sure that boy doesn't ruin her life the way her father ruined mine. I hope that man rots in jail for what he *did*."

She seems bothered and sighs loudly.

7

San Francisco

Houghton Fawcett looks at the cell phone in his hand and seems confused. He throws it on the sofa and grimaces.

"That boy of mine is a deceitful two-faced worm. He'll pay for this no doubt—when he least expects it—damn him."

Page **48**

Houghton hears a sound and turns around. He sees nothing and sighs. He seems frustrated and clenches his fist.

"Still think I'm telling you tall tales?"

Houghton spins around and sees Tiffany Johnson staring back at him from a huge mirror in his office. As he watches she steps through the mirror and gleefully comes toward him.

"You didn't tell me everything."

Tiffany laughs slyly and points her finger at him.

"You're on a need-to-know basis."

Houghton looks at Tiffany curiously as she circles him again and points to the mirror. He watches as she laughs.

"Your son is a piece of work no doubt."

Without warning the office begins to swirl in front of Houghton's eyes. He stands there unable to move as the room swirls for several seconds. Suddenly images begin forming and he realizes Loren and Vladimir are together in Loren's office. Tiffany grins broadly as she comes closer to Houghton and laughs.

"It seems your beloved son thinks he's got nothing to worry about after what he did—played you for a fool."

Houghton turns around as the office returns to normal. He watches as Tiffany wags her finger. She points at him slyly.

"What if I told you I know something awful about Loren that you don't—something that would change your life."

Houghton seems annoyed as he looks at Tiffany scornfully while she continues to snap her fingers as if dancing to a tune.

"Spit it out bitch—I'm tired of your games."

Tiffany wags her finger at Houghton again and smirks.

"Don't say I didn't warn you."

Tiffany watches his reaction and smiles broadly. Seconds later there is a blinding flash. Houghton seems unable to react for several seconds as Tiffany casually folds her hands in triumph.

"I told you it was quite a shocker."

Houghton seems about to faint from fright.

"It's not true—you're lying."

She watches as he leans against a nearby cabinet. A few seconds slip by as they look at each other. He finally speaks.

Page **49**

"Loren would never kill his older brother—not my precious Ralph. He knows how much I loved Ralph. He wouldn't dare."

Tiffany rolls her eyes mockingly.

"Is that so? Are you sure about that?"

Houghton spins around to face Tiffany.

"This is your doing—you're trying to confuse me."

Tiffany pretends to be offended. She dances around him several times as he seems about to explode with anger.

"I did no such thing. It was Loren. He did it all. Did it so he could get his hands on *your* company—*your* money."

She takes a step forward and stops.

"Tristan Montgomery Bell didn't kill your son. It was Loren who took Ralph's life. He lied to you—lied to you for years."

Houghton becomes enraged and tries to grab Tiffany but he falls against the sofa as she watches in joyful amusement.

8

Orchid Bay
Hampshire Street

Jason seems pleased with himself as he exits a diner and begins walking down the sidewalk. He begins to hum a tune.

"That stupid bitch better keep her mouth shut if she knows what's good for her. Tammy Cotler certainly doesn't want to get on my bad side—so much for her to worry about."

He hears someone behind him and turns.

"You and I have some talking to do."

Before he can say anything, handcuffs are slapped on his wrist as Roland O'Brien shoves him against a nearby store window. Jason struggles but Roland's grip is unyielding.

"I've got you Jason—you've finally crossed the line and now there's no way out. You and I are gonna dance plenty."

Jason shoots Roland an angry look.

"I have no idea what you're talking about. But if you don't get your fucking hands off me I'll really make your miserable life in this town extremely hard—won't even feel bad about it."

Page **50**

"Tammy Cotler says differently. It seems you've been accused of rape. Uh-huh. Imagine that—*you* of all people."

Jason rolls his eyes and begins laughing.

"That bitch is a liar. She's just mad because I turned her sorry ass down for a roll in the hay with yours truly. Fucking whore is certifiable. You've got nothing on me loser."

Roland seems ready to punch Jason as he looks at the handcuffs on Jason's wrists. He turns away for a second.

"Tammy Cotler is with one of my people right now. You should've worn a condom you moron. If your DNA is a match with what we found on her bed sheets—you're *so* fucked."

Jason and Roland glare at each other. Jason begins laughing loudly. He makes a lewd gesture with his tongue.

"You're just mad because I got your girl into my bed. If you had been servicing her like a real man—you'd still have her."

Roland explodes with rage and punches Jason in the gut several times. As Jason doubles over Roland kicks him.

"You lousy bastard—you destroyed my relationship with Marianne Singleton. She and I were supposed to get married."

Jason looks at Roland and begins laughing loudly.

"My penis said otherwise—played her good."

Roland angrily lashes out at Jason. He seems ready to hit him again when he notices Liana Danforth looking at them.

"Is everything all right?"

Roland looks at Jason angrily and at Liana again.

"Everything is fine—just dandy."

Jason gives Roland a knowing look.

"He just hit me."

Roland looks at Liana.

"He raped Tammy Cotler."

Liana seems horrified as she glances at Jason. Seconds later she enters her diner. Roland faces Jason again and winks.

"Uh-huh—you and I are gonna really have fun when I get you back to the station—oh yeah—you're really gonna enjoy what I have planned for you after what you did to Tammy Cotler."

Jason seems bored and turns away.

Page **51**

"What if I told you I know who killed your brother five years ago? Know their names and who they work for?"

"I'd say I was interested."

Marlisa Vigaro grins as Corey Danforth closes the door to his apartment and turns to face her. He notices her behavior.

"It's been a while since we spoke—as I recall you refused to spring me—said something about not wanting to deal."

Marlisa slowly runs her fingers through her hair and seems upset. She sighs loudly and grimaces. Corey notices.

"I couldn't—I had just gotten married. It would've been awkward. You were in jail. How could I explain it without having to go into detail about us? I just couldn't risk it. I'm really sorry."

Corey shoots Marlisa a suspicious look and sighs.

"Seems to me your marriage went south regardless in the end. I heard about you and Loren Fawcett—Adam Mills said Loren dumped you. You two seemed like the perfect couple."

"He turned out to be a toad."

"Uh-huh—I'll just bet."

Marlisa waves her hand in the air.

"He's why I'm here actually. His people were behind what *happened* to Allan. I think it's time justice was served."

Corey clenches his fist in anger.

"I figured as such—had the earmarks of a mob hit—but no one would believe me. Said I was delusional—laughed."

Marlisa reaches out to touch Corey's arm.

"I'm sorry I wasn't there for you when you needed me Corey—but I'm here for you now—for Allan too. I promise."

Corey glances at the window. He seems lost in thought for a few seconds. He turns to face her again with clenched fists.

"People still look at me like I'm a nutcase—they whisper behind my back—treat me like a zombie. It's been hard."

Marlisa reaches out to hug Corey.

"What if we get even with Loren Fawcett and his goons and get you the respect you deserve at the same time? Imagine how he would react if his children suddenly turned up missing."

Corey turns to face Marlisa and sighs.

"What do you have in mind?"

Marlisa smirks.

10

Orchid Bay

Hampshire Street Cafe

Liana closes the door to her diner and notices Sabine Norton looking at her curiously. Liana seems upset.

"What happened?"

"Roland O'Brien just arrested Jason Shappe."

"What did that boy do now?"

Liana lowers her voice to a whisper.

"He raped Tammy Cotler."

Sabine covers her mouth in shock and sighs.

"I always knew that Shappe boy would end up in trouble for something like that. His father spoiled him rotten—never made him earn anything—and now look where that has led to."

Liana gives Sabine a cautious look.

"I thought you liked him?"

Sabine seems to be trembling.

"I did—until I found out he was fooling around with Vina Phamler a few weeks after she got married to his hardworking cousin. Poor Paul, that boy had such bad luck with women."

Sabine leans closer to Liana.

"Before Vina, Paul was sweet on Daniela Koff. But then she up and got married to Lachlan Ball—and played him. Paul dodged a bullet with her but got snared by Vina a year later."

Liana reaches out to touch Sabine's arm.

"Paul stopped by the diner last week—seems he finally found someone decent—said he likes living in Half Moon Bay."

Page **53**

Sabine seems pleased and sighs.

"Lachlan Ball has found someone else too."

Sabine looks around the diner.

"I guess everyone is happy but Jason and that wretched whore Vina Phamler—oh how I hate her. She's the worst."

She seems pleased and tries to stifle a smirk.

11

Half Moon Bay

"Of course—I'll be there later this week. I'm so sorry this happened to you. I'll make sure you have the best lawyer."

Gwen Bartlett looks at Tammy staring back at her from an apartment in Orchid Bay. She looks bewildered and unkempt.

"It was awful—he was so angry."

She begins to cry.

"I never thought he could do something like that. People warned me that he wasn't good enough for me—but I didn't listen to them. I thought he really liked me. Then it all went wrong when I found out he had cheated on me—slept around."

Gwen shakes her head.

"It'll be alright. He's in serious trouble—no amount of his father's money can save him now. He's *persona non grata*."

Tammy wipes tears from her eyes and nods.

"His father isn't going to help him. He disowned Jason after he caught him in bed with his longtime girlfriend—he found them fucking in his bedroom like a pair of wild animals—*ugh*."

Gwen seems shocked at the revelation.

"He actually slept with his father's girlfriend behind his back? Played his old man for a fool—did the deed in his bed?"

Tammy nods several times. She gestures with her hand as she seems to remember private moments. She sighs.

"Jason liked having sex in public places—liked pushing buttons—creating a scene. Screwing his father's girlfriend in his bed was probably Jason's idea of sticking it to his old man."

Gwen watches Tammy's behavior.

"Don't worry cousin—he won't get away with what he did to you. He's going to pay for his actions—I guarantee it."

Tammy wipes another tear from her eye.

"That's what Roland O'Brien said when we met earlier. He swears he'll make Jason pay—make him sorry he raped me."

"Uh-huh—oh that's right—Jason broke up Roland and Marianne. Slept with her and bragged about their trysts on social media. Made sure Roland found out the worst way possible."

Tammy faces her cousin again.

"I just want him to pay for raping me."

Gwen nods in agreement.

12
San Francisco

"Don't worry—I got it. No mercy is to be shown to *those* you consider your enemies. Blood will be spilled until *those* you consider threats to you are dealt with. It is what it is."

A man shakes his head several times.

"Uh-huh. I'm ready."

He turns to look at a cable car passing by.

13
Orchid Bay
Downtown Police Station

"Just shut the fuck up already—you're not going anywhere for the next twenty years. I got you red-handed for rape."

Jason pounds his fists against the bars of his cell as he watches Roland fill out paperwork. Roland turns to face him.

"You've been playing with fire for years—but today you made a big mistake. Tammy Cotler is pressing charges—you're gonna see hard time for your actions. Hope you like being around a lot of horny old guys—many that like muscular young men."

Jason points his finger at Roland.

"I know my rights—you can't keep me here."

Roland waves his hand in the air and begins laughing.

"Can't I? Says who? In case you forgot I'm in charge not you. You're not going anywhere—I've got you—deal already."

Jason begins stomping around the small cell as Roland watches him become angrier. Jason stops and grins slyly.

"This is about Marianne Singleton isn't it? You're just mad I plowed your girl—rode her like a show horse—made her beg."

Roland grits his teeth and faces Jason. He stands up and walks over to the cell. He suddenly begins grinning broadly.

"Wait until you go to state prison—you'll be traded like a piece of chocolate—those shower incidents you hear about in the news will be your new reality—uh-huh—you just wait and see."

"I'm not going to jail—I didn't rape Tammy. She's my girlfriend—I can't rape my frigging girlfriend. I have rights."

Roland rolls his eyes knowingly.

"Ex-Girlfriend—she kicked your ass to the curb months ago after she caught you cheating yet again—royally busted."

Roland waves his hand in the air and smirks.

"This town has no secrets. Everyone knows everyone else's business as you well know. Face it—you're not going to sway this game to your reality—you're going to be charged with rape and I'll personally see to it you're sent to a state prison that has the worse of the worse housed within their walls—savage."

Jason grabs the bars of his cell.

"I have friends."

"So do I buddy—got friends in high places. Think about that while you wait to see what I've got planned for you."

Roland begins laughing and points to Jason as he leaves the room. Jason begins yelling loudly for several minutes.

14
Orchid Bay
Pearl Street Grub Hut

"She's still pissed at you Adam. That woman can certainly hold a grudge. Exactly what the hell did you do to her?"

Page **56**

Adam looks over at where Jayne Osborne is sitting alone and shrugs. He waves his hand in the air and laughs.

"How should I know? She and I had a thing—and then I cut her loose. It's not like she was serious with me—it was casual."

Ethan Vanwick rolls his eyes knowingly.

"Uh-huh—women play like they're good with a guy not being serious but it's a whole other story when they get dropped off at the curb and left to figure things out for themselves."

He sighs loudly and his face clouds over.

"I should know—been down that road plenty."

Adam waves his hand in the air.

"It was different with Jayne. We played house—but she had other guys on a string too—she had a rep for a reason."

Ethan notices Jayne glaring coldly at them.

"I think that maneater wants you dead."

Adam laughs and jabs Ethan.

"I'm not worried."

He takes another gulp of his iced coffee and stands up. He looks over at Jayne again and smirks. He glances at Ethan.

"I think Jayne and I should talk—clear the air and let what happened between us a while back not be an issue today."

Ethan gives Adam a warning look as he watches him about to walk over to where Jayne is sitting. He ignores Ethan.

"It's your funeral—don't say I didn't warn you."

Adam turns away from Ethan and walks over to Jayne. She seems ready to pounce as she faces him. He sighs loudly.

"I think it's time you and I bury the hatchet."

Jayne glares at him for a few seconds as a weird look comes over her face. Adam notices. She stifles a laugh.

"I haven't forgotten what you did—what *your* friends did to me at *your* party. I certainly haven't forgotten what happened to Steve Alsten—he's dead because of you—*you* had him killed."

Adam seems confused and gestures.

"What the fuck are you talking about Jayne? I had nothing to do with what happened—Alsten got shot by drug dealers."

He reaches out to grab her arm as she stands up.

"You better watch what you say about me around Orchid Bay—I had nothing to do with Alsten's death. He was mixed up with drug dealers and *they* killed him. That fucker caused his own death—*not me*. And as for saying my friends raped you—like seriously—who would believe one word that comes out of your lying mouth. Everyone in this lousy town knows you're a fucking slut—a vicious cunt that's bedded just about every guy that crossed your path—including yours truly. You're worse than your sister could ever dream about being—and that's saying plenty."

Jayne slaps Adam hard across the face.

"How dare you."

Adam angrily pulls Jayne toward him and smirks.

"Don't push me *bitch*—you don't want to get on my bad side—I'm your worst frigging nightmare. *I* take no prisoners."

Jayne jerks free of Adam's grip and leans toward him. He looks at her oddly. She smiles broadly as she whispers.

"It's *you* who should watch *your* step."

Adam seems enraged.

"Is that a threat?"

Jayne licks her lips and laughs.

"Like I said—do watch your step Adam—fatal accidents happen every day—people die—don't forget what happened to Caleb Corrington last month—he ended up dead—shot."

Jayne gives Adam a knowing look and walks away. He stands there for a few seconds. Ethan comes over to him.

"What did she just say to you?"

Adam slowly turns to face Ethan. He waves his hand and seems a bit nervous as his face drains of color. Ethan reacts.

"*She* threatened me—that *bitch* threatened me."

Ethan watches Jayne as she walks toward the parking lot across the street from the diner. He faces Adam once more.

"I told you that girl was bad news—she ruins every guy who gets between her legs—cold-blooded and psychotic."

Adam clenches his fist in a rage.

"No one threatens me and gets away with it—especially not some two-bit whore that thinks she's something special."

Page **58**

Ethan nervously grabs Adam's arm.

"What are you going to do to get even with Jayne? What kind of example are you gonna make out of that maneater."

Adam makes a slashing gesture with his hand across his throat and smiles broadly. He pulls out his cell phone.

"Two can play her sick game if that's how she wants to roll—and I know just the guys to call—just her type—*oh yeah*."

Ethan watches as Adam begins punching numbers into his cell phone. He turns to face Ethan. They share a grin.

15

San Francisco

"It was quite a show if I do say so myself. Your father was certainly having an animated conversation with someone."

Jared Lansing faces Loren and seems about to laugh as he turns the video off. Loren stares at the monitor for a few seconds before speaking. He seems unsure about what to say next.

"He wasn't talking on his cell phone—I checked. He was definitely talking to someone I couldn't see on the monitor."

Loren runs his fingers through his hair.

"There is no other explanation. My father actually believes that he's communicating with otherworldly beings."

Jared shoots Loren a curious look.

"What do you want me to do? He refused to talk to a shrink the last time this happened despite our repeated offers."

Loren laughs and looks at the monitor.

"I think we both agree that there are no such things as ghosts. My father is mentally ill. There *is* no other conclusion."

Without warning the door to Jared's office open as a cold gust of wind blows into the room. They look at each other as the door shuts on its own. Loren turns to face Jared again.

"Somehow he lost his mind and began believing in this ridiculous notion of seeing ghosts—and talking to them."

He runs his fingers through his hair and sighs.

"Nikola Orlov also has the same issues—certifiable."

Page **59**

He turns to face Jared and stifles a smile.

"I think we'd better decide what to do about my father's delusional ravings. It's obvious he needs help. This can't go on any longer—it's just a matter of time before he completely snaps."

Several feet away Tiffany stands with her hands on her hips. She seems amused at the conversation the two men are having as she turns to look at Jeremy Weissmann standing nearby. They nod in agreement and continue listening.

16
Orchid Bay
Hampshire Suite Rentals

Corey crawls out of bed and faces Marlisa with a sly grin. She reveals her exposed breasts and he reacts. She points her finger at him and laughs slyly. He looks down at his penis.

"It was just like old times—like no time passed since we last hooked up—plenty of wild times a decade ago."

Marlisa makes a lewd gesture with her finger. He watches as his penis becomes erect once more. She licks her lips.

"No one made me feel the way you did."

Marlisa climbs out of bed and comes toward Corey. They look at each other for a few seconds. She strokes his chest.

"Don't worry about anything—I'll make sure Allan's death is avenged. No one will be spared—especially Loren."

"I just want everyone that participated in my brother's death to be on a slab at a morgue in Frisco—an eye for an eye."

"I'll make it happen. It's only fair."

Corey clenches his fist again and nods.

17
Orchid Bay
Downtown Police Station

"I didn't rape that miserable bitch. She wanted me to fuck her—begged—so I did. The cunt knows she's lying about me."

Page **60**

Jason grips the bars of his cell as Sarina Wolper looks at him in dismay. She shakes her head and seems confused.

"I can't help you. You're being held without bail on account they think you're a flight risk. I'm sorry Jason."

Jason seems about to explode.

"That fucking bitch made up tales about me—we had sex and that was it—I never promised her anything afterwards."

He clenches his fists angrily.

"I swear when I get out of here I'm gonna fuck her so hard she won't be able to walk for weeks—I'll break her damn will."

He begins laughing as Sarina reacts.

"Talk like that won't help you."

Jason begins walking back and forth. He stops and faces Sarina again. He tries to smile but manages only a grimace.

"What about my father?"

"He said you're dead to him—warned me that you're not worth it—said you use everyone you know—lies endlessly."

Jason grips the bars of his cell again.

"That fucker—worst father anyone can have—I really hate him—hate his miserable fucking guts. I wish he was dead."

Sarina reacts and backs away.

"I'm sorry. I'll come by tomorrow."

Jason watches her leave and begins angrily pounding on the bars of his cell. The noise echoes for several minutes.

18

San Diego

"Uh-huh—I got it. Actually I'm on my way to Orchid Bay as luck would have it. It seems your sister-in-law wants me to work over her daughter's lowlife boyfriend—show him what happens when warnings are ignored. I'll be there tomorrow morning."

Adam looks at Sergei on his cell phone and grins broadly. He shakes his head and seems pleased. Sergei wags his finger.

"How's Jayne Osborne? Should I look her up?"

Adam gestures with his hand seemingly enraged.

Page **61**

"*Ugh*. I hate that wretched whore. She split town after her encounter with you and Sasha Levitov left her with so many warm memories. I thought I was rid of that miserable bitch for good. Then she waltzes back into town not long ago—and today proceeded to threaten me—said I'd better watch my step."

Sergei grits his teeth and grimaces.

"Don't you worry about her—Sasha and I will show her what happens to bitches who make threats. This time we'll push her to the brink of no frigging return—make her see the light."

Adam begins laughing and gestures with his hand.

"Do what you must—kill her if you have to."

Sergei shakes his fist at the camera before ending his video call with Adam. His cell phone rings once more.

19
Boston

"These people just don't know when to stop."

Jeremy Winterfield turns to face Miles Shefford as he gets into his car. He smiles as he looks at the street up ahead.

"I wonder what's going to happen when Houghton Fawcett gets wind of what is about to happen to his mighty empire courtesy of your handiwork. He'll have a coronary."

"It has been a long time coming is what I say. The family Fawcett destroyed so many lives with their criminal enterprising from one end of the country to another. Enough is enough."

Miles starts the engine of the car.

"I wish I could be there when he finds out Boleyn had help. That we helped—worked every angle to bring them down."

Jeremy makes a lewd gesture with his hand.

"Fawcett isn't my first rodeo by any means. I destroyed a scumbag named Carson Penney a while back after his troubled son ran over an old man in Castle Beach—and just last year I put the screws to a crooked doctor named Travis Nickerson from St. Thomas with a flurry of lawsuits after he attempted to blackmail me in order to get his son off for the murder of his girlfriend."

Jeremy stifles a laugh and seems bothered as he wipes sweat from his face. Miles nods in agreement and sighs.

"I do what needs to be done. It's as simple as that. These motherfuckers always think *they* are above the law. Always try the same game every time—blackmail to achieve their goals."

Miles runs his fingers through his hair.

"Uh-huh—agreed—Houghton Fawcett and his brood are responsible for the deaths of hundreds of people—some of which were out of greed while others were cold-blooded revenge."

"You think?"

They look at each other again.

20
Orchid Bay
Downtown Police Station

"Have you spoken with Tammy Cotler yet?"

Roland looks up from the stack of paperwork on his desk at Lachlan Ball. He glances at the hallway leading to the jail.

"Jason Shappe is in a mess of trouble—and he knows it."

Lachlan leans back in his chair and sighs loudly.

"That dude has been testing the waters for a long time now. I guess the dam finally broke. He fucked up royally."

Roland laughs and wags his finger at Lachlan.

"I'd say so. He's pissed that he can't talk his way out of this mess—no one can help him. Even his father isn't playing."

Roland stands and stretches as Lachlan sighs.

"I guess you've finally gotten your revenge after what he did to you—screwed up your relationship with Marianne."

"It's not about Marianne—but I would be lying if I deny getting a perverse sense of pleasure by locking him up after what he did. Used her just to get even with me—bragged after the fact knowing I'd get wind of it. Marianne tried to deny it but there were too many eyewitnesses to their frequent visits at that motel just past Paradise Pointe. Hurt like hell—but I dealt with it."

Lachlan bangs his finger on his desk.

Page **63**

"It was the same with Daniela—never thought something like that could happen to me. But time heals all wounds."

"How are you and Alison Orlonge doing? You two have been dating a while—I assume no trouble in paradise yet?"

Lachlan leans back in his chair again.

"We're fine. Her brother fixed us up actually."

Roland stifles a smirk.

"That must have pissed off Glen Orlonge when he found out about you. I heard he wanted to get back with his ex."

"Alison is done with Glen. Divorce papers were signed and delivered. He had no choice in the matter—forced to sign."

Roland walks over to Lachlan's desk.

"I assume you and Alison's kid brother are tight."

"Uh-huh—kid's got a good head on his shoulders. Knows how to live by rules—understands life—especially after."

Roland waves his hand in the air.

"That mess with Judd Vinette caused quite a scandal. But no one blamed him for what happened. Vinette was troubled."

Lachlan nods in agreement and stands. He walks over to Roland and taps him on the shoulder. They look at each other.

"Marianne just wasn't the one—sorry dude."

Roland nods and faces the hallway briefly.

"That motherfucker is gonna pay for what he did to Tammy Cotler—he's not gonna get away with it—no way."

They share a glance and nod in agreement.

21

San Francisco

"I'm tired of hearing about some imaginary teenage girl visiting you—enough is enough—just admit it's all a story."

Houghton clenches his fist as he looks at Loren. He turns to look at the mirror. Loren notices and shakes his head.

"There's no one in the mirror father."

Houghton runs his fingers through his hair.

"If Ralph were alive—he'd knock you around a bit."

Page **64**

"But *Ralph* isn't alive—is he? *He's dead.*"

"You killed him didn't you?"

Houghton circles Loren like an animal.

"She told me you did it—killed Ralph—told me you made it look like Tristan Montgomery Bell did it. But it was *you.*"

Loren turns away and grimaces.

"I've had it with your lies—had it with these bizarre stories about some dead girl. This is the end of the road father."

Houghton grabs Loren by the arm.

"What are you going to do? Huh? Kill me like you killed Ralph? Make it look like someone else did it? She said you'd try something like that—said I better watch out—watch *you.*"

Loren jerks free of his father's grip.

"There *is* no girl. She's a figment of your imagination."

"Is she? Or are you worried that she's real and knows what you did to my precious Ralph? You took the only person I ever loved on this planet—you killed him in cold blood and lied."

"Ralph was a loser—he had no concept of being who you thought he was—it was me that had the power—not Ralph."

Houghton flies into a rage and attacks Loren.

22
Orchid Bay
Hampshire Street Cafe

"I just want to talk—clear the air between us."

Julia Danforth glares at Vina Phamler.

"I know what happened between us won't ever be able to be changed. I'm aware my selfish actions caused the death of Samuel Grady at the hands of that demented creep that said he was my father. But I honestly had no idea that Roger Olof was *really* my father—no idea that my mother gave up Alexander Mansfred for adoption after she was raped a second time by Roger. I always thought my father was who my mother said he was—until Alexander showed up. When Alexander came looking for his birth mother—everything changed—I freaked."

Julia rolls her eyes knowingly.

"It's always someone else's fault isn't it Vina? No matter what you do, it's always someone else's fault when something goes wrong. You never take responsibility for your actions."

Julia notices people staring. She notices their concern but ignores it. She turns her attention to Vina once more.

"When Roger Olof made his presence known in Orchid Bay and you found out who he was—you pretended that Samuel Grady was your brother—hoped Roger would scare Samuel into leaving town—and for what? Because Samuel turned you down when you made a pass at him—scorned you? Once Roger found out Samuel wasn't his son—he killed him because he assumed he'd been made a fool of by Samuel—and you *let* it happen."

Vina rolls her eyes and seems bored.

"I have no idea what you're talking about."

Julia takes a step toward Vina.

"Of course no one knew at the time Roger was responsible for what happened to Samuel—*except* you. You knew what he was capable of and continued to play like you had no idea what was happening. And once Roger figured out Alexander was his long-lost son—he confronted him—and in a struggle he killed Alexander—snuffed out his life without so much as a second thought for his actions. Yet you still pretended you had no idea what was going on? Only when that whack job set his sights on killing your mother—planned to burn her alive in the basement of her home did you come clean. Seriously Vina—what kind of person are you? So far all I see is a woman that uses men, lies to her friends, treats everyone around her like crap—and now wants people in this town to act like you're someone decent? Sorry, I'm not that kind of person. I'll never forgive you causing Alexander Mansfred to lose his life—and that goes double for Samuel."

"Blame me all you want—I had nothing to do with what happened. Roger acted on his own—he's guilty—not me."

Vina and Julia stare at each other for a few seconds and then Vina leaves without another word. Julia seems annoyed as she watches Vina walk away. Her anger is clearly evident.

Page 66

"That bitch is going to get what's coming to her. And I know just the person to make it reality—painful if need be."

She pulls out her cell phone.

"I think it's time I call in a few favors."

She smiles broadly as an image appears.

23
Boston

"Boleyn isn't going to like these turn of events one bit."

Jeremy grabs his cell phone as he shakes his head several times. He seems distressed as he begins furiously dialing.

24
Orchid Bay
Boutique Apartment

Lachlan enters his apartment and closes the door. As he turns on the lights he's grabbed from behind. He feigns shock.

"I've got a gun and I'm not afraid to use it."

Alison Orlonge laughs and turns on the lights.

"Uh-huh—just wait until I get you alone in the shower later—then we'll see how brave you really are—how tough."

Lachlan grins broadly and kisses Alison.

"I'm a very dangerous man—nothing but wicked thoughts running through my mind at the moment—highly sexual."

Alison pulls Lachlan toward her and grins slyly.

"I'll be the judge of such threats."

Seconds later they kiss passionately as Lachlan lifts Alison into his arms and head up the stairs amid loud laughter.

TO BE CONTINUED

A Brief Look at the Third Episode

Long ago secrets begin to unravel while a jailed man begins making threats to those he once called his friends as dark events begin playing out threatening more than just one person.

Episode 3
Invisible Tapestry

1
Washington DC

"Do I know someone named Caroline Welsh?"
Maxwell Pendergraft leans back in his chair and sighs.

"*I did*—we were in college together. Her name at that time was Caroline Dey. She married some nerdy-looking dude."

He reacts as the monitor in front of him comes to life. A photo appears. Maxwell seems in shock. He gestures.

"*It can't be.* It happened only once—we were both drunk and ended up in the backseat of my car. She was engaged so we acted like it never happened. I attended her wedding."

Harcourt Styverson points his finger at Maxwell and stifles a smirk. He pulls up another photo and shows it to Maxwell seconds later. He snickers lightly and begins laughing.

"He's *your* son—his father—Dayton Welsh and I are really tight. My cousin is married to his sister. He just found out."

Maxwell runs his fingers through his hair.

"Does the kid know I'm his pop?"

Harcourt rolls his eyes knowingly and shrugs.

"Not yet—they are figuring out how to do it. They live in a little seaside village called Orchid Bay near Santa Barbara."

He gestures at Maxwell and smirks.

"It was quite a huge shock. Dayton and his girlfriend were planning a family—until the doctor gave him the bad news."

Harcourt walks over to Maxwell.

"Dayton is sterile—always been dry. No way could he be anyone's father. It was quite the life-changer—newsworthy."

Maxwell looks at the photo again. He sighs loudly as he faces Harcourt and stands. He waves his hand in the air.

"How do I figure into the picture?"

Harcourt gives Maxwell a knowing look.

"Dayton had a talk with Caroline and she confirmed she lost her virginity to you in the backseat of your car. Told Dayton she got drunk and you two did the deed—said she never said anything afterwards because she was ashamed of her actions. Admitted she married Dayton without telling him—didn't know she was pregnant until months later—assumed Dayton was the proud poppa. It wasn't until they talked that she realized."

"There's no doubt—I'm really this kid's pop?"

Harcourt looks at the photo and grins broadly.

"He's not a kid—he's a young man."

Maxwell runs his fingers through his hair again.

2

Pacific Coast Highway

"I'm tired of hearing that you can't spend the weekend with me at my father's cabin. No one will know. Least of all Carrie Booker—*ugh*—that girl is a real killjoy no doubt—blah city."

Marley Osborne pulls Kyler Vanwick toward her and sighs loudly as she embraces him. They then kiss passionately.

"I just don't want any drama."

Marley pretends to slap Kyler playfully.

"That bitch isn't married to you. I don't see what the big deal is—tell her you've moved on. Just tell her it's over."

Page **70**

Kyler zips up his jeans and seems annoyed.

"Look, you know my deal when we got together. I told you I was with Carrie—and you and I were only gonna be friends."

Marley shakes her fist at Kyler.

"I know what you said before—but we've been fucking for months now—playing Carrie for a fool. I'm sure she knows you've been stringing her along—on account of her rich daddy having all those connections in Orchid Bay. *Ugh*—I'm just so ready to let her find out about us—cry herself to sleep knowing we fucked."

"I'm not going to dump Carrie for you—besides what about you and Dash Grillo? Chump told me he loves you."

"He's away at college. Case closed."

Kyler steps out of his car. He looks around the area for several seconds and faces Marley again. Kyler grimaces.

"I think we should stop seeing each other."

Marley reacts. She seems enraged.

3
Orchid Bay
Mills Apartment

"Do I look like I give a fuck about what people think about my rep? People in this fucking town need to get a frigging life."

Adam Mills grabs Sabine Norton by the arm.

"You and I are not gonna change how we do things. I own you for better or worse—and don't you forget it, *bitch.*"

Sabine gives Adam a knowing look.

"I'm tired of how you treat me—I'm not one of your cheap back alley whores. I think it's time we go our separate ways."

Adam laughs and pulls Sabine toward him.

"What do you think would happen if everyone in this motherfucking town found out about us? Found out that you've been my lucky charm for the last three years—servicing my most intimate needs bordering on kinky. Found out that you and Graham Vanwick were lovers? Oh, imagine the tongues wagging for weeks if I showed them the videos I found—*scandalous.*"

Sabine seems frightened and grimaces as Adam begins laughing. He tightens his grip on her arm and laughs loudly.

"That Graham Vanwick freak show knew how to service his women without a doubt—used you—made you do things."

Sabine reacts and jerks her arm free.

"I thought you said you destroyed the videos."

Adam laughs and points at Sabine.

"I lied."

He looks at his erection.

"You and I have a date with my bed."

Adam grabs Sabine by the arm once again.

"I hope you're on the pill. I won't tolerate you telling me you missed your frigging period again—once was enough."

Sabine seems upset as Adam leads her toward his bedroom and whistles. Her forces her through the door and slams it shut before throwing her on the bed. He unzips his jeans.

4
San Francisco

"What's happening to me? Is Loren right? Am I losing my mind? Can it possibly be true? Is that teenage girl not real?"

Houghton Fawcett reaches out to pull the drapes across the window in his office. He stops suddenly and sighs.

"She said Loren *killed* Ralph."

A blast of cold air rushes past Houghton. He turns around suddenly and sees Tiffany Johnson staring back at him. They look at each other for a few seconds. Houghton rubs his eyes several times. She takes a step forward and points at Houghton.

"You're on borrowed time old man."

Houghton reacts to the comment unable to move.

"Loren has a crypt waiting for you at Colma."

Tiffany points at Houghton again and seconds later vanishes. For a few seconds he seems in shock and sighs.

"How could I have been so wrong about my own flesh and blood? He had everything—his life held so much promise."

He walks toward his desk and stops.

"How shall I even the score?"

He walks back and forth several times.

"Funny you should ask."

He slowly spins around and sees Tiffany standing directly behind him again. She smiles slyly and gestures at him.

"I can help you teach Loren a lesson."

Tiffany smirks and walks toward the mirror. She looks back at Houghton. He watches as she reaches out to touch the mirror lightly. Flashes of light illuminate the office for a few seconds. She turns to face Houghton again and smirks.

"Well? What are you gonna do?"

Seconds later she's gone. He clenches his fist and walks toward the door. Several feet away Tiffany reappears and smiles as she folds her hands. She seems pleased and laughs.

The Next Day

5
Pacific Coast Highway

"I think we should kill that whore—have our fun with her and then break her neck. Be done with her once and for all."

Sasha Levitov makes a lewd gesture with his finger.

"I'm so ready for some action between the sheets—got to keep my juices flowing—especially after what happened with my last girlfriend. Goddamn slut royally skipped out on me."

Sergei Lycov jabs Sasha and laughs.

"Your girl shacked up with your big brother. Alexei finally got out of the slammer after that crypt incident a while back and banged Pamela at your engagement party. Got to hand it to him for being bold—took what he wanted—seriously insulted you."

Sasha clenches his fist as Sergei smirks. Sergei jabs Sasha again. They look at each other briefly. Sasha seems annoyed.

"I hate him. I hate that fucker—brother or not."

Sergei pulls over by the side of the road and sighs.

"You two were splitsville the minute he got between her legs and plowed her. She's his property now. Saw them yesterday at Costco shopping—probably stocking up on condoms."

Sasha seems about to explode.

6
Orchid Bay
Osborne Apartment

"Uh-huh—we're still good together."

Ryan Pena winks at Jayne Osborne as he pulls on a pair of jogging shorts. He notices her reaction and grins slyly.

"Why exactly did you leave Orchid Bay the way you did. One day you were here and the next you were history."

"I just had to get away. Leave it at that."

Ryan strokes his erection poking through his shorts.

"I'm just glad you're back. I intend for us to have plenty of moments in the next couple of weeks—make lots of noise."

"I'll let you know."

He shoots her a concerned look. Jayne walks toward him and pushes Ryan toward the door. He notices and sighs.

"Is this your way of telling me you're expecting company shortly? I can take a hint if that's the case—a dolt I'm not."

He watches her walk down the hallway of her apartment toward the bathroom. He sighs and looks at his erection.

7
Orchid Bay
Greasy Spoon Diner

"Last time I saw a grin on your face was like—*like* never. I assume you and your girlfriend are hitting all the right chords."

Lachlan Ball playfully points his finger at Curtis Solle pretending to warn him about his comment. He laughs.

"She and I are quite happy. I couldn't ask for anyone nicer. It's been a while since I felt this way—well—especially after."

Curtis gives Lachlan a knowing look and sighs.

"Have the two of you set a date."

Lachlan playfully shoves Curtis and smirks.

"Don't you go there with me Solle—we're just getting to know each other—know our moods. Enjoy being together."

Curtis continues to tease Lachlan.

"Uh-huh—it's just a matter of time before you and that wonderful woman tie the knot. I got it on good authority."

Lachlan seems embarrassed and shrugs.

"I'm in no rush to get married."

Curtis looks at the street ahead and grins.

"Uh-huh—we'll see. Just saying—I'd be proud to be your best man if needed. I approve of your choice in a bed partner."

"Will you just leave it alone?"

Curtis leans toward Lachlan and laughs.

"I'm really happy for you."

Lachlan reaches out to hug Curtis.

"Thanks dude. I appreciate it. Really I do."

Curtis grabs Lachlan's arm.

"Name your first kid after me."

Lachlan pretends to punch Curtis.

"Will you stop already?"

Curtis makes a lewd gesture and grins.

8
Orchid Bay
Welsh Residence

"You've got to talk to me—what about exactly? If this is about Lloyd's relationship with Susan Osborne—leave it be."

Caroline Welsh seems annoyed as she looks at Dayton Welsh staring back at her from his car. She sighs loudly.

"Where are you exactly? You seem."

"I'm just outside of Orchid Bay."

Caroline notices Dayton's demeanor.

"What's going on Dayton? Is something wrong?"

Page 75

"I'll be there in twenty minutes."

Caroline looks at her cell phone as it goes blank. She turns to look at the driveway. She looks at the cell phone once more.

"I wonder what he's up to."

Caroline realizes Lloyd Welsh is standing in the doorway looking at her. He takes a step forward. He seems upset.

"What going on?"

Caroline shrugs. They look at each other for a few seconds as Lloyd comes toward her. He wraps his arms around her.

"Is dad OK?"

Caroline seems about to cry.

"He's fine."

"Are you OK?"

Caroline looks at Lloyd for a few seconds and laughs.

"I see Susan has rubbed off on you."

Lloyd shakes his head.

"I have no idea what you're babbling about."

Caroline leads her son toward the kitchen window. She looks out and seems nervous. He notices. Caroline sighs loudly.

"Your father is on his way. He said it was important. I think maybe he's found a solution to something he and I found out."

Lloyd shoots his mother a concerned look.

9
Orchid Bay
Greasy Spoon Diner

"I'm pregnant. I just thought you should know."

Carrie Booker looks at Marley curiously as her rival sits down next to her. Marley grins slyly as she watches Carrie's reaction. She slowly licks her lips and seems quite pleased.

"Aren't you gonna ask who's the daddy?"

Marley seems annoyed and grabs Carrie's wrist. She leans toward her and smirks. She tightens her grip and winks.

"It's Kyler."

Carrie reacts.

Page **76**

"I don't believe you."

Marley gestures with her hand.

"He's been fucking me for months—been fucking since we hooked-up at the junior prom. He knows his way around my vagina—refuses to use a condom whenever we fuck—told me he's tired of being with you—said you bored him—dullsville."

Carrie stands and faces Marley.

"You disgust me."

Marley makes a lewd gesture with her finger and stands. She licks her lips again. She notices a few people listening.

"His penis has a scar on the left side. Said he got it skiing when he was a kid. It's shaped like a saucer—oval to be exact."

Carrie seems about to faint. Marley smiles broadly as she licks her lips again. She raises her voice and laughs.

"He likes sensuous blowjobs—comes really fast when my tongue touches the head—said I've got a hold over him."

Carrie suddenly runs out of the diner.

10

San Francisco

"What do you mean he left? That old man never leaves without his limo—he's up to something no doubt."

Loren Fawcett looks at the cell phone in his hand for a few seconds. He turns to face Cujo Momoa and grimaces.

"OK—OK—just find him. I don't care what you have to do—just find him. I don't like not knowing his whereabouts."

Loren runs his fingers through his hair.

"Look—just find him—and stop telling me you'll try. I want him found or else. *How far could he have gotten.* Damn it."

He slams the cell phone down on a table and faces Cujo again. They exchange a concerned glance. Loren sighs.

"It seems my conniving father has managed to escape into thin air. Stupid employees can't locate him anywhere. No doubt he's up to something he doesn't want me privy to—*fuck.*"

Cujo seems confused. He gestures.

Page **77**

"What do you think your old man is up to? You had cameras installed everywhere. What about security?"

Loren clenches his fist angrily.

"Apparently every goddamn camera went down at exactly the same time. It just doesn't make any sense whatsoever."

Cujo takes a step forward.

"Unless he had help—paid someone?"

Loren faces Cujo.

"Who would dare defy me?"

Cujo waves his hand in the air several times.

"Money changes everything."

Loren begins laughing.

"My father is a cheap son-of-a-bitch. He wouldn't pay anyone if he didn't have to—unless he's being blackmailed."

Cujo lowers his voice and snickers.

"What about that teenage girl?"

"What girl? My father is a loon. There is no girl. He imagined her—made her real—at least in his mind anyway."

Cujo looks at Loren curiously.

"Did he?"

They look at each other.

11
Orchid Bay
Downtown Police Station

"Oh God—not again Lachlan—enough with the ear-to-ear grin every damn morning. I'm so close to punching you."

Roland O'Brien watches as Lachlan comes toward him.

"Go ahead—I can take you—pop you hard."

They begin laughing and pretend to shadow box.

"It's nice to see you happy. Alison Orlonge has worked her magic on you without a doubt—made you human again."

Lachlan shoves Roland and laughs.

"That offer still stands—I can take you."

"In your dreams bud—I boxed plenty in college."

Page **78**

Lachlan gives Roland a knowing look and laughs.

"Hey, that's one of Alan's lines. How is Alan Swinton doing anyway—haven't heard from him since he moved to Vegas."

Roland waves his hand in the air.

"He's doing fine. Sent me a message last week—said he and Maggie tied the knot. Said his brother was thinking of going back to singing. Independent clubs—artsy stuff mostly."

"Lane Swinton was quite the dude about town once he began singing. People kept pestering him for autographs."

Roland glances at the front door.

"Cara Tickerson had it bad for him until he fooled around with her sister. People talked for weeks about the vicious catfight that ensued between them just outside St. Anne's Church."

"Maria Tickerson left town right after. Last I heard she was living in Half Moon Bay with some musician or other."

Roland glances at the hallway.

"Have you paid our guest a visit yet?"

Lachlan reacts and sighs.

"I'm not in the mood to look at that frigging rapist. I might do something that I'll enjoy—like break his damn skull open."

Roland nods as he sits down at his desk.

12

Orchid Bay

Greasy Spoon Diner

"This isn't the time or place Erica—think before you say something you'll regret later. Plenty people are listening."

Erica Gersh seems about to slap Ryan as her rage builds. She turns to face Denise Stone. She mockingly points at her.

"You and her—are you serious? *Ugh*—talk about scraping the bottom of the barrel when it comes to finding a bed partner. She's got loser written all over her after spending time in the slammer. *Ugh*—I'm gonna be sick—used-up prison trash."

Denise reacts and glances at Ryan. She faces Erica again and grins slyly. She notices several people watching them.

Page **79**

"At least I didn't cause a scene at my ex's wedding begging him to leave his pregnant bride. Oh, and I didn't sleep with both of the Lorenzo brothers trying to decide which one was better in bed. Of course I also didn't sleep with my stepfather right after my mother's death in a car accident—talk about an "ugh" moment—not even Vina Phamler would stoop that low."

Erica slaps Denise.

"*You bitch.*"

Denise reacts and slaps Erica back as people begin whispering. She turns to face Ryan. She notices people pointing their cell phones at her. She grins and faces Erica. She laughs.

"Who do you think you are calling me names? I served time for passing a bad check—not fucking every guy in town. If I were you I'd fix the mess that is your life before you point fingers at anyone else. Seriously Erica, is there anyone in this town you haven't fucked yet—besides women and gay men of course."

Erica realizes she's being filmed and seems ready to burst out in tears. She runs out of the diner as Denise smiles.

"Was it something I said?"

Denise watches Ryan's reaction.

13

Morro Bay

"Of course I know what they're capable of when someone crosses them—but so what? I want them to pay—dearly."

Marlisa Vigaro watches Carlos Vente as he looks at the gun in his hand. She takes a step forward and gestures.

"I've been wronged and there's only one way to make things right—a message must be sent—one laced with blood. It's been a long time coming—Loren Fawcett needs reality."

Carlos looks at the gun in his hand again.

"I got no problem taking those guys out. I just want you to be aware of the risk. They'll attack with guns blazing."

Marlisa looks at the credit card in her hand and grins. She throws it at Carlos. She watches his reaction and snickers.

Page **80**

"Gather a team together and work your magic. One after another—I want them to meet the most grisly of fates."

Carlos stares briefly at the cell phone in his other hand.

"Who should I take out first?"

Marlisa licks her lips.

"Sergei Orlov. He's an easy target—not too bright if I recall. His sudden death will make them begin to wonder."

They exchange a glance.

"Who's second?"

"Cujo Momoa. Seems to me he's the hired gun behind a lot of what takes place with Loren and his people. Losing him will make it clear someone has gone hunting—gunning for them."

Carlos runs his fingers through his hair.

"You're one cold bitch."

Marlisa blows him a kiss and laughs.

"I'll take that as a compliment."

He looks at his cell phone again and grins.

14
Orchid Bay
Hampshire Street Cafe

"It's just not the right look. Are you sure I can't change his mind. Talk some common sense into that boyfriend of yours."

Kayla Larsen turns around to face her mother. She watches as Shirley Larsen gives her a knowing look.

"Leave it alone mother—Patrick doesn't need you telling him how to run his life. Besides he's not the type to listen anyway—he's made up his mind—knows what he wants."

Shirley wrings her hands.

"This is not what I envisioned for you."

"I'm well-aware of that—painfully aware. But it's my life and I don't think it's a mistake to let my boyfriend be himself."

Shirley reacts to the slight and grimaces.

"I only want the best for you."

Kayla glances at her cell phone.

"I know mother—but sometimes you've just got to let go and let your children live their own lives—wrong or right."

"Violet never gave me any trouble."

Kayla shoots her mother a knowing look.

"I'm not Violet—she and I are very different. She married a man she didn't love. I couldn't do that—absolutely no way."

"Violet and Aaron are happy together."

Kayla stifles a laugh.

"Uh huh I just bet. On her wedding day she barely spoke to him. It's been three years plus and she still lusts after Daniel Williams from Ocean Landing. Uh-huh—she's really happy."

Shirley throws her hands up in the air.

"Fine—but don't say I didn't warn you about what kind of life you're going to have with an unemployed loser."

Kayla notices people looking at them inside the small diner. Not far away she sees Liana Danforth tending to several customers and turns to face her mother again. She sighs.

15
Orchid Bay
Pioneer Trail Mall

"Marley Osborne is a fucking liar. She's slept with every guy in our school—teachers included. Seriously, she's a slut."

Carrie seems about to cry as Kyler grabs her by the arm. He pulls her toward him as she resists. He sighs loudly.

"I haven't been with her OK—she's just trying to split us up. She hates you—hates us together. Let it go already."

Carrie jerks free from Kyler's grip.

"How does she know about the scar on your penis?"

Kyler reacts. Carrie notices.

"Oh God—*it's true*. All of it is true. You've been fucking that piece of trash. *Ugh*—I hate you. We're through—*over*."

Kyler reaches out to Carrie but she roughly slaps his hand away and begins running out of the parking lot. He shrugs.

"What is the matter with women today?"

Page **82**

He clenches his fist. He flexes his muscles and sighs.

"That bitch is gonna pay for what she did when I find her sorry ass. She and I have some things to work through."

He pulls out his cell phone and begins dialing. Several seconds later Marley answers. She notices Kyler's anger.

"I thought it was time for Carrie to know about the two of us. That girl was living in a fantasy world—a sad fairy tale."

Kyler runs his fingers through his hair.

"You told her you were expecting my baby. What the fuck was that about? There's no baby. You're not pregnant."

Marley slides her fingers over her exposed breasts as she sees Kyler's reaction. She strokes herself several times.

"We're done. OK. We're over."

Marley stops stroking her breasts and seems angry.

"I don't take kindly to threats. You and I are done when I say we're done. Don't forget I know what you did last year."

Kyler seems bored and shrugs.

"Don't threaten me Marley. You've got plenty of really tawdry secrets that I know about too—starting with that incident involving Jessica Ball and your uncle. Of course there's also that situation between you and Ethan Vanwick's father last month."

Marley gestures with her hand. She smirks slyly.

"I wonder what your father would do if he found out what you did to get into college. He would be so disappointed."

The cell phone goes blank in Kyler's hand.

"I think it's time I call Spence Rojas. He'll know how to handle Marley. From what I recall they had something going for a while—until he caught her in bed with his grandfather. *Ugh*."

He looks at the cell phone and then begins dialing.

16
San Francisco

"Uh-huh—that's right it's me. It seems my two-faced son has been leading a double life for several years—pretending to be my dutiful son while killing his older brother in cold blood."

Houghton shakes his fist and grimaces as he looks at a cell phone in his hand. He continues talking for several more seconds before he merges into the shadows of a garbage-soaked alley.

"I'll see you in an hour—don't be late."

He nods several times and shuts off the cell phone. A few feet away a man's body can be seen. A screwdriver is sticking out of his chest. Houghton shrugs as he quickly walks past him.

17

Orchid Bay
Paradise Pointe Bluffs

"Here's his picture. He should be easy to find. I want a clear message sent. Make sure he heeds your warning."

Sergei gives Daphne Mills a sly look as he takes the photo from her. He winks at Sasha and faces Daphne again. He twirls the photo in his hand. She notices and seems nervous.

"Just give him a scare—don't kill him."

Sergei gestures with his hand and laughs.

"Point made—I'll play nice."

"No one must know I made this possible. Make sure that boy is alone when you pay him a visit. Orchid Bay is plenty full of ears—people like drama. Keep it at a minimum if you can."

Sergei stifles a smirk.

"I know Orchid Bay well. Adam and I spent quite a bit of time at Murphy's Bar and Grill—got into plenty of fights."

He turns to Sasha and points to the car.

"Make sure you have the brass knuckles ready for when we rendezvous with Dana's soon-to-be ex-boyfriend."

Daphne shoots Sasha a nervous look. She watches as they walk toward the edge of the bluffs. She grabs Sergei's arm.

"I want him breathing after you're done working him."

"I'll do my best. It all depends on his behavior."

Daphne seems bothered. She stands for a few seconds in silence before facing her car a few feet away. She sighs loudly.

"I hope I'm doing the right thing."

Page **84**

She glances at Sergei and Sasha briefly before getting into her car and driving away. She looks back several times.

18
Orchid Bay
Public Parking Lot

"I'm not dating anyone right now—just winging it."

Vina Phamler gives Roland a knowing look as he shuts the door to his car. She watches him walk away and sighs loudly.

"How about we meet for lunch tomorrow?"

Roland waves his hand in the air and continues walking across the parking lot. Lachlan jabs Roland and laughs.

"That girl never gives up. When she's done with one guy she moves on to another. She's a regular black widow."

"Vina Phamler is more than I can handle. She's more than any guy can handle. She ruins every man she becomes involved with. I pity the idiot who falls for her games—terrible."

Lachlan runs his fingers through his hair.

"Uh-huh—I agree. She tried to snare me but my mother quashed her schemes—protected me. She threatened Vina from what I heard—used her sordid past against her—shamed her."

"I'll just bet. Your mother is not one to mess with. She's fearless. Several months ago she single-handedly busted Gerald Olek's boy when he tried to sell her fake insurance. Said he was helping out his father's firm. She called his father right in front of him and humiliated that boy. He hasn't been the same since."

Lachlan begins laughing.

"I love that woman. After my marriage ended my mother was there for me—really helped me through the pain—listened."

He wipes sweat from his brow. They stop several feet away from a diner. Lachlan grabs Roland's arm. He grins slyly.

"Julia Danforth isn't dating anyone."

Roland shoots Lachlan a warning look and laughs.

"Don't you get started with Julia Danforth and me going out on a date—we're just friends—nothing more than that."

Page 85

Lachlan jabs Roland and lowers his voice.

"She's not Vina."

Roland stifles a smile.

"That I know. Everyone knows that."

They share a knowing look and enter the diner.

19

Orchid Bay

Lighthouse Park

"I don't appreciate your mother saying I'm a zero just because my ex-girlfriend slept with my father. Finding out Lyla Osborne was playing house with my father almost sent me over the edge. He and I haven't been the same since. My mother won't even discuss the issue publicly—it's as if it never happened."

Dana Mills strokes the back of Mark Corrington's neck.

"Seriously, your mother needs to stop judging me. I know I've not been a model of perfection. Hanging with Drew Phamler before he totally went off the deep end with Nina Holliday put a stain on my character that I'm still trying to erase. But Lyla getting horizontal with my father wasn't of my doing. It's on them, not me. I found out like everyone else when her mother tried to have my pervert father arrested for rape until she realized Lyla was already eighteen and wasn't considered a minor."

Dana runs her hands through Mark's hair.

"I don't care what my mother says about you—it won't change how I feel. I'm tired of her comparing every guy I like to my loser father. He's in jail where he belongs. End of story."

"Did your father really try to kill the mayor?"

Dana nods. She grabs her cell phone and sighs loudly.

"Said the former mayor was trying to frame him for some business deal gone wrong—at least that's what he says."

She begins going through her social media account as Mark shoots her a curious look. She stops suddenly.

"My father lies—he's a liar—he just can't help himself. I just don't know why he does it—maybe he's deranged."

Page **86**

She gives Mark her cell phone and points to a folder on her account. She looks at him as he clicks on it and sighs loudly.

"I saved all the stories that were on the news."

Dana watches as he opens the folder.

20

Santa Barbara

"It's all set. Loren Fawcett is about to get a nasty surprise he wasn't expecting. It's just a matter of hours until my guy begins his mission—blood is going to be spilled plenty."

Marlisa laughs as she faces Corey Danforth.

"I think you should've let me do the honors. Take those bastards out for what they did to Allan—sweet revenge."

Marlisa gestures with her hand.

"It's better this way. I hired a professional. I've used him in the past to twist some arms when needed. He's also skilled in taking problems out of the way for good. Loren will be beside himself with rage when he gets the news that one of his guys has been iced. He'll want to know who pulled the trigger—only to realize too late another death is already underway. Of course it's only a matter of time before further tragedy befalls him."

She begins laughing hysterically.

"I wish I could see the look on Loren's face when he gets the news about his precious cousin—shot by someone he doesn't know that has already begun hunting him like an animal."

Corey slowly walks over to where Marlisa is standing.

"I just want Allan's death avenged."

"It's just a matter of time before the first of many is given a free ticket to the morgue. By the time I'm finished with Loren Fawcett he'll beg for mercy—wish he was already dead."

"What happens if your guy is bested by one of Loren's goons? I've heard of his people—they're a vicious bunch."

Marlisa waves her hand in the air.

"I'm not worried. I hired the best—he truly enjoys his job. Loren won't know what he's up against until it's too late."

Page **87**

Corey reaches out and wraps his arms around Marlisa as she giggles. He kisses her neck and whispers in her ear.

"You've got a filthy mind Danforth."

"Uh-huh—I certainly do."

He points toward the hallway.

21
Orchid Bay
McKeon Beach Condo

"Denise Stone is fresh out of the slammer?"

Carter McKeon watches Erica's reaction and grins.

"She and I had some history—then she hooked up with William Gilliland—a few months before he met his maker."

Carter laughs noticing Erica's anger increasing.

"She insulted me—called me out in front of everyone as if she was some sort of saint. *Ugh*—how can Ryan stand her?"

Carter makes a lewd gesture with his finger.

"She certainly didn't waste any time landing in his bed. I guess it's true what they say—all a woman has to do is spread her legs and she can catch anything—even a lowlife like Ryan."

Erica reacts and stands up.

"I thought you were my friend Carter—someone who I could talk to—especially after how I've been treated lately."

Carter stands and grabs Erica's arm.

"I'm sorry—how about we start over. OK?"

They look at each other.

"She was really mean to me. Called me all sorts of vile names—and Ryan just let her do it. He just stood there."

"That's hardly news. Dense Stone has always been a bitch as far back as I can remember. She cares about no one other than herself—uses everyone around her—extremely selfish."

Erica slides her hands across Carter's chest. He notices and laughs. They stare at each other. He looks at his erection.

"This is where you promise me really good sex if I help you get even with Denise—punish her terribly for insulting you."

Erica's hand slide across Carter's swelling erection. She tugs at the waistband of his Lycra shorts. He laughs.

"OK—OK—I'm an easy yes. We've had some wild times in the past—you always deliver. What do you want me to do?"

Erica leans closer to Carter and whispers.

"Oh man—that's really vicious—seriously hardcore."

Erica slides her hand into his Lycra shorts and grins slyly.

"People will be talking for months when you're finished with her—she'll probably have to leave Orchid Bay for good."

Erica nods and passionately kisses Carter.

22
Orchid Bay
Downtown Police Station

"Do I look like I give a fuck about how this will affect you if I tell your father what you did? I'm through being nice."

Jason Shappe glares at Sarina Wolper.

"Either you get me out of here or your father is going to know what I know. Imagine his reaction when he finds out you embezzled a huge chunk of his bank account in order to finance a ridiculous online Bitcoin business venture several years ago."

Sarina reacts and turns away from Jason.

"You promised you wouldn't tell—said I could trust you when I told you what I did—the day you took my virginity."

"I lied."

He grabs the bars of his cell.

"Either you get me out of this hellhole or I'm going to turn your world upside down. I swear I will—I'll destroy you."

Sarina watches Jason as he shakes his fist at her and grins broadly. He notices her frightened reaction and smirks.

"You have one day—twenty-four hours."

Jason makes a lewd gesture with his finger.

"It's either you or me and I choose me. Friendship could only go so far in this life. Help me or I swear I'll crush you."

Sarina seems about to cry.

Page **89**

"I thought you were different—thought you really cared about me. I believed you. Believed every word you said."

"Dumbass bitch—stupid whore."

Sarina turns away. Jason seems enraged by her behavior and begins yelling loudly at her as she walks down the hallway.

"Twenty-four hours—then I let dear old dad know what kind of a daughter you really are. I'll destroy you Sarina."

He continues ranting for several minutes.

23
Orchid Bay
Welsh Driveway

"You can't be serious. It'll destroy his world."

Caroline looks at the folder in her hand and then back at her ex-husband. Dayton shakes his head and turns away.

"Do you have a better way?"

Caroline looks at the folder once more.

"Dropping a shocker like this will freak Lloyd out. We need to think of how we're going to explain to him that you're not his father. How this all happened—and that we didn't know."

They hear footsteps and turn around.

"How what happened?"

Lloyd stares at his parents blankly.

24
San Francisco

"How about we take this to the next step? Make it a point of discussion with my family. Tell them we're dating."

Lizette Richardson nods as she kisses Sergei Orlov and steps out of the car. He looks at her and laughs gleefully.

"There's nothing to worry about. Everyone likes you."

Lizette blows Sergei a kiss and smiles broadly.

"Who'd think you of all people would steal my heart the way you did last year—make me love you—cherish you."

Page **90**

Sergei wags his finger at Lizette.

"I stole you from my cousin."

Lizette laughs.

"You did no such thing—Igor and I were just friends. I never thought of him in that way. He's OK with us—said so."

Sergei rolls his eyes.

"What my cousin says and what he does is two very different things. He takes slights personally—makes threats."

Lizette gives Sergei a knowing look.

"I'll see you tomorrow."

Sergei nods. He watches as Lizette walks toward the crosswalk. As she begins crossing the street a black sedan heads toward Sergei's car in a rush. Bullets spray his car endlessly. He's shot multiple times. Blood is everywhere as the car drives off.

25
Orchid Bay
Hampshire Street Cafe

"I'm gonna tell her. I swear I will if you don't."

"Don't you dare—let it alone."

Lachlan grins broadly and glances over at Julia Danforth several tables away talking to a friend. Roland grimaces.

"Mind your own business—or I'll poke my nose into your business—leaving no stone unturned in your love life."

Lachlan sighs loudly. He glances at Julia again. He notices Roland's gaze focused on Julia. He points at Roland.

"We both know you like her—been eyeing her for several weeks now. Just ask her out already—she'll say yes."

"I'll hit you—I swear I will."

Lachlan winks at Roland and laughs.

"OK—OK—I'll let you handle your own affairs—for now anyway. I just want you to be happy—love your life again."

Roland shoots Lachlan a knowing look.

"I know you mean well. But I'm not ready yet to pursue anything with Julia Danforth. I just need time to myself."

Page **91**

Lachlan glances at Julia again and grins broadly.

"I got over my ex—you can get over yours."

Roland leans back in his chair.

"I'm completely over her. But I still need more time before I get back in the swing of things—figure out where I stand."

Lachlan nods and turns around again.

26

San Francisco

"What the hell happened to my little brother?"

Vladimir Orlov seems about to explode as he looks at Lizette. She appears to be in shock as she wipes away a tear.

"It all happened so fast. I got out of Sergei's car and was walking across the street to my doctor's office—when this sedan came out of nowhere and began shooting. It was horrible. The car was sprayed with bullets. The sedan sped off before I could react. All I could see was Sergei's body covered in blood—half his skull on the street. There was so much blood. I must have screamed so loud the cops heard me. They appeared out of nowhere."

Vladimir clenches his fists.

"He was killed by one of our rivals no doubt. They'll pay for this. When I find out who ordered a hit on Sergei—there'll be no place for them to hide. I'll crucify them myself. Their blood will quench my thirst for revenge. I'll show them no mercy—none."

Lizette seems confused and sighs.

"But why would anyone dare come up against us? They know what would happen once you exposed them. Your rep is known throughout the city—feared. Who would be so foolish?"

Vladimir clenches his fist again.

"Good question. Who would dare do such a thing?"

He walks back and forth for a few seconds as Lizette watches him. He stops and faces her. They look at each other.

"Whitney. It's got to be that bastard. He ordered the hit on my little bro. It all makes sense now—Whitney ordered it."

Lizette looks at Vladimir curiously.

"But no one knows where Todd Whitney is being kept. No one outside your family knows his whereabouts. He has no way to communicate with the outside world from his cell inside the Fawcett mansion. He's been there since you kidnapped him. As far as the world is concerned Todd Whitney has been dead for a year. He simply disappeared and was never seen again."

"He must have found a fink among us—got word out to someone to take Sergei out. That frigging bastard is going to pay for having my brother killed. I swear I'll kill him myself."

Lizette reaches out to grab Vladimir's arm.

"But who among us would rat you out? Who would dare cross your family? It just doesn't make sense for someone to risk their life and the lives of their families for chump change."

Vladimir pulls free of Lizette's grip and reaches for his cell phone. He looks at her briefly and seems a bit panicked.

"It has to be Whitney. He's been a thorn in our sides for years now. He should've been killed long ago. But Anton Levitov and his damn perverse behavior got the better of us all. Damn him for forcing us to keep Whitney alive in order for him to watch his precious daughter being raped weekly by Anton. His hatred for Whitney has caused us all to have a lapse in judgment."

Lizette wipes a tear from her eyes and shrugs.

"Maybe *we* should take Whitney out. Rub him out in the most painful way possible. But not before we make him watch his precious daughter being viciously strangled to death by Anton. He'll enjoy killing that girl as her father watches helplessly."

Vladimir nods in agreement and smiles.

TO BE CONTINUED

A Brief Look at the Fourth Episode

Murders begin occurring in one family with no end in sight as a slighted woman schemes to destroy her rival while another woman makes a fateful decision about her immediate future.

Episode 4
Imperfect Lives

1
New York City

"Why are you asking me about the business dealings of Wesley Mayfield, Pendergraft? I hardly knew the guy."

Scott Malone runs his fingers through his hair as he stares at Maxwell Pendergraft on his computer screen. He sighs.

"It's been several years—memory is a bit foggy when it comes to details on the yacht. That man had several screws loose from what I recall—seemed ready to snap—really rude."

Maxwell leans back in his chair.

"I just thought you might know—might have heard if he was mixed up with the mob? I was given some info a few hours ago. Mayfield's name showed up. I thought since you had dealings with him you might have heard something drop."

Scott rolls his eyes and smirks.

"Not a peep—he and I only met once—and he wasn't in the talking mood if you know what I mean—dude seemed up to something—really shady. At least that's what Sandra said in her book. You have a copy—Sandra said she sent you one."

Scott watches as Maxwell glances at a book several feet away on top of an ice maker and shrugs. Maxwell stands and walks over. He picks it up as he continues talking to Scott.

"How is it selling? Top of the list I assume?"

Scott points at Maxwell.

"Twelve last week—people are still lapping it up. Sandra is stoked—never thought it would last so long at the top."

Maxwell flips through the book and seems preoccupied as he continues talking. Scott notices and seems irritated.

"Look man, I don't have anything on Mayfield. Would you like Sandra to give you a call? She's out at the moment but will be back in about an hour or so—took our kid to the doctor."

Maxwell looks at the book again and shakes his head. He faces Scott once more and makes a gesture with his finger.

"OK—thanks anyway."

He points at Scott and smirks.

"I've got some vacation time coming. How about you and I meet up—I'll kick your ass on the tennis courts as usual."

Scott makes a lewd gesture with his finger.

"In your dreams buddy—I'll wipe the court with you."

He shakes his fist at Maxwell.

"I'll make you beg."

Maxwell laughs and makes a fist.

"I'll crush you."

Maxwell and Scott continue poking fun at each other about their tennis skills before ending the call a minute later.

2

San Francisco

Carlos Vente watches Cujo Momoa for several seconds as he walks toward his car in a parking lot. Carlos grins broadly as he watches the man get into an expensive European sports car.

"Sometimes things don't work out for some people. But death is a part of life. Good thing he has a family plot at Colma."

As Cujo starts the engine the car explodes.

Page **96**

"Autopsy is gonna be a mess no doubt."

Carlos begins laughing loudly as he drives away. People stare in shock as crowds begin gathering. Flames leap from the scorched car. Several fire trucks are heard in a distance.

3
Santa Barbara

"Perfect. I love how this is playing out. I'll be in touch with you shortly. Number three is not far away—one hour."

Marlisa Vigaro laughs as she shuts her cell phone off and turns to face Corey Danforth. He seems confused as she grins.

"Cujo Momoa is dead—car explosion."

Corey snaps his fingers several times as he comes toward Marlisa. They embrace. He notices her phone buzzing.

"Looks like you've got an urgent call. Someone named Steve Syverman? Dude seems pretty upset about something."

Marlisa waves her hand. Corey reacts.

"Aren't you going to answer it?"

"I'll call him back later. I have to decide who will be next on the chopping block. Third one will certainly sets hearts aflutter in the Fawcett household. The pieces of the puzzle will start to play on Loren's fragile mind when I take another of his kin out."

Corey seems confused and shrugs.

"I just want my brother's death avenged. I don't care who gets iced—take the entire brood out if need be. Whatever."

Marlisa slides her fingers through Corey's hair. She licks her lips several times and begins laughing gleefully. She walks over to a mini bar and pours herself a drink. She seems pleased.

"Cujo Momoa always had problems with the law going back to his high school years. No one will care he's dead."

She gestures with her hand.

"He killed one of his teachers at his senior prom—claimed self-defense but no one thought it was such. Everyone knew he hated that man. Broke his neck during a fight—walked away from it because of one of Houghton Fawcett's fancy lawyers."

Page **97**

Corey seems uneasy as he walks over to Marlisa.

"I remember that story. It was in the news for weeks. The trial was a circus. They put the dead teacher's memory on trial. It was terrible. The press had a field day—Momoa claimed all sorts of sordid things about the poor man. Destroyed his memory—his wife had to leave California. Of course there was that incident with a teenage girl. He skirted that one too—claimed he didn't know her—never met—said she lied—worked the jury plenty."

Marlisa takes a swig of her drink and laughs.

"Like I said—no one will miss Momoa."

She glances at her cell phone again as it begins buzzing once more. She gives Corey an odd look and gestures again.

4

Washington DC

"I wonder what was Wesley Mayfield's connection to the mob—and how does it connect to Tristan Montgomery Bell?"

Maxwell leans back in his chair and sighs.

"Shall we wait until you figure it out in a year?"

Maxwell spins around and realizes Tiffany Johnson is standing next to him. He seems unnerved and gives her a strange look as she glances at the book on top of his desk. She smirks.

"Mayfield was in deep with the Russian mob. Played with fire much too many times—crossed the line over and over."

Tiffany seems pleased as she leans over and whispers in Maxwell's ears. He reacts in shock. She points her finger at him.

"He was a piece of work no doubt—not a nice person by any means—met a grisly end in the Caribbean—in that terrible tragedy your friend witnessed. So many loose ends though—not everything has been dealt with—at least not yet anyway."

Maxwell stands up and faces Tiffany again.

"Well, are you gonna fill me in on the details about Wesley Mayfield and Tristan Montgomery Bell's connection?"

Tiffany seems pleased with herself as she looks at the computer screen. She notices Maxwell's reaction and laughs.

Page **98**

"What are you gonna do about your teenage son?"

Maxwell seems shocked at the remark.

"How do you know about that?"

Tiffany laughs and comes toward Maxwell again as he watches her circle him. He shakes his head several times.

"You *knew* about him didn't you?"

Tiffany gestures with her hand and nods.

"I know everything. There are no secrets that I don't know about. Starting with the tryst you had last night with that blonde you met at the Watergate building. She got played by you."

Maxwell gives Tiffany an odd look.

"I don't know what you're talking about."

"Uh-huh—play that game, dear Maxie—but we both know what I'm talking about, don't we? Told her you would call but you won't—just another one night stand for you—nothing serious."

"OK—OK—so what—I'm no saint—never claimed to be boyfriend material. I'm just not the serious type—shoot me."

Tiffany makes a lewd gesture with her finger.

"She works at Quantico."

Maxwell seems confused and sighs.

"Is that supposed to mean something to me?"

Tiffany winks at Maxwell.

5
Orchid Bay
Phamler Garden Condo

"You can't be serious? I won't do it—no way."

Tim Bergman shoots Vina Phamler a cautious look as he stands up. He walks to the door and suddenly stops.

"What happens if he overdoses?"

"He won't overdose. You'll just give him enough to knock him out. Once he's out I'll strip him to his birthday suit and take a few pictures of his penis. Make Kayla Larsen think I bedded her precious love. It'll end their relationship—case closed."

Tim runs his fingers through his hair.

Page **99**

"I don't like this—it's just too risky. This time you've gone too far with your schemes. This will end badly for you."

Vina rolls her eyes. She waves her hand in the air and sighs loudly. She points to the door. They look at each other.

"There's the door—use it."

Tim reacts. He shakes his head.

"Don't do it. If something happens to Patrick Clerke you'll end up in the slammer guaranteed. His parents will see to it."

"Are you still here? Get out. Be gone already."

Tim looks at Vina curiously and walks to the door. He stops briefly and turns around. He seems uneasy and sighs.

6
Los Angeles

Jayne Osborne grins broadly as she looks at the gun in her hand. She glances back at the gun store a few yards away.

"I've waited long enough for revenge."

She places the gun in its holster and turns around. She seems oddly pleased with her behavior. Her cell phone rings.

"They're gonna pay for what they did to me."

Jayne ignores her cell phone and looks at the gun.

"He may have thought he'd gotten away with what he and his friends did to me—thought I wouldn't get even with him."

She grins broadly and touches the gun.

"Revenge is a dish best served with a bullet from my gun."

Jayne begins laughing as she looks at the gun again.

7
Pacific Coast Highway

"He comes by here every day around this time according to Daphne. He gets a bite to eat before heading back towards Orchid Bay. It'll be a piece of cake—rough him up a bit."

Sasha Levitov grins slyly as he jabs Sergei Lycov sitting next to him in their car. He glances at his watch and shrugs.

Page **100**

"We'll brass knuckle the chump a bit. Make it clear to him he needs to stay clear of Dana Mills or else. Scare him."

Sergei's cell phone begins ringing. He answers it. Sasha watches as the color drains from Sergei's face seconds later.

"Oh fuck—like seriously? *He's dead? They're dead?* Is this some sort of joke? Quit playing games—it's not funny."

Sergei lets go of his cell phone. Sasha watches as it falls between their seats. He grabs it and begins talking. He reacts.

"Someone shot Sergei Orlov? Who? Why?"

His grip on the phone tightens.

"Cujo Momoa too—his car exploded?"

He wipes sweat from his brow.

"They were both killed less than two hours ago?"

He nods several times and sighs loudly.

8
Washington DC

"How does Wesley Mayfield figure into the Fawcett clan in San Francisco? Are you gonna tell me the details? Or am I supposed to figure this mess out all on my own—risk my life?"

Maxwell slowly turns to face Tiffany.

"Why is this family so important to you anyway?"

Tiffany shrugs and turns away.

"They just are—that's all you need to know right now."

They look at each other. Tiffany comes toward Maxwell. He seems uneasy. As he turns she grabs his arm. He reacts.

"Be careful—things are not what they seem."

Seconds later she's gone. He seems in shock as he looks about the room expecting to see her reappear. She doesn't.

"It must be incredible to have the power Tiffany Johnson has—knowledge of the ages—to be aware of everything that's going to happen—having the ability to prevent it beforehand."

Maxwell grabs his cell phone and heads for the door in a rush. He seems panicked as he runs toward the elevator.

9
Orchid Bay
Clerke Apartment

"I think we should go away for the weekend. Leave Orchid Bay behind for several days—you and I need some peace and quiet—from Vina Phamler for starters—and her constant effort to get into your pants. She's not gonna stop—she wants *you*."

Patrick Clerke playfully points at Kayla Larsen.

"Will you stop—Vina and I are old news. She knows there's no chance of us getting back together. I'm with you now."

Kayla seems annoyed and pulls Patrick toward her.

"I don't trust her—she's got her eye on you."

"You've been watching way too many streaming episodes of *Paper Dolls* online. The 1980s is long gone. Things change. Vina and I are not going to get back together. I'm just not into her."

"I'm serious about Vina—she's told plenty of her friends that the two of you belong together. Said you were her Prince Charming—the nicest guy she's ever met—ever slept with."

Patrick gestures with his hand.

"How many times do I have to say it—Vina and I are just friends—nothing more than that—she's just messing with you."

Kayla pulls away from Patrick. She seems upset.

10
Santa Barbara

"Third time is the charm. Number two really put a scare into that family. I'll send you the details for number three."

Marlisa nods a few times and grins broadly.

"Loren Fawcett will be brought to his knees. No one in his frigging family is safe—everyone is a target—kids included."

She shakes her head several times.

"Uh-huh—that's exactly what I'm saying."

She turns to face Corey as she shuts off her cell phone.

"Did you just say what I thought you did?"

"Loren Fawcett brought this nightmare upon himself. He'll regret the day he messed with me. I won't be ignored."

Corey seems uneasy as multiple videos of a car explosion streams on the local news. Several seconds later the news is interrupted by the reports of a shooting. Marlisa grins.

"It's not like anyone will really miss those losers. They were lowlifes—spent their entire lives hurting other people."

She sits down next to Corey and smiles.

11

San Francisco

"I want whoever is responsible found. I'll crucify them myself. No one fucks with my family and lives to tell about it."

Loren Fawcett seems enraged as he slams his fist on his desk and looks at the cell phone in his hand. He grimaces.

"Call his family. Tell them the details. Make sure they know what I plan to do to his killer. There'll be no peace until whoever is behind this is in the morgue—starting with Whitney and his whore daughter. Get Anton over here this second."

Loren clenches his fist angrily.

"Uh-huh—I *know* he's on a date with his latest girlfriend. Do I look like I care about his frigging sexual escapades with some random bimbo he picked up at a nightclub on Nob Hill?"

He leans back in his chair and sighs.

"It's time he and I talked about Todd Whitney."

He slams his fist down on the desk again.

"Get Alexei Levitov on the phone too. He has expertise in the Whitney family and their people. That idiot worked plenty of years for those fools before he came back over to our side."

He nods a few times and sighs loudly.

"Call me back in ten minutes."

He nods several times and shuts off the cell phone. He stares at photographs on the wall of his father and several other relatives. He stands and clenches his fist. He stares at the photograph of his father and older brother. He seems upset.

Page **103**

"My father certainly turned out to be a disappointment to me after everything I did to please him. He could never see it was me that was his rightful heir. Put all his faith in Ralph. Thought he would run his empire one day—thought I'd be happy to take orders from my worthless older brother—*ugh*—not a chance."

Loren shakes his fist at the photographs.

"Even after I put a bullet in my brother's head and played the role of dutiful son it was never enough. Dear old dad kept living in the past—focusing on his dead son as if he was still alive and not rotting in the ground. Damn him—damn them all."

He takes a step closer to the photographs on the wall. His rage seems to grow as he looks at the images again. He sighs.

"Of course that garbage my father has been spouting about talking to a dead teenage girl only made things worse."

He shakes his head and seems confused.

"Where the fuck is my father and what is he up to?"

Several feet away Jeremy Weissmann watches silently. He smirks several times watching Loren's behavior unraveling.

12

St. Thomas
United States Virgin Islands

"I wish I could help you. But there was nothing in our records about Wesley Mayfield. He was just a passenger on board that ill-fated yacht. As far as I know he never set foot in the Virgin Islands other than when the yacht was docked briefly."

Peter Zimmerman shrugs as leans back in his chair and faces Maxwell looking at him from the video screen on his computer. He nervously runs his fingers through his hair.

"What's going on? Why are you looking into this case? It's been years. The paperwork was filed long ago—closed."

Maxwell nods several times.

"Point taken—but a new wrinkle has shown up recently concerning someone he may have worked for besides Bell."

Peter runs his fingers through his hair again.

Page **104**

"I wish I had the answers you need. But this well is quite dry. It was just an unfortunate accident—crap happens."

Maxwell nods in agreement and the screen goes blank. Peter seems bothered and stands up. He looks out at the harbor and glances at the file cabinet at the other end of the room.

<h1 style="text-align:center">13
Los Angeles</h1>

"I've never met someone like you. You just have a way about you. I think maybe it's your thick Australian accent."

Donna Markway reaches out to stroke the unkempt hair of her latest boyfriend. She giggles as he grins broadly at her.

"I think my brother will really like you. He's coming for a visit in a week—coming from a photo shoot in Munich."

Silas Bell reaches out to kiss Donna.

"I'll be on my best behavior."

Donna stifles a laugh and pretends to slap Silas.

"My brother is not a prude."

Silas makes a lewd gesture with his finger.

"Is that so? Wait until he finds out we had sex on the Ferris Wheel at Santa Monica Pier in front of a crowd of thousands."

Donna pretends to slap Silas again.

"We never had sex at the pier in Santa Monica in front of thousands of people. I would've remembered if we had."

Silas pulls Donna toward him and grins.

"How about we make what I said come true."

Donna wags her finger at him.

"You always say the craziest things Heath."

Silas licks his lips sensuously.

"I think we should head back to my apartment. I've got some ideas—ideas which shouldn't be filmed on video."

Donna seems uneasy. She sighs.

"You're certainly not shy Heath Griffith."

Silas grins broadly and winks.

"I'm just a guy who's crazy in love with you."

<h1 style="text-align:center">Page 105</h1>

Donna notices his erection straining against his faded Levi's and strokes his cheek. He kisses her and smirks.

"My apartment is only ten minutes away."

Donna looks at his erection again and nods.

14
Orchid Bay
Downtown Police Station

"You can't keep me in here forever. There are laws against such things. I demand you release me this instant—or else."

"Or else what—you'll call your lawyer—or the media?"

Roland O'Brien begins laughing as he gives Jason Shappe a side glance. He gestures with his hand as Jason reacts.

"This is against the law—I didn't do anything wrong."

Roland spins around and makes a lewd gesture with his hand. Jason clenches his fists and shakes it fiercely at Roland.

"That bitch is lying. I didn't do what she said."

"Uh-huh—so says you. But your DNA says you did what Tammy Cotler said you did. You've fucked up for the last time."

Jason pounds his fist against the bars of his cell.

"You'll regret fucking with me O'Brien. I swear when I get out of here I'll destroy you. I'll make you wish you were never ever born—there won't be any place you can hide from me."

"Don't you get it yet—you're never getting out of here. You're going to spend the rest of your miserable life in prison."

Roland watches Jason's reaction and grins.

"Two other women came forward less than an hour ago."

Jason clutches the bars of his cell again.

15
Pacific Coast Highway

"Are you serious? Your mother didn't tell you about who your real father was—kept it a secret for your entire life."

Lloyd Welsh runs his fingers through his hair.

"She didn't know. Or so she said anyway."

He watches as Susan Osborne shakes her head.

"It was quite a shock to find out my real father was just some dude she had sex with in the backseat of his car right before she married my dad. When she told me what happened that night it sounded like she ripped off the storyline from an old episode of *Knots Landing* or *Falcon Crest*—and not in a good way either. At first I thought she was kidding around—just teasing me."

Susan seems confused and sighs loudly.

"What are you going to do?"

Lloyd stands up and faces Susan.

"I'm not sure yet."

Susan stands and hugs Lloyd warmly.

16
Munich

"I'll be there in a minute—soon as I change clothes."

Ashton Markway closes the door to his hotel room and begins taking his shirt off. He hears a sound and turns around. He reacts in shock as he sees Tiffany standing several feet away. She takes a step forward. They stare at each other for a few seconds while Ashton recovers from the shock of seeing Tiffany.

"It's been a while Ashton."

Ashton backs away nervously.

"Are you? Is this?"

Tiffany takes another step forward.

"You've certainly changed Ashton—quite photogenic if I do say so myself. Turning lots of heads everywhere."

Ashton stifles a grin and seems flattered.

"I can't complain."

There is a moment of silence. Tiffany sighs.

"You've got to go back to Los Angeles right now. Donna is in trouble. There's no time to waste—pack your bags."

Ashton seems confused.

"What? What are you talking about?"

Ashton throws his shirt on the bed nearby as he continues to watch Tiffany curiously. He seems unsure of what to do.

"Your sister is in serious trouble. Go to Los Angeles this very minute. Take the first flight out. Don't argue with me."

Seconds later Tiffany is gone.

17

San Francisco

"I don't give a fuck. Find him. I want that lover boy in my office before the hour is out. Damn it—stop arguing with me."

Loren slams his cell phone down on his desk as he turns to look at Anton Levitov. Anton seems nervous and shrugs.

"I told you my older brother would be hard to get to. He and his latest have been fucking like rabbits all over town."

Loren seems about to explode.

"You're one to talk cousin. Exactly how many has it been this week? How many whores have you fucked already?"

Anton makes a lewd gesture with his finger and winks.

"A gentleman never talks about his conquests."

Loren reacts.

"You and Alexei are trying my last nerve."

He points to a monitor on the wall streaming live news nonstop. Loren turns to face Anton again. He begins yelling.

"Two of our own are dead."

Anton gestures with his hand.

"I'm aware of what happened to Sergei and Cujo. Lizette is a mess. Cujo's ex and his children are in hiding as we speak."

Loren stands and comes toward Anton.

"This is Whitney's handiwork."

Anton shakes his head.

"Todd Whitney has been locked in a room with no access to the outside world—none. Your father made sure Whitney could never escape—never let anyone know his whereabouts."

Loren grits his teeth and points at Anton.

"I want him dead—kill him. Blow his brains out."

Page **108**

Anton shoots Loren a nervous look and smirks.

"His suffering knows no end since he's been our prisoner as you well know. He has had to watch his daughter submit to my will every day for a year now. Every day he watches me fuck his precious offspring like a cheap prostitute knowing he can't do anything to protect her. He's watched helplessly as I raw-dogged his daughter day after day—got her pregnant twice already."

Anton laughs gleefully as he snaps his fingers.

"The abortion clinic down the street has been seriously busy due to yours truly—turned Whitney's daughter into a slut."

Loren angrily grabs Anton.

"I don't give a fuck about your sexual escapades. That man has lived long enough—caused us too much problems."

Anton frees himself of Loren's grip. Loren suddenly grabs him again and begins shaking him violently. He grimaces.

"I want Whitney dead. Bring him to me. I'll shoot him myself. He must pay for what has happened—pay with his life."

Anton pushes Loren away. He sighs loudly.

18
Orchid Bay
Downtown Police Station

"He's not a bad guy. Can't you see that?"

Sarina Wolper watches Roland's reaction as she leans forward toward his desk. He rolls his eyes and turns away.

"Jason Shappe is a serial rapist. Or doesn't that make a difference to you. Is the sex between the two of you that good?"

"How dare you speak to me like that?"

Roland stands up and comes toward Sarina.

"I'm not going to let him out so he can skip town. His father called just before you got here. Made it clear his son would not hesitate to leave the country if it meant he'd remain free."

"His father hates him. He's got it out for Jason."

Roland gestures with his hand.

"Jason slept with his father's girlfriend."

Page **109**

Roland seems angry as he gestures with his hand again.

"I would be pissed too if something like that happened to me. Oh wait, it did. Jason bedded my girlfriend too—flaunted their behavior all over town. If I were you I'd consider it a blessing that you weren't raped. Shappe has quite the sordid record."

Roland runs his fingers through his hair.

"There have been two more cases—one of them a high school girl—perhaps you know her—Tracey Oakfield."

Sarina seems shocked as the name is mentioned. Roland notices and takes a step closer to Sarina. He points at her.

"According to what she said—Jason raped her last month after having sex with her mother—took her by the pool."

Roland pulls Sarina to him. He sighs loudly.

"If I were you I'd think about that for a second. Think about the fact Tracey is only fourteen. Think about how he forced her down on a folding chair by the pool and ravaged her like a wild animal—told her he'd kill her if she said anything to anyone about what he did. She told her mother less than an hour ago."

Sarina covers her mouth in shock.

19

Pacific Coast Highway

"You worry too much. My mother wouldn't dare try to hurt you. She knows how I feel about you—knows I love you."

Dana Mills leans over to kiss Mark Corrington.

"I can't help it Mark—you've stolen my heart. Made me fall hard for you—fall for your charming ways—and gentle smile."

Mark grins broadly.

"I'm not sorry—I'd do it again if I had to."

They kiss for a few seconds. He leans back on the blanket as he glances around the wooded area of a small park.

"Your mother gave me the oddest look earlier—acted like she was seeing things—seriously creeped the hell out of me."

"My mother isn't some sort of monster."

Mark sits up and faces Dana as she stifles a laugh.

Page **110**

"She just thinks you're not good enough for me after how my father turned out. There's nothing to worry about."

"I hope you still feel that way as I'm being lowered into the ground after having several bullets rip through my body."

Dana reacts and pulls Mark toward her.

"Don't you make jokes about something like that—no one is going to hurt you—especially not my mother of all people."

Mark rolls his eyes seemingly unconvinced.

20
Munich

Tiffany watches as Ashton boards a plane for Los Angeles. His face is wreathed with worry as he passes security. She slowly folds her arms across her chest and seems pleased.

21
Pacific Coast Highway

"What do you mean you had a change of plans? I thought we had a deal? I want that boy in the hospital—in a coma."

Daphne Mills seems upset as she listens to what is being said. She stops suddenly. She sighs loudly and pauses.

"*Oh*—I'm so sorry. I understand. Let me know when you can accommodate me. Again I'm so sorry about your loss."

She shuts off her cell phone and sighs loudly.

"Damn it—that Corrington boy caught a break."

She seems upset as she faces the ocean.

22
Orchid Bay
Mills Apartment

"I'm not playing your sick game Jayne. Get the hell out of my apartment before I call the cops—have you arrested for breaking and entering—threatening me with a toy gun."

Adam Mills watches as Jayne begins to circle him. He slowly backs away as she comes closer. She begins laughing.

"Is this gun a toy—how about we find out?"

Adam watches as Jayne's fingers dances on the trigger as she edges closer and closer to him. He begins backing away.

"Get the hell out of my apartment."

Jayne laughs loudly and takes a step closer.

"Un-huh—I bet you thought you got away with what you did to me. Thought once I left town you were home free—no one would ever hold you accountable for what you and those two losers did to me. But surprise—when I left town I moved to Los Angeles and learned how to shoot a gun—planned what I would do to you and your friends when I came back for revenge."

Adam reacts and gestures with his hand.

"I don't know what you're talking about. I think you should pay a visit to a shrink and get help for your problems—maybe two shrinks. Seriously, you're living in a demented fantasy world."

Jayne lunges at Adam. He falls backwards on the sofa. She climbs on top of him and jams her gun against his temple.

"You're going to tell me the names of your friends—and if you don't I'll fucking shoot you. Do I make myself clear?"

Adam seems in a panic as Jayne grins broadly.

"I'm going to start counting."

Jayne watches fear spread across Adam's face and begins laughing as he tries to wriggle free. She jams the gun against his head even harder—scraping away pieces of skin from his face.

23
San Francisco

"Bring Whitney to me—you have one hour. I want him at my mercy—want him to feel my wrath as I blow his frigging brains out for daring to come after our family with impunity."

Anton seems uneasy but nods. He turns to leave. Loren's cell phone rings. As Loren answers his demeanor changes and drops the phone. Anton walks toward Loren. He reacts.

"What happened? Did something else?"

Loren faces Anton and sighs loudly.

"Alexei—he's dead—shot. He was ambushed ten minutes ago with his girlfriend outside a Target store in Nob Hill."

They seem unable to react. Anton silently takes a step toward Loren. They look at each other as Anton's rage builds.

"I'm so going to enjoy killing the motherfucker that took out my brother. There won't be anywhere to hide—nowhere."

Loren looks at the video on his phone again.

"It was Whitney—that worm is behind everything. He ordered the hit—took out your brother—played us for fools."

Anton glances at the cell phone.

24
Orchid Bay
Mills Apartment

Blood oozes from a bullet wound to Adam's temple. His eyes are wide open—seeing nothing. His right hand is at an angle pinned under him as if reaching for something inside the back pocket of his bloodstained Levi's. There is an eerie silence inside the apartment as birds chirp happily outside in a nearby tree.

25
Santa Barbara

"I love it. I'm on cloud nine. Good work."

Marlisa dances as she holds her cell phone in front of her while Carlos on the other end of the video screen tells her about the deaths of Alexei Levitov and his girlfriend. Marlisa sighs.

"Who was the girl with him?"

"Don't know—don't care. She was in the way so I took her out as a precaution. Dead women tell no tales—it happens."

Marlisa waves her hand in the air.

"I agree. She was simply in the wrong place at the wrong time. People die every day due to gunshots—crap happens."

Carlos nods and faces Marlisa again. She watches as he seems nervous about something. He looks at a piece of paper in his hand and seems bothered. Marlisa gestures wildly.

"They are your next hit—no exceptions."

Carlos nods and faces Marlisa.

"Is it really necessary to kill Momoa's family?"

Marlisa clenches her fist in anger.

"I want them all dead before sunset tomorrow."

He looks at the paper again and nods in agreement.

26
Orchid Bay
Downtown Police Station

"I can't believe it—can't believe he lied to me."

Sarina reels in shock as Roland comes toward her. He puts his arms around her. She begins crying and faces him again.

"What now? What's going to happen?"

Roland nervously runs his fingers through his hair.

"Jason Shappe is going to face charges for raping Tammy as well as charges for raping a minor. He's looking at a long prison stay from what I can gather. Other charges are pending."

"I really believed him. He seemed so genuine with me."

Roland shakes his head and grimaces.

"So was **Ted Bundy** before he got busted for murder."

Sarina nods and looks at her cell phone as it buzzes. She notices it is Jason's father. She seems unsure what to do.

"What if there are more?"

Roland wrings his hands and shrugs.

27
San Francisco

Anton watches as a sheet covering his brother's body is pulled over his head. He slowly runs his fingers through his hair and faces the coroner—then the covered body again.

Page **114**

"What gun was used to kill my brother?"

Victor Kanjek shakes his head several times and glances at the covered body briefly. He faces Anton again and sighs.

"It's hard to say until I complete an autopsy. He was shot at close range as you saw. He knew his killer is my guess."

Anton clenches his fist. He seems about to explode as he bolts from the room and begins walking down the hallway.

One Day Later

28
Orchid Bay
Brandt Law Office

"I'm tired of playing by everyone's rules in this town. I'm through playing nice—being respectful—I'm rich—filthy rich."

Vera Holliday turns around and faces Daniel Brandt.

"Did you hear what I said? I'm rich."

Daniel nods and looks at the folder in front of him. He sighs loudly and stands up. He faces Vera. She shrugs.

"My father was a no-good bastard that ignored me my entire life. But at least he did something right before he kicked the bucket two months ago in Santa Barbara. I mattered."

Daniel shakes his head and sighs.

"Davis Osmond had another child besides you."

"I thought you said he was unmarried at the time of his death? You said he had no wife or children you knew about."

Daniel runs his fingers through his hair.

"I know what I said—but this morning I got an email from a lawyer in Los Angeles. He's representing your half-sister."

"I want my money—all of it—every damn penny."

Daniel looks at the folder again nervously.

"Apparently your father worked briefly with someone in Hollywood named Hayes Walston. He had a relationship with Walston's sister. They had a daughter named Amber. Her lawyer made it clear she intends to fight you every step of the way."

Vera walks toward Daniel and stops.

"That miserable hoity-toity bitch better watch her back. I won't let some slut take what's legally mine. I'll destroy her."

Daniel faces Vera with a worried look.

"Amber Walston is certainly not someone you want to mess with Vera. From what I read about her she's a piece of work. Her reputation in the film industry is not that of a forgiving person. She deals with people she considers rivals harshly."

Vera seems bored and rolls her eyes.

"I'm not impressed. She doesn't stand a chance."

She grabs Daniel's arm angrily. He notices.

"Where is my bitch of a sister at the moment? I want to meet her so I can tell her what I'll do if she dares provoke me."

Daniel seems nervous and looks at his watch.

"Her lawyer has already scheduled a meeting. We can do it by video call or live in person. She's willing to come to Orchid Bay. Currently she's in San Diego prepping a movie."

Vera gestures and sighs loudly.

"How about I pay her a visit on her own turf—make my dear sister aware who she's dealing with—scare her a bit."

Daniel seems upset and nods. He glances at the door and faces Vera again. Vera notices. She pulls Daniel toward her.

"Are you still with Zarina—still bored?"

Daniel pulls away from Vera.

"I thought I already made it clear about Zarina."

Vera gestures with her hand.

"What she doesn't know won't hurt her."

Daniel reacts. He seems nervous.

"We're going to be married in a few months."

Vera rolls her eyes knowingly.

"So what—that doesn't mean you and I can't play house in my bedroom on the sly. You're a very attractive man. It's a crime to waste your looks on someone as plain as Zarina Fuertes."

Daniel glances at his watch again.

"I already told you the answer is no. There is no future for you and me—none whatsoever. Let it go—stop trying."

Page 116

"What if I told Zarina that you and I fucked? Tell her how aggressive you can get between the sheets when provoked."

"I already told you there is no chance you and I are going to hook-up again. It's just not going to happen. Case closed."

Vera licks her lips several times.

"I like men who are aggressive in bed—men who make me feel helpless—men who won't take no for an answer."

Daniel walks to the door. He stops.

"I'm not Roger Olof."

Vera seems stung by the remark. She throws a folder at Daniel. He watches as the contents of the folder fall.

"How dare you mention his name after what he did to me and Vina Phamler? He was a monster—evil to the core."

Daniel smirks and reaches for the doorknob.

"Maybe you should remember that when you pursue a man like Roger Olof—you never know what he's like until it's too late—seems to me that might be a lesson to learn from."

He glances at Vera briefly and leaves. She continues to stand motionless for a few seconds enraged at his behavior.

29
Los Angeles

Ashton frantically hails a taxi from one of the busy terminals. He appears panicked as he jumps into the first one that stops. Several feet away Jeremy seems pleased and nods.

30
Orchid Bay
Mills Apartment

"I'm not surprised that this is the ending that befell Adam Mills. He led a pretty shady existence—made all sorts of enemies throughout Orchid Bay and the surrounding areas. I can only assume whoever took him out had plenty of reasons wanting him dead. I guess we should let his half-brother know his fate."

Roland watches as Lachlan Ball pulls a sheet over Adam's body. They look at each other. Roland shakes his head.

"Do you think he knew his killer?"

Roland nods and gestures with his hand.

"More likely than not he did—the question is—who hated Mills enough to pull the trigger. Might have to get help on this one—probe his sordid background for good measure."

Lachlan nods and looks at his cell phone.

"Albert Vanwick is calling—the press vultures have already begun to circle. Cue to the tabloid headlines to come shortly."

Roland rolls his eyes and sighs loudly.

"*Ugh*—I really can't deal with Vanwick or his rag of a newspaper right now—it makes *TMZ* look respectable."

Lachlan stifles a grin and nods in agreement.

31
San Diego

"Oh, is that right? She wants to meet in person. Well I think we should grant my bitch of a sister her wish—make nice."

Amber Walston turns to face Chase Banfield with a look of scorn. They exchange glances. He seems impatient.

"According to her lawyer her name is Vera Holliday. Said he informed her less than an hour ago. She's already salivating."

Amber makes a lewd gesture with her finger and grabs her cell phone. Chase grabs her by the arm. She pulls away.

"I'm not sharing one cent with white trash. My father was a lousy human being. He treated me like crap all my life."

She looks at her cell phone again.

"It's mine—all mine. He owes me plenty."

Chase glances at the folder on a table a few feet away.

"He left her everything. He left you nothing."

Amber throws her cell phone at Chase.

"Do I look like I give a fuck? I want what is owed me. I want it all and I won't let some small town zero play me for a fool."

Seconds later Amber's cell phone begins ringing.

"Who is it? Is it that slut? Is it her? Is that dumb bitch daring to call me to see if we can make a deal—make nice?"

Chase shakes his head and seems relieved.

"It's your client. She's returning your call from earlier."

Amber's demeanor changes as she takes the phone and begins talking. Chase nervously turns to look at the balcony.

32
Orchid Bay
Crystal Cove Estates

"I'm sorry for what my troubled son put your through. But he's a grown man and he has to face the consequences of his actions. I should've never spoiled him the way I did—but there's nothing I can do to change anything now. It is what it is."

Carlton Shappe runs his fingers through his hair as he faces Sarina. She seems upset. He walks over to her and sighs.

"Do you think there's more than one girl?"

Sarina nods and seems about to cry.

33
Los Angeles

Ashton jumps out of a taxi and heads toward an apartment building in the Los Feliz section of Los Angeles.

"Good. He's arrived. Maybe it's not too late."

Jeremy turns to face Tiffany as Ashton is seen knocking frantically on the door of an apartment. There is no answer.

TO BE CONTINUED

Page 119

A Brief Look at the Fifth Episode

Nothing is what it seems when several lives collide together while events linked to the past begin to unravel as a murderous killer stalks members of one family with sadistic revenge in mind.

Episode 5
Ships in the Night

1
Orchid Bay
Lighthouse Park

Kevin Alsten seems annoyed as he notices Lauren Corrington staring at a bunch of homeless people talking about something. The conversation seems heated. She takes a step forward and seems about to walk toward them. Lauren turns to face Kevin briefly and notices the curious look on his face.

"What do you think they're talking about?"

Kevin gestures with his hand.

"Maybe you should go over and ask them?"

Lauren gives him a sharp look and turns away.

"I bet it's about drugs—probably meth."

Kevin runs his fingers through his hair and sighs.

"Not every homeless person is a drug addict. Some have other issues. Many just had bad things happen to them."

Lauren rolls her eyes at Kevin.

"I never said they were all drug addicts. It's just that I heard there is a lot of drug activity in this park. Susan said."

Kevin seems upset at the mention of the name and grabs Lauren's arm. They look at each other for a few seconds.

"Susan Pisani doesn't know anything. She lives in a condo near Santa Barbara. The only drug dealing she's seen is when her loser boyfriend goes hunting for a score on Friday night."

Lauren jabs Kevin. He grimaces.

"You just don't like Kyle Martino—especially after he crashed your car last Christmas—wrecked it out by Silver Point when he tried to drive through the police barricades."

Kevin runs his fingers through his hair again and turns to look at the group of homeless people arguing loudly.

"Kyle is a fuck-up. Got cut off by his father when he dropped out of college—been sucking Susan's money ever since pretending he likes her. Dude is no good—*there* I said it."

Lauren pulls Kevin toward her.

"Do you think he's cheating on her?"

Kevin laughs.

"No doubt—old habits die hard with Kyle."

They look at each other again.

2

Los Angeles

A man stares at a huge poster in front of a distinguished movie theater. He stands there for a few minutes without moving as a few people walk by. He clenches his fist in anger as he continues looking at the poster. His rage seems to intensify.

3

Orchid Bay

Downtown Police Station

"I'm telling you—Jayne Osborne murdered Adam Mills yesterday. He warned me about her—said she threatened him."

Roland O'Brien shoots Lachlan Ball a look and faces Ethan Vanwick. He watches as Ethan shakes his fist in the air.

Page **122**

"She did it. He said she told him she was gonna get him for what happened last year. Dude was scared for his life."

Lachlan leans back in his chair.

"What happened last year? Care to elaborate?"

Ethan looks at Lachlan and then at Roland. He wipes sweat from his brow. He glances at the front door and sighs.

4

San Francisco

"Of course—I'm game. Just tell me when and where you want to meet. My cousin's death was no accident—I know his bitch ex is responsible despite what everyone is saying."

Simon Momoa rolls his eyes knowingly.

"She used him to get to Loren. Dated Cujo for a year and then kicked him to the curb—said he cheated. He took it as an insult to his name. Damn whore is to blame for what happened next—became addicted to having kinky sex with prostitutes."

He angrily clenches his fist.

"What? Are you seriously asking me a question like that about my cousin? Did he cheat? Does it matter? Who cares?"

He wipes sweat from his brow and nods.

"OK—sure—he banged his secretary—said she was always making a play for him so he took her in one of the stairwells."

He makes a lewd gesture with his finger.

"He had no way to explain himself before that slut threw him out—afterwards she claimed he raped her—made it up."

He clenches his fist again. He sighs loudly.

"She's trash. Uses men like tissue paper and tosses them out the door when she's done with them. She's had so many boyfriends over the years she makes **Britney Spears** look like **Julianne Moore**. That horrible bitch needs to be taught a hard lesson and I know just the right person to make it happen. No doubt in my mind she's responsible for what happened."

He snickers as he listens to the voice on the other end of the line. He waves his hand in the air and gestures a bit.

Page **123**

"Even now she's still trying to get back at Cujo despite him being dead—making up stories—smearing his reputation."

He seems about to explode.

"I want her dead—the sooner the better."

He nods several times.

5

Pacific Coast Highway

"How about we go surfing out by Paradise Pointe?"

Lauren reaches out to touch Kevin's hand as it rests on the steering wheel. He doesn't respond. She snaps her fingers.

"Are you paying attention to me?"

He continues to ignore her as he drives.

"I asked you a question?"

Kevin pulls the car over and faces her.

"I've figured out what I want to do with my life."

Lauren seems confused. She sighs.

"What are you talking about?"

He runs his fingers through his hair.

"I want to make a difference."

Lauren seems about to laugh at the comment.

"Congratulations **Nathan Hale**. What do you have in mind for a career—being a hero—rescuing people in distress?"

Kevin turns to look at several homeless people walking toward a small park up ahead. He shakes his fist and sighs.

"Make fun of me all you like—insult me. But I think I might be able to change a few lives. Someone has to care. Sometimes all it takes is one person—look at **Greta Thunberg**. She was just one person at first—now her movement is a force to be reckoned with around the world. Even **Jane Fonda** is a fan. Said so in interviews—praised Greta for her efforts to improve society."

Lauren glances where Kevin's gaze is focused for a few seconds before she faces him again. She lowers her voice.

"I didn't mean anything by it. I'm sorry."

Kevin runs his fingers through his hair again.

Page **124**

"What if someone like me could make a difference in someone's life? Change how society sees homeless people."

Lauren leans back in her seat and grimaces.

"They don't want help. People have tried. Homeless people like being outside. They don't want to follow rules."

Kevin clenches his fists. Lauren notices.

"Uh-huh—says who—the people who pretend they want to help but in reality all they want is the government to give them money which they spend on themselves all the while claiming they're helping the people which never amounts to anything."

They look at each other for a few seconds. Kevin wipes sweat from his brow as he glances at the road ahead.

"The shelters in this state are a joke. They claim to have space for everyone on the streets. But that couldn't be further away from the truth. The shelters are nothing more than a flophouse. No one ever gets out of the system despite what has been reported. I have it on good authority some of the shelters here in California purposely sabotage the chances for a homeless person to get off the street for good because they need people on the street to validate the large amounts of money they receive from the government every year. For the record—it's not a secret by the way—everyone knows what's going on but they play dumb and act like they want to curb homelessness in this country."

Kevin pulls out his cell phone.

"Are you going to tell me that it hasn't occurred to the government to build more shelters—create more places for homeless people to live—curb the population on the street by making sure people have room and board instead of spending every night sleeping by a bus stop? The truth isn't pleasant."

Images appear on Kevin's cell phone.

"This shouldn't be happening in America. It's a stain on who we are as a country. People should care. Do something."

Lauren reaches out to touch Kevin's hand.

"What about the mentally ill? What about them? They can't work. Who would hire someone with mental issues?"

Kevin shoots Lauren a cautious look.

"They should be housed—and they still would be if **Ronald Reagan** hadn't shut down so many mental hospitals in order to give selfish rich people tax cuts. It had a trickle-down effect."

They look at each other once more.

6

Orchid Bay
Falling Pines Memorial Park

"Why did we have to meet here? This place is not on one of my "must visits." What kind of trouble have you gotten into Sarina? Is it that creep Shappe? Is he why we're meeting?"

Sarina Wolper looks at Dirk Veriteke and grimaces.

"Jason Shappe is a problem waiting to happen."

Dirk shoots Sarina a knowing look.

"Uh-huh—tell me something I don't already know. That dude has been a thorn in my side for years—tried to frame me for causing that accident by Paradise Pointe that crippled my cousin and led him to kill himself once he realized his fate. Shappe is a piece of garbage—pure and simple—scumbag extraordinaire."

Sarina seems about to cry as she grabs Dirk's arm.

"He threatened me—said he would expose that whole Bitcoin mess I was involved with not long ago. He's desperate. I know he'll do it. He raped Tracey Oakfield. She came forward and fingered him after he got arrested for raping Tammy Cotler."

Dirk runs his fingers through his hair.

"What do you want from me?"

Sarina smiles slyly and opens her purse.

7

Marble Hills

"There's nothing to worry about. You've taken care of everything. Maddie Gormley is up to the job. No worries."

Gina Bentley turns around to face Pierce Colby. They stare at each other for a few seconds. He walks toward her.

Page **126**

"You know how your brother gets when things don't go exactly the way he expects them to—Logan Airport awaits."

"My brother is over the moon that Wesley Madison gave him a role in his new movie. I've never seen Eddie get so excited about anything before. You'd think he was twenty again."

Pierce gestures with his hand and laughs. He takes a step toward Gina. They share a glance before he gestures.

"I dare you to tell Eddie Kane what you just said."

Gina shakes her finger at Pierce.

"I plan to tell him. Count on it dear husband. I'm not afraid of my brother. Unlike some people I could mention."

Pierce reacts and seems annoyed. He grimaces.

"I'm not afraid. I'm cautious. I've heard plenty about your brother since I became part of the family—scary stuff."

"Uh-huh—most of which my brother probably started himself to keep everyone in Marble Hills on their heels."

Pierce grins broadly as he embraces Gina passionately.

"Didn't your brother box in college?"

Gina rolls her eyes and shakes her finger at Pierce.

"Why don't you ask him yourself if you dare?"

Pierce winces and turns away.

8
Los Angeles

"Call Sandra King—make sure she's coming on the next flight. I can't have the writer of the book that my movie is based on not show up—oh—make sure to get her a first class seat."

Wesley Madison leans back in his chair as he looks at his assistant on the video monitor. Margo Sampler nods several times as she shuffles a few pieces of paper on top of her desk.

"Get her hubby a seat too. Dude is really annoying but I can't risk anything. Make sure he feels like he's important."

He rolls his eyes and sighs.

"Dude can't stop talking about himself. Always has to be the center of everything—nonstop male Karen attitude."

He snaps his fingers several times.

"Oh, and don't forget to call my dad and tell him to meet me for lunch. Make sure he knows I've got plenty to gab about."

Margo looks up several times and sighs loudly.

9
Orchid Bay
Mills Driveway

"Uncle Adam is dead? Who killed him?"

Dana Mills reels in shock as she looks at her mother for a few seconds. She watches as Daphne Mills hides a smirk.

"Jayne Osborne."

Dana shakes her head and seems confused.

"I thought she left town."

Daphne looks at her cell phone.

"Apparently she came back with revenge in mind. At least that's what Ethan Vanwick is saying. He said she did it."

Dana rolls her eyes.

"*Ugh*—who'd believe anything he said."

She watches her mother scrolling through the messages on her cell phone and seems annoyed. She grabs her mother's arm. They look at each other briefly. She turns away.

"I bet *he* did it."

Daphne shakes her head.

"Why would Ethan kill his best friend? Those two go all the way back to grade school. Always getting into trouble—stealing and breaking into stores throughout their high school years."

"Uh-huh—*exactly*."

Daphne turns to face her daughter.

10
Honolulu

"Did you think you'd get away with it? Did you think I wouldn't find out? Wouldn't seek revenge after the fact?"

Carmen Pendleton takes a step toward Shirley Beecroft as the younger woman seems unfazed. They look at each other for a few seconds. Carmen raises her hand and sighs loudly.

"*Get out*. It's over. You lose. I win."

Shirley rolls her eyes in contempt and grins.

"You're making a huge mistake."

Carmen grabs Shirley by the arm.

"Is that so?"

Shirley pulls away.

"I have friends."

Carmen begins to laugh.

"Do you know who you're talking to? I have friends everywhere. Don't dare cross me, *bitch*—the results will be most unpleasant. I'll destroy you—run you into the ground."

Shirley walks to the door and stops.

"You've been warned."

She leaves and slams the door behind her.

Carmen shakes her head and turns to face a huge window fronting Waikiki Beach. She seems irritated and shrugs.

"The nerve of that bitch thinking she could outsmart me like I'm some sort of moron. I should've known the moment I caught her in bed with Alexander she was willing to do anything to get what she wanted. Luckily my son tossed her aside for the next flavor of the month. Bitch took it badly if I recall."

Carmen stifles a smile and glances at a cell phone lying a few feet away on top of her desk. She slowly walks over and picks it up. She begins rapidly dialing. She seems upset and stops.

11

San Francisco

A drone hovers over a large house surrounded by tall trees and expansive lawns. Several large objects are dropped on the property. Sounds of explosions are head as fire engulfs the entire house and area. More explosions are heard amid screams.

Page **129**

12
Orchid Bay
Downtown Police Station

Jason Shappe watches as Sarina comes toward him. She seems oddly quiet. He lunges at her through the bars of the jail.

"Well? Are gonna spring me from this hellhole?"

Sarina faces him. He watches as she takes something out of her purse. She looks at him and sighs loudly. He reacts.

"I'm going to make good on my threat if you don't help me get out of here. I'll destroy you. Ruin your frigging life."

Sarina shakes her head and looks at the object in her hand. She faces Jason. He notices the bottle in her hand.

"What the fuck is that?"

As he watches she holds the bottle toward him and sprays a mist-like substance in his face. He begins gasping for air.

"It was either you or me—and I choose me."

He claws at his throat for a few seconds and then falls against the bars of his cell. Sarina puts the bottle into her purse and begins calling for help. Seconds later Lachlan runs toward her and tries to open the cell as he reacts. He slowly reaches out and turns Jason over. He's dead. Lachlan faces Sarina in shock.

"He's gone."

Sarina reacts as Lachlan stands.

"What the hell happened?"

Sarina shake her head.

"He just started freaking out—saying he couldn't breathe. It all happened so fast. Then he just fell against the bars."

Lachlan turns to look at Jason again.

13
Honolulu

Carmen shuts off her cell phone and walks toward a mini bar several feet away. She stops briefly and sighs loudly.

"Who the hell is paying her? She's nobody."

Page **130**

She stares blankly at the cell phone for a few seconds.

"I hope his fucking penis was worth it."

She seems about to laugh.

14
San Francisco

"*This just happened*? There were no survivors?"

Loren Fawcett reacts and turns to face Vladimir Orlov standing a few feet away. He nods several times before he ends the call. He runs his fingers through his hair and sighs.

"The Momoa hideout was just bombed. The entire estate was blown up. Apparently a drone was seen hovering above."

Vladimir clenches his fist.

"Still think it was Whitney?"

Loren shakes his head.

"That wretched worm begged for his life yesterday when confronted. Swore he had nothing to do with what happened to Cujo and the others. Anton made a side deal with him."

Vladimir takes a step forward.

"What sort of a deal?"

Loren's cell phone begins ringing.

15
Washington DC

"Of course I'm coming Sandra—wouldn't miss it for the world—especially since you wrote a role for me in the movie."

Maxwell Pendergraft leans back in his chair.

"I'm leaving DC in a couple hours. Got a few things to wrap up and then I'm off to the airport—should be there by four."

He turns to face a woman standing nearby. She seems annoyed and buttons her blouse. He rolls his eyes knowingly.

"I'll call you later. Say hi to your lazy hubby."

He grins and shuts his cell phone off. He faces the woman with an odd look. Patrika Monvez wags her finger at him.

"I thought we were going to spend the weekend together at Cape Cod. You said you wanted to get to know me better."

Maxwell shoots her a cautious look.

"Things change."

She seems upset and grimaces.

"I thought you and I had an understanding."

"We're just friends—nothing more."

Maxwell stands and walks over to her. He takes her hand and smiles weakly. He sighs as she gestures. He turns away.

"I think you should look elsewhere for Mr. Right. I'm just spoiled. I'll never be faithful—never be husband material."

Patrika pulls her hand away and seems upset.

"Is this what I think it is?"

Maxwell shakes his head and sighs.

"I'm sorry. I should've told you weeks ago."

He watches as she becomes enraged.

"You said I was the only woman in your life. Said you were done chasing women for the time being. Was it all a lie?"

Maxwell seems confused.

"I never said you and I were exclusive."

He runs his fingers through his hair.

"Like I said—I'm sorry."

Patrika angrily slaps Maxwell and leaves without saying another word. Maxwell rubs his cheek for a few seconds.

16
Santa Barbara

"This is the beginning of the end for Loren Fawcett. A few more of these events and he'll be begging for mercy."

Marlisa Vigaro licks her lips as she talks to Carlos Vente on her cell phone. She points at him on the screen and laughs.

"I think it's time we took out Loren's main guy when it comes to breaking people's arms. Crucify the bastard."

Carlos looks at the list in his hand.

"Kevin Kulkovich is about to meet his maker."

Marlisa licks her lips again and gestures at Carlos for a few seconds. He notices the star by Kevin's name. He winks.

"Uh-huh—I know. Make sure he suffers before I blow his fucking head off. Make him beg if need be—tease him a bit."

Marlisa begins laughing gleefully.

"He and I have history. He knocked me around after I threatened to expose Loren for the lying snake he was. I want that bastard to suffer before you put a bullet in his head."

Carlos looks at Kevin's photo again.

"Your wish is my command."

Marlisa seems pleased.

17
San Francisco

"What did this kid do?"

Kevin Kulkovich shrugs as he faces Sergei Lycov.

"Got no idea—does it matter?"

He looks at a wharf up ahead.

"Cujo wanted to send this college graduate to the morgue before the end of business day yesterday. Obviously Cujo's death put a crimp in his plans—it's up to us to finish off the kid."

Sergei makes a lewd gesture with his finger.

"Any word on who iced Cujo?"

Kevin seems upset.

"Not a peep."

He clenches his fist.

"Vladimir Orlov is freaking out."

Sergei jabs Kevin.

"He was one of Vlad's personal favorites—cold-blooded and relentless. Lizette Richardson is a close second."

Kevin reacts to the statement. He looks at the gun lying nearby and sighs loudly. He runs his fingers through his hair.

"Her guy also met his end. Someone is fucking with us no doubt. Clearly trying to see how far to push Loren Fawcett."

Sergei shakes his head knowingly.

Page 133

Orchid Bay
Downtown Police Station

"This just got complicated in so many ways."

Lachlan and Roland share a glance and watches as the covered body of Jason Shappe is carried out of his cell. They watch as several coroner attendants begin wheeling the body down the hallway. Roland sighs loudly and faces Sarina.

"Tell me again exactly what happened."

Sarina wipes a tear from her eye and faces Roland. She seems in shock over what just took place. Lachlan shrugs.

19
Honolulu

Carmen walks back and forth as she glances at the cell phone in her hand every few seconds. She seems upset as she walks toward the balcony. She stops suddenly and grimaces.

"I want that ungrateful wretch served before the day is over. She tangled with the wrong person. She has to pay."

Carmen continues standing motionless for a few seconds as she watches the pristine image of Diamond Head in a distance from her balcony. She clenches her fist and turns away.

"She's probably making a play for some dumb jock college dropout at the beach. She likes those types—muscle heads."

There is a few seconds of silence.

"OK—stop wasting time with excuses. Find her and make her aware I plan to destroy her. Make her beg for mercy."

She grins slyly and walks back into her condo.

"Uh-huh—exactly what I was thinking—sex tapes."

She looks at a pile of paperwork on top of a desk nearby and suddenly seems to come up with an idea. She shrugs.

"What about her mother—how about we sue her too. A few extra lawsuits will really send a message no doubt."

She nods several times and seems pleased.

"Just bring that bitch to me the minute you find her. I don't care what her frigging deal is—I'm going to crush her."

Carmen gestures with her hand.

20
New York City

"It was nice of your mother to come by and watch Andrew for a week. I owe her—I'm sure she had other plans in motion."

Scott Malone rolls his eyes knowingly.

"My mother loves playing grandma. Told me forever she wanted a grandchild. Made me feel guilty plenty—worked it."

Sandra King jabs Scott and laughs.

"Admit it—you love having your mother always sticking her nose in your business—makes you feel wanted—loved."

Scott grabs one of the pieces of luggage from a nearby carrier with a grimace. He faces Sandra and waves his hand.

"I'll admit no such thing—end of story."

Sandra jabs Scott again and winks.

"Perhaps your mother should come live with us?"

Scott seems appalled and reacts.

"My mother loves living in Rhode Island. I *like* her living in Rhode Island. She needs her own space. Leave it at that."

Sandra playfully jabs Scott again enjoying his discomfort at showing emotions. She glances at the airport entrance.

"Wesley Madison invited me to his house in Malibu. Said it was really secluded. Said hardly anyone ever around."

Scott seems irritated.

"You're not going anywhere with that guy."

Sandra fakes being upset.

"Says who?"

Scott grabs Sandra by the arm.

"I forbid it."

Sandra pulls Scott toward her and smirks.

"What if I say no?"

Scott clenches his fist and gestures wildly.

"I'll pound him—I swear I will."

Sandra kisses Scott.

"I like it when you get jealous."

Scott gestures with his hand and sighs.

"He's nothing."

They share a look.

21
Honolulu

"What did your friend say? Is he coming?"

Shirley looks at Gaston Bauer as he shuts off his cell phone and faces her. She seems impatient as she watches his reaction.

"He's really busy—got a cousin's death to deal with at the moment. Nevertheless Carmen Pendleton will be dealt with."

Shirley angrily grabs Gaston's arm.

"Is he going to set her up for a drug bust or not?"

Gaston laughs and gestures with his hand.

"He's got a better idea."

"Well? What is it?"

Gaston glances toward Chinaman's Hat in a distance.

"Kidnap Alexander Pendleton—demand a hefty ransom."

Shirley rolls her eyes and seems bored.

"Is that all? I expected more from your friend. Especially after you said he was well-connected to the Russian mob."

Gaston gestures with his hand again.

"Simon is tight with those guys. But like I said they have other things going on at the moment. Carmen Pendleton isn't exactly a top priority to them. But don't you worry your pretty little head about anything—when your dumbass boy toy ex turns up missing it'll throw Carmen for a loop. She'll cough off plenty of dough to make sure her precious offspring is returned safely. But things won't end exactly the way she hopes. Sad how so many kidnappings end in tragedy. Murders happen—reality check."

Shirley seems shocked and recoils.

Page 136

"Are you saying what I think you're saying Gaston?"

Gaston laughs loudly and points at Shirley.

"Do you think they'll kidnap the boy wonder and not finish him off after the ransom is paid? Dead men tell no tales."

Shirley sighs loudly and seems upset.

"But he—we were close once."

Gaston makes a lewd gesture with his finger.

"So were we. But things change."

Shirley pretends to slap Gaston in mock anger.

"You cheated on me with my sister."

Gaston licks his lips and smirks.

"It happened once OK—like deal already."

He points his finger at Shirley again.

"As I recall the boy wonder cheated on you more than once. Slept with several of your friends—got one pregnant."

Shirley grimaces and sighs again.

"OK—OK. He was a dog."

Gaston winks at Shirley. He laughs.

"Did she keep the baby?"

Shirley shoots Gaston a knowing look.

22

San Francisco

"Uh-huh—exactly. I'm dealing with my cousin's death as you know. His family was just blown up as well. Someone's going to pay dearly for it—probably more than one person."

Simon nods several times.

"Regardless—I agree this other matter in Hawaii needs our attention. One of our people has been exposed despite our best efforts. She wants to even the score with her former boss."

He gestures with his hand.

"Of course—book two flights—first class."

He seems impatient.

"This loser is finished once you arrive in the islands. His mother will know we mean business immediately—bet on it."

Page **137**

Simon moans loudly as he looks down at a young woman positioned between his legs giving him a blowjob.

"That rich kid won't see it coming. By this time tomorrow he'll be with you and Clyde—and dead within a few days."

He begins laughing. He looks at the woman positioned between his legs and hastily motions for her to stand up.

"What about the body?"

Simon begins laughing loudly.

"Pendleton's body will be found with a bullet in his head courtesy of you—most likely severely beaten as well I assume."

He laughs again as he motions for the woman standing nearby to go to his bedroom. He makes a lewd gesture with his finger as she nods. He grins as he faces Cameron Hodge.

"His mother will get the message loud and clear when she gets a call from the local police informing her that her son has been found with a bullet in his head and plenty broken bones."

He looks at the hallway and grins broadly.

23
Orchid Bay
Hampshire Street Cafe

"I guess you don't have to worry about Jason Shappe anymore Tammy—on account of what I just heard—tragic."

Tammy Cotler seems confused as she turns to face Liana Danforth. Liana realizes Tammy is unaware of the news.

"Jason Shappe is dead."

Tammy reacts. Liana leans closer to Tammy.

"He died about an hour ago. According to what I heard he simply began gasping for air and died. Heart attack I guess."

Tammy seems unable to speak.

"Sarina Wolper was with him when it happened. She's in shock. Lachlan Ball immediately ordered an autopsy from what I heard. No waiting for a day like usual. He wants answers."

Tammy folds her hands in front of her.

"I hope he rots in hell."

Page **138**

Liana reaches out to comfort Tammy.

"Even the Lord Almighty doesn't want to deal with the likes of Jason Shappe is my guess. Disgusted I assume."

They look at each other.

24
Honolulu

Shirley slams the door shut to her apartment and looks at the package in her hand. She seems in shock and sighs.

"This is the last straw. Damn her."

She rips open the package and gasps.

"Carmen Pendleton is going to pay dearly. I wonder how she'll feel when her precious offspring turns up missing."

Shirley seems about to explode as she looks at the folder in her hand. She walks toward the balcony of her small apartment facing a grove of trees across the street. She sighs loudly.

"I think it's time I up the ante."

She grimaces and reaches for her cell phone.

"Sorry Alexander—revenge is more important to me than you are. Your demise will be your mother's fault—not mine."

She turns and faces a small kitchenette.

"I just got a package from Carmen Pendleton—I'm being sued. She just declared war. I'm on board with your plans."

She nods several times and smiles broadly.

"That's right—I'm on board."

She glances at the folder once more.

25
Boston

"It's so nice to see you David. It's been a while."

David Sherwood smirks as he notices how Justine Ross is looking at him. She slyly slides her arm around his waist.

"You're still eye candy. It's just not fair. You look like you just got out of high school—temptation city. I hate you."

Page 139

David laughs as he watches her fingers play with the buckle on his belt. They stare at each other for a few seconds.

"My brother still has no idea you bedded me back in high school. You never told him did you? Kept your mouth shut."

David laughs loudly. He reacts and pulls away.

"I like living. If Parker found out about us he'd finish me off no doubt. He warned me about hooking-up with you."

Justine points her finger at David.

"That was ages ago. It was no big deal."

David reacts to the comment.

"I was your first."

Justine rolls her eyes.

"You didn't do anything I didn't want you to do. You were the hottest guy in high school. I wanted you to be my first."

She pulls David close to her once again and sighs loudly.

"Are you single? Please tell me you are."

David laughs loudly again.

"No ring on my finger—still single."

Justine seems pleased.

"I wouldn't mind spending a few nights in your bed while I'm in Los Angeles for the premiere. You would call the shots."

David seems uneasy and shrugs.

"What about Parker?"

Justine gestures with her hand.

"What about him?"

She tugs at one of the buttons on his Levi's.

"Who says he has to find out."

David grins and nods in agreement.

26
Philadelphia

"Uh-huh—I understand. I'm wrapping up a few things here before I head out to Frisco and launch my attack on Fawcett."

Trevor Boleyn nods as he stares at Jeremy Winterfield on his cell phone. He gestures with his hand and shares a laugh.

"Loren Fawcett tried to block sales of his stock to yours truly but I got around it nevertheless—sucked up another 18 yesterday despite his best efforts. That fucker is probably beside himself wondering who I am—and what I'm up to. Fuck him."

Jeremy shows Trevor a newspaper headline from a recent copy of *The New York Times*. A look of shock seems to overcome Trevor as he notices the headline. He turns away briefly.

"I see I'm not the only one gunning for the Fawcett clan. I wish I knew who was behind these murders. Congratulations to them whoever they are. No one deserves it more than those wretched creatures. Death is too good an ending for them."

Jeremy wipes sweat from his brow.

"Word on the Internet is that the killer is none other than Todd Whitney. Conspiracy theories are all over the place."

Trevor rolls his eyes.

"Todd Whitney is dead."

Jeremy makes a gesture with his hand.

27
Orchid Bay
Downtown Police Station

"I don't know anything. Adam and I weren't on speaking terms as you know. We split up a while ago. He cheated."

Roland sighs loudly as he looks at Tabitha Bairstow. He leans back in his chair. He seems confused by her behavior.

"Ethan Vanwick says—says you made threats after Adam said he would release some tapes he had of the two of you."

Tabitha rolls her eyes knowingly.

"Ethan Vanwick is a frigging liar. That jerk is no better than Adam Mills. He has a record as you well know—theft."

Roland leans forward. He seems upset.

"No one is saying Vanwick is a saint. Nevertheless he said there were tapes of you and Mills getting friendly in bed."

"I never slept with Adam. Kyle Derringer was my first."

Tabitha turns to face Roland and seems upset.

"I've had nothing to do with Adam Mills for months—and I certainly had nothing to do with what happened to him."

Roland watches her walk to the door.

"We're not done yet."

Tabitha stops.

"Talk to my lawyer."

He watches her leave.

28
Orchid Bay
Greasy Spoon Diner

"Look—I know someone iced Mills at his pad. But so what? He pissed off a lot of people. Made plenty enemies in town."

Lachlan reacts as Kyle Derringer takes a bite of his burger seeming not to care about what happened to Adam Mills.

"There's talk going around."

Lachlan gestures with his hand.

"Talk that you threatened Mills. Made it clear to him you'd squash him if he continued to pester Tabitha Bairstow."

"Uh-huh—I knocked his lights out just recently. Dude was getting in our faces too much and I did what had to be done."

He stands and faces Lachlan. He flexes.

"As you can see I'm a tall guy—muscular build. I flattened that weasel because he wouldn't stop talking trash. I admit it."

He sits down again and smirks.

"No regrets on my part. I enjoyed seeing the look on his face when he ended up on the floor. It was wonderful—knowing he knew he had been bested by yours truly. Deal already."

Lachlan looks at his cell phone and sighs.

29
Boston

"I assume you're on the pill? Wouldn't want any surprises in the next couple of weeks. Not ready to be a daddy."

Justine pulls David toward her and grins.

"You haven't changed one bit."

He laughs as he finishes zipping up his jeans. She watches as he grins and faces her. She reaches out to kiss him.

"I'm on the pill. I have a life."

David runs his fingers through his hair.

"What's the deal with Taylor Pendleton anyway?"

Justine rolls her eyes.

"We got together again last year but it fizzled out rather quickly thanks to Chandler Penney's whore of a sister."

David reacts and laughs.

"Taylor and Eden Penney hooked up?"

He makes a lewd gesture with his finger.

"Isn't she still in high school? I could imagine the trash-talk all over Castle Beach and Marble Hills—R rated no doubt."

Justine pretends to slap David.

"Eden just started college. She's eighteen. Not that it matters much—from what I heard she spread her legs plenty all over Marble Hills—even scored with law enforcement types."

"If only I was a few years younger."

Justine seems shocked at the statement.

"How many women have shared your bed since you left Castle Beach? Should I start guessing at one hundred?"

David grins slyly.

"Higher."

They look at each other. Justine pulls David toward her again and seems bothered by something. She sighs.

"Is my brother really happy living in Los Angeles?"

David looks at her curiously.

"What do you mean?"

Justine slides her finger across David's lips.

"He won't come home—even to visit—says he's too busy whenever I ask—insists we visit him in California instead."

David pulls away and grimaces.

"He's fine. Enjoys working at Paramount Pictures—met someone there from Marble Hills actually—Donna Markway."

Page 143

Justine reacts. David notices.

"He never said anything about it. My firm works with her father—Gable Markway. He comes by several times a month."

David shoots her a knowing look and sighs.

"Doesn't he have a famous son?"

Justine seems bored.

"He does—but I've never met him."

She turns to look at her cell phone for a few seconds. She pulls up a few photographs of Ashton Markway online.

"Jeremy Winterfield said he's really nice. They met at a gala in New York last year. Plenty of big names showed up to raise money for some charity that helps people using drugs."

David grabs his jacket from the sofa.

"Wasn't Winterfield the dude that took down Carson Penney—put the fear of God in him for what his son did?"

Justine shakes her head.

"He doesn't talk much about it."

David glances at the door.

"I guess we should head to the airport."

Justine follows David out of the hotel room as he closes the door behind them. They walk toward the elevator.

30
Orchid Bay
Phamler Garden Condo

"Are you sure this will knock him out."

Gregory Maarsen looks at the glass vial in his hand and smirks knowingly. He nervously hands it to Vina Phamler.

"It's perfectly safe. No one has ever died from the stuff I supply. It'll knock him out—just as you wanted—no issues."

Vina still seems unsure but nods in agreement.

"How long does it last for? One hour? Two?"

Gregory makes a lewd gesture and laughs loudly.

"Ten Minutes. Then he awakens. That's the best I can do with what you have in mind. It's up to you from that point."

Page 144

"What if I slip him a few extras?"

They share a sly glance between them.

"I don't recommend it unless you want the coroner asking questions. Not to mention your local police department."

Vina reacts and sighs loudly.

31
Santa Barbara

"Kulkovich is stalking his next victim unaware he's also being stalked. I love it. Right before he kills his latest he'll meet his maker. This is gonna be quite the reality show no doubt."

Marlisa glances at her cell phone.

"What about the other guy with Kulkovich?"

Marlisa seems bored and yawns loudly.

"Do you even need to ask?"

She snaps her fingers.

32
Orchid Bay
Downtown Police Station

"Jayne Osborne has pulled a disappearing act."

Lachlan glances over at Roland and nods.

"Where do you think she went?"

Lachlan leans back in his chair and sighs.

"She knew we were looking for her."

Roland stands up.

"I think it's time we call the State Police."

Lachlan reaches for the phone as Roland walks toward the door. He runs his fingers through his hair. He seems worried.

TO BE CONTINUED

A Brief Look at the Sixth Episode

Events begin to unravel for several couples while murders begin to pile up in San Francisco where not everything is what it seems as a life hangs in the balance due to one woman's actions.

Episode 6
Summer Fantasy

1
San Francisco

"What the fuck? Who the hell is this chick?"

Carlos Vente seems confused as he watches a young woman get out of her car. Casually without a worry in the world she opens fire. Kevin Kulkovich dies instantly as he is shot in the forehead by the young woman. As Sergei Lycov tries to exit the car he is shot several times by the woman. As he lies in the alley gasping to breathe she walks up to him and laughs. Seconds later a bullet can be seen protruding from his temple. Carlos watches as she calmly walks away as if nothing happened. He sighs.

"Is she one of Marlisa Vigaro's people?"

He reaches for his cell phone.

2
Los Angeles

"Oh man, this is gold. It reads like fiction—so sad that it's based on a true story. This kid lived through a nightmare."

Wesley Madison turns to face Harper Brynton with an odd look on his face. He glances back at the open script on his desk.

"I can get this made for Paramount or Universal. It has Oscar potential. Finding the right actors is essential no doubt."

Wesley seems confused and sighs.

"How come I never heard of this story before?"

Harper seems pleased as he glances at the script lying on top of the desk titled *The Bobby Driscoll Story*. He sighs.

"I came across his story while doing a thesis on child stars from the 1930s and 1940s. What happened to him was like a horror movie. **Bobby Driscoll** was like a male version of **Judy Garland**. Had so much talent—but **Walt Disney** treated him horribly when he reached his mid-teens—allowed his staff to sexually abuse Bobby from what I heard—apparently it happened in front of stars like **Ruth Warrick** and **Jane Wyman**. But they never said anything about it until years later. Sort of tells you what kind of women they were—cared more about their precious careers than the welfare of a child. His parents were no images of perfection either—they treated him like a bag of money and nothing more. One of the worst stage parents ever. **Mary Astor** could relate no doubt. Rumor has it that **Howard Hughes** had a "thing" for Bobby—as in pervert—predator—rapist probably—and when he was rejected by the kid—that disgusting creepy bastard forced Disney to terminate Driscoll's contract out of spite."

Harper clenches his fist in anger. Wesley notices. He glances at the script again. He faces Wesley once more.

"Hughes later claimed he just didn't like child actors. But everyone knew there was more to the story—including Disney. Disgusting excuses for human beings—Disney has a really dark rep according to biographer **Marc Eliot**. Check out his book online. Not for the faint. Anyway, poor kid was blacklisted for years afterwards by Disney—couldn't get major roles in movies or television. Unfortunately he turned to drugs to numb the pain and ended up on the streets—homeless. He was discovered dead in some rundown building in New York. He had so much promise but because of unscrupulous adults in his life he lost his way."

Wesley watches as Harper pulls out his cell phone and seconds later photographs of the long-ago film actor appears.

3
Orchid Bay
Derringer Apartment

"I told him how I felt. It wasn't a secret. Everyone knew I hated that creep. He deserved what happened. Good riddance."

Kyle Derringer faces Tabitha Bairstow and grins.

"I only wished I was the one who killed that bastard."

Tabitha reacts.

"Don't say that—people might think you did it."

Kyle waves his hand in the air.

"Fuck them—I'm not sorry and won't pretend to be a bit sorry that fucker is in the morgue. He got what he deserved."

Tabitha reaches out to embrace Kyle.

"I'm just so worried."

Kyle looks at Tabitha curiously.

"Why? I didn't do it."

Tabitha strokes Kyle's chest.

"Do you really think Jayne Osborne shot him?"

Kyle runs his fingers through his hair.

"Ethan Vanwick says she did. Said she made threats that she was gonna take him out—send him to Falling Pines."

Tabitha slides her arms around Kyle's waist.

"What if she didn't do it?"

Kyle shoots Tabitha a curious look.

4
Orchid Bay
Phamler Garden Condo

"I thought I made myself clear. I'm with Kayla now. She and I are together. You and I are over—just friends. I think from now on we shouldn't have anything to do with each other."

Patrick Clerke looks at the tray of Chinese food in front of him and sighs. He waves his hand at Vina Phamler as she tries to slide her arms around his waist. He aggressively pushes her away and is about to head to the front door when she slyly trips him.

"I won't let her have you."

Vina jumps on top of Patrick and forcibly administers an injection into Patrick's neck. He looks up at her in shock.

"What did you do?"

Seconds later he begins losing consciousness and lies back silently. Vina grins triumphantly. She begins to unbuckle his belt and unzips his Levi's. She slides her fingers across his underwear and moans loudly as she strokes his penis. She seems pleased with herself and reaches for a camera. Less than a second later Patrick begins to shake violently. Vina reacts and panics.

5

St. Thomas

United States Virgin Islands

"I thought you said you couldn't go to Coral World? Said your mother wouldn't let you—said you broke curfew?"

Niels Anderssen faces Byron Blakely with a grimace. He waves his hand in the air and walks toward the window.

"I'm going—*count* on it. Like seriously."

Byron seems intrigued and laughs.

"Remember what happened the last time you didn't do what you were told. My mother's freak ex kidnapped you."

Niels laughs and shakes his fist.

"If I recall he was after *you*."

Byron reacts and seems upset at the comment.

"How come you never told me what happened with Brent Crawford? You always change the subject whenever I ask."

Niels seems uncomfortable.

"I told you what happened already. I was held by your mother's ex and his freak show pal. They thought I was you."

Byron takes a step toward Niels.

Page **150**

"Yeah—yeah—I know all that. But how did the friend of my mother's ex end up at the bottom of the cliff dead."

Niels waves his hand in the air.

"I don't know. He was chasing me and then he wasn't. It wasn't until later I found out he fell—slipped off the bluff."

Byron gives Niels a suspicious look and sighs.

"What about that FBI guy? How did he find where those two goons were stashing you? Did he ever tell you?"

Niels shakes his head. He sighs.

"I assume Brent Crawford's sister told him."

Niels glances at his computer.

"Whatever happened to her anyway?"

Byron makes a flying motion with his hand.

"She left the island right after the police closed the case. I think she went back to the mainland—or maybe to Europe."

Bryon drops his voice to a whisper.

"Her story never really added up about what happened with her brother—seemed like a bad episode of one of those old prime time soaps like *The Colbys* that they show on Hulu."

Niels glances at the mirror.

"Facts are stranger than fiction."

Byron seems confused at the comment.

6

Santa Barbara

"She's not one of my people. I hired *you* not *her* or *anyone* else. She must be working solo—probably an ex-girlfriend."

Marlisa Vigaro looks at Carlos on her cell phone. She seems a bit impatient as she nervously walks back and forth.

"This *person* definitely puts a wrinkle in my plans to even the score with Loren Fawcett. No doubt he's freaking out."

She glances at the ocean and grimaces.

"Did you see where she went?"

She watches his reaction and sighs loudly.

"Plan B goes into effect immediately."

Page 151

Marlisa glances at a list of names on top of a nearby counter. She smiles as she faces Carlos once again and laughs.

"Simon Momoa."

Carlos watches as Marlisa snaps her fingers.

"With him dead there will be no Momoa family members left to wreck havoc in San Francisco—take the bastard out."

Carlos nods in agreement as the phone call ends.

7

Los Angeles

"I agree. This project is certainly something I want to film next year. Start looking for actors to play **Bobby Driscoll** as a child and teenager—but keep it quiet for the time being. A certain studio certainly won't be pleased with us after what they did to the real-life Bobby—a nightmare in the daylight no doubt."

Harper makes a lewd gesture with his finger.

"Fuck them. They ruined his life and tried to cover up what they did for over half a century. Blamed him every chance they got. It's about time the world knew what really happened to that poor kid—turned a promising young actor into a homeless drug addict—then made it look like they had nothing to do with it."

Wesley runs his fingers through his hair.

"I'm going to clear my schedule for this project. *The Bobby Driscoll Story* is the first film to begin filming next year."

"Should I start looking for directors too?"

Wesley gestures with his hand as his cell phone begins buzzing. He grabs it and smiles as he sees his caller.

"Well, well, well. Wonders never cease. Are you in Los Angeles already? I assume you're coming to the premiere?"

On the screen he sees Simon Spencer making a lewd gesture with his finger as he begins laughing. He gestures.

"Of course I'm coming. I wouldn't miss it for the world. It's been ages since we last saw each other. Five years exact."

Wesley shakes his fist at Simon.

"I see you haven't changed one bit."

Page **152**

Simon rolls his eyes.

"No reason to."

He grins broadly and waves his hand toward the screen showing a wedding ring on his finger. He appears happy.

"Yours truly is a married man as of last month—got myself hitched to my college sweetheart. She's perfect—absolute."

Wesley seems pleased at the news.

8
Orchid Bay
Phamler Garden Condo

"Who are you calling?"

Tim Bergman looks up at Vina as he begins dialing. On the floor next to him Patrick is struggling to breathe. Vina gasps.

"You can't do that. I'll be arrested."

Tim shoots Vina a nasty look.

9
Orchid Bay
Downtown Police Station

"Have you located Adam's killer yet?"

Roland O'Brien seems a bit irritated as he watches Ethan Vanwick slam the front door and come toward him. He sighs.

"And who would that be?"

Ethan stops suddenly and clenches his fists.

"Jayne Osborne."

Lachlan Ball stands and faces Ethan.

"It appears Adam Mills had plenty of enemies—not just Jayne from what we've learned. Shall we discuss Adam and his list of problematic relationships with the local townsfolk?"

Ethan makes a lewd gesture with his finger.

"Spare me the theatrics. Jayne Osborne is your killer. That chick is certifiable. What the fuck are you waiting for? I bet she's already in Mexico. Is this what we pay taxes for? Well, is it?"

Lachlan walks to the door and opens it.

"Get the hell out before I toss you in the slammer."

Ethan seems about to laugh.

"And then what—have me killed like Jason Shappe? Oh yeah the so-called good townsfolk are having a field day with what happened to him. Which one of you jerks took him out?"

Lachlan seems about to explode as he angrily grabs Ethan and forces him out the front door. He slams the door shut.

"Can you believe that guy?"

Roland shakes his head several times.

"I never liked him."

He shakes his fist at the air.

"I'm surprised no one has tried to kill him."

Lachlan stifles a laugh.

10

San Francisco

"Well, if it isn't my favorite party guess? What brings you to Frisco sweet thing? Do you want to book a hotel room? We could finish what we started at Adam's party—go all the way this time I assume—make a moment of us getting horizontal."

Jayne Osborne seems oddly calm as she looks at Sasha Levitov while he finishes off a mug of beer. She leans over and whispers in his ear. He reacts and begins laughing loudly.

"I'll rock your world hard—leave an impression that won't be forgotten anytime soon. Yours truly has quite a history."

Jayne seems to stifle a laugh.

"We'll see."

Sasha licks his lips.

"Oh we will no doubt—guaranteed."

He looks down at his swelling erection and smirks.

"I know a quaint little motel down the street."

Jayne slides her fingers across Sasha's lips and moans.

"I hope you have plenty of condoms."

He seems ready to explode with excitement.

11
Orchid Bay
Parkview Hospital

"What did he take?"

Tim turns to look at Vina as Lance Veltrope faces them. They watch as she pulls out a syringe and hands it to Lance.

"He took this?"

Vina and Tim look at each other.

"She injected Patrick with it—assumed it was safe."

Lance reacts and turns to face Patrick.

12
St. Thomas
United States Virgin Islands

"I'll see you tomorrow—if you're not grounded."

Niels watches as Byron begins walking toward the staircase a few feet away before he closes his bedroom door.

"Finally—I thought he'd never leave."

Niels spins around and seems startled as he sees Tiffany Johnson standing near his computer. She points to it.

"I'm going to need your help."

Niels stands there for a few seconds almost as if he's not sure what he's seeing is real. He takes a step forward.

"It's been a while."

Tiffany gestures with her hand.

"I have a problem and I'm going to need your help in accomplishing my goal. There's no time to waste."

Niels rolls his eyes.

"Just tell me what to do."

Tiffany folds her arms across her chest.

"It involves someone you know."

Niels looks at his computer.

"Maxwell Pendergraft."

Page **155**

Tiffany nods and motions for Niels to sit down in front of his computer. He walks toward her and stops. He sighs loudly.

"I spoke with Gina Bentley."

Tiffany nods.

"I know."

Niels reacts and shrugs.

"Did everyone really think she was mentally ill because she said she saw you? Why didn't anyone believe her?"

Tiffany stifles a laugh.

"Would you believe I existed if you hadn't witnessed what you saw in person? No one believes until they come face to face with someone like me. Once that happens there's no turning back even for the most stubborn types who say ghosts aren't real."

Niels sits down in front of the computer.

"I didn't believe until I saw you."

Tiffany nods in agreement.

13
San Francisco

Sasha lies naked on top of a bloodstained bed staring upwards at nothing. Blood oozes from a bullet wound in his forehead. Except for the ticking of a nearby clock the room is silent. In his outstretched hand are a few packets of condoms.

14
Orchid Bay
Downtown Police Station

"Are you serious? We'll be right there. Make sure she doesn't leave the hospital—that goes for Tim Bergman too."

Lachlan looks at his cell phone and sighs. He faces Roland with a look of disgust on his face. Roland seems confused.

"What happened? Or do I have to ask?"

Lachlan grabs his jacket.

15
Los Angeles

"Tiffany Johnson told me you were in danger—said for me to come right away. I took the first flight out of Europe."

Ashton Markway runs his fingers through his hair. He watches as his sister sighs loudly. Donna Markway turns around and looks at the mirror as if expecting to see Tiffany looking back at her from the other side. She faces her brother once more.

"I don't know why she told you I was in danger. I'm fine. I have nothing to be concerned about. I'm not in danger."

At that moment there is a blinding flash. They both react in shock as Tiffany appears before them seconds later.

"I say differently."

Donna continues standing motionless as Ashton runs his fingers through his hair again and takes a step forward.

16
Orchid Bay
Parkview Hospital

"Is he going to be okay?"

Kayla Larsen seems about to fall apart as she looks at Lance. He glances at Vina and Tim—then faces the hallway.

"I had his stomach pumped and induced a coma to give his body a chance to recover. It was a close call—very close."

Kayla turns to face Vina.

"You hateful bitch—you tried to kill him."

"I did no such thing."

Lance shoots Vina a cautious glance and sighs. He turns to face Kayla again with a worried look on his face. She notices.

"Can I see him?"

Lance nods and faces Vina.

"The police are on their way as we speak."

Vina turns around to look at the front door. She notices it is blocked by two security guards. They seem ready to fight.

"I haven't done anything. It was an accident. He fell on a syringe. It happened—nothing but an accident. Deal already."

Kayla lunges at Vina but is restrained by Lance.

"Tim *said* you gave Patrick an injection. You did this to my boyfriend. You tried to end his life because he didn't want you. He told you the two of you were finished. You're a vicious horrible person who should be locked up for the rest of your life."

Kayla angrily points at Vina.

"No one in this town has forgotten what happened to your half-brother because of your vicious lies. You killed him whether you pulled the trigger or not. Why are you still here in Orchid Bay anyway? No one likes you. Shouldn't you be in Los Angeles where all the freaks are? Fucking every guy you meet? Ugh—*bitch*."

Vina is about to answer when she notices Roland and Lachlan entering the emergency room in a rush. She panics.

17

San Francisco

"Is this some sort of joke? Are you fucking with me? Both of them are in the morgue. Shot? Ambushed? What the fuck?"

Loren Fawcett clenches his fist as he faces Vladimir Orlov and seems about to explode. Vladimir looks at his cell phone.

"According to an eyewitness Kulkovich and Lycov were shot by a woman—a beautiful woman to be exact. Just walked up to them and opened fire and walked away—not a worry in the world from what it appeared to the eyewitness. They were in a diner across the street. Madness ensued immediately afterwards as the woman got in a car and took off. The cops got nothing."

Loren pounds his fist on top of his desk.

"A fucking cunt took out two of our best—two trained killers I might add. Something isn't adding up. Someone knows something. I want that damn witness found—brought to me."

He leans back in chair and grimaces.

"That cunt is gonna regret fucking with my people. I think we have our smoking gun. She's responsible for everything."

Page **158**

Vladimir runs his fingers through his hair.

"I think that's a bit of a stretch. One lousy bitch can't be behind what's been happening—too many moving parts."

"Do you have a better idea?"

They look at each other.

18
Los Angeles

"It just seems so unlike Heath. He's a sweet guy."

Ashton grabs Donna by the arm.

"You heard what Tiffany said. Heath Griffith isn't his real name. He lied to you. Do you think Tiffany would lie about something like this—to *you* of all people? I believe her."

Donna glances at the mirror again.

"She said his real name was Silas Bell. Said he killed the mother of his half-brother's son and several police officers in the US Virgin Islands. Said he killed four people in Florida and killed a father of two in Phoenix after carjacking him. He raped a woman in San Diego before killing her—killed her son when he came home early. She said he also killed a doctor in Australia."

"Heath Griffith—Silas Bell—he said."

Ashton notices the computer on a desk nearby seems to be turning itself on. As they watch in amazement the keyboard on the computer begins typing in a password and seconds later the screen comes to life. As they watch they see a pre-teen boy staring back at them from his bedroom in the US Virgin Islands.

"Hi, my name is Niels Anderssen. Tiffany Johnson told me to contact you about Heath Griffith's true identity and crimes."

They both seem in shock at the scene unfolding.

19
San Francisco

Carlos watches as Simon Momoa crosses the street and is about to head up the driveway to his house. Carlos smirks.

Page **159**

"No better ending than a home explosion to put a damper on plans for a quiet dinner with his latest flame—life happens."

He pulls out his cell phone and begins dialing.

20
Orchid Bay
Downtown Police Station

"I didn't do anything. It was an accident. I thought I told you so at the hospital. It was all a big misunderstanding."

Lachlan seems annoyed as he looks at Vina and Tim and grimaces. She attempts to stand up but Lachlan motions her to remain seated. She rolls her eyes as Tim remains oddly silent.

"Do you know how much trouble you two are in at the moment? Have you any grasp of reality? A man is fighting for his life because of what you did. If I were you I'd drop the Karen attitude and begin to deal with what is happening to you and your friend. Both of you are going to be charged—you for attempted murder and him for being an accomplice to an attempted murder. If I were either of you I would seriously begin thinking of hiring a lawyer—one that specializes in murder by poison."

Tim jumps up suddenly in shock.

"I told her not to do it."

Lachlan gestures at him angrily.

"Uh-huh—but you didn't tell anyone. You kept your mouth shut knowing she was going ahead with her scheme to break up Patrick and Kayla by making it look like Patrick was an unfaithful boyfriend. Tell me how that makes you innocent?"

Tim angrily faces Vina.

"Tell him I warned you. Tell him."

Vina smiles slyly.

"He knew what I was gonna do and encouraged me. He hated Kayla because she blew him off. Told him she didn't date nerds with no game. Said he was a loser—a pathetic dweeb."

Tim reacts and faces Lachlan.

"None of what she said is true. She lies."

Page **160**

Lachlan stands and faces them. He points at Vina as he walks toward her. They watch as he leans close to Vina.

"Do you think you're playing out some role on one of those long ago beloved prime time soaps where everyone always managed to scheme their way out of a long jail sentence for killing someone they hate by playing dumb? Well, do you?"

He watches Vina's reaction. She seems to be enjoying the drama she has created. She licks her lips and yawns loudly.

"How much longer are you going to run your mouth? I have things to do—people to meet. How about we call it a day?"

Lachlan begins to laugh.

"You're not going anywhere. Both of you are gonna spend the night in the slammer. Welcome to your new home."

Vina jumps up and heads for the door.

"I'm leaving."

As she runs toward the door she sees Roland standing at the front door with his hands folded in front of him. He laughs.

"I'm six feet tall. I work out daily at the gym. You're staying put. Deal with it. Don't make me have to restrain you."

Vina licks her lips as her eyes fall to the buttons on his snug-fitting jeans. She sighs loudly as she approaches him.

"How about we work things out in your bedroom like I offered previous? I'll give you a blowjob that will leave you paralyzed with lust. You know you want to fuck me. I'm game."

Roland glances at Lachlan. Vina notices.

"Oh my God—now it all makes sense why you didn't take me up on my offer. You and him—*ugh*—what a waste of a virile young man—you and *him*—gross. Wait until I tell Alison."

Roland grabs Vina by the arm.

"When they send you to one of the State prisons you're gonna wish you'd never tried to kill Patrick Clerke. I've heard plenty of stories about how some women in prison treat troubled beauty queens like yourself—you'll be passed around to the highest bidder—until they tire of you. Imagine if one of those women feels you insulted them at some point—think of what they'll do to you at night in your cell—so alone—so helpless."

Vina jerks free of Roland's grip.

"How dare you talk to me like I'm some sort of common criminal? Have you forgotten who I am? My family owns this town—my mother's father—my grandfather founded Orchid Bay and made it what it is today. You have no power over me."

Roland grabs Vina's arm again and uses his strength to subdue her. He pushes her against the wall. He grins broadly.

"I think it's time you learn just how powerful you really are in this town. A few nights in jail ought to knock some sense Into that feeble brain of yours. Your Karen act just ran out of gas."

He forcibly pushes her toward the door leading to the hallway. Try as she might Vina cannot break Roland's grip on her arm. His grins as he applies more force as they reach the door.

21

San Francisco

"Damn it—this fucking slut is gonna pay for what she's done today—first Kevin and Sergei—then Sasha—now Simon."

Loren seems enraged as he throws his cell phone on the sofa. He turns to face Anton Levitov. Anton looks at the gun in his hand and grins. He strokes the gun several times and sighs.

"I'm going to enjoy killing this bitch. No one insults us like this and lives to tell about it. Her rental car has been found."

Loren clenches his fist.

"Who hired her?"

Anton shakes his head.

"I'm working on it."

He looks at the gun in his hand.

"The name on the rental application is Scarlett O'Hara."

Loren reacts.

"Is this supposed to be a joke?"

Anton seems confused.

"No—that's the name that was on the application. She paid cash. The rental agent said she was really sweet—polite."

Loren grabs Anton and shakes him violently.

"You're such a dumb fuck Anton—don't you read? Scarlett O'Hara is not a real person. She's a character in a novel called *Gone with the Wind*. You got played royally by this clever cunt."

Loren lets go of Anton.

"Out of my sight this instant—be gone."

Anton gestures with his hand.

"It doesn't matter one way or the other as far as I'm concerned—I'm going to find her and put a bullet in her head."

Loren points to the door and begins yelling.

22

Orchid Bay
Parkview Hospital

"He'll pull through. Don't worry."

Kayla seems about to cry as she faces her father. Sidney Larsen pulls his daughter toward him. He glances at Patrick lying a few feet away. Sidney strokes Kayla's hair and whispers.

"Patrick is strong. He'll come through this soon enough. He has to. How else will I get to know the kind of man he is?"

Kayla looks at her father curiously.

"I thought you didn't like him?"

Sidney gestures with his hand and laughs.

"I never said I didn't like him."

"But you implied it—said he had a rebellious streak in him—said he needed to show respect for his elders. You said more than once I could do better—said he had a sharp tongue."

Kayla laughs and points at her father.

"That's why I like him—he's just like you."

Sidney glances at Patrick again.

"OK—OK—I guess I said what you said I did. Nevertheless I can see how much you care for him so I'm willing to give him a chance. If he makes you happy that's all I really want. Lord only knows Violet's marriage hasn't been a bed of roses—far from it actually. It seems there's trouble brewing in paradise. Violet told me today she's thinking of calling it quits—wants a divorce."

Page **163**

Kayla rolls her eyes and sighs loudly.

"I should say I'm shocked. But I'm not. Violet just isn't cut out for the life of a dutiful wife. Everyone knew it but her."

Sidney nods in agreement.

23
Orchid Bay
Derringer Apartment

"Do you think Jayne Osborne is going to get arrested for murder if they can find her? I heard she skipped town."

Kyle lays back in bed seemingly exhausted.

"You and I just got through a marathon hour of intense lovemaking and that's what you're thinking of at the moment?"

Tabitha seems irritated.

"I can't stop thinking about what happened. Adam Mills was a terrible person. He slept with most of the women in Orchid Bay. Scored with several high school girls from what I heard—got one of them pregnant actually—paid for her abortion. But even he deserves justice. Jayne Osborne needs to be punished."

Kyle runs his fingers through his hair.

"I don't care if they ever find her. I'm just glad that piece of trash is on a slab in the morgue. He got what he deserved."

Kyle grins he watches his penis becoming erect.

"I'm alive he's dead. It's as simple as that. Case closed. Life is for the living and right now all I want to do is resume what we've been doing for the last hour plus. I'm horny as fuck."

Tabitha angrily pushes Kyle away.

24
Orchid Bay
Hampshire Street Cafe

"I'm not a bit surprised she tried to kill Patrick Clerke."

Sabine Norton takes a sip of coffee.

"She never got over being dumped like trash."

Liana Danforth shakes her head.

"He wasn't even her type. She likes guys that are wild and live on the edge. Patrick is mellow and trusting. Her type is a guy like Jason Shappe. Those two were made for each other."

Sabine rolls her eyes.

"Adam Mills."

She leans over to Liana and whispers.

"I heard he and Vina Phamler hit the sheets plenty."

Liana seems disgusted and sighs.

"What some skanky women in this town won't do to keep themselves on the top of every list of any guy with a pulse."

Sabine stifles a smirk.

"There's talk about Adam Mills circulating plenty. Word is he tried to rape Jayne and she shot the bastard. Blew him away and then skipped town. Certainly couldn't blame her if that's what happened. That man was the embodiment of pure scum. He was mean and conniving—always trying to get one over on some unsuspecting innocent. I applaud Jayne for taking him out."

Liana seems bothered.

"You don't know if Jayne killed him."

Sabine rolls her eyes.

"Of course she did it. Who else could it be?"

Liana seems nervous as she looks at the front door.

"Kyle Derringer."

Sabine gasps.

"Why would he want Adam dead?"

"He made a play for Tabitha Bairstow again—tried to force her to have sex with him. Kyle was livid when he found out."

Liana notices a customer entering the cafe.

"Apparently he still thought Tabitha was his girlfriend and made it clear he wouldn't tolerate Kyle being in her bed."

Sabine seems bored and yawns.

"Kyle is all talk and no action. The man is a saint. He helps out at the homeless mission on Rose Lane. He takes kids camping every summer so they can experience the great outdoors."

She makes a lewd gesture with her finger.

"He has no black marks on his name. Unless you count the time he popped Adam for telling lies about him. As far as I'm concerned Jayne Osborne is the only suspect they should be searching for in Orchid Bay. I bet she's halfway to Europe already or Australia—just saying. That woman has money to burn—family money to be exact. If she was innocent why isn't she here to defend her good name? Face it—she killed that lying bastard."

Liana shakes her head and goes to help the lone customer sitting at the front counter. Sabine pulls out her cell phone.

25
Orchid Bay
Pioneer Trail Beach

"How many times do I have to say it—we're done. You cheated on me. I know it and Marley Osborne knows it."

Carrie Booker glares at Kyler Vanwick.

"It's over. I'm done with you."

Kyler angrily grabs Carrie by the arm.

"I love you Carrie. You can't just throw me away like I don't matter. We have history. Marley Osborne means nothing to me. I thought I made that clear. She lies. She's not pregnant."

Carrie pulls away from Kyler.

"You and that man candy slut have been having a sexual relationship for months. Like I said we're done. Get lost."

Kyler runs his fingers through his hair.

"It meant nothing. She means nothing to me. It just happened once. That's it. She knows I'm with you—only you."

Carrie turns away. She seems annoyed.

"I'm sure Marley will take you back. Welcome you into the back seat of her car. Spread her fucking legs—give you a thrill."

Kyler watches as Carrie begins walking along the surf. He clenches his fist and pulls out his cell phone. He sighs loudly.

"I swear I'm going to kill that whore. No one will blame me either. Everyone knows Marley Osborne is a slut—a filthy slut to be exact—slept with her cousin's boyfriend—broke them up."

Page **166**

He notices Carrie talking to someone.

"I'm going to teach that slut a lesson she won't forget for trying to interfere in my life. She's been nothing but trouble from the moment I fucked her in the backseat of her father's car."

The line is picked up.

"I need to see you right away."

He watches as Marley Osborne licks her lips.

"I know you'd see things my way."

Kyler sighs loudly.

"Meet me at Paradise Pointe."

Marley licks her lips again.

"Why don't you just come over? We can pick up where we let off before Carrie Booker started acting like she was better than every other girl in this town—told everyone the two of you were official—warned us about defying her—threatened."

Kyler seems annoyed.

"I said Paradise Pointe and that's final."

Marley blows a kiss toward the cell phone and smirks.

"I like it when you take charge."

She slides her fingers across her exposed vagina.

"I'm on the pill by the way."

Kyler shakes his fist.

"One hour."

He ends the call.

26

San Francisco

"I'm not going anywhere with the likes of you."

Igor Levitov grins as he tightens his grip on the arm of a terrified young woman. He leans closer to her and laughs.

"Or what—you'll scream for help? Do it at your own peril. I have my orders. Dead or alive it doesn't matter to me."

Nancy Blyden shakes her head.

"When Loren finds out you're a dead man."

Igor begins to laugh loudly.

Page **167**

"Who do you think ordered that you be taken into my custody? Seems like you've been quite the woman about town haven't you—several secret meetings that Loren Fawcett wasn't privy too? Did you screw those guys in suits you met with? Those nerdy types were probably quite boring in bed—unprepared."

Nancy seems confused.

"What are you babbling about?"

Igor twists Nancy's arm backwards. She grimaces.

"Did you order a hit on your ex?"

Nancy reacts. Igor seems to become angrier.

"Did you have Cujo Momoa killed?"

"I have no idea what you're talking about."

Nancy seems bored.

"He and I were over ages ago."

She stifles a smile.

"I'm Loren's girl now. I've been his girl for months now. He took me away from Cujo. Those are the facts—deal already."

Igor watches her defiant behavior intensify.

"Uh-huh—Simon said you only hooked-up with his cousin to get to Loren. That makes you a slut—an unpaid prostitute."

Nancy lowers her voice and smirks.

"You're just mad because I never gave you a tumble. Big strong guy like yourself and you couldn't get me into your bed."

Igor seems enraged at the slight.

"You need to be taught a lesson about respect."

He hits her across the face with his fist. He laughs as she reacts to the blow. He hits her again. She seems about to cry.

"You'd better hope you had nothing to do with Cujo's death—or I swear your death will be most painful. I will take you out myself—broke every bone in your body before I put a bullet in that worthless skull of yours. And I'll enjoy doing it too."

"I had nothing to do with Cujo's death. Like I said—he and I were over. He accepted it and moved on with his usual groupies from that bar on Nob Hill—and I moved on with Loren. He said he was happy for me—said Loren was better for me anyway."

Igor tightens his grip on Nancy's arm.

Page **168**

"Simon Momoa said he had evidence you were behind Cujo's death. He was supposed to meet with Loren when he was killed earlier today. Loren is pissed about these turn of events. He's really hurt you slighted him. Wouldn't be the first time one of his "girls" tried to pull one over on him. But as you know they always end up dead when he exacts his revenge—bodies riddled with bullets—mutilated—dumped in some alley where even the homeless won't dare go. This will be your fate if he thinks you had Cujo snuffed out. Him and Cujo were tight—like brothers."

Nancy suddenly seems nervous. Igor notices.

27
Orchid Bay
Paradise Pointe Bluffs

"I want you out of my life. Do you hear me? We're over Marley. I'm done with you or I swear I'll frigging hurt you."

Marley reaches out to slide her fingers along the buttons of Kyler's jeans. She sighs loudly as he pushes her away.

"She's all wrong for you. You're a guy that likes to fuck for hours at the beach. Carrie likes quiet picnics. *Ugh*—blah."

Kyler pushes Marley against her car.

"I said we're through. I'm done with you. I'm moving on with or without Carrie. Nevertheless you and I are finished."

Marley grabs Kyler. She seems angry.

"I won't allow you to throw me away like you've done to almost every girl in Orchid Bay once you've had your fun."

She strokes his belt buckle.

"We belong together and you know it. You always push me to the edge with your demands—and I always give myself to you—always let you indulge your fantasies. But if you think I'll be cast aside—think again. I know things about you. Lots of things you don't want anyone to know. What do you think the police would do if I told them it was you *not* Jason Shappe that raped Tracey Oakfield? How do you think they'd react if they found out you threatened her and made her say Jason Shappe did it?"

Page **169**

Marley watches as Kyler reacts and grins broadly.

"She told me what happened between the two of you that afternoon at her home. After you fucked her mother you found her by the pool and fucked her. Oops—raped her. Her mother still doesn't know the details about what you did to Tracey—at least not yet. But that can change. You're *so* finished Kyler—face it."

She begins to unzip the zippers on his Levi's. He watches her silently and then without saying anything he grabs her throat. As he strengthens his grip she cried out but he joyfully continues tightening his stranglehold until she begins to lose consciousness. He watches as she falls limply against his chest and smiles. He lets her fall to the ground seconds later. As he stands above her in triumph he wipes sweat from his brow and seems relieved.

"I was done with her anyway."

He turns to face the edge of the bluffs and casually pushes her body over the precipice a few feet away. As she falls toward the rocks below he turns away—not bothering to look.

28
Honolulu

"I don't care who you are. I'm not going anywhere with you. Carmen Pendleton and I have nothing to talk about."

Eugene Ledyard grabs Shirley Beecroft by the arm and pushes her against the door. He leans closer to her and grins.

"Carmen Pendleton decides whether the two of you have anything to talk about. Your opinion has no value—none."

Shirley tries to wriggle free of Eugene's grip.

"I know people—very bad people."

A fist smashes into her jaw. Eugene smirks.

"Do I look like a boy scout?"

He punches her again—this time with more force. As she reels from the assault he forces her toward the elevator.

"You had better show me more respect or I'll have to teach you a lesson. One you won't like—but of which I'll enjoy."

Shirley tries to reach for her cell phone.

"Did you not understand what I just said?"

Eugene forcibly grabs her cell phone and slips it into the back pocket of his jeans. He faces her again. He seems angry.

"One more stunt like that and we going to have a lot more to talk about—starting with how much physical pain I should inflict on you before you start playing by Carmen's rules."

Shirley seems unbothered by Eugene's threat.

"It's you who should be worried. You're just a dumb jock who services Carmen when she needs a tumble. When my people find you there'll be no escape. This island isn't big enough for you to hide from them—they're already on the way as we speak."

Eugene rams his fist into Shirley's jaw again as they get into the elevator. He hits her repeatedly as the doors close.

29
Los Angeles

"I can't believe I was so wrong about Heath. He was just so polite—so respectful. I thought he was the man of my dreams."

Ashton rolls his eyes knowingly.

"Dude is a freak show—no matter how hot you thought he was—he a lot of mental issues to keep endless shrinks busy."

He glances at the computer and then at Donna.

"Niels Anderssen said someone was on their way to keep an eye on you. Said Tiffany ordered it. Said it was someone you already knew from Marble Hills. Someone you could trust."

Before Ashton can continue the doorbell rings. Donna and Ashton look at each other. They face the door and seem nervous as the doorbell rings again. Ashton slowly walks to the door.

TO BE CONTINUED

A Brief Look at the Seventh Episode

A man and woman pretend to be a couple which unnerves a romantic rival while one woman's schemes to exact revenge leads to tragedy as another woman is reunited with an old friend.

Episode 7
Reality Show

1
Honolulu

"I'm going to have you arrested for rape."

Eugene Ledyard looks at Shirley Beecroft as he buttons his jeans. He glances at the back door of his van. He grins.

"One word to the cops and I'll kill you."

Shirley watches as he leans closer to her.

"Not one word, *bitch*—or they'll find your fucking body lying face down on some godforsaken beach. Count on it."

Shirley notices semen dripping from her exposed vagina and clenches her fist. Eugene grabs her arm and twists it.

"I'm not a nice man when provoked. You needed a lesson today and you got it. What happened was your fault."

"Carmen Pendleton is going to pay for what you did to me—nothing is going to stop me for talking. Do you hear me?"

Eugene looks at his erection swelling under his jeans and begins laughing. He angrily grabs Shirley's arm once more.

"Maybe round two is needed to set you straight on what happens to cheap sluts that overplay their hand at blackmail."

Eugene strengthens his grip on Shirley's arm. He watches her react and begins laughing. He shakes his other fist at her.

"Not one word about what happened between us to Carmen or anyone else—or I'll make sure you suffer before I put a bullet into your head and dump your worthless body on the North Shore where brain-dead surfers will find your bloated corpse."

Shirley wipes a tear from her eye.

"You won't get away with what you did."

Eugene hits her across the face in a rage. He hits her again several more times. She cries out in pain and is hit again.

"I'm beginning to lose patience with you."

He angrily punches Shirley again. Blood trickles down her nose as he grins. As she turns away he hits her once more.

2
Orchid Bay
Parkview Hospital

"I'm going to make sure Vina Phamler gets what she deserves for what she did to you. She'll pay—I swear."

Kayla Larsen sheds a tear as she watches Patrick Clerke lying motionless a few inches away. She reaches out to stroke his hair and seems about to cry. She hears a noise and turns to see her father in the doorway. Sidney Larsen walks over to her.

"Go get a cup of coffee. I'll stay with him."

Kayla looks at her father curiously.

"Seriously I got this. Go get a cup of coffee. You need a break anyway. He's not going anywhere. I'll keep watch."

Kayla stands and embraces her father.

3
Orchid Bay
Downtown Police Station

"I'm here to talk to my client."

Lachlan Ball leans back in his chair and sighs loudly.

"I see the saying 'lawyers chasing ambulances' is not just a tall tale as people assume. I was expecting you to show your face here sooner or later. Sad what some people will do for money when an opportunity presents itself. Don't you agree Miles?"

Miles O'Rourke rolls his eyes knowingly.

"Still nursing that bruised ego from high school I see. Get over it already. I bedded your girl on prom night. It happened."

Lachlan stands up.

"You forced yourself on her if I recall. Got her drunk and took her back to your uncle's beach house and fucked her."

Miles points his finger at Lachlan.

"Someone had to fuck her Lachlan—lord only knows she wasn't going to get laid by the likes of you—boy scout to the end—nothing sadder than a virginal girl on prom night."

Lachlan clenches his fists.

"I ought to bust you again like I did before."

Miles laughs loudly.

"Go ahead and try—I'll have you arrested for assault."

At that moment Roland O'Brien steps between them. He pushes Lachlan away and faces Miles. Miles reacts and sighs.

"I won't tolerate a two-bit pathetic zero backtalking me. He needs to know his place. I carry plenty weight in this town."

Miles seems irritated as Roland stifles a laugh.

"Being a sleazy lawyer carries no power anymore. Your cousin simply isn't going to be granted bail—reality bites."

Miles seems about to explode.

"I won't tolerate this kind of behavior."

Roland stifles a laugh again.

"You'll tolerate it and like it O'Rourke. Your cousin is a flight risk facing a serious charge of attempted murder. I have no intention of making it easy for her to skip town. Deal already."

Miles glances at Lachlan.

"Judge Norton will say otherwise."

Roland shakes his head.

"I have already spoken to Howard. He agrees with me that Vina Phamler is a flight risk if released. No bail—end of story."

Miles glances at Lachlan again. He sighs loudly.

"You two are gonna pay for this slight. I swear I'll make sure you end up sweeping the streets of Orchid Bay for a living."

Lachlan steps forward and points at Miles.

"If I were you I'd think about that before you act. In case it slipped your mind this office has a camera recording everything that happens—audio and video if you must know. Seems to me it's you who should be worried. Lawyers being disbarred have become commonplace in this country. The question *is*—exactly where you fall on that list—given your association with a certain politician presently in jail as we speak for accepting bribes."

Miles reacts and turns to face the door. He stops.

"I'm going to make sure both of you pay."

He leaves slamming the door angrily.

"He hasn't changed one bit since high school."

Roland nods in agreement.

4

Los Angeles

"I can't believe you're here. It's been a while."

Donna Markway hugs Maxwell Pendergraft warmly as her brother stands nearby. Maxwell faces Ashton Markway and they shake hands. He looks around the room. Silence permeates the apartment as the three of them share an awkward moment.

"I assume Niels Anderssen made clear the situation with Silas Bell. That guy is dangerous. Murder is a sport for him."

Donna nods and glances at Maxwell.

"Seeing Tiffany after all this time certainly brought back a lot of memories. It's almost like no time passed at all."

Maxwell laughs and faces Ashton.

"Over the last few years Tiffany Johnson and Jeremy Weissmann have been helping me with select cases. It was odd at first but I've since become accustomed to her frequent visits."

Donna seems confused and glances at the computer. She runs her fingers through her hair. Maxwell notices and laughs.

Page 176

"I assume you're wondering about Niels Anderssen—and how he and Tiffany know each other. How that came about?"

Donna nods. She glances at Ashton.

"It did cross my mind."

Maxwell laughs and seems amused.

"Niels Anderssen lives in the US Virgin Islands. Apparently he was the victim of a botched kidnapping gone wrong a while back—mistaken identity. For whatever reasons which I'm still not sure about Tiffany became personally involved and sent me to retrieve him. But Niels had a surprise of his own that threw Tiffany for a loop afterwards. Apparently the boy wonder can see ghosts. At the beach where I rescued him he saw Tiffany standing on the beach after his rescue. Wouldn't let it drop no matter how much I tried to dissuade him. He even sketched her for me. The first time I saw the sketch I almost had a heart attack. I knew he'd seen her and didn't know what to do. He wouldn't listen to anything I told him so Tiffany confronted him and got him to promise he would never reveal what he knew. I assume from that day they've been in touch. He's wise beyond his years and Tiffany relies on him to complete certain tasks that need his specific expertise—which are computers. From what I know he also contacted Gina Bentley—and she filled Niels in on what initially happened between her and Tiffany years ago in Marble Hills."

Donna reacts to what Maxwell is telling her. She leans against the wall. Ashton turns to face Maxwell. He sighs.

"Did she say why Silas Bell is after Donna?"

Maxwell wrings his hand nervously.

"I'm on a need-to-know basis at this point. But from what I've learned about Bell—he's a character. His father was a wealthy adventurer named Travis Montgomery Bell. He was killed in an explosion in the Caribbean a while back. I was involved with that case—that's how I met Sandra King. Silas Bell was in a mental hospital in Australia at the time but escaped. He showed up in the Virgin Islands and tried to kill his brother—but ended up killing his brother's ex-girlfriend instead. He vanished immediately after."

He wipes sweat from his brow and shrugs.

Page 177

"I assume you figure into his murderous plans somehow but have no idea why at this point. Tiffany isn't saying."

Ashton takes a step forward.

"So what's the plan? Wait until that lunatic makes his move and tries to kill my sister? Wait like sitting ducks?"

Maxwell gestures with his hand.

"You won't be alone. One of my guys is on the way. He's tough as they come and won't let anything happen to you."

Ashton nervously turns to look at the door.

5

San Francisco

"I want this woman found. This murderous cunt must pay for what she's done. I just got word that Simon Momoa was killed in an explosion at his home. That damn whore is gonna pay."

Loren Fawcett clenches his fist as he walks back and forth in his office. He stops and sighs. He looks at his cell phone.

"On another issue—has my father been located?"

He shakes his head and glances at the door.

"I want him found ASAP. I don't care what it takes. Find that old man and bring him to me—use force if necessary."

He clenches his fist again.

"Should you beat him? Do whatever it takes."

He grimaces and sighs once more.

"I want him found. He's been a thorn in my side for years now. I think it's time he was dealt with—dealt with harshly."

Loren gestures with his hand.

6

Orchid Bay
Pioneer Trail Mall

"Where's Carrie?"

Kyler Vanwick turns to face Carolyn Mills.

"How the fuck should I know?"

Page **178**

Carolyn sits down near Kyler. She smirks slyly.

"I thought you two were a couple?"

Kyler rolls his eyes.

"You thought wrong. She and I are over."

Carolyn reaches out to touch Kyler's hand. He notices.

"She was all wrong for you anyway."

Kyler seems irritated by her comment and sighs.

"I suppose you think you're a better fit for a fucked-up guy like me—one with a lot of baggage—relationship issues."

Carolyn leans closer to Kyler.

"I know what you like—you like fucking nonstop in the backseat of your car. No strings attached of course—just sex."

Kyler grins broadly.

"Is that supposed to be a bad thing?"

Carolyn licks her lips.

"Not in my book it isn't. A guy that doesn't like fucking in the backseat of his car is weird—probably has mommy issues."

Kyler laughs loudly.

"I go no mommy issues. My mother doesn't give a fuck about me. Told me she wishes I were in college already."

Carolyn licks her lips again.

"What about Marley Osborne?"

Kyler reacts.

"Don't mention that frigging slut to me again. She messed things up between Carrie and I. Told her I was a fucking dog."

Carolyn stifles a laugh.

"Marley has had her eye on you from the beginning. It's no secret she wants you all to herself. Told everyone who would listen she was going to try to get pregnant by you. Make you marry her and be a family. That girl is certifiable no doubt."

Kyler makes a lewd gesture with his finger.

"I'm not the marrying type."

"Good—I just want you to screw me in the backseat of your car. Use me to set Marley straight about the kind of guy you are when it comes to relationships. Carrie might see you in a new light—see you as a rebellious guy that doesn't give a fuck."

Kyler grins broadly and stands up. He grabs Carolyn by the arm and makes a lewd gesture with his finger. She giggles.

"I think I'll take you up on your offer."

Carolyn nods and follows Kyler to the elevator.

7
Los Angeles

"Guys I want you to meet Bradford Styverson. He works with me in DC and is the younger brother of one of my best friends from college. He won't let you down. I trust him."

Donna seems unable to look away from the man standing before her as Maxwell closes the door. Her eyes immediately fall upon his tight clothing which seems to fit his muscled body perfectly. Bradford extends his hand as she continues to gawk. Ashton rolls his eyes and turns to Maxwell. He sighs loudly.

"I think my sister is pleased with your selection."

Maxwell pulls Ashton aside.

"Bradford is the best. He's extremely professional. You have nothing to worry about. Donna will be in good hands."

Ashton turns to face Donna and Bradford again. Maxwell looks at his cell phone and seems upset. He faces Ashton.

"I have to go—something has come up."

Ashton nods and watches as Maxwell leaves. He turns around and realizes Donna and Bradford have left the room.

8
San Francisco

"What do you have to say for yourself?"

Loren seems enraged as he faces Nancy Blyden. Igor Levitov forces her forward into the office. She sighs loudly.

"I'm not going to ask you twice."

Nancy tries to look away.

"I don't know what you're talking about. I'm one of your girls—nothing more. I've been loyal to you Loren—only you."

Loren walks toward Nancy and Igor. He grabs her by the neck. He seems about to lose control. He shakes her violently.

"Are you working with that cunt that killed Cujo?"

Nancy shakes her head several times.

"I told you I don't know what you're talking about. I had nothing to do with what happened to Cujo or the others."

Loren punches Nancy in the face. He looks at Igor and points to the door. He gives Nancy a sharp look and laughs.

"Take her to the stairwell and do what is necessary. Use as much force as you feel is needed. Make sure she suffers."

Igor grins and forces Nancy toward the door.

"Please—Loren—I love you."

Loren begins laughing. He grabs Igor by the arm.

"Film it. I want to see her life being taken. See her beg for mercy before you put a bullet in her head. I need a good laugh."

Igor nods as Nancy begins screaming for help. Loren walks toward her and punches her several more times. He grimaces as he sees her reaction. He angrily hits her again in the jaw.

9
Orchid Bay
Pioneer Trail Mall

"Just look at her—she thinks by staring at you I'll just disappear into nothing. That girl needs to get a life—pathetic."

Denise Stone sighs as she faces Ryan Pena again.

"What does she think will happen if she stares? You and I are just friends—I know she knows we're not a real couple."

Ryan gestures with his hand.

"I'm actually glad she found us together."

He makes a lewd gesture with his finger and snickers.

"I was tired of her anyway. Our sex life had reached a point of no return. I'm into adventurous sex—she wasn't."

He makes a lewd gesture with his hand.

"Some women just never seem willing to accept that the man they share a bed with doesn't love them—never did."

Page **181**

Denise reaches out to touch Ryan's hand.

"How about we do something that will piss Erica off and cause her to have a meltdown? Make her completely lose it."

Ryan glances at Erica Gersh sitting at a cafe a few yards away. Denise leans closer to Ryan and begins whispering. Ryan nods gleefully. He kisses Denise lightly then passionately.

"This is going to be so much fun."

They stand in unison and walk over to where Erica is sitting with Julia Danforth. Denise watches Erica's reaction.

"Erica dear—I wanted you to be the first to know—Ryan and I are getting married next month. I hope you can attend."

Erica reacts as she watches Denise slide her fingers across the outline of Ryan's erection straining against his Lycra shorts. A second later Denise licks her lips sensuously and grins slyly.

"I know you like Ryan but he's mine now. Sorry dear—I win and you lose. He'll only be in my bed from today forward."

Without waiting for a response Denise and Ryan walk away holding hands as Erica seems about to explode with rage.

The Next Day

10

Los Angeles

"Your life seems so exciting. Protecting all those sleazy politicians must be a chore—they all have so many secrets."

Bradford stifles a laugh.

"They certainly have behavioral issues that I personally don't find appealing. So many hotel room deals from some of the most prominent—many of them behave like movie stars."

Donna gestures with her hand.

"The stories I could tell about some of the biggest names in the movie business. Not the nicest people by any means."

Bradford leans back in his chair and glances at the pool a few feet away. He runs his fingers through his hair and sighs.

"This life of mine is a killjoy for relationships."

Donna seems confused and shakes her head.

"I assumed you would have women lining up to spend every night they could in your bed. Wanting to get to know you better if only for one night—just to be in your presence—you being so charming and all—so incredibly easy on the eyes."

Bradford begins laughing.

"You think I'm charming? Think I'm easy on the eyes? It's all news to me. I assumed women found me boring—too rigid."

Donna glances longingly at Bradford's muscular body as he sits opposite her—naked except for a pair of shorts that seem much too tight for a man of his height—but of which makes him even more attractive regardless—makes his chances of getting laid incredibly easy without a doubt. Donna stifles a laugh.

"You're definitely not rigid by any means Bradford—if anything you're very relaxed—quite comfortable in your own skin. I love your shorts by the way—you could be a print model for those magazines with guys that seem too perfect to be real."

Bradford throws his head back and laughs.

"I'm definitely enjoying the compliments. I just threw this on at the last minute if truth be known. I usually go hiking in these back in DC—holds everything in place—much nicer than Lycra."

He grins and stands up to model the shorts. Donna seems mesmerized as she looks at Bradford in awe. Her eyes fixate on the outline of his penis against the tight fabric. It's clear to her he's not wearing underwear. He sits down as she sighs loudly.

"Do you have a girlfriend at the moment?"

Bradford shakes his head.

"Last relationship I had was a year ago. I was told I spent too much time working—she took up with a gym instructor."

Donna reaches out to touch Bradford's hand.

"I'm sorry."

He gestures with his hand.

"She wasn't the first. I've been in a lot of relationships since I became a bodyguard. Lots of lonely nights wondering what it is wrong with me. Why I can't seem to find love."

They share a glance. Donna stands. She seems upset.

"If you were my boyfriend I'd cherish you. Treat you with the utmost respect. Love you for being you. Never take a moment for granted. Make you happy every day of your life."

Bradford nods. He stands up and faces Donna.

"I believe you would make a wonderful girlfriend and never let a moment slip by. Never treat me like I didn't matter."

Donna hugs Bradford warmly. They look at each other for a few seconds. She realizes his erection is pressing against her thighs. Bradford begins apologizing immediately but she tells him he has nothing to apologize for and hugs him again.

11

Santa Barbara

"Any word on who this mystery woman is? I assume she must have a lurid connection to Loren Fawcett. Ex-girlfriend perhaps—or one of the girls he employs to walk the streets?"

Marlisa Vigaro walks back and forth as she looks at Carlos Vente on her cell phone. She seems impatient and stops.

"Loren must be freaked out at this moment. He hates not having control. Knowing that there's someone going around killing his people is really getting to him. Wait until he finds out that it's not her he should be so worried about—it's me."

Marlisa stifles a laugh.

"I'll have your next target shortly. Right now I'm just enjoying seeing Loren at wit's end—a couple of steps away from completely losing his mind. But wait until he realizes who's been behind his people being sent to the morgue—wait until he comes to the realization that not one of his people will be spared."

She begins laughing hysterically.

"Of course what I have planned for him will be even worse than what his people endured. His pain is only just beginning."

She seems to suddenly get an idea.

"Actually I think we should move forward with our next target. Kidnap Lizette Richardson—but don't kill her. Definitely rough her up for good measure—use her to send a message."

Page **184**

She dances around the patio a few times and stops.

"She'll be killed—painfully of course. That two-bit whore and I have history dating back years—insulted me plenty every chance she got. Her death will be used to scare his remaining people—make them aware of what their own fate will be when they too are taken out by you on my orders. By the time Loren Fawcett realizes I'm behind everything he'll be at my mercy."

She begins laughing hysterically again.

12
Orchid Bay
Paradise Pointe Bluffs

"Do you think she slipped? Fell accidentally?"

Roland looks at Lachlan and sighs.

"No way—there are scuff marks at the edge. Someone did this intentionally. It looks like we have a second murder case in our hands—first Adam Mills and now Marley Osborne."

Lachlan faces the bluffs once more.

13
Honolulu

"I want that miserable bitch found by 5 o'clock today. She and I have unfinished business to attend to—namely that I plan to sue her and her low-rent family into homelessness—destroy them all—run them out of the islands and back to redneck Texas. "

Eugene stifles a smile and nods.

"I think she flew the coop. She's probably in Texas already hiding at her grandfather's farm—shacking up with her cousin."

Carmen makes a lewd gesture with her finger.

"I don't give a damn about who she's shacking up with. I want her found. There will be no escape from my wrath."

Eugene pulls out a set of keys from the back pocket of his jeans and hands it to Carmen. She seems confused and sighs.

"What the fuck is this? Explain yourself."

"I found this outside her studio apartment. Like I said I think she fled the islands. She's not in Hawaii anymore."

Carmen throws the keys at Eugene.

"Her mother lives in Kaimuki. Get me the owner of her apartment building on the line. Tell him I want to buy the building and don't take no for an answer. Once I buy the building I'll throw her bitch of a mother out on the street. If that wretched girl thinks by leaving the islands I would leave her family alone—wait until she finds out how far I'm willing to go to destroy her."

Eugene wipes sweat from his brow.

"Your wish is my command."

Carmen glances at the paperwork on top of her desk a few feet away. She points to the paperwork and faces Eugene.

"Serve her mother with notice of my impending lawsuit against her and her daughter after you talk to her landlord. Make sure you smile when you give it her to her—laugh in her face."

Eugene nods in agreement as Carmen smirks.

14
Orchid Bay
Parkview Hospital

Kayla is sitting next to Patrick who is still in a coma. She holds his hands as a tear trickles down her cheek. Sidney stands at the door and seems concerned as he looks at his daughter.

15
Orchid Bay
Hampshire Street Cafe

"Look at her—she's dug her claws into Ryan. He has fallen into her web. That filthy skank is gonna pay for going after my boyfriend. How dare she think she can get away with stealing my man? He's mine—everyone in Orchid Bay knows it. Ryan and I were supposed to get married—he promised me that we'd tie the knot. Promised me we'd start a family—become parents."

Erica glances at Sabine Norton and sighs loudly.

"I hate her. If I had a gun I'd take that skank out once and for all. She should never have come back to Orchid Bay."

Sabine stifles a smirk and shrugs.

"You've got to get hold of yourself. She's got him now. *He* is a willing participant. He's going to marry her shortly."

Erica slams her fist on top of the table.

"She'll never marry Ryan—I won't allow it."

Sabine turns to look at Ryan and Denise holding hands at a table by the entrance of the cafe. Erica's anger seems to grow as she realizes they are kissing passionately. She faces Sabine again and whispers as Ryan and Denise continue kissing.

"She'll never marry Ryan Pena—I swear it."

Sabine reacts and seems worried.

16
Los Angeles

"I just want to apologize again for earlier. If I offended you I'm sorry. My intention was never to make you think that I was hitting on you. It won't happen again. Again I'm sorry."

Donna turns around to face Bradford.

"You did nothing wrong Bradford—you having an erection is a perfectly normal experience. I wasn't offended in the least. In fact if truth be known it was sexy. I meant everything I said to you yesterday about you being attractive. You looked incredibly hot in those shorts—the commando look definitely works for you."

He watches as her eyes fall on his shorts.

"Don't for a second think that you offended me earlier. You are so sweet—wonderful in every way—considerate."

Bradford grins but seems uneasy.

"Nevertheless from now on I'll behave professionally. I just think it would be best. I'm supposed to be protecting you—not wondering if we could have a relationship at some point."

Donna reacts. She takes a step toward him.

"Are you interested in us being in a relationship?"

Bradford seems embarrassed. Donna takes his hand and reaches out to touch his lips with her finger. She sighs.

"I wouldn't say no if you were interested in pursuing a relationship with me. I would be honored actually. Like I said I think you're a good man—to be respected and cherished."

Bradford faces her and seems pleased.

17
Orchid Bay
Welsh Driveway

"You can't keep avoiding me Lloyd. We have to talk about this situation. It happened. There's no turning back now."

Lloyd Welsh turns to face his mother and sighs. Caroline Welsh watches as her son digs his hands into the front pocket of his Levi's. She reaches out to grab his arm. He turns away.

"I was young—just a little older than you. He was really charming and handsome—rebellious—a college guy—and before I knew it I was in the backseat of his sports car. Then he was on top of me—saying how much he loved me—and then he was inside me. Then it was over. It was obvious to me at that point he was drunk so we promised not to mention it again—to go on with our lives. I married your father and pretended I didn't lose my virginity to this incredible guy who I later found out was named Maxwell Pendergraft. Your father never suspected and when I found out I was pregnant I assumed it was his. I never saw a reason to suspect Maxwell had fathered my child and not your father. I'm sorry—I'm not perfect—but even though your father isn't your biological father he loves you—that won't change."

Lloyd runs his fingers through his hair.

"I know my father loves me—and he'll always be my father as far as I'm concerned. I'm not about to throw away all those years we shared together when he thought he was my dad."

Caroline seems relieved and sighs.

"I'm truly sorry you had to find out this way."

Lloyd runs his fingers through his hair again and sighs.

Page 188

"So who is this Maxwell Pendergraft dude? Does he know about me yet? Does he want to meet me? Does he care?"

Caroline pulls out her cell phone.

"He knows and wants to meet you. He's wrapping up some business in Los Angeles and then plans to swing over to Orchid Bay to see you—but only if you want to. He doesn't want to intrude on your life—doesn't want to complicate things."

Lloyd takes a step toward his mother.

"What does he look like?"

Caroline shows Lloyd her cell phone.

"These are photos of Maxwell when he was a senior in high school. He sent me these earlier. There are some recent ones also. He lives in DC but was originally from a small town outside of Boston called Castle Beach. He has a younger sister who lives in Maine and a father who lives in a care facility."

Lloyd looks at the photos of Maxwell when he was in high school and smiles broadly. He faces his mother and sighs.

"He was quite the looker."

Caroline stifles a laugh and turns away.

"He still is—the years have been good to him."

She shows him several recent photographs. Lloyd shakes his head and laughs. He makes a lewd gesture with his finger.

"I bet he gets laid endlessly."

Caroline gestures with her hand.

18

Los Angeles

"What do I know about being a father to a teenage boy? I'm in way over my head. What a frigging mess. Damn it."

Maxwell flips through photographs of a teenage boy.

"What a babe—like father like son."

Maxwell turns around in shock and sees Tiffany Johnson looking at him. She waves her hand in the air and grins slyly.

"Lloyd Welsh is no different than you when you were sixteen—if I recall you were quite promiscuous—troubled."

Page **189**

She licks her lips several times and points at Maxwell as he looks at the photographs again. He leans back on the sofa.

"He's a kid—what does he know about women? He's probably still a virgin. He looks innocent in these photos—just a sweet teenage boy who's just finding his place in society."

Tiffany makes a lewd gesture with her finger.

"He lost his virginity on his fourteenth birthday—banged the older sister of his best friend. She was seventeen."

Maxwell reacts and watches as Tiffany seems gleeful as she tells him lurid details about his son. He stands up.

"Does he have a girlfriend?"

Tiffany nods and gestures with her hand.

"He does—they've been together for two months now. He took her virginity on the night of the junior prom if you must know. She didn't want to but he insisted—he popped her in the backseat of her car. Your son is quite a charmer if I do say so myself. He knows how to get what he wants. But he's a nice guy regardless—always helps people out in their time of need."

Maxwell runs his fingers through his hair.

"You could have told me about Lloyd long ago—why didn't you? Why did you keep it a secret for so damn long?"

Tiffany rolls her eyes and sighs loudly.

"You were on a need-to-know basis about Lloyd Welsh. If I had told you—what do you think you would've done?"

Maxwell shakes his head.

"I don't know—probably contacted him—try to explain what happened all those years ago with his mother and me."

Tiffany points at Maxwell.

"That's exactly why I didn't tell you—can you imagine what would've happened if I had told you about Lloyd before he found out the truth? He would've been destroyed by the revelation that his whole life was a lie—probably ending up using drugs—or worse—taking his own life—unable to cope."

Maxwell walks toward the balcony of the hotel room. As he looks out at the Los Angeles skyline he sighs again. He turns to face Tiffany once more. They look at each other silently.

Orchid Bay
Lane Parking Lot

"That wretched boy will be out of my daughter's life soon enough. Once he's alone I'll make my move. All I have to do is put one bullet in his empty skull and he'll no longer be a thorn in my side. Dana will get over him soon enough and then I'll push her in the direction of someone that is more socially acceptable."

Daphne Mills watches as her daughter kisses Mark Corrington and drives away. As Dana Mills is out of sight she steps out of her car and approaches Mark. He reacts.

"You and I have to talk."

Daphne glances at the parking lot.

"We need to clear things up between us for Dana's sake. How about we meet at Rocky Ledge Bluffs in fifteen minutes?"

Mark seems confused.

"I'm not going to stop seeing Dana."

Daphne gives Mark a sharp look and turns away.

"I wouldn't think of ever asking you to stop seeing my daughter. I think we know it would be a huge waste of time."

Mark runs his fingers through his hair.

"Whatever."

Daphne appears to be irritated.

"I'll see you at Rocky Ledge in fifteen minutes."

Mark nods and watches as Daphne drives away. He shakes his head and seems confused by her behavior. He grimaces.

20

Los Angeles

"That damn bitch gave me the slip—I haven't heard from her in days. Who does she think she is? Damn wallflower."

Silas Bell looks at the hot dog on his plate and is about to take a bite when he notices a woman staring intently at him.

"Did you ever stay at a classy hotel in the US Virgin Islands called Windward Passage? I could swear we've met before."

Silas shoots Diana Munroe a cautious look but smiles and motions for her to sit down next to him. He gestures briefly.

"And you would be?"

"Diana Munroe. I was there for a book signing and I remember passing someone who looked like you in the hallway outside my room. I never forget a face—a handsome face."

Silas grins broadly and nods.

"Uh-huh—that was me. I was there for a much-needed vacation. Lovely hotel—island was quite the tourist trap."

Diana laughs and waves her hand.

"I'm not sure if you recall a story about a group of people ending up on an island being chased by killer brothers and then getting rescued by the Coast Guard. I was one of those people."

Silas takes a bite of his hot dog and shrugs.

"I don't follow news that much."

Diana leans closer to Silas and sighs loudly.

"Married—divorced—single—gay?"

Silas stifles a laugh.

"Single—but definitely not gay."

Diana seems pleased.

"I live right down the street in Hancock Park."

Diana reaches out to stroke his shoulder.

"I'm not looking for anything serious. No strings attached in case you're wondering—just sex—raw and unrestrained."

Silas stands and looks at the half eaten hot dog. He faces Diana and makes a lewd gesture with his finger. She laughs.

"I'm down for anything—definitely a fan of raw-dogging."

He quickly follows her out of the diner.

21

Honolulu

"I guess I should let Eugene know that bitch is dead. She must have crossed someone else on this island no doubt."

Page **192**

Carmen sighs loudly as a local reporter named **Sam Spangler** details the gruesome find of a woman's body found washed up on the rocks at Black Point. Graphic details are given about the condition of the body. Carmen seems pleased.

22
Orchid Bay
Pointview Police Station

"I don't give a damn what jurisdiction they have. I want my cousin brought here—and then released immediately."

Miles seems irritated as he shakes his fist.

"O'Brien has pushed the limits of his power. He's had it for sweet Vina a while now. He wanted to get between her legs but she told him to take a fucking hike. That guy has a problem."

Grant Volker rolls his eyes as he leans back in his chair while Miles sighs loudly as he reaches for his cell phone.

"I intend to make him regret daring to arrest one of the most upstanding citizens in this town. He's a bastard—a creep that thinks he can make a play for a woman who doesn't want him and then have her arrested on fake charges. It's absolutely outrageous this sort of thing can happen to my cousin. Someone of her standing should never be called out by a working stiff."

Grant runs his fingers through his hair.

"I'm sorry—my hands are tied. Roland O'Brien is within his rights to hold Vina Phamler indefinitely. It is what it is."

Miles clenches his fist and looks over to where another police officer is sitting at her desk. Marilyn Waaysend pretends to ignore Miles as he stares at her. He faces Grant again.

"I'm going to crush that bastard O'Brien if it's the last thing I do. He'll regret crossing the Phamler family. His pathetic life is about to become a fucking nightmare—I swear it."

Grant stands and faces Miles.

"Threats like those will get you a nice stay in the slammer for several years. If I were you I'd refrain from such actions."

Miles walks to the door and stops suddenly.

"I swear I'll make him pay. He's finished."

He leaves slamming the door behind him as Grant and Marilyn look at each other. Marilyn seems worried and sighs.

"I guess we better let Roland know about our visit from Miles O'Rourke. Vina Phamler strikes again. That woman always seems to find ways to make everyone's life a living hell."

Grant nods in agreement and gestures.

23
Orchid Bay
Parkview Hospital

Sidney is sitting besides Patrick's bed when he notices that Patrick appears to be waking up. Patrick opens his eyes and seems confused where he is. Sidney immediately stands up.

"I'll go get Kayla right away."

Patrick still seems confused as he watches Sidney leave. He looks around the hospital room not sure where he is as Kayla runs into the room with tears streaming down her cheeks.

24
Honolulu

"Oh yeah—you're the best—you always got my back when I need you most. What would I do without you Veronica?"

Veronica Thibault grins broadly as she tousles Eugene's hair. She leans over to kiss his exposed penis. He moans loudly.

"I'm still charging you full price."

Eugene winces and seems upset at the slight.

"I never doubted it for a minute—despite me being such a loyal customer. How many years now—oh yeah—two years."

Veronica slides her finger across Eugene's lips.

"A girl has to make a living."

As Eugene is about to respond his cell phone begins to ring. He glances at Veronica and seems upset. He grimaces.

"That woman is impossible—certifiable."

Page **194**

Veronica rolls her eyes knowingly and climbs out of the bed as Eugene reaches for his cell phone. She slides her finger over her exposed vagina. His erect penis springs forward.

"I'm coming after you again. The minute this call is over I'm coming for you. I won't show an ounce of mercy."

Veronica seems pleased as she watches him grimace when he answers the phone. On the other end Carmen is livid.

"Where are you? Have you heard the good news? It's all over the island as we speak. Shirley Beecroft got herself iced."

Eugene looks at Carmen and seems bored.

"Someone took out dear Shirley? What a pity? How sad for her family. I assume her mother knows—probably crying her eyes out as we speak. Oh well—she still has other children."

Eugene stifles a laugh as he glances at Veronica.

"What's our next move?"

Carmen sighs loudly and glances at the TV again. She licks her lips as she looks at **Sam Spangler** discussing how Shirley was found by some surfers. She can't seem to take her eyes off the TV as she hears Eugene's voice on the phone. She moans loudly.

"That man is so sexy. Too bad he's married—the things I would do to him if he were single—every sexual act possible."

Eugene reacts and seems about to gag.

"As I was saying—Shirley is dead—what is our next move concerning her family? I assume her mother is still a target?"

Carmen faces Eugene again and nods.

25
Orchid Bay
Rocky Ledge Bluffs

"End of the road Mark—enough is enough. I tried to warn you but you wouldn't listen to reason. This is your fault."

Mark looks at the gun pointed at him and seems frozen as Daphne points at him and gestures. He glances at the ocean below unsure what he should do. Daphne stifles a laugh.

"You're just the wrong guy for my daughter."

Mark glances at the ocean again and sighs loudly.

"You'll never get away with this—no matter what you tell Dana—she'll know you were involved somehow. She already hates you—once she figures it out you're gonna be sorry."

Daphne seems enraged by the comment.

"This is why I don't like you—you turned my daughter against me—lied to her—made her believe your reality."

Mark shakes his head several times as digs his hands into the front pockets of his jeans. Daphne looks at the gun in her hand again. She takes a step toward him. He notices.

"I did no such thing. It was you. You did it all—you and your brother-in-law. Uh-huh—Dana knows about you and Adam getting horizontal multiple times while you were still married to her father. She knows about the abortion you had. She knows the daddy was her uncle. She told her father—he knows too."

Daphne reacts. In a fit of rage she shoots Mark twice. She smiles broadly as she watches him fall from the cliff into the ocean below. She looks over and begins laughing as she sees his body floating in the waves. She looks at the gun in her hand and then back at the body below. She seems pleased with the turn of events and looks at Mark's car parked nearby. She sighs.

26
Orchid Bay
Parkview Hospital

"I'm so glad you're going to be okay. I love you. No one is ever going to hurt you again. I won't allow it. I simply won't."

Kayla repeatedly kisses Patrick on his cheek as her father stands nearby but says nothing. Patrick lies back on two pillows and seems to be enjoying the extra attention. Kayla kisses him yet again and tousles his hair briefly. She seems about to cry.

"Not a day will go by I won't tell you I love you. This was a close call. I came so close to losing the most wonderful man I've ever known. I'm just so glad Vina Phamler wasn't able to make good on her vile plans. That woman is a horrible monster."

Page **196**

Patrick sighs and glances at Kayla.

"Did she really try to kill me?"

Kayla clenches her fist and shakes it several times.

"She did—if it wasn't for Tim Bergman you'd be dead right now Patrick. She intended to let you die rather than let anyone know what she did—that woman actually tried to prevent Tim from calling an ambulance. She claimed it was an accident."

Patrick reacts as Kayla kisses him again.

"I could get used to being kissed all the time if you must know. Just saying—all this attention is really a crowd-pleaser."

Kayla kisses Patrick several more times.

"I meant what I said earlier Patrick. I'm never taking you for granted ever again. Even my dad has had a change of heart where you're concerned. He kept you company when I had to run errands in case you were wondering. I didn't want you to be alone for even a second and he was more than gracious about it."

Patrick glances at Sidney.

"Thank you."

Sidney nods in agreement.

"I've hired a lawyer from Boston. He was recommended to me by a business associate. He will make the Phamler family beg for mercy. Vina Phamler is going to be punished for what she did. It's about time someone stood up to her and her family—they've made a mockery of justice in this town for much too long."

Patrick seems confused.

"What about Tim Bergman?"

Sidney and Kayla look at each other.

TO BE CONTINUED

A Brief Look at the Eighth Episode

Scheming individuals plot against others in various locations as two people thrown together realize they have plenty in common while a murderer finds out too late actions have consequences.

Episode 8
Fantastical Worlds

1
Orchid Bay
Parkview Hospital

"I want Tim Bergman released immediately."

Patrick Clerke faces Kayla Larsen with a determined look as she shakes her head. He slowly tries to sit up in bed.

"I'm not going to testify against him. Get Roland O'Brien on the line right now. Tell him I want to see him about Tim."

He turns to look at Sidney Larsen.

"I want him released."

Sidney and Kayla look at each other. Sidney reaches for his cell phone and faces Patrick. Kayla seems confused.

"He knew what Vina Phamler was going to do. He didn't say anything. He let that monster carry out her sick plot."

Patrick waves his hand in the air.

"I don't care. He saved my life. I'd be dead if he hadn't called the ambulance. I owe him that much. Get Roland on the line right away. Tim made a mistake but he's no killer."

Sidney begins talking to Roland and shrugs.

"That's right he's awake. He wants to see you."

Sidney glances at Patrick. He nods a few times and then faces Kayla. He walks over to Patrick and looks at the phone.

2
Los Angeles

"You're a frigging machine. Four times and you still want more. I've never met a man that was so demanding in the sack after two hours—except Maxwell Pendergraft of course."

Silas Bell angrily looks at Diana Munroe.

"Who the fuck is this Maxwell Pendergraft jerk—is he your boyfriend—I thought you said you were single and available?"

Diana licks her lips and sighs loudly.

"Maxwell isn't my boyfriend—he's not boyfriend material by any means. He can't keep his dick in his pants long enough to care about any woman if truth be told. He's just a good time."

Silas seems irritated and grimaces.

"That fucker is a loser. I'm here now. You don't need anyone else. I'm a frigging wonder in the sack. I love to fuck."

Diana strokes his chest and sighs.

"You certainly are a wonder in bed. I'm glad I'm on the pill after what just took place between us. You made it clear from the moment we met you were not using a condom. Said I had no choice in the matter. I like a strong forceful man in my bed—even if he refuses to wear protection. I have no regrets at all."

Silas laughs loudly and pulls Diana under his body again. He winks slyly. Seconds later he plows into her again. He grins as she lets out a loud moan while he aggressively slams her.

3
Orchid Bay
Hampshire Street Cafe

"She's not my girlfriend anymore. I thought I told you we were over. She's dead—a stiff. I heard it was suicide."

Carolyn Mills seems bothered and sighs. She watches as Kyler Vanwick grabs a handful of French fries and grins slyly.

"I'm with you now. Like I said Marley and I were over before she took her own life. It's not my fault she ended it all because I told her she meant nothing to me. That's life."

Carolyn looks at her cell phone.

"Marley didn't kill herself. She was murdered."

Kyler seems bored and shrugs.

"I still don't care."

Carolyn watches Kyler wolf down his burger. As he eats she looks at her cell phone again. She shakes her head.

"I wonder who killed Marley."

Kyler turns to face Carolyn seemingly annoyed.

"I thought I told you I didn't care."

Carolyn stands up.

"I think it was someone she knew."

Kyler stops eating and looks at Carolyn.

"Or probably she hooked up with a trucker. She was fond of guys that lived on the rough—liked to be smacked around."

Carolyn reacts at the comment.

"No woman likes to be smacked around Kyler—you sound like all those guys that get in trouble for marital abuse."

"Keep believing that women just want a gentle dude to share her bed with. Read a bit and you'll learn plenty."

Carolyn sighs loudly and turns to leave.

"You're a disgusting pig."

Kyler makes a lewd gesture with his finger.

"Uh-huh—until you need me between your legs—then I'm a wonderful guy. Yeah—you made my point perfectly."

Carolyn storms out of the diner.

4
San Francisco

"That's right—I'm planning an extended stay. Lots of deals to focus on—starting with taking down Houghton Fawcett."

Page **201**

Trevor Boleyn turns to face a window looking out at the San Francisco Bay and smirks. He nods a few times and laughs.

"Exactly—when that murderous lunatic finds out he's lost his entire empire he'll lose his mind—most probably suicidal."

He clenches his fist and shakes it.

"Uh-huh—it would be a fitting end to his life."

He begins laughing and nods again. In an ornate mirror facing a mini bar a teenage girl and boy seem pleased. Trevor walks toward the mini bar and continues talking on his cell phone as Tiffany Johnson and Jeremy Weissmann glance at a clock on the wall and nod. They watch as Trevor swallows a shot of whiskey and seem annoyed as he ends his call. He grimaces.

5

Orchid Bay

Parkview Hospital

"Uh-huh—that's right—I won't do it. He saved my life. I want all charges against Tim Bergman dropped this instant."

Roland O'Brien seems confused as he looks at Patrick and Kayla. Patrick points at Roland. He seems visibly upset.

"He had a lapse in judgment—so what."

Roland nervously runs his fingers through his hair.

"I hope you know what you're doing."

Patrick turns to look at Kayla.

"I want to see him the moment he's free."

Kayla nods and faces Roland.

6

Los Angeles

"You've done nothing wrong. You have a right to pursue a relationship with a woman you like. We're both consenting adults and don't have to answer to anyone. I'm game if you are."

Bradford Styverson looks at the door.

"What about your brother?"

Page **202**

Donna Markway gestures with her hand.

"My brother likes you—said you were really nice."

Bradford sighs loudly.

"What about what people will say?"

Donna pushes Bradford up against the wall.

"I don't care what people think."

He seems nervous as she pulls his head toward hers and kisses him lightly on the lips. He reacts. She kisses him again.

"I've liked you from the moment I met you. You were so hot. First thing I noticed was how nice you looked in jeans."

Bradford grins broadly.

"I've had those jeans since high school. My ex-girlfriend bought them for me. She was wonderful—loved poetry."

He suddenly seems sad and turns away.

"She was killed in an auto accident the night after we made love for the first time. It took me a year to adjust."

Donna pulls Bradford toward her and hugs him warmly.

"I'm so sorry for your loss."

She hugs him again.

"Tell me about her. What was she like?"

Bradford pulls out his cell phone.

7
Orchid Bay
Vanwick Apartment

"I want her gone. I don't care how you get rid of that trashy slut—I just want her gone—away from Orchid Bay."

Erica Gersh licks her lips as she looks at Ethan Vanwick and slides her fingers across his erect penis. She sighs loudly.

"I want Ryan back—and as long as that scheming bitch is sharing his bed he won't come crawling back to yours truly."

Ethan watches Erica's finger and laughs.

"What's the deal with Ryan? That fucker cheated on you every chance he got. He bedded all your friends. Made sure you knew he had done the nasty with your own skanky cousin."

Page 203

Erica reacts and shoots Ethan a sharp look.

"I know his history. But he's the only man I want in my bed. No matter what he does I'll forgive him. He knows it too."

Ethan looks at his naked body and grins.

"The only man you want in your bed?"

Erica points her finger at Ethan.

"You're just a distraction if you must know the truth. Don't read more into it than that Ethan. I assure you there's not going to be a repeat performance. Ryan is the only guy for me."

Ethan stifles a laugh.

"Does he think the same about you? I would place bets that he feels that he can and will continue to screw whomever he feels attracted to—so many rumors out there to look into."

Erica grabs a robe and climbs out of bed. She turns to face Ethan. He watches as she strokes her breasts and smirks.

"I delivered today. Tomorrow you need to deliver on your promise. I want that bitch run out of town immediately."

Ethan climbs out of bed naked and comes toward Erica. He looks at his penis sticking out in front of him and laughs.

"I'm not done with you yet."

Erica tries to resist as Ethan grabs her by the waist but he subdues her immediately. He forces her toward the bed.

"I have needs—and until I'm completely satisfied you're not going anywhere. This is how I make a deal—I must get what I want on my terms or we're gonna have serious problems."

He forces Erica down on the bed and pulls the robe off her body in a frenzied rush. She tries to fight him off but he subdues her again and seconds later plows into her as she cries out.

8

San Francisco

"Oh man, look at him go. Cujo Momoa was certainly a wonder with the ladies. He just keeps going and going."

Loren Fawcett laughs and faces Vladimir Orlov as they continue looking at multiple videos on a large TV monitor.

Page 204

"He taped all his sexual encounters apparently. These copies are just a few of thousands. He went through young girls like candy. He fucked so many I don't know how he had time to service his ex. She was clueless to the end—thinking he was the perfect husband—faithful and loyal. Such a stupid woman she was without a doubt. She certainly got played royally by Cujo."

He begins laughing as he stops the video.

"Cujo apparently would befriend girls who had run away from abusive homes and bring them to his private apartment. He would then rape them for hours before tiring of them. Once he had no more use for them he would strangle them to death slowly—making sure they knew without a doubt they were going to die by his hand. He would laugh as he succeeded and they succumbed. The joy I saw on his face as he killed one particular girl was something to behold. She fought him repeatedly as he raped her over and over—and afterwards he was so insulted by her slighting him he violently strangled her. He forced her down on the floor and sat on her chest as he squeezed the life out of her. As with all his girls her body ended up in a landfill according to what Cujo stated was his usual way to dispose of the bodies of the girls whose lives he took. Seriously, my admiration for that man has grown since I came across these tapes in Cujo's safe deposit box. He was a god—never thought twice about using the misery of vulnerable young girls to service his sexual needs."

Vladimir begins laughing and gestures.

"I agree. I want copies of those tapes. Cujo was what every sane straight man aspires to be. I'm gonna miss him—miss his charming personality with women. His death must be avenged."

Vladimir pulls out his cell phone and sighs.

9
Orchid Bay
Downtown Police Station

"Vina Phamler was fit to be tied when you sprung Tim Bergman a few minutes ago. She threatened you repeatedly."

Page **205**

Roland rolls his eyes and faces Lachlan Ball.

"Uh-huh—she probably thinks threatening me is a turn on of some sort. That woman should have a reality show."

Lachlan makes a lewd gesture with his finger and laughs as he glances at a folder on top of his desk. He picks it up.

"Speaking of reality shows."

He waves the folder in the air and grimaces.

"Well, it looks like Jason Shappe died of natural causes after all. According to his autopsy he had an asthma attack."

Lachlan flips through the rest of the folder and lays it on top of his desk with a thud. He faces Roland and snickers.

"Who knew that disgusting creep would suddenly drop dead because of something as minor as an asthma attack?"

Roland seems bothered by something.

"It just seems too easy."

Lachlan stands up and stretches.

"Sometimes the simplest explanations make the most sense. That bastard had an asthma attack and croaked."

He stifles a laugh.

"No one in Orchid Bay will shed a tear."

Roland runs his fingers through his hair and sighs.

"What about his father?"

Lachlan laughs.

"Not a peep from him. I guess he has no plans to pay for his son to be laid to rest in Orchid Bay. Shappe's body will most likely be cremated—and his ashes scattered—in the city dump."

He walks toward the door and seems pleased.

"I know I should behave like I care even if I don't—but I just can't. Jason Shappe was a disgusting piece of garbage that never spent one second thinking about anyone other than himself."

Lachlan makes a lewd gesture with his finger again.

"As far as I see it Orchid Bay is better off without having to worry about when Jason Shappe would go after another young girl. I'm sure Tracey Oakfield is doing cartwheels right now."

Roland reacts at the mention of Tracey's name.

"I ought to call her and see how she's doing."

Page 206

Lachlan nods and reaches for the doorknob. As he does he sees Carolyn Mills standing in the doorway looking upset.

"I think I know who killed Marley Osborne."

Lachlan and Roland share a look.

10
Los Angeles

"Maybe I should inform Maxwell Pendergraft about the turn of events concerning—you know—us getting together."

Donna looks at Bradford and shakes her head.

"Maxwell is the most open-minded person out there. He's no saint by any means—has left a trail of broken hearts all over the US and Europe. He goes through women really fast."

They share a laugh. Donna grins.

"Don't worry—he'll be fine with us getting together. Your older brother is one of his closest friends. You're family."

Bradford pulls Donna toward him.

"It's been a while since I have lived—I just want to live—to experience life again. My luck with women has been dismal."

He watches Donna's reaction.

"I've only been with nine women my entire life. My first girlfriend left me for her best friend's college-age brother."

He runs his fingers through his hair.

"My second girl died. The third and fourth cheated on me with my friend and my cousin. The fifth used me to keep her family in the dark about being a lesbian. Sixth through nine said I was a bore—worked too much. Not good for anything."

Donna pulls Bradford's head toward her and kisses him on the lips. She kisses him again and gently takes his hand.

"I haven't had the best luck either. My first boyfriend raped me—he was murdered by the father of another girl he raped and killed. The next four boyfriends all turned out to be losers—four more followed exactly the same way. My latest is why you're here. He turned out to be a fraud—a murderer."

Bradford stifles a laugh and kisses Donna.

Page 207

"Uh-huh—I know all about Silas Bell—also known as Heath Griffith. He has quite the history—reads like a soap opera from the 1980s. *Bare Essence* comes to mind. Caught it on one of those cable channels that rerun old prime time soaps—I also watched some of the episodes of *Pasadena* and *Pacific Palisades*. I had plenty of time on my hands last summer if truth be known."

He laughs as he sees Donna's reaction.

"Guys watch soaps too—they just don't admit it."

Donna gestures with her hands.

"I watch that channel also—as well as the one that reruns crime shows from the 1980s. *Simon & Simon* were one of my favorites. I also liked *Hardcastle and McCormick. Tucker's Witch, MacGruder & Loud, Cover Up* and *Whiz Kids* were good too even though they didn't last long—cancelled after just one season."

They share a laugh and kiss once again.

11
Orchid Bay
Parkview Hospital

"I'm glad you're okay. I'm so sorry about what happened. I should've said something. I just didn't think Vina would actually go through with what she said she wanted to do. She blamed everyone but herself for what occurred. She made threats."

Patrick and Kayla look at Tim Bergman and shake their heads in unison. Patrick sighs and offers his hand to Tim.

"All is forgiven. No worries."

Kayla watches as they shake hands.

12
Orchid Bay
Downtown Police Station

"Do you think she's telling the truth? She is a Mills after all. That family has had trouble with the truth—and reality."

Roland runs his fingers through his hair.

"Carolyn Mills isn't like her cousins. I think she's telling the truth. Kyler Vanwick certainly fits the profile. That boy has been in trouble so many times I lost count. He thrives on chaos."

Lachlan looks at the front door.

"But is he capable of killing someone?"

Roland grabs his cell phone.

"Everyone is capable of committing murder."

He sighs loudly and stands up.

"There's plenty cases of children committing murder—and getting away with it. It all depends on how good a liar they are and how despicable their lawyer is. It all hinges on lawyers."

Lachlan stifles a laugh.

"I second that."

"But Kyler Vanwick is hardly a child. He's months away from turning eighteen. He has a bad rep around town already."

Lachlan gestures with his hand.

"When are you gonna pay him a visit?"

Roland shrugs and nervously looks at his watch.

13
Honolulu

"I don't care what that woman tells you—serve her with eviction papers and make it clear she has twenty-four hours to vacate her home before the local police become involved."

Carmen Pendleton smiles as she looks at Eugene Ledyard on her cell phone. He grins. She notices an incoming call.

"Serve Alana Beecroft with those damn papers and make it clear what happens if she doesn't leave her frigging home."

She grimaces and answers the other call.

"Carmen Pendleton?"

Carmen nods and seems annoyed.

"Who the hell are you?"

Cameron Hodge stifles a laugh.

"Listen up, *bitch*—we've got your son. His life depends on what you do. Things will get gruesome if you dare defy us."

Carmen watches as Cameron forces Alexander Pendleton to face the camera. It's obvious he's been beaten—his face bruised by several black and blue marks. Clyde Matheson smirks as he lands a vicious blow on Alexander's jaw. Carmen reacts.

"Your son dies if you call anyone."

Cameron waves a hunting knife in the air and laughs.

"Hunting season is right around the corner. Seems your son has been selected to be our first kill. *But*—and that's a big but—*if you do what we tell you*—your son will be spared."

He begins to laugh as he punches Alexander again.

"The clock is ticking—you decide—tick tok."

The screen goes blank. Carmen stands there for a few seconds unable to move. She looks at the cell phone again.

14
Orchid Bay
Pioneer Trail Mall

"She's not going to get away with it. How could she do it? How could she kill him? Oh my God—*Mark*—oh Mark."

Dana Mills seems in shock as she looks up at her friend sitting across from her at a cafe in the mall. Vivien Bernsay reacts as she watches Dana. She drops the phone on top of the table.

"Is everything all right?"

She watches as Dana glances at her cell phone.

"She did it—she killed Mark."

Vivien grabs the phone and gasps.

"Is this real?"

Dana nods.

"It has to be. I haven't heard from Mark in hours. It's not like him not to call. I just thought he was busy. He taped his meeting with my mother—sent it to me as she shot him."

Vivien grabs her cell phone and begins dialing.

"Who are you calling?"

Vivien looks at Dana's cell phone again.

"Who do you think?"

Dana seems confused as Vivien begins talking to Lachlan seconds later. Dana begins to cry—softly at first—then louder.

15
Los Angeles

Ashton Markway stands in the doorway as Bradford and Donna kiss passionately. Bradford seems embarrassed and sighs loudly. They face Ashton as he shoots them a warning look.

16
Orchid Bay
Bay Street Condo

"How much longer are you going to be here?"

Janet Virella turns to face Houghton Fawcett and seems annoyed. He looks at her with a scowl and mutters something under his breath. She walks over to him and grabs his arm.

"I don't give a fuck that you're my biological father—my real father to be exact. I don't play the pity game. Not after finding out you knew about me my entire life and only decided to make it known when it served your purpose and bank account."

Houghton shakes his fist at Janet.

"How dare you speak to your father like that?"

Janet points her finger at Houghton.

"Oh please—who do you think you're speaking to? I want you out of here by tomorrow. Or else I call precious Loren."

She takes a step forward.

"Call my dear brother and tell him that you've been hiding out here after he played you for a fool. What's it gonna be?"

Houghton stands and snarls at Janet. They stare at each other for a few seconds. Houghton angrily points at Janet.

"I'm your father—show some respect child. Your elders should be respected—especially when they gave you life."

Janet begins laughing as she circles Houghton—enjoying the look of discomfort on his face. She takes another step.

"Uh-huh—maybe you should have thought about that before you hid the fact I was your bastard child. The question I have for you is simple—how many other siblings do I have that I don't know about. Of course excluding Loren—and dear departed Ralph. What is it old man? Are there other bastards out there?"

Houghton shakes his fist at Janet again.

17

Los Angeles

"You have a five o'clock appointment with a reporter named Karl Bretche. He's a handful. Don't piss him off."

Martin Knappson turns to face Wesley Madison. He's talking on his cell phone. Martin walks over to him and sighs.

"Did you hear what I said?"

Wesley waves his hand in the air.

"Uh-huh—loud and clear. I won't piss him off."

Martin looks at a stack of scripts lying on a coffee table nearby. Wesley faces him with a grin and gestures.

"I'll charm that jerk. Don't worry."

Martin seems uneasy as he faces a huge window. In a distance Century City looks like a postcard. As Martin watches Wesley drops his cell phone on a nearby sofa. He sighs loudly.

"That was Andrea. We've been having problems as you know. I have a lot of bridges to mend after the things I said."

Martin rolls his eyes. He seems irritated.

"I never liked her."

Wesley points his finger at Martin and sighs.

"We've talked about this before."

He looks at the cell phone.

"I've waited a long time to find someone like her and you're not going to do anything to mess it up. Is that clear?"

Martin stifles a smirk as he turns away.

"I wouldn't think of it. It's your funeral all the way."

Wesley walks over to Martin. He faces him directly and looks Martin straight in the eye. They stare at each other.

Page **212**

"I know what happened with Diane previous. You told her I was too busy for a serious relationship. Made it seem like I wasn't into her. Told her I was skipping around—lied to her."

Martin seems uneasy.

"She wasn't right for you Wesley. She just wanted to be with you because of who you know. Everyone knew it but you."

Wesley gives Martin a sharp look.

"I let what happened with Diane Linderson not become an issue between us despite what you did to push her away. I won't play that game again Martin. I can make my own decisions when it comes to handling my issues with women. Stay out of my business unless I ask for advice. I mean it. This stops today."

He wrings his hands.

"I assume we understand each other."

Martin nods and sighs loudly.

18
Orchid Bay
Downtown Police Station

"This just happened?"

Vivien glances at Dana and faces Lachlan.

"Uh-huh—Dana's mother killed Mark Corrington. She shot him. Shot him out by Rocky Ledge Bluffs. It's all on video."

Lachlan looks at the cell phone again.

"Where is your mother now?"

Dana shrugs.

"I don't know."

Lachlan stands. He glances at the door.

"Where exactly is Rocky Ledge?"

Vivien and Dana look at each other.

"Up the coast a bit—near Santa Barbara—right where these huge rocks come really close to Pacific Coast Highway."

Lachlan begins scrolling on his cell phone.

"What's going to happen to my mother? Is she going to be arrested? My dad is already in prison—and my uncle is dead."

Lachlan turns to face Dana. He seems bothered.

"What about your grandparents?"

Dana shrugs. Vivien comes toward Dana.

"She can stay with me. My mother won't mind."

Lachlan nods and heads to the door.

19
San Francisco

"You'll pay for this—there will be no place you can hide that Loren Fawcett won't find you. He'll crucify you."

Carlos Vente begins laughing as he glances at Lizette Richardson tied to a chair. He laughs louder as he faces Hobson Crusoe and winks. Without warning Lizette is punched in the jaw by Hobson—his muscular arms delivering a severe blow to her face. She cries out as Hobson lands another crushing blow.

"Do you know why you're here Lizette? Are you aware how utterly useless you are to me right now—any idea at all?"

Lizette fearfully looks at Hobson.

"I can be your girl—*help me.*"

Carlos begins laughing again and points.

"Hobson is gay. He does dudes not prostitutes."

Lizette reacts as Carlos slowly walks toward Hobson and passionately kisses him. They share another passionate kiss and then Carlos faces Lizette. He laughs loudly. She grimaces.

"Uh-huh—he's an animal in the sack."

He licks his lips.

"He's twenty-four and can go all night."

He takes a step toward Lizette.

"Loren Fawcett is headed for a fall. He just doesn't know it yet. But I assure you he will soon enough. As you can see there are cameras in this room. Imagine what is coming next."

Lizette seems panicked.

"I'm not afraid of you or Todd Whitney."

Carlos reaches out and grabs Lizette by the throat.

"Todd Whitney? You think he's behind this?"

He leans closer to her and laughs.

"Todd Whitney is dead, *bitch*. He has nothing to do with what has been happening. No wonder Loren is such a failure at everything he does. He's surrounded by morons like you."

Lizette stifles a smile.

"Todd Whitney isn't dead."

Carlos twists Lizette's neck and laughs.

"Like I care either way—it doesn't change the fact of the situation you're in right now. I have big plans for you."

He glances at Hobson and smirks.

"In addition to being an animal between the sheets my man Hobson enjoys killing people. Loves watching their faces as he stabs them to death—loves to hear them scream for mercy."

He jabs Lizette in the chest.

"He's also an amateur filmmaker. My man Hobson has cleverly filmed every person he's ever killed. Watches his victim's deaths over and over with a bowl of popcorn and laughs his head off as the screaming begins. Oh—the joy he gets from his work—I pity you actually. What he has planned for you will certainly give him plenty of laughs in the coming months following your death at his hands. It'll be quite the show. I guess the moral of the story is we all have to die sooner or later—and today it's your turn."

He begins laughing as he sees her reaction.

20

Los Angeles

"Don't worry—I'll be there. Just got to wrap up a few things here and I'll be on the first flight out—four days tops."

Wesley nods several times while he walks back and forth as Martin stands a few feet away looking a bit agitated.

"Of course—Andrea is coming with me."

Wesley gestures with his hand.

"She's wonderful."

He nods a few more times and grins.

"Uh-huh—right back at you."

Page **215**

He runs his fingers through his hair and smirks.

"I agree—London is nice this time of year."

He turns to look at Martin as he shuts off his cell phone. Wesley notices Martin's sour expression but ignores it. At that moment his cell phone rings. He glances at Martin briefly with an odd expression as he listens to the voice on the other end.

21

Orchid Bay

Hampshire Street

"I'm on my way as we speak. This town is really beginning to seem like a bad movie where people keep turning up dead."

Roland nods and gestures with his hand.

"Let me know if Mark Corrington's corpse turns up."

He walks toward a nearby parking lot when he sees Tracey Oakfield coming toward him. She seems distraught.

Roland takes a step toward her.

"Is everything all right?"

Tracey seems about to cry.

"*I lied*—I lied about Jason Shappe."

Roland seems confused.

"What are you talking about?"

Tracey turns to look at several people walking by them on the street. She faces Roland again and drops her voice to a low whisper. Roland reacts as Tracey begins to cry softly.

"Jason Shappe didn't rape me. Kyler Vanwick did."

Roland runs his fingers through his hair.

22

Orchid Bay

Greasy Spoon Diner

"How dare you. I had nothing to do with that wretched boy's death. My lawyer will see to it that you end up in court for slandering me. I'll fucking destroy you. Do you hear me?"

Page **216**

Lachlan stifles a laugh and gestures at Daphne Mills.

"You might as well admit it. You've been fingered for what you did by none other than the deceased. Maybe next time you shouldn't have left so many clues behind—starting with making threats against Mark Corrington's life. Oh, did I mention he taped his own murder. Uh-huh—he taped his meeting with you—taped you shooting him at Rocky Ledge. Imagine that—the judge is gonna love this no doubt. And wait—*so* will your lawyer."

Lachlan begins laughing as he faces Daphne.

"Uh-huh—he's gonna love this no doubt. The question that he will have to decide upon is how much time you're gonna have to spend in the slammer. I'm guessing years—decades."

Daphne struggles against the handcuffs on her wrist as she's forced into a police car. People stare at the scene from the entrance to the diner. Several point at Daphne accusingly.

23

Los Angeles

"I'm fine with you and my sister—got no issues with my sister hooking-up with you. Just be aware she's a handful."

Donna pretends to slap Ashton.

"I'll remember that crack dear brother."

Ashton laughs and faces Bradford.

"It's your funeral buddy."

He stifles a laugh and looks at his watch

"I have to go. Parker Ross and I have lunch plans."

Donna faces Ashton.

"Tell Parker I said hi—OK?"

Ashton nods and leaves. Donna turns to face Bradford and sighs loudly. They embrace for a few seconds. She looks at him and seems bothered by something. He notices and sighs.

"What's wrong?"

Donna pulls Bradford toward her.

"I won't hurt you like the others did. I promise I won't."

Bradford runs his fingers through Donna's hair.

Page **217**

"If only I'd met you years ago. Imagine if we'd met when we were teenagers. Imagine the two of us against the world."

Donna looks at Bradford and smiles broadly.

24
San Francisco

"I want her found. Do you hear me? Search the fucking city from top to bottom. Don't leave a stone unturned."

Loren slams his cell phone down on his desk and walks toward a window overlooking San Francisco Bay. He seems upset as he hears the door to his office open. He turns around to see Vladimir standing there with a folder in his hands. He sighs.

"Is there any word on Lizette Richardson?"

Vladimir shrugs and takes a step toward Loren.

"As I said earlier—she was kidnapped at gunpoint at a diner in broad daylight by a young man. He was described by a patron as being muscular and very attractive. Our eyewitness stated he was wearing jeans and a leather vest. Said he had a snooty disposition—said he seemed to be waiting a while."

Loren clenches his fist and glances at the door.

"I want him found. I'll kill that motherfucker myself. No one goes after one of our own and lives to brag about it."

Vladimir seems annoyed and turns away.

"I still say this is Todd Whitney's doing. That man has to die—he's a threat to us as long as there's breath in his body."

Loren waves his hand in the air.

"Oh, he'll get what's coming to him soon enough. Once I locate my father I plan to ice Whitney. He's a liability that must be dealt with before he causes anymore trouble. His whore of a daughter must also be dealt with. Anton will be given the task to snuff them both out. Make them beg before they expire."

Vladimir seems excited by Loren's comments.

"I just think it's time they both ended up in a landfill. Once Todd Whitney is no longer among the living we can go after that murderous bitch that has eluded us so far—and crucify her."

Vladimir faces Loren. He clenches his fist and sighs.

"There's also the question about what to do about your dear old dad. You have to face the inevitable. He's a liability."

Loren stifles a laugh and points at Vladimir.

"I've already made a decision concerning my father if you must know. I know what must be done. He will be dealt with."

Vladimir seems pleased and grins broadly.

Two Days Later

25
Honolulu

"What did that bitch say when you called her earlier?"

Cameron closes the door behind him and faces Clyde. He seems irritated. He walks over to where Alexander is tied to a chair. His face is badly bruised from being punched repeatedly.

"She said she'd have the money by later today."

He grabs Alexander by the throat.

"You better hope that mother of yours loves you—or you're gonna end up with a bullet in your head. I guarantee it."

Without warning he punches Alexander in the face. His rage is evident as he lands another blow. Alexander winces each time he's punched but says nothing. Cameron laughs loudly.

26
Los Angeles

"Call the theater again. Make sure they have everything they need. I don't want any surprises later. Nothing can go wrong today. This movie is my ticket for respect in this industry."

Wesley faces Martin and sighs.

"Margo Sampler will be here shortly. Have her check the guest list once more. I don't want any last minute no-shows."

Martin nervously looks at his cell phone.

"Is there anything else? What about **Ron Howard**?"

Page **219**

Wesley gestures with his hand.

"Said he can't wait to see what I did with Sandra King's book. He tried to get the film rights but I beat him to it."

Martin looks at his cell phone again and seems pleased as he looks at the screen. He hides a smile as he faces Wesley.

27
Orchid Bay
Downtown Police Station

"Should I ask how our three guests are doing?"

Roland looks up as Lachlan enters. He waves his hand in the air and stifles a laugh. Roland watches as Lachlan walks toward his desk. He seems bothered about something.

"Word on the street is that Kyler Vanwick is gonna claim he was set up to take the fall for what Jason Shappe did."

Roland reacts and stands.

"That piece of trash can play every scenario he wants and still he won't get himself out of a rape and murder charge."

He runs his fingers through his hair.

"George Osborne is fit to be tied from what I hear. He wants to take Kyler out himself—threatened his life on more than one occasion since yesterday. Said Kyler needs to be given the electric chair for what he did to his daughter—and to Tracey."

Lachlan leans back in his chair.

"I'm surprised the local media is laying low."

"I was thinking the same thing."

They share a knowing look.

28
Orchid Bay
O'Rourke Law Office

"Are you serious? Are you actually trying to blackmail me in order to help your cousin? This won't end well for you."

Miles O'Rourke waves his hand in the air.

"I'm serious Volker. What do you think people will do if they find out about your involvement with an underage girl from a little nobody town up the coast called Ocean Landing?"

Grant Volker takes a step forward.

"Go ahead—it happened years ago. I was twenty and she was almost eighteen. Even her loser father didn't care that his daughter and I fucked on the night of her senior prom."

Miles leans back in his chair and snickers.

"I wonder what Melissa Barrow would say to that? Shall I call her and see? How about it? How about we ask her?"

Grant takes another step forward and smirks.

"How are you gonna do that O'Rourke—through a fake medium? I guess you didn't do your research. Melissa Barrow was involved with a situation a while back involving a murderous priest. She killed him—tongues wagged plenty for months."

They stare at each other for a few seconds.

"Guess what O'Rourke—this little blackmail stunt is going to cost you dearly—I'm going to file harassment charges against you—I hope you have your ducks in a row—I know I do."

Miles watches as Grant shows him his cell phone and grins broadly. He seems pleased as Miles realizes the implications of being filmed after making a blackmail threat. Grant snickers.

"Get yourself a lawyer O'Rourke—quickly."

He leaves without saying another word. Miles sits there for a few seconds in shock. He runs his fingers through his hair.

29
Los Angeles

Martin looks at a photo of a young woman in front of him and stifles a smirk. He turns and faces his cell phone again.

"Uh-huh—make sure it looks real."

He watches as the man staring back at him holds up several photos. He licks his lips several times and laughs.

"He's dumb—he'll never figure it out."

He points toward his computer proudly.

Page **221**

"There is no limit with what I can do. When I'm done you'll have that gorgeous man all to yourself Martin—at your mercy."

Martin seems pleased as he waves his hand in the air. He touches himself several times. Several moans escape his lips.

"I want him in my bed. I've wanted him for over a year. But each time some bitch got in my way—turned his head."

Oliver Grimke makes a lewd gesture with his finger.

"He's yours once I remove this pesky last obstacle in your path. You have isolated him from his friends already from what you've said. It's just a matter of time now. Once he's alone again you can work your magic—bed him and make him yours."

Martin touches himself again.

"I've just got to have him all to myself. I can't focus anymore. I want him so badly. It's maddening actually."

He faces Oliver again and sighs.

"He and I belong together. There's a connection between us. I've known it from the moment we met. He likes me."

Oliver licks his lips several times.

"I want to be invited to your wedding."

Martin nods. He seems pleased.

30
Orchid Bay
Downtown Police Station

"O'Rourke just did this? Openly threatened you in order to get his cousin out of prison? I didn't think he was that stupid to try something so blatantly criminal. I guess there's more Phamler blood running through his corrupted veins that we assumed."

Lachlan runs his fingers through his hair.

"It seems O'Rourke spent too many hours thinking about how to help Vina without focusing on reality. His behavior today could bring an end to his law career—dumb move no doubt."

He leans back in his chair and sighs loudly.

"What are you gonna do? Get him for trying to blackmail you. This can get messy. O'Rourke is sleazy—proudly corrupt."

Page **222**

Grant seems bothered and clenches his fist.

"I know he'll play dirty. But I have insurance. I taped our meeting. Every second of what took place is safely on video."

Lachlan begins laughing loudly.

"Oh man—I bet O'Rourke thought he had you cornered and then you turned the tables on him. He's so fucked."

Grant pulls out his cell phone.

"I never like him anyway."

He hands Lachlan his cell phone.

"What you think about his chances in front of an honest judge? Losing his precious law license is just the beginning."

Lachlan nods and begins watching the video.

31
Los Angeles

"Of course I'll go—love movie premieres. Not short notice at all. When should I come by your pad? I can be there in less than an hour if needed. I'm actually staying at a motel on Beverly."

Silas grins and gestures.

"Uh-huh—I've got a tux. Don't worry."

He nods a few times. He glances at a table a few feet away and smiles broadly. On top of the table is a small handgun.

TO BE CONTINUED

A Brief Look at the Ninth Episode

Consequences have actions as several people in various locations find out the hard way while two sisters square off when lots of money comes into play as a scheming employee plays with fire.

Episode 9
Mirror Images

1
Orchid Bay
McKeon Beach Condo

"I thought you'd forgotten about me?"

Erica Gersh watches as Carter McKeon closes the door to his condo and faces her. He makes a lewd gesture with his finger and signals her to come toward him. He pulls out a folder.

"Oh ye of little faith—I'm a man of my word."

He glances at the folder and snickers.

"It seems Denise Stone really played her cards well in the slammer. Made lots of close friends—hopped a lot of beds."

Erica licks her lips and seems pleased.

"How many of the guards did she service?"

Carter gestures with his hand.

"She made the rounds—both male and female."

Erica reacts. Carter smiles broadly.

"That woman made everyone she came in contact with a willing participant. Plenty of action was had between her legs."

Erica takes a step forward. She snaps her fingers.

"Wait until Ryan finds out his soon-to-be wife is a cheap thrill for anyone willing to give her what she wants. *Ugh*."

Erica attempts to grab the folder from Carter's hand. He laughs as he grabs her arm. He pushes her against the wall and uses his strength to make a point to her. He laughs loudly.

"Ryan is a fucking puss. You're my girl now."

Erica tries to push Carter away.

"I want Ryan. Not you."

Carter laughs and rips Erica's blouse.

"Ryan is yesterday. I'm today."

Erica watches as Carter yanks her bra off and pushes her toward his bedroom. He begins whistling as he strengthens his grip on her wrist. His anger is evident as he forces her through the door to his bedroom and locks the door. He laughs.

"Imagine what Ryan would do if I told him you attempted to run his best girl out of town. It's over between the two of you on account of what I know. Face it—you're my whore now."

He begins to undress as Erica glances at the window. Carter notices and begins laughing. He grabs Erica again.

"It's a two story drop—there's no way out of here."

He forces her down on his bed against her will.

"I think you should know I like it rough—and yeah I intend to play by my own rules where you're concerned sweet thing."

He begins laughing as he sees her reaction.

2

Orchid Bay
Clerke Apartment

"I hope it's OK that I invited my sister to help. She just split with her husband. I thought the change of scenery would be nice for her until she decides what to do about her marriage."

Patrick Clerke nods as he faces Kayla Larsen. Kayla opens the door to his apartment and ushers him inside. He seems upset as she reaches out to brace him. She notices and sighs loudly.

"Uh-huh—lots of TLC is coming your way."

Page **226**

Patrick gestures with his hand.

"I can take care of myself. I'm not an invalid."

Kayla reaches out to kiss Patrick. She helps him sit down on the sofa just as Violet Lorenzo comes through the front door with several large pillows. She notices the exchange between Kayla and Patrick. She comes toward them and smiles.

"I hope these helps."

Patrick turns and faces Violet.

"I'm sure they will Violet. Thank you."

She walks toward her sister.

"How about I go get something from the mall? There's plenty of really decent vegan cafes there—everything healthy."

Kayla nods and watches Violet leave. She notices Patrick's reaction to Violet's comment about vegan food. He sighs.

"You're gonna eat whatever my sister brings back and like it. That's an order. Not one whiny complaint out of you."

"I'm not making any such promises."

Kayla pulls Patrick towards her and kisses him.

"I'm really glad you're OK."

Patrick grins.

"I second that."

"Your father asked me to go out on his boat with him when I'm feeling better. Said there are plenty of great fishing areas around the Channel Islands—mentioned his father lived there during the 1970s while he worked as a stunt double for an actor named **James Houghton** on a series called *Code R* that ran on CBS for one season. Said he visited his dad a few times and got to hang with the cast. Stated it was the highlight of his life as a six-year-old—told me it led to his fascination with the ocean."

Kayla seems pleased and kisses Patrick again.

3

San Francisco

"Lizette Richardson is dead—murdered. This just came a minute ago. Front desk said it was hand delivered by courier."

Page **227**

Loren Fawcett glances at the flash drive for a second as Anton Levitov hands it over. He watches Loren's reaction.

4
Honolulu

"Spare no expenses Eugene. He's all I have. Scrape this miserable island from one end to another—but find him."

Carmen Pendleton grimaces as she watches her cell phone go blank. She paces back and forth nervously and as she turns around she sees Tiffany Johnson standing before her. Carmen reacts in shock as the apparition takes a step forward.

"This is what happens when you play with fire Carmen. You and I have had this discussion before. I warned you."

Carmen continues to stand as if in a trance while Tiffany slowly circles her for a few seconds. Tiffany suddenly stops.

"This is not what I expected from you."

Carmen watches as Tiffany takes another step forward. She glances at a photo of Alexander Pendleton nearby.

"Your behavior brought this about. *You* are the cause of what Alexander is experiencing. *You* did this. You have no one else to blame but yourself. Of course there's the troubling matter with Eugene Ledyard. He's not what he appears to be."

Carmen shakes her head and sighs.

"What are you talking about?"

Tiffany points at Carmen once more.

"He's a killer."

Carmen seems confused.

"I don't know anything of the sort."

Tiffany angrily grabs Carmen by the arm.

"He killed Shirley Beecroft."

Carmen shakes her head.

"That slut left the island—went back to Texas."

A flash of light shades Tiffany's face.

"Did she? Or did Eugene Ledyard tell you she did."

Tiffany lets go of Carmen's arm and sighs.

Page **228**

"I'm putting you on notice. You're heading down the wrong path. The same path Howard Madison went down before his unfortunate demise at Glass Owl. There will be no escape if you refuse to heed my words. This is your last warning."

Carmen seems unable to move.

"I had nothing to do with what Eugene Ledyard did. I didn't tell him to kill her. He's responsible for her death."

Tiffany grabs Carmen's arm again.

"I'm not going to argue with you. You know what you have to do—what is expected. If you fail you'll regret it."

Tiffany looks at a photo of Alexander.

"I know what I have to do—and *so* do you."

Moments later she's gone. Carmen stands there for a few seconds and finally grabs her cell phone. She begins dialing.

5
Orchid Bay
Downtown Police Station

"I want to see my cousin. I have rights—she's my client and you have no choice. Unless you want to face the local press and explain how you're preventing me from doing my job."

Lachlan Ball stares at Miles O'Rourke and stifles a laugh as he stands up. He walks over to Miles. Miles takes a step back clearly intimidated by Lachlan's height. He sighs loudly.

"Decent people like my cousin shouldn't be held to such low standards by the likes of you. Vina Phamler is worth more than you and your kin will ever be worth. Facts are facts."

Lachlan gestures with his hand.

"Uh-huh—so you say O'Rourke—but at least no one in my family is facing murder charges at the moment. Yeah—that's right—and oh—by the way—your cousin isn't really a Phamler is she? Everyone knows she's Roger Olof's bastard daughter."

Miles reacts. His rage is evident.

"How dare you talk about my cousin like that? It was never proven she was Olof's daughter. No DNA test was ever done."

Page **229**

Lachlan grins broadly and glances at Roland O'Brien sitting a few feet away. He points to a computer nearby.

"How about we test your theory right now? How about it O'Rourke? I know someone at a clinic that specializes in DNA."

Miles is taken aback and seems about to explode.

"I'm *so* going to enjoy destroying you."

Lachlan begins laughing.

6

Los Angeles

"I'm sorry. There's no other way to tell you."

Ashton Markway seems unable to move as he stares at the young woman in front of him. Karen Eberhardt notices his shocked reaction. She watches as he shoves his hands into the front pocket of his faded Levi's. He sighs loudly and shrugs.

"Why didn't you tell me?"

Karen looks down at her stomach. She's in the last months of pregnancy. She seems about to cry as she faces him.

"I was afraid you would hate me."

Ashton runs his fingers through his hair.

"I could never hate you."

He seems confused and sighs loudly.

"We only slept together once."

Karen looks at her stomach again.

"I haven't been with anyone else. You were my first."

Ashton runs his fingers through his hair again.

"How come your mother didn't tell me?"

Karen wipes a tear from her eye.

"She respects you too much Ashton—knew you didn't consider me your girlfriend—said she didn't want to drop a bombshell that could destroy her chances of working with you in the future—wanted me to tell you in person—before I had."

Ashton glances at Karen's stomach.

"What's going to happen now?"

Karen turns away. Ashton grabs her arm.

Page **230**

"Wait—do you think I wouldn't want anything to do with our baby? Is that what you think of me? That I'm just some guy who sleeps around and couldn't care less if I impregnated a virgin—that I couldn't be bothered to be responsible after."

Karen seems unsure what to say.

"I didn't want you to think I trapped you. When we spent the night together at your hotel room you made it clear we were not a couple. Told me you were sexually active and didn't want a serious relationship with anyone—especially a virgin like me."

Ashton turns to look at the driveway.

"I'm going to be there for you. I won't pretend that I'm not the father. You have my word. Everything is going to be OK."

Karen seems relieved and throws her arms around Ashton and hugs him warmly. He glances at her stomach again.

7

Honolulu

"That dumb bitch better not screw with us or she'll be sorry. The death of her son will be the least of her worries."

Cameron Hodge clenches his fist in anger as he faces Clyde Matheson sitting a few feet away. They glance at the hallway leading to several rooms. Cameron smirks.

"The boy wonder is going to meet his maker shortly. It'll be quite the show. Then we deal with that scheming bitch."

A movement catches Clyde's eye and as he turns around he sees Tiffany standing a few feet away. Cameron reacts.

"What the fuck?"

Clyde seems in shock.

"How did you get in here?"

Tiffany takes a step forward and laughs.

"What if I told you I came through the mirror? Would you believe me? Or would you think I was yanking your chain?"

Cameron begins laughing and approaches Tiffany. He looks at the front door. It is still locked. He seems annoyed.

"I asked you a question. I want an answer."

Page **231**

Tiffany glances at both Cameron and Clyde. She watches Cameron flexing his muscular arms as he prepares to assault her. Clyde stands up and takes a step forward. He seems pleased.

"How much is Carmen Pendleton paying you?"

Tiffany seems about to laugh.

"How much is Loren Fawcett paying you?"

Cameron reacts in shock to the name and winces.

"I think you need to be taught a lesson when it comes to respecting how angry a man can become when provoked."

He lunges at Tiffany. She stands motionless as he begins to struggle to breathe. Seconds later he falls at her feet—dead. A few feet away Clyde reacts to seeing Cameron dropping dead.

"I'm *so* out of here."

Clyde runs toward the front of the beachfront home and tries to open the door. As he turns around he realizes Tiffany is standing next to him. Before he can open the door he begins struggling to breathe. He gasps several times for air before he collapses. Less than a second later he's dead. Tiffany stands above him and seems satisfied. A few feet away a dark shadow approaches Cameron's corpse as his soul leaves his body. The dark shadow then turns into a claw-like creature and devours him as his soul cries out for mercy. Seconds later the same fate befalls Clyde as the claw-like creature hungrily devours his soul and disappears. Tiffany walks down the hallway and opens the door to the room where Alexander Pendleton is being held. He reacts as he sees her. He watches as she touches the ropes binding his wrists and feet. They fall away instantly. His eyes widen.

"How did you do that?"

Tiffany doesn't answer. Alexander remains seated unsure what is happening. As he watches she walks toward a huge mirror and steps through it. He reacts again at what he just witnessed and rubs his eyes several times. He stands up and stretches.

"Is she? No. It can't be."

He looks at the mirror again as if expecting the apparition to return. He runs his fingers through his hair and cautiously peeks out of the room. He notices the empty hallway ahead.

"What the hell just happened?"

He looks back at the mirror for several seconds and then bolts from the room. As he runs into the living room he sees the bodies of Cameron and Clyde lying motionless on the floor. He stops briefly to look at them before opening the front door and running down the rocky beach. He looks back a few times.

8
Orchid Bay
McKeon Beach Condo

"Not another word about Ryan Pena. That fucking loser is off limits—do you hear me? He's no longer your concern."

Carter grabs Erica by the hair and pulls her toward him. He looks down at his erect penis and laughs. She tries to push him away as he becomes more aggressive while he licks his lips.

"You and I are couple now. And couples fuck. They fuck morning to night. I'm gonna use you to service my needs until I become bored. Then you'll be kicked to the curb like the slut you are. Of course by that time Ryan and Denise will be married—and who knows—expecting their first kid. You'll just be known as a cheap thrill for every guy in Orchid Bay who wants a piece."

Erica finally manages to push Carter away.

"I hate you—do you hear me?"

Carter laughs and grabs Erica again.

"Go tell it to someone who gives a damn. You and I are gonna really push boundaries. When I'm finished with you there isn't going to be anyone in this town that won't know how much sex we had together. Yeah—that's right—I intend to make sure our encounters are filmed. *Oops*—did I forget to mention what just happened between us is on film. Uh-huh—you're gonna be a big star on the Internet—Orchid Bay's very own porn star."

Erica reacts and looks around the room.

"I'm going to kill you."

Carter slides his hands around Erica's neck. He seems to be losing control as Erica feels herself losing consciousness.

Page **233**

"No one threatens me—especially a two-bit whore."

He tightens his grip and forces her down on the sofa. As she tries to break free he plows into her again. She cries out as he begins raping her. His laughter echoes throughout the room.

<h1 style="text-align:center">9</h1>

San Francisco

"Bring Todd Whitney to me. He and I have to talk."

Anton stifles a grin and nods. Loren watches him leave and turns to face Vladimir Orlov. He wrings his hands.

"There's no way all of this isn't tied to Whitney in some way. Too many of my people have met grisly ends. He knows something. It's time he answers for what he brought upon my people. He will talk or that bastard will endure my wrath."

Vladimir grins broadly as he glances at a huge butcher knife laid out on a coffee table nearby. Loren notices.

"We should have taken Whitney out a long time ago. He and his whore of a daughter have no value to us anymore."

Loren runs his fingers through his hair.

"Speaking of having no value to anyone—any word on the whereabouts of my dear old dad? I don't like the idea of not knowing what he's up to. Frankly, I think it would be better if he was dead—lying in a crypt at Colma—at rest—next to Ralph."

Loren clenches his fist and sighs loudly.

"Ralph is the cause of all my problems. Once I took him out I assumed my father would dote on me—instead he seemed to spend more time focusing his attention on my dead brother instead of realizing I was his future—damn him to hell."

He points at the butcher knife.

"I want him dead—the sooner the better."

Vladimir seems about to laugh.

"I'm glad you've finally come to your senses about your old man. He's served his purpose to you and the family. But facts are facts—he's become a liability—talking about some dead girl stalking him simply made his situation worse—much worse."

<h2 style="text-align:center">Page 234</h2>

Loren nods in agreement and faces Vladimir.

"When I locate my father I think it's time he and I have a long talk—about my future and his death at my hands."

He looks at the butcher knife nearby.

10
Orchid Bay
Bay Street Condo

"Has anyone ever told you that you're a whiny bore—like seriously, you are so fucking dull old man—enough already with your constant whining about dear Loren—blah—blah—blah."

Houghton Fawcett glares at Janet Virella.

"You ungrateful bitch—show your father respect."

Janet grabs Houghton by the arm.

"I want you to leave."

Houghton jerks free of Janet's grip and looks at the door before he turns to face her again. He raises his fist in the air.

"I could have you killed."

Janet begins to laugh and points at the balcony.

"I was just thinking the same thing."

She gestures toward the balcony and smirks.

"Do you think a man your age could survive a fall from a twelve floor condo? I wonder how many bones would break."

She walks to the front door and opens it.

"Get the hell out or else."

Houghton points at Janet.

"I'll get you for this. I swear I will."

Janet waves her hand in the air and laughs.

"Blah—blah—blah—*get out.*"

He stands motionless for a few seconds and walks to the door. He stops and faces her. She seems bored and sighs.

"Are you still here old man?"

Without warning Janet shoves him through the doorway and slams the door. She smiles and walks toward a mini bar.

"That old man is more trouble than he's worth."

Page **235**

She hears him cursing in the hallway and begins laughing as he pounds on the door. She walks over to the door.

"I'm going to call the cops old man."

He continues to swear at her.

"I'm going to count to ten—then I call."

She begins counting and hears his voice trailing as he walks down the hallway. She glances at the mini bar again.

"No wonder my brother freaked out."

She begins laughing.

11

Orchid Bay
Condo Elevator

"I like her. I really like her. She's got spunk—won't allow the likes of you to push her around. Isn't she your daughter? The one you refused to acknowledge for years—denied her."

Houghton realizes Tiffany is standing next to him. He seems about to explode as she continues to mock him.

"Oh—how the fortunes have fallen for the mighty—oh what shall you do now? Being homeless is such a terrible way to live—especially if that person is you. I guess Loren made good on his threat to freeze your credit cards—such a wonderful son."

Houghton clenches his fist as he glares at Tiffany.

"You could have told me what he was up to."

Tiffany pretends to wipe tears from her eyes and laughs.

"I thought I already told you I don't work for you. In fact I know something else that you don't—and it's quite a shocker."

Houghton watches as Tiffany circles him. She seems unable to contain her joy as she watches his confused reaction.

"What if someone you thought was dead—wasn't?"

Seconds later he's alone in the elevator again. Houghton watches as the door slowly opens and several people enter. He walks toward the sidewalk and faces the condo once more.

"What if someone I thought was dead wasn't? What the hell is that supposed to mean? Damn that miserable girl."

Page **236**

He begins walking down the street muttering loudly while several people turn and stop to look at him—and whisper.

12
Los Angeles

"I still can't believe my book is actually a movie."

Sandra King embraces Wesley Madison as Scott Malone stands a few feet away. He seems ready to attack Wesley.

"It's hard to believe it happened just three years ago."

Wesley shoots Scott a look and notices Martin Knappson coming into his office. He hands Wesley a thick folder.

"Paramount and Sony passed on the **Bobby Driscoll** script but Universal said they are leaning toward yes. Disney is certainly not pleased. Pissed would be a better word if truth be known."

Wesley waves his hand in the air.

"Ask me if I care either way."

Scott notices Martin looking at him. He shoots him a nasty look and sighs. Martin continues staring at Scott. He smiles.

"You should be in the movies. You certainly have the right look no doubt. Has anyone ever told you how hot you are?"

Scott grabs Martin by the collar. Martin seems excited by Scott's aggression as Sandra shoots Scott a cautious look. Scott shakes Martin and seems to want to punch him in the jaw.

"I don't do dudes—*ugh*—*you*—like seriously."

He lets Martin go and seems disgusted.

"I'll wait downstairs."

Sandra watches him go and faces Wesley. He seems upset as he glances at Martin. Martin leaves without saying a word.

13
Pacific Coast Highway

"I intend to show that bitch half-sister of mine who I really am from the minute we meet. I'm gonna royally crush her."

Vera Holliday licks her lips and laughs.

Page **237**

"I hope you warned her I plan to skin her alive."

Daniel Brandt shakes his head.

"I did no such thing. I thought I told you she was a nasty piece of work. She creates enemies wherever she goes."

Vera points her finger at Daniel.

"Have you met me?"

She makes a lewd gesture with her finger.

"That bitch is gonna be a blubbering mess when I start going after her character—starting with her messy DUI arrest. That cold-hearted freak show ran over two sisters in Tarzana last summer and tried to blame them for her hitting them. Said they purposely stepped in front of her car because they wanted to make some extra cash—when it was actually she—in a drunken haze mowed them down like trash and just kept going."

Daniel runs his fingers through his hair.

"I know all about what Amber Walston did. She paid off the judge apparently—the case was dropped and she walked."

Vera stifles a snicker.

"She paid him off by getting between his legs. I know how women like her work their game. Use a man who has a frigid wife to further their endeavors—oldest trick in the book for someone with her mindset. She's just one step above a prostitute."

Daniel shoots Vera a cautious look.

"You better leave such talk at the front door. That woman will sue you for comments like that. She has a history of suing anyone who utters a bad word about her—enjoys doing it."

Vera grabs Daniel's arm.

"I thought I made it clear to you I'm gonna crush her. I've been doing a lot of research on her. Three days is a long time to have to wait—she'll regret not agreeing to meet me sooner."

Daniel shakes his head and sighs.

"She said she was busy."

Vera makes a lewd gesture with her finger again.

"Uh-huh—she was busy alright—probably making good on her deal to keep the judge's penis happy. *Ugh*—I bet he's really old—somewhere in his late seventies—wrinkled and limp."

Page **238**

Daniel seems disgusted by her comment and turns to look at the freeway exit up ahead as they approach Brentwood.

"I'm warning you. Be really careful what you say to Amber Walston. She made it clear she intends to destroy you."

Vera waves her hand in the air.

"It is she who will be destroyed by yours truly."

Vera glances at Daniel again and slyly slides her hand between his legs. She smiles as her fingers probes the outline of his penis. He pushes her hand away. He seems irritated.

"I thought I already told you."

Vera eyes fall on Daniel's penis straining under the confines of his fitted suit and laughs as she notices he has an erection. She licks her lips several times and gestures to him.

"Why don't we just pull over by the side of the road and let me give you a blowjob. You know you want my tongue on your dick. We both know how much you enjoyed it back in the day."

Daniel pulls his car over to the side of the road.

"I'm not going to say it again. You and I are no longer a couple. I'm with Zarina now. There's nothing more to talk about. I've moved on—you need to find someone else—Roland O'Brien for starters. He's single—hasn't been with anyone lately."

Vera rolls her eyes in disgust.

"*Ugh*—he's a goody-goody. That man never does anything wrong. I bet he asked permission before he and his ex-girlfriend had sex. No way do I want someone that sensitive—dullsville."

Daniel runs his fingers through his hair.

"Ethan Vanwick?"

Vera mimics sticking her finger down her throat.

"He's a loser—and he's bad in bed."

Daniel starts the engine of his car and sighs.

"Fine—whatever Vera—but you and I are not getting back together. It's simply not going to happen. Leave it be."

Vera seems upset and pouts.

"I won't take no for an answer. Do you hear me? I want you back in my bed and I'm going to have my way. It's obvious we belong together and once Zarina realizes it she'll adjust."

Page **239**

Daniel sighs loudly and faces Vera. He looks at the street ahead and watches several cars drive past. He grimaces.

"When we get back to Orchid Bay I'm going to find you another lawyer Vera. I think you and I need some time apart."

Vera becomes enraged and slaps Daniel.

14
Orchid Bay
Downtown Police Station

"I heard you were looking for me. Something about what happened to Adam Mills? I assume I'm the prime suspect?"

Lachlan and Roland seem in shock as they look at Jayne Osborne standing in the doorway. She seems oddly calm.

"Where have you been all this time?"

Jayne stifles a laugh.

"I was in Phoenix. That's where my boyfriend lives if you must know. He and I went camping. He likes the outdoors."

She giggles as she takes a step towards them.

"I had absolutely nothing to do with what happened to that miserable wretch Adam Mills. I was with my boyfriend the entire time I was away. No cell phone service for miles around."

Lachlan leans back in his chair.

"You were seen leaving his home the day he was found dead. Neighbors reported the two of you had words together."

Jayne gestures with her hand and smiles.

"I paid him a visit the afternoon he was iced. He and I had unfinished business to attend to before I left for my trip."

Lachlan stands up and gives Jayne a sharp look.

"What sort of unfinished business?"

Jayne glances at Roland.

"I warned him to stay away from me—told him to keep his friends away from me too. I made it clear he and I were over."

She turns to face the front door.

"He was alive when I left. Sorry to burst your bubble but I had nothing to do with what happened to that damn loser."

She watches their reaction and stifles a smirk.

"Look—let's get real OK—I'm not even going to pretend I'm upset he's lying under a pile of dirt at Falling Pines."

She begins to laugh.

"Orchid Bay should hold a parade."

She turns to look at the front door again.

"Do you want to talk to my boyfriend from Phoenix?"

Before they can answer she walks to the door and seconds later a young man about thirty steps forward. Roland and Lachlan try to control themselves from laughing out loud as they look at Evan Molloy. His shirt and cowboy hat looked like it was bought from a tacky costume site online while his jeans were so tight it was a wonder he could walk. To make matters worse it appears he was not wearing underwear—going commando no doubt.

"Evan Molloy meet Orchid Bay's finest. Evan and I are gonna meet the folks then we're headed back to Phoenix."

Lachlan turns to face Roland.

"Should we insist she remain in Orchid Bay?"

Roland glances at Evan again—still desperately trying to keep from laughing. He faces Jayne and Evan with a loud sigh.

"I expect you to remain in Orchid Bay for the time being until I decide otherwise. A murder was committed and someone is clearly responsible—you are hereby ordered to stay put."

Jayne looks at Evan and then at Roland.

"I didn't kill that motherfucker."

Roland stands up and walks over to where Evan and Jayne are standing. Evan takes his hat off. Roland stifles a smile.

"I'm not going to tell you again."

He turns and walks to the front door.

"I think this concludes us talking further."

Jayne storms out the front door with Evan right behind her. As Roland closes the door he faces Lachlan and laughs.

"If that dude is straight I'm Santa Claus."

Lachlan mimics Evan and feigns being insulted.

"I like girls. Really I do—don't I look straight?"

They begin laughing loudly and pretend to hold hands.

"Oh my—what if someone thought we were gay—gay and in a secret romance? Oh what would people say—oh my."

Lachlan stops laughing and sighs.

"Do you think she killed Adam Mills?"

Roland runs his fingers through his hair.

"I guess we have to talk to the neighbors again. I think we should also get hold of the security cameras from the beauty shop across the street. Video footage doesn't lie. People do."

Lachlan wipes sweat from his brow.

15
Orchid Bay
Pioneer Trail Mall

"Tough break dude—I heard you found out your dad wasn't really your dad. I'm here if you want to talk about it."

Lloyd Welsh faces Gary Hachter and grimaces.

"Does everyone in Orchid Bay know my business?"

Gary pats Lloyd on the back.

"Don't sweat it—I've got your back."

Lloyd sighs loudly.

"Thanks. I appreciate it."

Gary nods and sits down next to Lloyd.

"On another note I finally got Lana Dempsey last night. It was long in coming. She told me for weeks I'd never get her after I popped her younger sister—but she had to eat her words."

Lloyd salutes Gary and laughs.

"She was one of the last holdouts in Orchid Bay."

Gary makes a lewd gesture with his finger.

"She's nothing now—courtesy of yours truly. I raw-dogged her in my car outside Falling Pines despite her begging me to not insult her the way I did her sister. So I did her the same way."

He laughs and jabs Lloyd.

"She's freaking out that I impregnated her."

He jabs Lloyd again.

"She's just another slut now."

Page 242

He wipes sweat from his brow and smirks.

"That was my one goal before I headed off to college in the fall—that I would pop her like I did her sister. There's nothing worse than a girl flaunting her virginity to horny high school guys who just want to get laid countless times before they head off to college to bag even more babes before they marry one they actually like—one that isn't a raging slut—or used-up trash."

Lloyd seems upset and grimaces.

"I'm gonna meet my real dad in a few days. He's in Los Angeles for a movie premiere or something from what he said."

Gary lowers his voice.

"Your real dad knows movie people?"

Lloyd nods and gestures.

"I think so. Or so he says anyway. I'm not sure exactly. I only spoke to him briefly on the phone. Said he was looking forward to meeting me. I have some old photos of him that he sent my mother. He was quite the looker in high school."

Gary rolls his eyes knowingly.

"Oh-oh—is he fat and ugly now?"

Lloyd shoots Gary an odd look and laughs.

"He also sent present-day photos too. He's still a chick magnet if you must know. Maybe he and my mother will hook-up again when he comes to Orchid Bay. He's single—no kids."

Gary notices Lana Dempsey coming toward them. He seems nervous as she approaches. Lloyd acknowledges Lana.

"How's everything Lana?"

Lana notices Gary ignoring her.

"I'm fine. Hello Gary."

Gary faces Lana and smirks.

"Are you and Edward still going to the dance?"

Lana reacts and seems hurt.

"Edward found out about what happened last night. He doesn't want anything to do with me—said I was a slut."

Gary stifles a laugh.

"Tough break—he was a jerk anyway."

Lana glances at Lloyd. She seems about to cry.

"Everyone is talking. Everyone thinks I spread my legs like my sister did. You tricked me. I didn't even want to have sex."

Gary stands up. He grabs Lana's arm.

"It's over OK. It happened and now it's over. You and I are just friends. What happened between us meant nothing."

Lana jerks free from Gary's grip and runs toward the elevator a few yards away in a rush. Gary turns to face Lloyd.

"I never promised her anything after I fucked her in the backseat of my car. I'm just not that kind of guy. I don't want a girlfriend—she was just a distraction. She was fully aware I only wanted to pop her because I popped her sister. I told her more than enough times she was gonna lose her virginity to me."

He begins to laugh.

"She was lame if it matters."

Lloyd reacts as Gary eyes a girl standing by the elevator and licks his lips. He faces Lloyd again and stifles a snicker.

"She and I had some good times previous."

Lloyd watches as Gary walks away.

16
Honolulu

"I was just a hired help. It wasn't my idea."

John Alohu faces Eugene Ledyard and laughs. He notices several police officers walking past his desk. Eugene is handcuffed and seems pissed off. John leans forward.

"I'm all ears. Spill your guts. Whose idea was it to kill Shirley Beecroft? Was it Gaston Bauer—her ex-boyfriend?"

Eugene seems confused and sighs.

"I don't know anyone named Gaston Bauer. I'm talking about Carmen Pendleton. She's behind it all—paid me."

John shakes his head.

"I suppose you have proof of your claim?"

Eugene nods. He stifles a laugh.

"I kept records. I have it all—tons of stuff on Carmen."

John stands and gestures to another cop.

San Francisco

"This is it Whitney—no more reprieves. I know for a fact you're behind the rash of killings of my people. I warned you and you defied me. Killing Lizette Richardson was the final straw. I'm fully aware how poetic it is that you had her killed—her being the one that was responsible for the death of Thomas and his family in the Bahamas. But revenge will cost you your own life."

Todd Whitney struggles to free himself from Anton's grip as Loren takes a step toward him. He seems pleased as he grabs Todd's neck with his hand. He shakes Todd's head back and forth and starts laughing. He lets go and glances at Anton. He laughs loudly seeing a huge grin wreathed across Anton's face and makes a slashing gesture with his hand across his neck. Anton nods as Todd panics. He begins to struggle to free himself.

"I had nothing to do with what happened to your people. I'm innocent. I'm being set up—probably by you yourself."

Loren spins around and angrily punches Todd in the chest.

"How dare you insult me like that?"

He hits Todd again as Anton restrains him.

"You have insulted my family for the last time."

He motions for Anton to kill Todd. Todd cries out several times as Anton's fingers tighten around his neck. Anton laughs loudly as his strength increases around Todd's neck. He watches as Todd struggles to free himself as his life ebbs away. Anton laughs even louder as he sees Todd's eyes rolling back in his head as he tightens his fingers even more around Todd's neck. Loren stands a few feet away and seems pleased as Anton seems to relish his power over Todd. Todd stops struggling as he begins to lose consciousness while Anton laughs gleefully. Todd goes limp in Anton's hands and falls against him. Anton laughs yet again but seems disgusted by Todd lying against his body. He grabs Todd and breaks his neck. Todd's body falls to the floor. Anton wipes his hands against his jeans and faces Loren in triumph.

Page **245**

"I assume the city dump is the next step for Whitney?"

Loren stifles a laugh and gestures at Anton.

"Put the stiff in a box with dog poop from my kennels in Chinatown. It's not like Todd will complain about the smell."

Anton begins laughing and points at Todd's body lying at his feet. He seems disappointed as he kicks the corpse.

"I thought he would put up more of a fight. But he just gave up. It's as if he wanted to die—be put out of his misery."

Anton makes a lewd gesture with his finger.

"When I get back from the dump I'm gonna pay Bridget Whitney a visit. She and I have some unfinished business to attend to. And yeah as I'm fucking her I'm gonna let it drop I killed her father. Killed him with my bare hands and enjoyed it."

They begin laughing loudly.

18

Los Angeles

"What happened earlier with Scott Malone had better not happen again—I already warned you about your behavior."

Martin seems bored and sighs loudly.

"I was paying him a compliment. He should be flattered that someone like me thinks he's hot—boyfriend material."

Martin licks his lips.

"The things I could do to him."

He makes a lewd gesture with his finger.

"I bet he looks like a Greek god in the shower."

Wesley slams his fist down on his desk.

"You have no right to hit on someone you don't know. This is your final warning Martin. I would really hate to lose you but you simply refuse to behave professionally when it comes to my clients—making one inappropriate comment after another that causes me to have to clean up your mess afterwards. He was not the first—but he better be the last. Is that clear Martin?"

Martin nods and looks at the door.

19
Honolulu

News cameras flash as Carmen is led toward a waiting police car. Tourists seem confused while the police surround the car as it drives away from a fancy condo in Waikiki Beach.

20
Los Angeles

"Is this real? Is Carmen Pendleton being arrested for conspiracy to commit murder? This must be a mistake."

Gina Bentley seems in shock as she faces Pierce Colby. He runs his fingers through his hair. Gina grabs her cell phone as Pierce turns the television in their hotel room off. She sighs.

"I wonder if Eddie knows about Carmen."

At that moment there is a blinding flash of light as Tiffany suddenly appears. They both turn to look at her in shock.

"Carmen Pendleton became what she despised most. She became Howard Madison. I had warned her about where she was headed. I'm glad she finally did the right thing and decided to make amends for the choices she made. It was either her or her son—she chose her son. I guess there's hope for her after all."

Gina reacts at the mention of Alexander's name.

"Is my half-brother OK? Who exactly was Carmen involved with—and how was Alexander involved? Earlier *Inside Edition* said something about a conspiracy to commit murder—said she hired an ex-con to kill someone she fired—did she really do that?"

Tiffany nods several times and smirks.

"That's just half the story."

Less than a second later Tiffany is gone.

"Maybe I should call Alexander—see if there's anything I can do. I better let Eddie know what just happened too."

Pierce suddenly grabs Gina's arm.

"I'm sure he already knows."

She looks at her cell phone and sighs.

Page **247**

"I'll call him anyway—just in case. The premiere of Wesley Madison's movie is just a few hours away. It'll spoil everything if he finds out from some tacky reporter on the red carpet."

Pierce seems nervous and shrugs.

21
Orchid Bay
Pioneer Trail Mall

"You should have used a condom? I asked you to."

Gary laughs as he buttons his jeans.

"I like raw-dogging all my conquests. Like deal already."

Jennifer Alsten aggressively jabs Gary in the chest.

"What if I tell my brother?"

Gary laughs as he combs his hair.

"Tell him—I don't care. He's probably raw-dogged plenty of girls. He's got a reputation around Orchid Bay for being really naughty when he was in high school. He's certainly no saint."

Jennifer seems annoyed as she buttons her blouse while Gary looks at her and licks his lips. He takes a step forward.

"How about a second round—I'm hard."

Jennifer glances at Gary's erection straining under his jeans and sighs loudly. She angrily gestures with her hand.

"I've got things to do."

Gary reacts and laughs loudly.

"Ouch—I got told off by one of my repeat deals."

She pretends to slap him.

"I let you—and don't you forget it. You didn't get anything I didn't want you to have. I hope we understand each other."

Gary pretends to be offended.

"Wow—you certainly know how to crush a dude's ego with just a few words. I might need counseling after today."

Jennifer slides her arms around Gary's waist. She looks at him for a few seconds before kissing him lightly on the lips.

"You'll do just fine. There's no doubt in my mind you'll find another easy mark before the day is over. I believe in you."

Page **248**

Gary gestures slyly and laughs. He winks at Jennifer as he hugs her warmly. They stare at each other and kiss again.

"I'm still going to tell my brother."

Gary begins laughing and kisses Jennifer again.

22
Los Angeles

"I asked you a question—who the fuck sent you? I didn't ask for an escort to the premiere tonight—just get the fuck out of my sight before I call the cops and report you for hooking."

Amir Iskandar seems insulted and sighs.

"My name is Amir Iskandar. I'm a lawyer. I was sent here by Daniel Brandt to discuss your case against Amber Walston."

Vera Holliday rolls her eyes and sighs.

"I only want Daniel Brandt as my lawyer. Get lost."

Amir stifles a smirk and sighs.

"I never said Daniel wasn't your lawyer. He sent me to help you. Seems your half-sister is bringing out the big guns to make sure she crushes you tomorrow. She's out for serious blood."

Vera clenches her fist and begins yelling.

23
San Francisco

Houghton Fawcett steps out of a taxi and looks at the mansion across the street. He seems pleased as he pulls out a cell phone and begins dialing. A few seconds later he grins.

"Uh-huh—it's me—I'm ready."

He faces the mansion located in Pacific Heights for a few seconds. He nods several times and begins laughing loudly.

TO BE CONTINUED

A Brief Look at the Tenth Episode

Tragedy seems to befall certain people when least expected as a father and son confront reality with events that are beyond their control as a murderous psychopath makes an appearance.

Falling Pieces

1
Orchid Bay
Pioneer Trail Mall

"I guess I'll be seeing you sometime later this week."

Jennifer Alsten sighs loudly as Gary Hachter begins walking up the stairwell. She runs after him and grabs his arm.

"I just want you to know all the girls in Orchid Bay are really gonna miss you and Lloyd Welsh when you guys leave for college. It just won't be the same around here—dullsville."

Gary seems pleased and smirks.

"Wow—that's such a sweet thing to say."

He makes a lewd gestured with his finger.

"I appreciate you saying that—especially after how Lloyd and I treated you and every girl in Orchid Bay. The last two years have been incredible—you girls just made it so easy for us."

Jennifer pulls Gary toward her.

"We were all mad at first when we found out you and Lloyd had organized a ratings system for every girl in town. Set us up to compete against each other in losing our virginities."

Gary laughs loudly and kisses Jennifer.

"Lloyd and I took you girls down within a month. We both got laid at least twice every afternoon after school for weeks."

He kisses Jennifer again. She sighs loudly.

"You took me in the girl's locker room at school."

Gary stifles a smirk.

"You told me you were still deciding."

He watches her reaction.

"I told you a decision had been made."

Jennifer hugs Gary warmly.

"I'm really gonna miss you Gary."

He laughs and glances at the door.

"What about you? Where are you headed?"

Jennifer wipes a tear from her eye.

"Pepperdine—I think—or San Francisco State."

She wipes another tear from her eye.

"I didn't get into UCLA."

They look at each other again.

2

Los Angeles

"I'm serious—you should take a few photos. This could be a side gig for you. You would easily book print ads here and in New York. Clothing companies would kill to have you wearing their clothing—especially jeans—fitted suits and shorts too."

Maxwell Pendergraft climbs out of bed and turns to face Juliet Haskelle. He nervously runs his fingers through his hair.

"I'm not a model. I like to eat."

Juliet laughs and comes toward him.

"You're thinking of runway models. Print models just have to be hot—with a photographer that knows what to do."

Maxwell points at Juliet.

"I assume that would be you?"

Juliet embraces Maxwell with a kiss.

"I could do wonders for you—with one photo."

Page **252**

She pulls Maxwell closer to her and grins slyly.

"Does Ashton Markway ring a bell?"

Maxwell watches as Juliet's fingers slide between his legs. He moans loudly and looks at her again. They kiss once more.

"Let me think about it. Modeling just isn't something I ever thought about. I'm also not a young man anymore."

Juliet pretends to slap Maxwell.

"You're thirty-four."

Maxwell pulls away from Juliet and grimaces.

"I'll let you know tomorrow. Really I will. Right now I'm just focusing on attending the premiere for my friend's movie."

Juliet looks at Maxwell's exposed penis.

"I think you owe me."

Maxwell begins laughing.

3

San Francisco

"Uh-huh—they have no clue what happened. Hobson really did a number on Lizette. He promised her he wouldn't kill her and then too late she realized he had lied. She was scared—it was funny actually—someone like her that had caused so many people to lose their lives—knowing she was gonna die by his hand freaked her out royally. When Hobson stuck her the first time—he laughed as she screamed. She begged for mercy but he kept ramming her with his knife. He toyed with her over and over as he stuck her with the knife and was aware she was losing a lot of blood. Finally he just slit her throat and it was over. He tossed her bloody corpse in a landfill and came back to my apartment and we celebrated by fucking all night long like horny teenagers."

Carlos Vente licks his lips as laughs.

"He's got so much energy."

He looks at Marlisa Vigaro and smirks.

"Who's next?"

Marlisa laughs and points.

"Vladimir Orlov."

Page **253**

Carlos reacts and gestures with his hand.

"That motherfucker has been on my radar for years now. I hope he has his affairs in order. Funerals are so depressing."

Marlisa twirls around and giggles.

"I want him grabbed on the street when he goes for his usual lunch deal. Eliminate anyone with him. Take that bastard to Golden Gate Bridge. I think it's more than fitting for him to end up in San Francisco Bay with a concrete block tied around his foot as he plunges to his death courtesy of you and dear Hobson."

Carlos watches as Marlisa twirls around again.

"It is a fitting end considering how many people met their fates exactly the same way because of that fucking bastard."

Carlos clenches his fist and grimaces.

"I myself know of one such person. Orlov personally orchestrated his death. Hugh Blandwick was his name."

Marlisa turns around as Corey Danforth comes up behind her and kisses her on the neck. She faces Carlos again.

"Before Orlov takes his final bow I expect you and Hobson will work him over pretty good. Broken bones are a must if you were wondering. Right before you throw him off the bridge feel free to stab him in the back. I mean that literally by the way."

Carlos grins broadly and gestures.

"Your wish is my command."

Marlisa seems pleased and blows Carlos a kiss.

4
Orchid Bay
Hampshire Street Cafe

"Where is she? She needs to tell me herself."

Liana Danforth seems a bit irritated as she looks at Matthew O'Rourke. He takes a step closer and points at her.

"She and I had a good thing going until you stuck your fucking nose into our business and messed everything up."

Liana is about to answer when Roland O'Brien enters the diner. Matthew clenches his fist as Roland walks toward him.

Page **254**

"I think you'd better leave. You're obviously not wanted here. Take your drama elsewhere—like back to that office you share with you equally annoying brother. I'm going to count to ten and then you and I are gonna have a really big problem."

Matthew glares at Roland.

"Police abuse is a crime if you forgot."

Roland stands several inches away from Matthew as Liana seems nervous while she watches their reactions to each other.

"I'm going to count to ten."

Matthew rolls his eyes as Roland begins counting. He notices Roland flexing his arms. He looks at Liana and then storms out of the diner. Roland looks at Liana and begins to laugh as a few customers clap. He notices Matthew outside talking on his cell phone and faces Liana again. She seems relieved.

"Apparently Julia came to her senses and kicked Matthew to the curb after she found out he was getting horizontal with Loretta Osborne. It seems Loretta likes to keep her relationships with the men in this town in the family—first she went after the Lorenzo twins and now it's those O'Rourke brothers. *Ugh*. I bet she's gonna try to score with the Derringer twins next."

Roland stifles a laugh and wags his finger.

"Albert and Anson Derringer are only sixteen."

Liana wipes sweat from her brow.

"When has that ever stopped Loretta before?"

Roland reacts and leans closer to Liana.

"If you hear anything of the sort let me know. Those boys are underage. If she goes near either of them I'll bust her."

Liana wags her finger at Roland and smirks.

"You'll be the first to know."

Roland glances at the mostly empty diner.

"Speaking of Osborne family members—I had a visit from Jayne Osborne—and her boyfriend—so-called if you must know. It was quite the show. In she walked telling me she had nothing to do with the death of Adam Mills because she was shacking up with this dude she says she's involved with. Except of course the dude she's pretending to be involved with is gay—*so* gay."

Liana seems confused and shakes her head.

"Jayne knows he's gay right?"

Roland gives Liana an odd look and sighs.

"I assume—there's no way that woman would ever waste her time with a guy that wasn't into her. This dude probably spends all his time at gay bars trying to pick up a sugar daddy."

Liana notices the front door of her diner opening.

"Oh-oh—Jayne and her "boyfriend" have decided to pay my diner a visit. Oh the joy. No doubt she'll be her rude self."

Roland turns around as Jayne Osborne and Evan Molloy walk into the diner. As he watches them he stifles a laugh.

5
Orchid Bay
Clerke Apartment

"You really think I should give Aaron another chance? He won't change. He refuses to seek help—says he's fine."

Violet Lorenzo gestures with her hand.

"He lies. Tells me everything is going well—then I find him in the garage in a funk—literally catatonic—depressed."

Patrick Clerke slowly runs his fingers through his hair and sighs as he watches Violet. She wipes a tear from her eye.

"I'm at the end of my rope with him. He's been a good husband. He's never cheated. Never lifted a hand to me but he just can't seem to face he needs help. I left him when he refused to come with me for counseling. He said he didn't need to talk to anyone. Made it clear he just needed some time to adjust."

Patrick lowers his voice.

"Do you want me to talk to him?"

Violet reacts and turns away.

"It won't do any good."

She wipes another tear from her eye and grimaces.

"I just need to face reality. My marriage is over."

Patrick reaches out to comfort Violet.

"How about I have a word with his brothers?"

Page 256

Violet faces Patrick and sighs loudly.

"Neither of them is aware of his problem. I didn't want to betray Aaron so I never told them. His parents don't know either. They think I just walked out on Aaron because he lost his job."

Patrick grabs his cell phone.

"I'm gonna call Aaron. Invite him over to talk."

Violet glances at the phone and winces.

6

San Francisco

"The hunter becomes the hunted."

Hobson Crusoe grins as he watches Vladimir Orlov come out of his mansion in Pacific Heights and get into a limo. As the car leaves the driveway a cadre of men dressed in black surrounds the limo. The driver of the limo is shot as well as every security detail present. Hobson steps out of his car and struts over to the limo as Vladimir is pulled from the back seat. Hobson laughs.

"Not a good day to be you sir."

Vladimir struggles to free himself.

"How dare you."

Hobson punches Vladimir in the jaw.

"I was thinking the same thing sir. I assure you what we have planned is gonna raise plenty eyebrows—bet on it."

He laughs loudly as Vladimir is handcuffed and forcibly pushed into the back of another limo waiting nearby. Hobson signals his team to firebomb the mansion with drones. As drones begin launching from the street Hobson gets into the back of the limo with Vladimir and punches him in the jaw several times.

"This is the end of the road dear Vladimir. You and you ilk are done—finished. I bet you never thought you'd see this day but everything must come to an end. Today is your swan song."

Vladimir curses under his breath and is punched several more times by Hobson. Hobson points at Vladimir and laughs.

"A one way trip to San Francisco Bay from the Golden Gate Bridge is coming your way—courtesy of concrete shoes."

Page **257**

Vladimir reacts as Hobson begins laughing loudly with glee as he details what he has planned. He lowers his voice.

"Oh—uh-huh—yeah—if this sounds familiar it should. If you recall you gave Hugh Blandwick the same deal. I've waited for a long time to return the favor. Payback is a bitch sir."

He punches Vladimir again.

"High Blandwick was my half-brother in case you were wondering motherfucker. When you killed him you signed your own death certificate. It's only fitting you suffer the same fate as my half-brother. You took his life and I'm going to take yours."

He makes a lewd gesture with his finger.

"Oh and by the way—I killed Lizette Richardson. I cut her up like the filthy slut she was. She screamed and screamed but to no avail—oh the joy of hearing her begging me for mercy as I stuck her again and again until I slit her motherfucking throat."

Vladimir reacts as Hobson continues laughing.

"I hope where you're going you suffer for all the people you killed. If I could have you die a thousand deaths I would enjoy killing you each and every time. But alas you only have one life and I intend to take it from you like you did Hugh. The good thing is no one will miss you when you're gone. You'll just be another piece of trash taken off the street and dumped in the bay."

Vladimir opens his mouth to speak and is hit by another punch by Hobson. Vladimir notices the Golden Gate Bridge in a distance and panics. Hobson punches him again and grins.

"In case you were wondering—your dear old dad was grabbed just prior to you being picked up. He was shot in the head and dumped in a landfill. Your wife and children were with him from what I was told—oops—they met the same fate. When we finish what we started there won't be any Orlovs or Fawcetts left in this city. No one will be spared. Cujo Momoa and his entire ilk found that out the hard way—revenge is a dish best served soaked with blood. PS—if you think Cujo's man in Hawaii was spared—think again. Gaston Bauer met his end while jogging at a popular park near Diamond Head yesterday. Seems he fell onto someone's knife. Injuries from a sharp blade are always fatal."

Page 258

Hobson watches Vladimir's reaction as he pulls out a huge knife. He revels in seeing Vladimir exhibit fear. Hobson slowly waves the knife around and passes it close to Vladimir's face.

"In case you were wondering who's behind what's been happening recently. Spoiler alert—it wasn't Todd Whitney."

Hobson notices Vladimir trying to reach into his jacket and lands another punch to his jaw. Vladimir howls with pain and is hit even harder by Hobson. Hobson grabs Vladimir by the throat.

"You don't stand a chance motherfucker. You're going to die—deal with it already. No one is coming to save you."

Hobson reaches for his cell phone.

"There's someone who wants to wish you goodbye. I think you'll recognize her. At one time you actually liked her."

As Vladimir watches, the cell phone in Hobson's hand suddenly reveals a condo in Santa Barbara and Marlisa.

"Hello Vladimir. So sorry to be talking to you like this but as you know you and Loren brought this upon yourself."

She begins laughing seeing his expression.

"Uh-huh—it was all my doing. I think you know the expression—hell hath no fury like a woman scorned. You knew I wouldn't take what Loren did to me lightly. You knew I'd get even with him sooner or later. And yeah—I intend to make Loren Fawcett pay dearly for the lies he told me—hell hath no fury."

She blows him a kiss as the phone call ends.

7
Orchid Bay
Downtown Police Station

"I brought you some muffins for lunch. Just so you know I'm expecting a huge return on my investment tonight."

Lachlan Ball leans back in his chair and laughs as Alison Orlonge gives him a kiss. She points at him threateningly.

"I'm gonna collect—count on it."

Lachlan looks at the muffins and then Alison.

"What if refuse? What if I say no? What happens?"

Page **259**

Alison slowly runs her fingers through Lachlan's hair and whispers in his ear. He reacts and pretends to be afraid.

"That's cruel—boyfriends have rights."

Alison kisses Lachlan again.

"I say differently."

They kiss again just as the front door opens. They notice a man walking towards them. He has something in his hand.

"I was told to give this to you."

He hands Lachlan a flash drive. Lachlan seems confused as he looks at the flash drive. Ellery Hopkins sighs.

"I own a store across from the apartment building where Adam Mills lived. The security company I hire to monitor my store made this available to me earlier today. Apparently they found something they think I should bring to your attention."

They look at each other for a few seconds and then Ellery leaves. Alison and Lachlan stare at the flash drive. Alison sighs.

"What do you think is on the footage?"

Lachlan shrugs and glances at his computer.

8

Los Angeles

"I won't be ignored—call Daniel immediately."

Amir Iskandar shoots Vera Holliday a knowing look and glances at the files in his hand. She takes a step forward.

"I thought I told you to call him."

Amir faces Vera.

"I'm not your employee."

Vera angrily grabs Amir by the arm.

"I don't like your tone."

Amir jerks free of Vera's grip.

"I'm not your employee. I'm your lawyer."

He gives her a harsh look.

"Is that clear?"

Vera nods. She glares at him for a few seconds as he opens his briefcase. He pulls out some paperwork and sighs.

Page 260

"Here's the file on what your half-sister wants. For starters she wants nothing to do with you—made it very clear."

Vera rolls her eyes and grimaces.

"The feeling is mutual I assure you."

They look at each other.

9
Orchid Bay
Clerke Apartment

"There's nothing wrong with me. It's just been hard since I lost my job. I feel useless—got nothing to live for anymore."

Violet reacts and faces Aaron Lorenzo.

"What about me? What about our marriage?"

Aaron faces Patrick and sighs.

"I'm a mess. I admit it."

Violet takes Aaron's hand.

"Let me help you—talk to me."

Aaron runs his fingers through his hair.

"I'm a loser. I have nothing."

Violet pulls Aaron toward her.

"You're not a loser. Losing your job at the bank isn't the end of the world Aaron. They closed the location you were at—it happens. It wasn't your fault—they lost the lease—they had to let everyone go—including you. There are other jobs and banks."

Patrick stands and walks over to Aaron.

"How about I help you? We're practically brothers-in-law anyway. I have friends at Pioneer Trail Mall. They were looking for someone to manage the mall when Claire Vanwick retires next month. I think you'd be a perfect candidate to replace her. Everyone likes you—and you're really good with children."

Patrick gestures with his hands.

"You coached the Derringer twins to a championship two years ago—without your help they wouldn't have made it."

Violet hugs Aaron warmly and gestures.

"How about you give it a try?"

Page **261**

Aaron looks at Patrick and nods several times.

"No wonder Kayla is so sweet on you."

Violet and Patrick share a glance. He stifles a smile as he picks up his cell phone. He begins dialing as Aaron watches.

10
Orchid Bay
Hampshire Street Cafe

"This is an outrage. How dare you humiliate me in public like this? I didn't know Adam Mills. He was nothing to me."

Lachlan shakes his head and looks at Sabine Norton as he slaps handcuffs on her wrists. She turns to look at several people staring at her. Liana seems shocked as Sabine yells loudly.

"I'll get you. Do you hear me?"

Lachlan glances at the onlookers nearby.

"Uh-huh—that kind of behavior will certainly help your case. Making threats at the cop arresting you says plenty about what I saw on that security tape earlier. Face it—you're busted and there's no way out and no one to blame but yourself."

Sabine glances slyly at Alison.

"Lachlan is just upset I dumped him. He wasn't much in the bedroom—didn't know anything about pleasing a woman."

Alison makes a lewd gesture with her finger.

"Lachlan would never dare touch someone as vile as you Sabine—but the bigger question is a mystery—what exactly did Adam Mills have on you that made you want to take his life?"

Sabine lunges at Alison in a fit of rage.

11
San Francisco

"Hello son."

Loren Fawcett spins around to see his father standing in the doorway of his office. Father and son stare at each other for a few seconds. Houghton Fawcett seems pleased and grins.

"I assume you didn't think you'd have to worry about your old man once I left—but as you can see I'm back in the flesh—and ready to exact payback for what you did to Ralph years ago."

Loren gestures with his hand.

"I told you I don't know what you're talking about. Ralph's death was caused by Tristan Montgomery Bell. He did it—took out your son—my brother. He did it not me. Case closed."

Houghton wrings his hands.

"Except for what that girl told me you did."

Loren takes a step toward his father.

"There is no girl."

He runs his fingers through his hair.

"You made her up—created her in your mind."

Houghton circles Loren.

"Did I? Are you sure about that?"

Loren seems confused as Houghton grins.

"She's here. Uh-huh—that's right."

Loren turns to look around the room.

"I don't see anyone."

Houghton slowly turns around to face Tiffany Johnson standing a few feet away from Loren. She stifles a laugh.

"This is it father—I'm calling Karl Trebleton."

As he grabs his cell phone a hand reaches out. He reacts in shock. Tiffany watches as the cell phone drops from Loren's hand. They stare at each other for a few seconds. Houghton seems pleased and realizes someone else is in the room with them. Jeremy Weissmann walks toward Houghton. He reacts.

12
Orchid Bay
Pointview Police Station

"What the hell happened to you?"

Grant Volker stares at Erica Gersh in shock as she closes the front door to the police station. He watches as she takes a step forward. Her appearance is noticeable. She seems afraid.

Page **263**

"You've got to help me Grant. I've got no one else."
Grant watches as she glances at the front door. Erica sighs loudly and faces Grant again. She raises her hand to her face.
"He's been raping me. He swears he'll kill me."
Grant stands and glances at his cell phone.
"I warned you about Ethan Vanwick."
Erica seems confused and shakes her head.
"Ethan Vanwick? He's a jerk but he's no rapist."
Erica touches her lips with her finger.
"It's Carter McKeon."
Grant runs his fingers through his hair.

13
Los Angeles

"I could stay here forever. The scenery is perfect."
Donna Markway faces Bradford Styverson and leans against him as they look at the ocean. He stifles a laugh.
"I can't believe we have this beach to ourselves. Where are all the people? I thought this place would be packed tight."
Donna points her finger at Bradford.
"Too far out from Malibu—no sushi joints for miles."
She pulls him toward her and hugs him warmly.
"My parents are gonna love you."
Bradford seems concerned and sighs.
"What if they think we're moving too fast? We barely know each other. They might think I'm up to something."
Donna wags her finger at Bradford.
"There isn't a sneaky bone in your body."
She pokes him in the chest.
"I think you should be worried about them asking when we're gonna tie the knot and present them with a grandchild."
Bradford looks at Donna and laughs.
"You and I haven't even slept together yet."
Donna slides her finger across Bradford's belt buckle.
"I think we should change that tonight."

Page **264**

Bradford watches as Donna's fingers fumbles with the buttons on his jeans. He sighs loudly and stifles a laugh.

"Shouldn't we get a hotel room?"

Donna looks at Bradford and seems confused.

"Why would we need a hotel room?"

Bradford runs his fingers through his hair.

"Your brother lives with you."

Donna pokes Bradford again and smirks.

"He doesn't care what we do."

Bradford nervously wipes sweat from his brow.

<h2 style="text-align:center">14
San Francisco</h2>

"What did you do to Loren?"

Houghton glances at Jeremy and then at Tiffany. As the apparition stifles a smile Houghton looks at the open door. For a few seconds Tiffany stands silently without uttering a word seemingly enjoying the trauma she just caused. She grins.

"He said you were lying—so I made a believer out of him by showing something that was happening as we speak."

Houghton seems confused.

"And what is that?"

Tiffany wags her finger at Houghton.

"You'll find out soon enough. But beware—it won't be news you'll be comforted by—the grim reaper is nearby."

Houghton notices Jeremy is just inches away from him. He begins backing away. Tiffany notices his behavior and begins laughing. She points at Houghton mocking him repeatedly.

<h2 style="text-align:center">15
Orchid Bay
Hampshire Street Cafe</h2>

"What just happened in here? Was there a fight? Did Kyle Derringer work that loser Ethan Vanwick over with his fist?"

Page 265

Liana shakes her head as she faces Colby Lorenzo.

"Sabine Norton was just arrested."

Colby stifles a laugh and faces Liana again.

"You're joking right? She's wallflower."

Liana notices Sawyer Lorenzo standing besides his twin brother. She points toward several smashed tables and chairs.

"Lachlan Ball showed up and arrested her for killing Adam Mills and she lost it. She attached his girlfriend and they went at it for a few minutes. Alison Orlonge is not one to be messed with. It was like a scene from a movie—Sabine was worked over."

Colby and Sawyer look at each other and laugh.

"Seriously, what *really* happened?"

Liana gives them both a sharp look and points at Tammy Cotler sitting nearby. Colby and Sawyer turn to face Tammy.

"Sabine Norton killed Adam Mills—not Jayne Osborne as everyone in Orchid Bay assumed? But she skipped town—she did it—she had to—Sabine and Adam? Sabine hated Adam."

Tammy nods several times.

"Apparently there was security tape showing that Adam was alive when Jayne left his pad. They were arguing at the entrance of his apartment building before Jayne left. It seemed like she was warning him—cursing him out at the same time."

Tammy glances at Liana.

"Right after Jayne left Sabine is seen on security footage going up to Adam and showing him something in her hand. He grabbed Sabine and forced her into his apartment. Less than ten minutes later she's seen leaving alone. According to the coroner Adam Mills was dead when Sabine left his apartment."

Colby runs his fingers through his hair.

"Who would have thought Sabine Norton was capable of killing anyone. She always seemed so sweet and docile."

Liana gestures with her hand.

"Something must have happened between them. Adam was a pervert—taped all his sexual escapades according to my brother. He would brag about it whenever Corey would see him at Andy's Bar. It just seemed so fantastical—I guess it wasn't."

Sawyer makes a lewd gesture with his finger.

"I'm glad Sabine killed him actually. Adam Mills was a creep and everyone knew it. He and I got into it after I caught him having sex with my girlfriend on the night of the junior prom."

He clenches his fist.

"I beat him good—broke his nose."

Liana glances at Tammy.

"I guess Sabine did everyone a favor."

Colby and Sawyer share a smile as Liana looks at the broken furniture lying everywhere a few feet away and sighs.

16

Los Angeles

"Your brother just called—said he'll be late."

Gina Bentley turns around to face Pierce Colby and seems nervous. She looks at herself in the mirror. Pierce sighs.

"Said he had a problem with his tuxedo—said it didn't fit right. Was gonna look for another one in Beverly Hills."

Gina knowingly stifles a smile.

"He just wants to go to Beverly Hills. Walk down Rodeo Drive like he's a big star. I spoke to Alden Washington earlier. He said Eddie was impossible—wanted to see Hollywood too."

Pierce comes toward Gina. He grins.

"Who knew Eddie could be so dramatic?"

They share a laugh.

17

San Francisco

"What the hell happened to you?"

Anton Levitov closes the front door to his condo and turns to face Loren. Loren seems frightened as his eyes keep darting back and forth as if expecting someone to suddenly appear.

"What's going on? You look like you just saw a ghost."

Loren spins around and grabs Anton by his collar.

Page **267**

"She's real. That fucking girl is real."

Anton pushes Loren away from him and sighs.

"What are you talking about?"

Loren turns to look at the front door.

"I saw her. I saw Vladimir."

Anton runs his fingers through his hair.

"Vladimir?"

Loren looks at his arm and shudders.

"That *thing* touched me. I saw things—horrible things. It was like one of those movies that aired on late night cable back when we were kids. My father just stood there and watched."

Anton grabs Loren and shakes him.

"What the fuck are you talking about? Not one word of what you said makes sense Loren. What girl? What things? Is your father back in town? I thought he skipped after you threatened to put him in one of those padded hospitals for crazy people."

Loren looks at his arm again.

"Have you heard from Vladimir?"

Anton shakes his head.

"I talked with him this morning."

Loren looks at his arm yet again and grimaces.

"He's dead."

Anton reacts.

"What?"

Loren wrings his hands.

"I saw it happen. I saw him die. When that vile thing touched me I saw Vladimir. His feet were chained to concrete blocks as these two men laughed at him. They were on the bluffs near the Golden Gate Bridge. Vladimir was scared. I could see it in his eyes as they forced him toward the bridge. It was horrible."

Anton grabs Loren again.

"What men? Who were they?"

Loren shakes his head several times.

"I don't know—they were not our people. Mercenary types I assume. That vile creature forced me to watch as they brought Vladimir to the bridge. They threw him over and laughed."

Page **268**

Anton seems about to explode as he watches Loren while he continues to recount what happened. Loren sighs loudly and looks around the room again. Anton notices and gestures.

18
Orchid Bay
Pointview Police Station

"Erica Gersh is a liar. She's nothing but a two-bit whore and everyone knows it. She and I had moments together. Is it my fault she likes it rough. I threw her out of my condo earlier and told her never to come back—said she was lousy in bed."

Grant glances at Marilyn Waaysend as he watches Carter McKeon make a lewd gesture with his finger. He laughs loudly.

"I demand you call that fucking slut and make her take back her words. I'll destroy her—destroy you if need be."

Carter shoots Marilyn a cautious look.

"I'll get you too—count on it. I have lots of friends in high places. I'm rich—really rich. No one fucks with me—no one."

Grant leans back in his chair.

"Care to say that on tape Carter?"

Carter begins laughing hysterically.

19
Boston

"Uh-huh—the final nail in their coffin is almost ready for the Fawcett clan. Within a couple of hours their entire estate will be yours. You'll own everything—every stock—every real estate holding—every penny. You'll own Fawcett Enterprises."

Jeremy Winterfield stares at Trevor Boleyn on his phone and seems pleased. He notices the Golden Gate Bridge in the background as Trevor clenches his fist. He seems upset.

"Have you located Houghton Fawcett yet? Word on the street is that he skipped town. Had a falling out with his son—no one seems to know where he absconded to. I want him found."

Page **269**

Jeremy grins slyly and holds up a photo.

"This was sent to me earlier. Houghton Fawcett had a confrontation with his son earlier. From what I was told it was certainly dramatic—like an episode of *The Colbys*. Loren tore out of his office after being confronted—described as suicidal."

Trevor stifles a smile and snaps his fingers.

"Suicide has a nice ring to it—fitting end to someone with no morals. It would certainly be welcomed by yours truly."

Jeremy points at Trevor and laughs.

20
San Francisco

"Oh how sad—he looks so scared. Poor thing—poor little Vladimir reduced to half the man he once was just before he took a header off the Golden Gate Bridge. Love how you stuck a butcher knife in his back right before you pushed him to his death. His screams were pitiful to hear—you would have thought he would have cursed you or something—not beg for mercy like a whiny schoolgirl. The moment dear Vladimir hit the water was so reality TV. That wretched bastard knew he was gonna die and then he was gone—gone to the bottom of San Francisco Bay."

Marlisa begins laughing as she pops open a bottle of champagne and faces Hobson. She hands him a glass and turns to look at the video on the monitor again. She seems pleased.

"That disgusting creep was always trying to score with me. He was a pig. He deserved to die the way he did. Good on you to remember what he did to your half-brother. Nothing more fitting than getting the same sendoff he gave poor Hugh."

Marlisa glances at her watch. She seems nervous as she faces Hobson again. He notices and stands. He gestures.

"Carlos should be here soon. He had to wrap up the last part of what took place today—take out Vladimir's little brother at his church. Make sure the entire Orlov clan is no more."

Marlisa giggles and takes another sip of champagne.

"I heard Loren had an incident at his office."

Hobson seems confused and sighs loudly.

"What are you talking about?"

Marlisa turns to look at her glass of champagne again.

"I heard from my sources that Loren tore out of his office in a panic. He was seen running down the hallway as if he'd seen a ghost—took the stairs and not the elevator. I was told he was rambling incoherently—talking about a girl or something."

Hobson shakes his head.

"I have no idea."

Outside they hear sirens and realize that the area around the Golden Gate Bridge seem to be abuzz with police activity.

"I guess they found Vladimir."

They begin laughing.

21

Los Angeles

Crowds gather in Westwood while search lights beam back and forth as limousines begin showing up. Sandra King and Scott Malone are seen at the entrance talking to **Jonathan Vigliotti** of CBS—who is decked out in a black suit and blue tie. Nearby Wesley Madison is speaking to **Tom Llamas** of NBC about his film based on Sandra's book. Crowds begin screaming when several well-known celebrities make their appearances. Seen walking toward the entrance are Diana Munroe and Silas Bell. His eyes dart back and forth as if looking for someone specific in the crowd. Diana waves to the crowd and smiles.

22

Boston

"Are you busy? I have someone I want you to meet."

Jeremy slowly looks up from the paperwork on his desk as his daughter steps aside and smiles. Andrea Winterfield seems pleased as Kelvin Penney takes a step forward. Jeremy reacts.

"What the fuck? Is this a joke?"

Page **271**

Andrea seems upset and faces Kelvin.

"Meet Kelvin Penney."

Jeremy clenches his fist.

"I know who he is. Do you?"

Andrea seems confused and sighs.

"What are you talking about?"

Jeremy seems about to explode as he glares at Kelvin. He stands up and faces his daughter again. She seems annoyed.

"Kelvin and I met at Boston University in a political science class. We hit it off right away. He's from Marble Hills."

Jeremy clenches his fist again.

"Castle Beach—he's from Castle Beach."

Andrea stares from at her father.

"Yeah—so what—he was born there but grew up in Marble Hills. He knows one of my closest friends—Marla Sherwood."

Jeremy runs his fingers through his hair.

"Kelvin is the son of Carson Penney. Does that name ring a bell for you Andrea? I destroyed his father—ruined him."

Kelvin takes a step forward.

"I know what you did sir. But I hold no grudges. My father was hardly ever there for me if truth be known. He was focused on Chandler for my entire life—ignored my sister and me—and we all know where that led to. I'm aware what Chandler did to Orville Pendergraft and to Ivy Patterson before he passed."

He watches Jeremy's reaction.

"I probably would have done exactly the same thing you did if I were in your shoes sir. Losing everything was actually a blessing for me—I spent the last several years having a normal life and focusing on being a good person. I'm not perfect but I'm nothing like my brother. Both my sister and I have had a pretty good life in Marble Hills. There I said it—I'm not ashamed."

Jeremy appears speechless.

"Seriously daddy do you think I'd go out with a guy that was a vapid loser with no character—it's just not my style. Every guy I have dated had to measure up to you. You are the best father I could ever ask for—tough and sensitive—but fair."

Jeremy seems taken aback by Andrea's comment and sighs loudly. He runs his fingers through his hair again.

"I never thought you paid any attention to what I was all about. I just assumed you thought I was boring and stuck up."

Andrea begins laughing and walks over to where her father is standing. She hugs him warmly and then kisses him.

"You're definitely not boring."

Jeremy looks at Andrea curiously.

"What about stuck up?"

Andrea points at her father.

"Don't push it."

They hug again.

"I'm just concerned."

Andrea jabs her father and laughs.

"I know you are—but you didn't raise me to be afraid. I know what I'm doing. Kelvin is the one for me. Deal already."

Jeremy nervously turns to look at Kelvin.

23
San Francisco

"You won't get away with this. My brother will come after you. He's not gonna rest until you're a stiff in the morgue."

Carlos starts laughing loudly.

"Obviously you don't pay attention to the news bud. I took out your brother less than two hours ago. He's dead."

Victor Orlov reacts. He sighs loudly.

"You're lying."

Carlos laughs again as he looks at Victor. Victor is hogtied and lying on the floor. Victor kneels next to Victor and shows him video footage of Vladimir being thrown from the Golden Gate Bridge. He begins laughing loudly seeing Victor's reaction.

"Oh don't you worry precious Victor—you're going to be seeing your dear departed brother soon enough—I assure you."

Carlos points at Victor and laughs again.

"It's been my pleasure taking your people out."

He stands and kicks Victor in the face.

"Your family has been a scourge on this city for too long. I have enjoyed taking them out one by one. In case you haven't figured it out I'm a vigilante. I enjoy my work—I *so* enjoy sending scumbags like you to the morgue. Your brother got what he deserved. He killed a friend of mine by throwing him off the Golden Gate Bridge. It was only fitting he received the same in return. Of course my boyfriend added his own touch by sticking a butcher knife in your brother's back before he sent him over the edge. Your brother begged for mercy—it was so pathetic to listen to a grown man begging for his life like a sissy. But my boyfriend was having none of it. Justice was gonna be done regardless."

He kicks Victor in the face again.

"You actually thought by becoming a priest you would avoid the same fate as the rest of your family? Like seriously? What kind of priest ignores what his family has done? Do you think you wouldn't be judged as a fake by the almighty? Changing your name won't help. He won't be fooled when you come before him shortly. By this time tomorrow the police will be combing your room looking for clues—wondering how someone got into the church and took you out. But don't you worry your pretty little head about this quandary. I'm a pro at my job. Idiot cops in this city will never know I was involved. I'm like a ghost—I'm here and then I'm not. You however will still be dead. Sorry dude."

He laughs and kneels down to grab Victor's hair. He yanks his head back in a rage and shoves his gun into Victor's mouth laughing gleefully as he sees Victor's reaction realizing his fate.

"Living is easy—dying is a bitch."

Seconds later Carlos pulls the trigger.

24
Los Angeles

"It's odd that I haven't heard from Heath Griffith—oh sorry I mean Silas Bell. Not one call or text from him. Does he know?"

Bradford puts his arms around Donna and sighs.

Page **274**

"He's no fool by any means. He probably saw us together and changed his plans. I assume he had his reasons for dating you—none of which had to do with being in a relationship."

Donna smiles and strokes Bradford's chest.

"Maybe he saw your muscles."

Bradford laughs.

25
Orchid Bay
Pioneer Trail Mall

"I heard what happened at my sister's cafe earlier with Matthew O'Rourke. That guy just doesn't know when to take a hint and get lost. He slept with Loretta Osborne and then tried to lie about it. Rumor has it she aborted his child. He demanded she get rid of it or he would destroy her. That guy is just pitiful."

Roland looks at Julia Danforth and nods.

"His brother is no peach either."

They share and laugh. Julia faces Roland.

"Where does the case against Vina Phamler stand?"

"She's going to trial. Patrick Clerke isn't backing down. Neither is Kayla Larsen. She wants Vina behind bars for the next couple of decades. There's no love lost between those two."

Julia stifles a smile and nods in agreement.

26
Los Angeles

Massive crowds continue to surround a movie theater in Westwood as Gina Bentley and Pierce Colby arrive amid flashes of cameras. Right behind them Victoria de Hoya and Laura Wiley are seen talking to reporters. News trucks are everywhere.

TO BE CONTINUED

Page 275

A Brief Look at the Eleventh Episode

The lives of several people begin to unravel upon the realization of reality where the tables are turned on more than one person while a deranged man stalks his brother at a movie premiere.

Episode 11
End Games

1
Los Angeles

"Oh look, there's **Kevin Bacon** and **Kyra Sedgwick**."

Gina Bentley looks toward where Pierce Colby is pointing as they see photographers descend upon them. She sighs.

"Wait, is that **Prince Harry** and **Meghan Markle** chatting with Kevin and Kyra? I didn't know they knew each other?"

Pierce jabs Gina and grins.

"Are you gonna ask for an autograph?"

Andrew Perez from ABC Miami begins talking to Prince Harry as they watch several correspondents from local talk shows aggressively push through the throngs of people waiting.

2
Orchid Bay
Downtown Police Station

"Is Sabine Norton changing her tune or is she still insisting she had nothing to do with what happened to Adam Mills?"

Page **277**

Roland O'Brien leans back in his chair and smirks.

"She made threats—warned me I would pay."

Roland gestures at Lachlan Ball and grins.

"She said it in front of her lawyer."

Lachlan seems amused.

"Which one of the O'Rourke brothers took her case? I'm leaning toward Matthew. That man has no shame whatsoever."

Roland points at Lachlan and laughs.

"He warned me that I'd regret arresting his client. Said she was not guilty—tried to make her look like a virginal innocent."

Lachlan makes a lewd gesture with his finger.

"Did they find the sex tapes Ethan Vanwick said Adam Mills had in his possession? Vanwick said there were hundreds."

Roland rolls his eyes and sighs loudly.

"What Vanwick says and what is true is not exactly the same thing. That man is no stranger to telling tall tales."

Lachlan nods and sits down.

"I heard that Jayne Osborne and her "boyfriend" called it quits about an hour ago—something about them not having much in common—except that they both liked guys of course."

Roland roars with laughter and waves his hand in the air mimicking Evan Molloy. Lachlan blows Roland a kiss.

"I assume that the cowboy boyfriend is headed back to Arizona to play house with his latest. Poor Jayne—rejected."

They both laugh. Lachlan looks at his cell phone.

"I got a call earlier. Some dude I've never heard of before. He said he has info I might want—said it won't be free."

Roland stands and glances at the door.

"We don't pay for info."

Lachlan leans back in his chair.

"He's in jail—busted for selling drugs to high profile clients in Half Moon Bay. Said the info he had was about the death of Jason Shappe—made it clear Shappe's death was murder."

Roland turns around to face Lachlan.

"How much is he asking for?"

Lachlan glances at his watch and shrugs.

3
Orchid Bay
Vacant Plot of Land

"Why are we stopping here Kevin? You said you had a surprise for me. I assumed you have been house shopping."

Kevin Alsten faces Lauren Corrington.

"I own this lot—bought it earlier."

Lauren looks at the empty lot and grimaces.

"Are you serious? Why would you waste money on this old parking lot? It's been an eyesore for over a decade now."

Kevin jumps out of his car.

"I know—isn't it great? This time next year there will be a homeless shelter with 1000 rooms. I made a deal with Lacey Vanwick—convinced her to give me the land really cheap."

Lauren seems confused.

"I didn't know you and that strange old woman knew each other. It's a known fact she hardly speaks to anyone in town."

"When she found out what I wanted to do she agreed without hesitation. I think she just wants to be remembered for something other than being a rich widow with no friends."

Lauren grabs Kevin by the arm.

"What about us? I thought you were going to ask me to marry you—settle down and start a family—live the dream."

Kevin turns to face Lauren.

"I'm sorry. But this is important to me. I want to make a difference in people's lives. Can't we do both? Have a family and create a future for the less fortunate up and down the coast."

Lauren notices how happy Kevin seems.

4
Los Angeles

"Where is my annoying brother? I thought he'd be here by now? He said he wanted me to meet his new girlfriend."

Justine Ross turns to face David Sherwood who points at her brother several yards away in the massive crowds in front of a movie theater in Westwood. Parker Ross waves to his sister and David as he and Jenna deWilde come toward them. David and Jenna seem nervous and Parker realizes at that moment they already know each other. He seems upset. Justine notices.

<h2 style="text-align:center">5
Orchid Bay
Pointview Police Station</h2>

Carter McKeon walks toward his car in a nearby parking lot. A single shot rings out. He falls against his car as he sees a woman coming toward him. As he gasps for air he watches as she points her gun at him. A second shot rings out as blood sprays from his chest. He slides to the pavement. Erica Gersh grins.

<h2 style="text-align:center">6
Orchid Bay
Clerke Apartment</h2>

"Where you do think you're going?"
Patrick Clerke turns around and faces Kayla Larsen. She seems annoyed as she walks toward him. He grins slyly.
"I'm going for a walk around the block."
Kayla suddenly grabs Patrick by the arm.
"You're not going anywhere."
Patrick seems confused.
"You can't stop me from taking a walk."
Kayla tightens her grip on his arm.
"Is that so?"
Patrick glances at the door.
"I have rights."
Kayla slides her arm around Patrick's waist.
"I say differently."
They look at each other.

Page 280

"I just want a breath of fresh air."

Kayla pulls Patrick toward her. She kisses him several times. She runs her fingers through his hair and sighs loudly.

"You're not going anywhere until your doctor says you're completely recovered. That's just the way things are."

Patrick rolls his eyes.

"I feel fine. No issued whatsoever."

Kayla whispers in Patrick's ear.

"You're going to follow orders."

Patrick faces Kayla seemingly upset.

"What if I say no?"

Kayla shoots him a cautious look.

7

Los Angeles

"How nice to meet you again—how have you been?"

Armand Bell faces Victoria de Hoya in the lobby of a movie theater in Westwood. They share a nervous glance.

"I feel like a mouse in a maze."

Victoria reaches out to hug Armand.

"I know how you feel."

Armand nervously looks at the crowd as if he's looking for someone he knows. Victoria notices and leans closer to him.

"There's plenty security—your deranged brother wouldn't dare show his face here. No one can seriously be that stupid."

Armand nods but continues looking around.

8

San Francisco

"Have your people made their move on Loren Fawcett's wife and children yet? I want them eliminated within the hour."

Carlos Vente swallows the drink in his hand and faces Marlisa Vigaro. He notices Hobson Crusoe stroking his gun.

"They have about ten minutes left."

Page **281**

Hobson laughs and looks at the gun again.

"Fawcett's wife and two children are set to meet their maker the minute they exit the garage. A drone is waiting in some trees at the estate next door. One shot and it's over for the wife and brats. There won't be anything to find when the coroner pays a visit. Nothing but charred body parts and burnt toys."

Hobson begins laughing loudly.

"I'm so going to enjoy watching our handiwork over and over as I relax with a glass of Scotch in front of a monitor."

Marlisa seems pleased and twirls around several times.

"Igor Levitov and his brother are next."

She points at Carlos.

"I want them to suffer."

Carlos turns to face Hobson and stands.

"My man and I will do you proud I assure you. It seems that both brothers have quite a history of raping women."

Hobson looks at the outline of his penis straining against the fabric of his faded jeans. He licks his lips several times.

"It's only fair we return the favor."

Marlisa makes a lewd gesture with her finger.

9
Orchid Bay
Studio Apartment

"Have you heard from Erica recently?"

Ryan Pena laughs as he grabs his jeans and looks at Denise Stone lying naked on his bed. He stifles a laugh.

"I think she's got her hands full with Carter McKeon from what I heard Ethan Vanwick say yesterday. Vanwick says she threw him over for McKeon. Said Erica told him to get lost."

Denise grabs her bra nearby and grimaces.

"McKeon is certifiable."

Ryan laughs and pulls on his jeans.

"He makes me look like a frigging priest."

Denise licks her lips knowingly.

Page **282**

"You're definitely not priest material—racked up too many sexual encounters in the last two weeks with yours truly."

Ryan laughs and points at Denise.

"You corrupted me."

Denise slowly slides her fingers between her legs as Ryan notices. He looks at his erection and begins laughing.

"I was just an innocent bystander."

Denise gestures with her fingers again as the doorbell rings. Ryan seems confused and walks to the door. He opens it.

"Erica—what are you doing here?"

He watches as Erica's eyes fall to his erection and then the gun in her hands. Ryan takes a step backwards. Erica smirks.

"We belong together. You and that whore are through. I demand you throw her out on the street. She's nothing."

Ryan looks back at Denise still lying in bed and then at Erica. He backs away as he realizes the gun is pointed at him.

"I thought I told you we're over."

Erica takes another step.

"I want her gone—do you hear me? I want that bitch out on the street. You and I are going to be married tomorrow."

"What are you talking about?"

Erica notices Denise getting out of bed.

"She's trash. She was in jail. *Ugh*."

She raises the gun and laughs.

"As long as she's alive you and I won't ever be able to be happy. She has to die—don't you see? I have to end her."

Ryan steps in front of Erica. She notices.

"Get out of my way Ryan."

Ryan suddenly reaches for the gun.

10
Orchid Bay
Pointview Police Station

"It must have happened right after he and I spoke. Are the cameras working today? I think we already know the culprit."

Page **283**

Marilyn Waaysend faces Grant Volker and nods.

"Where do you think Erica Gersh is at the moment? Do you think we should let Ryan Pena know? She's been carrying a torch for him for weeks—fantasizing they're still a couple."

Grant nods and reaches for his cell phone.

11
Los Angeles

"I had to come—baby or no baby."

Larisa Lopez hugs Sandra King as Ward Brady shakes hands with Scott Malone. Sandra looks at Larisa who is clearly in her last months of pregnancy. Sandra gives Ward a knowing look and smirks. He proudly makes a lewd gesture with his finger.

"We've been busy no doubt—just can't keep my hands off my beautiful wife. Baby number three is already on my mind."

Larisa jabs Ward and faces Sandra.

12
Orchid Bay
Downtown Police Station

"OK—I'm on my way. I'm about ten minutes away."

Lachlan faces Roland. He grimaces.

"Carter McKeon is dead. Grant Volker thinks Erica Gersh is responsible. He thinks she went to pay Ryan Pena a visit."

Roland runs his fingers through his hair.

"Does Ryan know?"

Lachlan shakes his head.

"Volker hasn't been able to reach Pena. Denise Stone isn't answering her phone either. Pena's landlord has been notified."

They share a look. Lachlan turns to leave.

"What about the drug dealer? Are you still planning to pay him a visit tomorrow in Half Moon Bay? Hear him out?"

Roland runs his fingers through his hair again and sighs.

"I'm still deciding. I'll let you know later today."

Lachlan nods and looks at his cell phone.

"Volker is already at Pena's studio apartment near Bay Street. He says Erica's car is parked down the street a bit."

Roland sighs loudly and watches Lachlan leave.

13
San Francisco

Police are everywhere looking at a burned out area of what once was a mansion. Flames leap from the charred ruins as more police cars arrive with two coroner vans and a K9 unit.

14
Los Angeles

"I didn't bring you with me so you could stare at some lousy skank. Seriously, like how rude can you be Heath?"

Diana Munroe seems upset as Silas Bell continues staring at Donna Markway and Bradford Styverson standing about thirty feet away talking to Gina and Pierce. Diana jabs Silas several times as he continues to stare. She glances at Donna.

"Is she your ex? Did she dump you?"

Silas faces Diana.

"Shut your fucking mouth."

Diana reacts.

"How dare you talk to me like that?"

Silas grabs her arm and pushes her into a corner.

"You women are all the same."

Diana jerks her arm free of his grip.

"I want you to leave."

Silas grabs her arm again and forces her toward a private bathroom a few feet away. Several people notice but turn away when flashbulbs begin flashing as they see Wesley Madison and Alden Washington talking to several reporters. Nearby Eddie Kane is seen talking with Simon Spencer. Donna comes over and gives Simon a hug and then introduces Bradford to everyone.

Page **285**

15
Orchid Bay
Studio Apartment

"I heard a shot and—I found them like this. The girl saw me and turned the gun on herself. I couldn't stop her."

Lars Eisenmann wipes sweat from his brow and faces Grant as he notices Lachlan briskly walking toward them.

"It all happened so fast."

Grant takes a step forward and sees Ryan lying on the floor with a bullet hole in his chest. His jeans are unzipped and bloody. He sees Denise lying in bed—a bullet hole clearly visible near her exposed breasts. Erica is lying several feet away as blood pours from her mouth. Grant turns away and faces Lachlan.

16

San Francisco

"I'm so sorry. There was nothing I could do. A drone just came out of nowhere—the place blew up within seconds."

Igor Levitov glances at Loren Fawcett.

"I'll call Anton."

Loren nods as Igor leaves his office. Loren seems in shock as he stares blankly at the monitor. He hears laughter.

"What the fuck?"

He turns around and reacts as he sees Tiffany Johnson standing with her hands on her hips. She takes a step forward and points at him. Tiffany watches his reaction to seeing her again.

"*You* did this—*you* killed them—*you* caused your family to lose their lives. You and your father both—birds of a feather."

She takes another step forward and stops.

"Nothing comes without a price—no matter how much you think you've got everything figured out—reality never goes as planned—starting with how you murdered your brother."

Loren reacts to the comment. Tiffany laughs.

"Did you think you'd get away with what you did? Did you really think no one would find out what you did to Ralph?"

Loren looks at his desk. She notices.

"I don't have a frigging clue what you're babbling about. My brother died in a blizzard. He was stupid and got careless."

Tiffany points at Loren.

"How about we ask Ralph?"

As Loren watches in shock Ralph Fawcett appears next to Tiffany. Loren takes a step backwards. Tiffany gestures.

"How about I ask Ralph what happened the day he died in his cabin as a blizzard blanketed the mountain with snow."

Loren seems unable to move as the apparition of his brother comes closer to where he's standing. He sighs loudly.

"OK—OK—*I did it*. I killed my brother."

Tiffany mockingly begins clapping as Ralph grabs Loren's arm and spins him around. His face contorts with anger.

"I pity you brother—pity your fate."

Seconds later he is gone. Loren faces Tiffany.

"I'm on to you—this is some sort of blackmail scheme. But it won't work. Not one red cent—do you hear me—*bitch*."

Tiffany grabs Loren's arm and laughs.

"I'm *so* going to enjoy what I have planned for you."

She watches his reaction as her grip tightens.

"This day isn't over yet by any means *dear* Loren. Your misery is just beginning. How about we get started—shall we?"

He jerks free of her grip and runs to the door. She snaps her fingers and watches as the door seemingly vanishes.

"Like I said your misery is just beginning."

Loren watches as the room is shrouded in mist.

<h3 style="text-align:center">17
Los Angeles</h3>

"I was done with you anyway."

Silas looks at Diana lying on the floor in one of the stalls of a private bathroom and shrugs. He faces the door and smiles.

Page 287

"She made me kill her. Goddamn bitch just wouldn't shut her motherfucking mouth. Kept yammering and yammering like a banshee. Enough was enough—something had to give."

He looks at himself in the mirror.

"I think it's time I pay my little brother a farewell visit."

He stifles a smirk and leaves seconds later.

18
Orchid Bay
Hampshire Street Cafe

"I would never have thought she of all people would resort to something like this. She killed three people. Gossips are gonna have a field day with this story no doubt. I can just see the headlines in the local paper tomorrow—*ugh*—no thanks."

Alison Orlonge faces Lachlan.

"Did she leave a note?"

Lachlan shakes his head and sighs.

"I think she just snapped when Carter McKeon pulled the rug out from under her. She told Grant Volker he raped her."

A second later Alison notices Tabitha Bairstow and Kyle Derringer entering the diner. She turns to face Lachlan again.

"Janet Virella said Erica dated Kyle for a while. Said he cut her loose after a month—claimed she wouldn't leave him alone for weeks afterwards. I heard he was scared of her moods—heard she threatened him with a gun—told him she'd silence him."

Lachlan seems about to laugh.

"Janet lies. Kyle went out with Erica once. Said it was just a one night stand deal. Said she told him he was lame."

Alison glances at Kyle and Tabitha.

"They seem happy."

Lachlan reaches out to take Alison's hand.

"She's pregnant."

Alison reacts. Lachlan winks.

"I think it's time you and I get busy too and make a baby together. Take a romantic trip up the coast—no cell phones."

Alison leans over to kiss Lachlan several times.

"What about those women you say you've been having sex with behind my back—will you kick them all to the curb?"

Lachlan stifles a laugh.

"I was thinking of marrying one of them actually."

Alison kisses Lachlan again and laughs.

"It would be quite a show if you *did* have a throng of women whom you've been having sex with on a regular basis."

Lachlan pulls Alison towards him.

"I'm a one woman sort of guy."

He grins slyly and gently strokes her face.

"I like what we have together."

Alison seems pleased and kisses Lachlan.

19
Orchid Bay
Greasy Spoon Diner

"I just want to apologize. I was wrong."

Jayne Osborne looks up from the burger she's eating to see Ethan Vanwick standing before her. Jayne sighs loudly.

"I appreciate it. Thank you."

Ethan digs his hands into the front pockets of his jeans.

"I should've known Sabine Norton was capable of killing Adam when he told me he had been filming their trysts."

They stare at each other for a few seconds.

"He filmed all his sexual encounters."

Jayne seems disgusted and gestures at Ethan.

"How about we talk?"

Ethan nods and sits down.

20
Los Angeles

"This is great. I can't wait to meet the actor who played me in the movie. Thank you for inviting me to the screening."

Page **289**

Sandra leans over to hug John Smythe as people snap photos wildly. Boris Birney stands several feet away.

"If it hadn't been for you I wouldn't be here. No one else had a clue what was happening to us on that island."

They hug again. John faces Scott and shakes his hand.

"I second what my wife said. You rock."

John seems pleased as more photos are snapped from people standing behind crowd barriers. Several feet away they notice Maxwell Pendergraft coming toward them. Scott grins broadly as they shake hands and hug. Sandra hugs Maxwell warmly as photographs continue to be snapped by eager fans.

21

San Francisco

"Wake up motherfucker—the party is about to begin and I wouldn't want you to miss what me and my boyfriend have planned for you. Its going be quite the show I assure you."

Igor realizes he's naked and tied to a cot in what appears to be a cellar. He tries to turn around but is unable to. Hobson walks toward him and grins. He reaches out and grabs Igor by the hair and jerks his head backwards. He punches him in the jaw with his free hand. He begins laughing and punches Igor again.

"You and I are gonna have a party. You should know I like it rough—really rough. I plan to work you over plenty before I put a bullet in your head. Turnaround is fair play buddy. We both know how much you like raping women—how you enjoy inflicting pain in your helpless victims before you kill them. Well, guess what motherfucker. I plan to give you what you gave them."

Igor tries to push against the ropes tying him to the filthy cot but is unable. Hobson angrily lands a kick to Igor's face.

"You're not going anywhere."

He begins laughing as he leans close to Igor.

"When they find your bloated corpse they'll know you were played hard before you bought it. I intend to work you."

Igor curses under his breath. Hobson notices.

Page **290**

"My brother is going to get you good. He's a fucking freak. He'll find you no matter where you hide. You're dead—*do you hear me*—dead. It's over. There won't be a place you can hide on this fucking planet. You'll regret messing with our family."

Hobson begins laughing loudly.

"Do I look like a fool motherfucker? My people are looking for your brother. He's gonna get what you're getting when we find his sorry ass. No one is getting out alive. Not you and not your miserable wretch of a brother. Say your prayers loser."

Igor watches as Hobson comes toward him again. He realizes at that moment that Hobson is naked. He reacts as he watches the younger man climb on top of him. He grimaces as he realizes Hobson's erect penis is brushing against his thighs.

22
Orchid Bay
Pioneer Trail Mall

"I was thinking—asking actually."

Roland turns to face Julia Danforth while several people walk by them as he slowly takes her hand. He seems nervous.

"I was thinking maybe you and I should go away for the weekend. See if we can make it work without everyone in town watching us like a hawk. See if you like me enough to date me."

He notices her reaction and sighs.

"Separate rooms of course—I'll be the perfect gentlemen without a doubt. You have my word. I won't try anything."

Julia stifles a laugh and gestures.

"I have no doubt you'll be a boy scout the entire time. I just wasn't expecting you to take such a bold move. You've made it clear we were just friends for so long. I just thought."

Roland wipes sweat from his brow.

"It's Lachlan. He made me see the light. Said I needed to stop being so focused on what happened with Marianne. Said for me to give it a shot with you—see if you could stand me."

Julia reaches out to touch Roland's hand.

"You've got no flaws Roland. There is nothing wrong with you whatsoever. I would be incredibly honored to date you."

Roland seems pleased and stands.

"I hear Ocean Landing is nice this time of year."

Julia nods and stands. She takes his hand.

"I'm so honored you've made this decision about us. I promise I will never disrespect you the way Marianne did."

Roland pulls Julia toward him and hugs her.

"I'm not worried."

They look at each other as Roland's cell phone begins buzzing. Julia watches as he reaches into the front pocket of his jeans and seems worried as he stares at the phone. He sighs.

23
Orchid Bay
Greasy Spoon Diner

"I'm glad we had this talk."

Ethan looks at Jayne and stands. He faces her again as he nervously shoves his hands into the front pockets of his jeans.

"I also want to apologize for how I treated you in high school. I forced myself on you even though you said you didn't want to have sex. I took your virginity and then made you have sex with all my friends. I was a Class A jerk—I admit it. Sorry."

Ethan notices Jayne's reaction.

"I hope one day you can accept my apology."

Jayne stands and faces Ethan.

"It takes a real man to admit his faults. I accept your apology. It was a long time ago—you're a different person now. I can see that you mean what you say. It's in the past as far as I'm concerned. You and I have a long history together—sexual and otherwise. But one thing I can say is that you never hit me. You were always gentle when we got together—showed respect."

Ethan runs his fingers through his hair.

"I don't like violence—never have. It's just not my style. I have two sisters. I saw what they experienced—learned."

Page **292**

Jayne hugs Ethan again and kisses him lightly.

"Would you like to come over later? Have dinner and talk? I would understand if you say no—so much has happened."

Ethan seems confused.

"What about your cowboy?"

Jayne stifles a laugh.

"That wasn't real. It was just for show."

Ethan gestures with his hand and smirks slyly.

"You knew he was gay right?"

Jayne laughs.

"Uh-huh."

They share a laugh.

"Should I bring a bottle of wine with me?"

Jayne nods and reaches out to hug Ethan again.

"I think you should know I can't cook."

Ethan wags his finger at Jayne.

24
Los Angeles

"These guys lived the life no doubt."

Armand silently stands in a room off the lobby of the main theater where hundreds of photographs with Hollywood royalty adorn the walls—photographs of such screen legends as **Mary Astor, Lauren Bacall, Ingrid Bergman, Humphrey Bogart, James Cagney, Charlie Chaplin, Gary Cooper, Bette Davis, Errol Flynn, Lillian Gish, D. W. Griffith, Jean Harlow, Robert Harron, Grace Kelly, Vivien Leigh, Jayne Mansfield, Marilyn Monroe, Gregory Peck, Mary Pickford, Wallace Reid, Gloria Swanson, Elizabeth Taylor, Shirley Temple, Olive Thomas, Lana Turner, Rudolph Valentino** and **Natalie Wood** among many others who made the film industry during its golden era. Armand notices a memorial to **Loni Anderson** a few feet away mentioning her recent passing and her contribution to the entertainment industry as footsteps are heard. As he turns he realizes Silas is standing behind him. He hears laughter and reacts in shock.

Page **293**

"It's the end of the road brother dearest."

Silas holds a gun against Armand's back and grins.

"I've waited so long for this moment. That afternoon in Tasmania the day of your birthday should've been your swan song if it hadn't been for your bitch of a mother. Damn her."

He laughs as he looks at the gun.

"This will make headlines no doubt."

He watches as Armand glances at the door.

"It's locked. No one knows we're here."

"You won't get away with this. They'll catch you."

"Maybe—maybe not—but you'll be dead nevertheless. Of course that leaves your son. He's next. Once I turn your lights off I'm gonna pay that precious little boy a visit. One shot—just one shot and he's done for. With him gone our father's entire fortune is mine. Mine alone. Just like it was intended to be before you came along and fucked up everything for me. I deserve it all."

Armand nervously glances at the door.

"We have a sister. Our father had another heir."

Silas becomes enraged.

"There is no other heir. I'm the only heir—will be the only heir after I take you and your wretched brat out. It's just me."

Armand shrugs and lowers his voice.

"She lives in New York."

Silas angrily pushes Armand against the wall and sighs.

"You're lying. Making it all up to save your miserable life knowing there's nowhere you can run. I win and you lose."

At that moment Armand grabs for the gun in his brother's hand and they fall to the floor. Seconds later it goes off.

25
San Francisco

Igor cries out as Hobson's forceful thrusting intensifies. The younger man laughs loudly with glee. Igor is unable to free himself from the confines of the ropes binding his wrists to a filthy cot as Hobson recklessly rapes him showing no mercy.

Page **294**

26
Los Angeles

"Was that a gunshot?"

Gina looks at Maxwell curiously.

"Sounds like it."

Moments later there is a scream as a door opens and Armand stands motionless holding a gun in his hand. Security descends upon him and he turns over the gun. He glances at the room and points to where Silas is lying. He is gasping for air as several guards rush over to him. He struggles to catch his breath as words seem unable to come from his mouth. He sighs.

"Damn you to hell."

His eyes close seconds later.

27
Orchid Bay
Clerke Apartment

"You're just lucky I'm a nice guy."

Kayla reaches out to kiss Patrick and smiles.

"Uh-huh—I know."

She kisses him again.

"But you never stood a chance of leaving regardless of what you thought. I simply wouldn't have allowed it."

Patrick laughs loudly as he pulls Kayla toward him.

"That sounds like a threat."

Kayla strokes Patrick's cheek and grins.

"It was."

Patrick looks at the door.

"Good to know."

They kiss.

"Once you and I are official I think you should know something. I intend to be a really naughty husband. I know I said it before but I'll make good on my threat. Uh-huh—I said it."

Kayla runs her fingers through Patrick's hair.

"How naughty are we talking?"

Patrick makes a lewd gesture with his finger and grins.

"Extremely naughty—no holds barred."

Kayla suddenly pushes Patrick down on the sofa.

"You better not go back on your word."

They begin laughing.

28

Los Angeles

Photographers descend on a movie theater in Westwood as news outlets appear to be everywhere while police escorts thousands of people from the area. Sandra and Scott stand at a corner several streets away with Maxwell as searchlights continue to play across the sky. Two coroner vans drive past them.

"This is a nightmare."

Maxwell faces Sandra and sighs.

"It appears that Armand's brother cornered him in one of the rooms in the lobby of the theater and they fought."

Maxwell glances at the theater in a distance.

"Diana Munroe is dead."

Scott seems upset. He faces Sandra and then Maxwell. He wipes sweat from his brow. Several people walk past him.

"That bastard strangled her."

He clenches his fist.

"She didn't deserve this."

Maxwell nods.

"That's why he pretended to like Donna Markway. He was gonna use her to get to his brother. He knew Armand would be at the premiere. That was his plan all along—until I threw a wrench into his plans—hired Bradford. He must have met Diana Munroe at a party—and then used her the same way he used Donna."

Scott turns to look at Maxwell.

"That sounds like a bad B movie script."

Maxwell nods in agreement.

29
San Francisco

Loren seems panicked as he is chased by two skeletons. He screams several times as he's grabbed repeatedly amid laughter. He smashes into something and realizes it's one of the skeletons. The ghoulish entity pulls him close to its bony head as it seems to be sucking breath from his body. He begs for mercy but the skeletons only intensify their assault. Unable to run anymore he falls against one of the skeletons again. The entity reaches out and begins tightening its grip. He cries out in fright but is unable to free himself from its embrace. With the little energy he has left he breaks free and runs through glass doors toward an open balcony. At the last second he realizes where he's standing. Loren curses loudly as he falls headfirst to his death.

30
Los Angeles

"I guess the movie premiere you mentioned you had tickets to, made the news. Someone got shot by a lunatic."

Vera Holliday watches as Amir Iskandar comes toward her from the bedroom. He's not wearing any clothing.

"I got the better of the deal."

Vera giggles as her eyes remain focused on his erection jutting out in front of him. She motions to him to come and stand in front her as she sits on the sofa. He grins slyly and walks toward her. He watches as she strokes his rigid penis and sighs.

"Who knew a lawyer guy like you could be so aggressive between the sheets. You broke me earlier—took me so easily."

Amir laughs and licks his lips.

"You forced my hand. I told you I'm not the kind of guy that gets led around by a sexy woman. I *do* the leading."

Vera reaches out to kiss Amir's erect penis.

"You could've worn a condom earlier."

Page **297**

Amir laughs again and glances at his penis.

"Is Daniel Brandt still your guy?"

Vera slides her tongue across the exposed head and sighs loudly. He watches as she kneels in front of him. He winks.

"I'm not Daniel. I'll take you to the edge and never give it a second thought. I won't tolerate you playing silly games."

Vera sighs loudly and faces Amir.

"Do you have a girlfriend?"

Amir throws his head back and laughs.

"Would it matter if I did?"

Vera sensuously strokes his erection. Seconds later his stiff penis is lodged deep inside her mouth halfway down her throat. He lets out a loud sigh as her tongue begins probing.

31

San Francisco

News cameras are everywhere as a coroner places Loren's body into the back of a van. Several members of a camera crew try to get a still shot of his limp hand sticking out from under a bloody white sheet. A few people stand around whispering.

32

Orchid Bay

Welsh Residence

"Isn't that the man you told me was your father?"

Lloyd Welsh faces Susan Osborne as she points at the man being interviewed by **Steven Fabian** of *Inside Edition*.

"He said he was going to be at a screening for one of his friends who wrote a book that was turned into a movie."

Susan watches the headline flash across the screen.

"Someone got shot."

Lloyd watches as several clips of the event at the movie theater is replayed. People are seen running from the lobby as police descend on the area. Lloyd wipes sweat from his brow.

Page **298**

"Did they say who bought the farm?"

Susan shoots Lloyd an odd look.

"Some guy named Silas Bell. Apparently he managed to get past security. He then killed his girlfriend and tried to take his half-brother out. They fought and he ended up dead."

Lloyd sits down near Susan.

"I bet a whole bunch of pond scum lawyers are breaking traffic laws to get to that movie theater—ready to squeeze every dollar they can from anyone who feels a bit traumatized."

Susan knowingly wags her finger at Lloyd.

33
San Francisco

"Did you use a condom?"

Hobson turns to face Carlos and laughs loudly.

"I had myself a seriously good time."

He licks his lips.

"Igor Levitov put up quite a fight. That man made it clear I wasn't going to fuck him—said he'd break my neck first."

Hobson makes a lewd gesture with his finger.

"He was wrong."

Carlos sits down next to Hobson.

"He cursed and begged me to stop but I just kept riding that motherfucker like a show horse. He finally surrendered to yours truly and then I rode him really hard for an hour. I went through so many condoms—most of them broke if truth be told. I taunted him that I might impregnate him before the hour was over. When I finally lost interest I took out my gun and plugged him twice in the head. He cried like a frigging girl when he saw me walking toward him with my gun. There I was with my dick sticking out in front of me like an arrow after having had an incredible sexual encounter with this man and all he could do was cry like a bitch—terrified I was gonna kill him. I expected him at least to say thank you for a good time before he ended up with a bullet in his brain. People today are selfish. I felt *so* insulted."

He begins laughing loudly.

"I threw his bloody corpse in the city dump—stuffed his mouth full of used condoms. It was quite the visual no doubt."

Carlos looks at his cell phone.

"I guess I should call Marlisa Vigaro."

Hobson stifles a laugh.

"Been there done that. She laughed for a full minute when I told her how Igor cried like a girl when I got on top of him."

He makes a lewd gesture with his tongue.

"I taped it—every wonderful minute."

Carlos runs his fingers through his hair.

"Loren Fawcett is dead."

Hobson reacts.

"Does Marlisa know?"

Carlos shakes his head.

"I don't know."

He sighs loudly.

"He took his own life."

He runs his fingers through his hair again.

"Apparently he took a leap from the balcony of his office after finding out his family's fate courtesy of our drones."

Hobson roars with laughter and gestures.

"I *so* love happy endings."

Hobson mimics someone falling as Carlos stifles a laugh. A second later his cell phone begins buzzing. Hobson sighs.

34
Los Angeles

"I guess Silas Bell no longer poses a threat to me."

Bradford turns to face Donna. She watches as Ashton Markway comes toward her from the backyard. He sighs.

"The police believe he acted alone. It seems he just wanted to kill his half-brother. Those two had serious issues."

Bradford embraces Donna. She sheds a tear.

"What about the woman with him? Who was she?"

Page **300**

Ashton runs his fingers through his hair.

"Diana Munroe."

He looks at his cell phone.

"She was one of the people that were on that island with Sandra King. Apparently Silas used her to get into the theater."

Donna turns around to face Bradford.

35
San Francisco

"I don't believe it. That boy would never kill himself. He would never do such a thing. His children were just photographs to him—told me plenty of times. Someone pushed him."

Houghton Fawcett clenches his fist.

"I want you to find out what really happened. Get that wretched whore to talk. Fuck her over and over if you have to. I want answers. Do you hear me? Break her fucking neck."

Anton Levitov nods and leaves the room. Seconds later Houghton notices Tiffany standing on the other side of a huge ornate mirror in his office. He grimaces. She stifles a laugh.

"Death comes for everyone at some point."

Houghton shoots her an icy glare as she takes a step toward him. She gestures with her hand and mocks him.

"He screamed before he hit the sidewalk."

Houghton reacts.

"It was *you*."

Tiffany wags her finger at him.

"He fell. Case closed."

He seems enraged as he reaches out to grab her. He falls against a coffee table as she begins laughing with glee.

TO BE CONTINUED

A Brief Look at the Twelfth Episode

Not everything is what it appears as more than one individual with plenty to lose get what they deserve while several couples make plans for their future together amid unplanned events.

Episode 12
New Beginnings

1
Los Angeles

"Are you looking forward to tomorrow?"

Maxwell Pendergraft turns to face Sandra King. He runs his fingers through his hair and sighs. Scott Malone grimaces.

"You're one brave dude—meeting some kid who you didn't know existed a month ago. He's probably got issues."

Maxwell sighs loudly and nods.

"He seemed fine when I spoke to him."

He turns to look at a display window fronting a large bookstore. Maxwell notices a huge photo of **Anne Frank** facing a collection of her writings. He wipes sweat from his brow.

"My problems are nothing compared to other people and the traumatic experiences they had or were forced to endure."

He points at the photo and sighs again.

"Imagine what she went through before she realized she was going to die. Imagine how she must have made peace with the realization that she was never going to become an adult."

Scott glances at the photo and gestures.

"If only she had known how famous she would become. If only she knew that her story would one day become the second highest selling book in world history—the highest selling work of nonfiction—a billion copies and counting—quite a record."

Sandra jabs Scott and grins.

"I didn't know you read her book."

Scott looks at the display window once more.

"One of the all-time best reads."

Maxwell runs his fingers through his hair again just as Scott's cell phone begins to buzz. Sandra shoots him a look.

"Do I have to ask who's calling at this hour?"

Scott looks at his cell phone.

2

San Francisco

"You didn't have to kill him. I planned to deal with my son in my own way. Exact revenge for what he did to Ralph."

Houghton Fawcett faces Tiffany Johnson.

"You ruined everything."

Tiffany takes a step toward Houghton.

"I didn't kill your son."

She stifles a smirk.

"He fell."

She takes another step.

"He couldn't handle what he did—couldn't handle the consequences for his actions surrounding Ralph's demise."

She grabs him by the arm.

"Loren Fawcett got what he deserved."

He reacts as visions begin forming. He seems unable to free himself from her grip as he watches Lizette Richardson being murdered by an unknown man. Houghton calls out as he helplessly watches her being stabbed repeatedly. Her screams echo in his ears as he watches a black shadow emerge and hover over the corpse until a mist emerges. The mist cries loudly as it is gobbled up by a claw-like creature. He reacts and screams.

Page **304**

"What the hell was that thing?"

Tiffany tightens her grip on Houghton.

"I think you know."

As he watches he sees Igor Levitov being raped repeatedly by the same unknown man who killed Lizette. He reacts as he hears Igor calling out—begging for mercy as he is raped multiple times as his assailant laughs gleefully. He continues watching as the man tires of Igor and then walks over to him with a gun in his hand. Houghton watches as the man shoots Igor twice in the head and stuffs the corpse full of used condoms. He sighs.

"I'm going to kill that fucker."

Tiffany stifles a laugh and points.

"You don't even know who he is—or who hired him."

Houghton shakes his head and seems confused.

"Who does he work for—Whitney?"

Tiffany begins laughing.

"I'm not playing twenty questions with you."

As Houghton watches he sees Loren running around his office in a panic as he's chased by two skeletons. He sighs.

"I've seen enough of this nightmare."

Tiffany seems pleased as the scene continues playing showing Loren looking a bit confused as he runs without looking toward the balcony and falls on one of the chairs. The fall propels him over the railing. As Loren falls he curses loudly. Houghton winces as he sees his son fall from the balcony. As he continues to watch the macabre scene he realizes that a black shadow seems to emerge from nowhere and hover above his son's broken body. As a mist emerges it is viciously grabbed by the claw-like creature and though it fights—the claw-like creature envelops the mist within its embrace and soon vanishes. Houghton cries out as he realizes what happened. He turns around to face Tiffany.

"You did this to my Lizette and Igor—you allowed that thuggish fag to do unspeakable things to them. It was you."

Tiffany releases her grip on Houghton's arm.

"I had nothing to do with it. They brought what happened upon themselves. There's a price for everything you do."

Page **305**

She looks at the mirror and seems pleased.

"Maybe you should think about that."

Seconds later she's gone. Houghton seems in shock as he relives what he just witnessed. He looks at his cell phone.

3
Los Angeles

"Where do we stand now?"

Amir Iskandar faces Vera Holliday as he pulls on his jacket. He grins at her. He watches as she comes over to him.

"I asked you a question."

Amir gestures at her and sighs.

"I'm your lawyer."

Vera seems upset.

"Is that all?"

Amir stifles a laugh.

"What do you want from me?"

Vera pulls Amir toward her and slides her fingers over the outline of his penis straining under his fitted suit. She sighs.

"I think what happened between us should continue. I like strong men. You know how to handle a woman—how to keep me in line—how to set boundaries. More importantly you know how to fuck—I really like a man that constantly breaks rules."

Amir pulls away from Vera.

"I'll think about it."

She reacts. He notices and smirks.

"I have a girlfriend."

Vera becomes enraged.

"You fucked me even though you have a girlfriend? How dare you use me like that? You're a disgusting creep."

Amir laughs and pulls Vera toward him.

"Shut up. Just shut up. You wanted me as much as I wanted you. We fucked—end of story. Like deal already."

He kisses her passionately and laughs.

"My girlfriend and I have an arrangement."

Page 306

He kisses her again and gestures.

"The two of you can become friends. Share me."

Vera seems appalled and grimaces.

"I'll do no such thing."

Amir points at Vera and grins.

"If I insist upon it it'll happen."

Vera reaches out to slap him. He grabs her arm and pulls her toward him again. They stare at each other for a second.

"I'm *so* done with you. *Ugh*, what nerve."

Amir pushes Vera up against a wall and kisses her.

"You're done when I say you are."

He kisses her again. Vera resists at first but then embraces his advances and they kiss intensely for several minutes.

4

San Francisco

"I guess it's time I pay Fawcett a visit tomorrow."

Trevor Boleyn seems pleased as he glances at the news on a large monitor in his hotel room. He reaches for the remote.

"Offer my condolences."

He walks toward the door and stops.

5

Orchid Bay

Hampshire Street Cafe

"*Ugh*—that woman is so disgusting."

Liana Danforth faces Tabitha Bairstow as they watch Loretta Osborne kissing the Lorenzo twins. Liana grimaces.

"Word is she dumped the O'Rourke brothers."

Tabitha makes a gagging gesture with her hand.

"I hope both of them know where to go for STD info when she dumps them again for the newest flavor of the month."

Loretta notices them looking at her and blows a kiss as she resumes kissing the brothers. Tabitha reacts to the slight.

Page **307**

"Kyle said she came onto him about a week ago at the supermarket—told him she wanted to give him a blowjob."

Liana seems shocked and turns away.

"He thought she was kidding at first. She wasn't."

Tabitha seems irritated.

"I know Kyle isn't a saint but Loretta redefines the word whore. Is there any man she hasn't had between her legs?"

Liana makes a lewd gesture with her finger.

"Her gay cousin's ex is a good guess."

They begin laughing and point at Loretta.

6

San Francisco

"I should have done this a long time ago."

Anton Levitov slowly opens the door to a room where a frightened girl is lying on a bed. She jumps up as the door opens and seems panicked as he closes the door. He faces her.

"You and I have a date."

Bridget Whitney backs away as he grabs her arm. He angrily throws her to the floor and kicks her. He laughs.

"Today is your swan song, *bitch*."

He grabs her again and throws her toward the wall and smirks. He sees her fear and seems to enjoy his power over her as he grabs her once more. He unzips his Levi's and laughs.

"Say your prayers."

He hears a noise behind him.

"I couldn't agree more."

He spins around to see Tiffany standing on the other side of a mirror on the wall. She takes a step toward him. He seems confused as he watches the strange scene unfold before him.

"What the fuck?"

Tiffany takes another step as he grabs Bridget again and curses. He twists Bridget's arm backwards and laughs loudly with glee. Anton spins Bridget around and faces the entity again. He seems unafraid as he watches Tiffany take another step.

Page 308

"Let go of her."

Anton stands motionless for a few seconds.

"I'm not afraid of you."

At that moment something grabs Anton by the arm. He reacts in fright as he turns and faces Jeremy Weissmann.

"She's not going to ask again."

Anton ignores the request and laughs. His laughter dies in his throat as a bolt of electricity surges through his body. Less than a second later he releases his grip on Bridget's arm just as Jeremy's grip on Anton's arm increases. As Anton tries to push the entity away another bolt of electricity tears through his body. Anton screams loudly as Jeremy looks at Tiffany and smiles.

One Day Later

7
Orchid Bay
Pioneer Trail Mall

"I got to hand it you—you beat the odds. You fucked almost every woman in Orchid Bay since you moved here from Monterey and then scored up and down the coast as well and still somehow managed to score a virgin for your first serious relationship. I never thought the day would come where I'd see you commit to one woman—much less someone like Tabitha Bairstow—especially given your sexual history with her sisters."

Kyle Derringer laughs loudly and jabs Lachlan Ball.

"She's the one—plain and simple."

He grins broadly and sighs.

"I intended her to be just another nameless girl in my bed for a one-night stand—but something happened that night."

He shoves his hands into the front pockets of his jeans.

"I was coming out of a diner on Rose Street when I saw Adam Mills arguing with her. Apparently he was pissed that she found out he had slept with Loretta Osborne the night before."

Lachlan notices Kyle's anger building.

"He blamed her for what he did saying she wouldn't put out so he had to look elsewhere for some bedroom action."

Kyle sighs loudly and grimaces.

"I walked over to where they were and told Adam I'd put him in a coma if he didn't leave Tabitha alone. He took a swing at me and I clocked him hard on the jaw. Tabitha and I left him there on the street and went to my apartment. I had no intention of bedding her—it just happened. It was no secret I'd been with her older sister when we were in college together—and had a threesome with her twin sisters a few years later. I then slept with her cousin and her cousin's mother. My sexual history is an open book in Orchid Bay—I'm just not Prince Charming. But Tabitha needed someone to talk to and we talked—for two hours. Then it happened. I put my arms around her and we kissed. I looked at her and told her I wanted to make love to her. I made it clear I'd be gentle with her from start to finish—make her first time something she'd remember. But I made sure she knew this was just a one-night stand to me. I wasn't interested in getting serious with her. She nodded and didn't try to fight my advances—she simply took my hand and asked me where my bedroom was. By this time I had a massive erection as I lifted her into my arms and took her to my bedroom. As I undressed her I treated her with respect knowing she was so vulnerable at that moment and then I took off my shirt and jeans. I recall how amazed she seemed as she saw my penis sticking out in front of me like an arrow. I remember laughing loudly as I walked toward her. She was mesmerized no doubt—seeing a man's penis up close for the first time. I pulled her to her feet and kissed her again and made it clear she was safe with me—saying I wouldn't hurt her."

Kyle runs his fingers through his hair.

8

Los Angeles

"I'm on my way—got a few things to wrap up and then I plan to brave traffic on PCH. I should be there in an hour."

Page **310**

Maxwell nods and faces Scott Malone.

"I guess I'll see you in New York."

Scott nods in agreement and pulls Maxwell toward him. They hug warmly as Sandra King watches. Scott then points at Maxwell and shoots him a sharp look. He gestures wildly.

"I hope it works out with the kid."

Maxwell jabs Scott.

"I do too."

Maxwell hugs Sandra.

"Keep him in line—he needs a strong hand to prevent him from making a fool of himself—or getting arrested—again."

Scott shakes his fist at Maxwell in mock anger.

9
Orchid Bay
Pioneer Trail Mall

"She looked at me and said she was glad I would be her first. Saying it would be an honor to lose her virginity to a man like me. She said she had no problem with me being involved with her sisters and cousin—saying I was a single man and didn't owe any woman anything. She made it a point to say I didn't owe her anything either and that she just wanted me to be happy after it was over. It was incredible for a man to hear a woman say she didn't want anything from him except for him to have a good time in the sack and didn't owe her anything afterwards."

Kyle runs his fingers through his hair.

"As I put her down on the bed she looked up at me and said for me not to treat her like a virgin—saying she knew I'd been with hundreds of women and simply wanted me to do what I felt was appropriate when I made love to her. That it was important that when I was done with her I had no regrets taking her virginity. I remember laughing as I told her I've never had regrets after taking a woman's virginity. Saying again I'd been with hundreds of women and don't regret any sexual encounter I had. I made it clear my behavior was always that of a gentleman."

Page 311

Lachlan jabs Kyle and laughs.

"No one in Orchid Bay can ever say you're not a nice guy. I myself know firsthand that you have always been there for your friends in their time of need. Women love you—especially the ones you took to your bed and pleasured. I think only Adam Mills had issue with you. Of course he blamed you for bedding Tabitha Bairstow before he could make her one of his girls. He never stopped talking about his loss—that dude hated your guts."

Kyle grimaces and seems irritated.

"That fucking piece of dirt was unrelenting in pursuing Tabitha after she and I moved in together. He refused to accept that she had moved on—was my girl now. Sabine Norton did what so many others wanted to do. I had fantasies about killing that fucker—if you must know—I just wanted him out of my life. When I heard he had been killed I laughed for a whole minute. I was glad he was dead and no longer going to be a thorn in my side or Tabitha's for that matter. She chided me for being so happy—but understood my mood knowing that Mills was out of our lives forever—that we could actually live—make plans."

He clenches his fist and faces Lachlan.

"Yesterday I went to Falling Pines and pissed on his grave. I let it rip like a waterfall. There I was—a thirty-two-year-old man whipping out his dick and peeing on his twenty-nine-year-old rival's grave. I felt so liberated. I had won. He had lost. I was alive and he was dead. Tabby was upset when I told her but I had no regrets. I think I might pay Sabine Norton a visit and thank her."

Lachlan shoots Kyle a sharp look.

"Leave it be. Don't open that keg of gunpowder."

Kyle runs his fingers through his hair.

10

San Francisco

"This can't be happening to me. Anton is dead. Burned alive from what the coroner said. Made it clear he suffered."

Houghton runs his fingers through his hair.

"My entire family is gone. Killed like dogs on the street. I'm going to crucify that miserable fag—make him scream."

He hears laughter and looks up to see Tiffany standing about ten feet away. She stifles a sly smile. He grimaces.

"Get away from me—haven't you caused enough trouble for me already? Be gone creature—I'm not in the mood."

Tiffany makes a mocking gesture with her hand as she takes a step forward. Houghton pulls out a gun and laughs.

"I thought I made it clear."

Tiffany takes another step and smirks.

"What are you gonna do old man—shoot me? Have you learned nothing from our encounters? You can't kill me."

Tiffany lowers her voice.

"But *I* can kill *you*."

Houghton looks at the gun and sighs.

"I think I'll chance it anyway."

He fires.

"Hasn't anyone ever told you not to play with dangerous toys? Someone could get hurt—namely you old man."

Tiffany watches as the gun in Houghton's hand turns into a pile of dust. He reacts. She laughs and takes a step forward.

"Anton Levitov is where he should be."

She laughs slyly.

"He'll have plenty of time to think about all the things he did wrong—all the women he raped—and killed. But you'll be happy to know he has friends where he went. He had quite the reunion with Loren—Vladimir—Lizette—Kevin—and Cujo."

Houghton reacts and grimaces.

"Get out. Go away."

Tiffany wags her finger.

"I thought I told you the last time we spoke that the worst is yet to come. No time like the present for a nasty surprise."

Houghton seems confused as Tiffany snaps her fingers and opens the door. Seconds later he gasps as he notices a man dressed in a suit standing in the doorway. Tiffany laughs.

Page 313

Marble Hills

"It's so good to be home. I don't think I'll forget what happened for quite a while. I'm sick of answering questions."

Gina Bentley watches as Pierce Colby wraps his arms around her and stifles a laugh. They look at each other.

"Eddie called me at the airport."

Gina notices the look of concern on Pierce's face.

"Why? What's wrong?"

Pierce runs his fingers through his hair.

"Alec Martel wants out of the loony bin in Bangor. Eddie said he tried to forge release papers two days ago. Martel failed to convince the staff that Eddie was OK with such a questionable situation. Eddie is on his way there as we speak—something about making sure this never happens again. Martel apparently thought he could pull a **Meryl Streep** performance and hoodwink everyone with his direct-to-video acting. He was wrong."

At that moment they see Maddie Gormley standing at the door leading to the hallway. She seems nervous and sighs.

"Welcome back—I hope the premiere was everything you hoped it was. I know you were looking forward to it."

Gina and Pierce exchange glances.

"I'll tell you all about it later."

Maude nods and seems uneasy.

"There's someone here to see you. Said someone named Tiffany told her to come here—said you would know."

Gina and Pierce look at each other. They watch as Maddie gestures to someone nearby. They react as Bridget nervously walks toward them. They share an awkward moment.

12
Los Angeles

"Are you sure you really want to leave DC behind? I don't want you to think I'm pressuring you to stay here with me."

Bradford Styverson nods and kisses Donna Markway. He pulls a strand of hair away from her forehead and gestures.

"It's my choice—I made the decision."

He kisses her again.

"Last night was incredible between us. I never thought I could experience such joy. I certainly don't want to go back to DC and not see you again. I can always get a job in Los Angeles."

He pulls Donna toward him.

"Unless you think I shouldn't?"

Donna slides her finger across Bradford's lips.

"I was hoping you'd want to stay. Ashton will be over the moon no doubt. He made it clear he thought you were definitely boyfriend material—said my days of picking toads were over."

Bradford grins and kisses Donna's hand.

13
Orchid Bay
Pioneer Trail Mall

"I spent my entire adult life hopping from bed to bed simply because I felt empty. No matter how many times I fucked the latest flavor to catch my eye it didn't make me feel better. Right after college I backpacked all over Europe and must of slept with close to six hundred women. I probably have a kid out there I don't know about. But regardless it did nothing to improve how I felt about myself. I had a voracious sexual appetite until I met Tabitha. I went through women like tissue paper. Once I was done with my latest I tossed her aside and moved on to the next. It was no secret to anyone the kind of guy I was. Fuck them and dump them was my motto. But Tabitha changed all that. She was so giving—just wanted what was best for me. The first night we spent together was heaven. She saw how aroused I became as I held her while she cried about how Adam was treating her. I couldn't hide my erection straining under my jeans. She knew what was going through my mind. At that point I told her I wanted to make love to her—needed to be with her."

Kyle sighs loudly and stifles a smile.

"It was the start of me realizing I had found the woman I always wanted. Caring and loving—but still able to let me be myself and not feel trapped. I've never looked back since."

Lachlan mockingly sticks his finger in his mouth as he pretends to be disgusted. He jabs Kyle several times.

"What are you trying to do buddy—ruin the image of every guy out there who isn't as sensitive as you are?"

Kyle points at Lachlan.

"Deal with it."

Lachlan stands.

"I'm got to get back to the station. But know this brother from another mother. I'm glad for you—you deserve to be happy after all the women you bedded and seriously disappointed."

Kyle stands and looks at Lachlan.

"How would you like to be introduced to my fist?"

Lachlan pulls Kyle toward him and hugs him warmly.

"Just say when and I'll send you to the hospital."

They laugh loudly and hug each other again.

"How about you come over later with Alison? We can watch a scary movie—say *Salem's Lot*—the 1979 version with the freaky graveyard scene that scared us to death as kids?"

Lachlan shoves Kyle playfully.

"I'm game. But if you try to cuddle afterwards I'll pop you really hard in the jaw—guaranteeing a trip to a plastic surgeon."

Kyle flexes his muscles and points at Lachlan.

"You'll put up with my cuddling and like it buddy."

They begin laughing again.

14

San Francisco

"That's right motherfucker. I own everything. Not a dime is left to your name. I've already secured your mansions and fleet of cars. Your business is mine too. Bank account is in my name as well. You have nothing—not a fucking penny—it's all mine."

Page **316**

Houghton reacts. Tiffany seems pleased as she laughs watching the scene play out. Trevor Boleyn grimaces.

"I think there's one last thing you should know before I kick you out of my building. You have dear Loren to thank for everything that's befallen you. He framed me for what he did and brought this upon you and your wretched brood. But it was *you* that orchestrated your downfall—you and Wesley Mayfield."

Houghton stands motionless as he realizes Trevor's real identity. He turns to face Tiffany. She laughs mockingly.

"Uh-huh—I knew. In fact it was me that made all of this possible old man. Right after the yacht belonging to Tristan Montgomery Bell met its demise I happened upon the scene."

She faces Tristan Montgomery Bell.

"He was clinging to part of what was left of his yacht and had no one. Everyone else managed to get on the lifeboats but him. He was fucked. I knew it and he knew it so we made a deal as he treaded water. I save him and he redeems himself by doing my bidding. It was perfect. One moment he was treading water and the next he was being pulled up on a lifeboat by some Dutch survivors of another disaster several miles away. They just thought he was one of their own and didn't think twice about it. He was rescued along with the Dutch survivors and taken back to the Virgin Islands. From there Tristan and I began orchestrating your destruction—orchestrating the destruction of your entire empire. Bit by bit your company was taken—all the while you thinking it were the Whitney brothers. It was so entertaining watching you lose everything you got by ill-gotten means. Of course along the way I found out you had so many other enemies vying to destroy you. And yes—I could have stopped them—but why would I do that when they were doing my work for me."

Houghton sighs as Tiffany seems about to laugh.

"Watching Cujo Momoa get what he deserved was sheer pleasure—as was the demise of Lizette Richardson. Of course witnessing Igor Levitov experience some of what he forced upon his victims was intoxicating. His rapist spared him no mercy."

She smirks and points at Houghton knowingly.

"Of course Anton's fiery demise was exactly what he deserved. He screamed like a girl as he was burned alive."

Houghton reacts. Tiffany notices.

"So sad—none of your kin went out in a heroic blaze of glory as you imagined—just taken out like day-old trash."

Tiffany begins laughing as she faces Houghton.

"Where are you gonna live old man? I have it on good authority that you're officially homeless—so sad—oh *so* sad."

She mockingly wags her finger at him.

"How about you call Janet Virella?"

Houghton shoots Tiffany a sharp look.

"How do you know about her?"

Tiffany stifles a laugh.

"Figure it out."

She takes a step toward Houghton. Tristan wrings his hands and seems to relish Houghton's downfall. He laughs.

"Time is money—*my* money. I want you gone from my building in the next two minutes or else I won't be responsible for your safety. I might have a sudden blackout and accidentally throw you off the balcony because you refused to leave."

Tiffany watches Houghton's reaction.

"You should leave right about now. If you were to fall from the balcony who could say it wasn't suicide—just saying."

Houghton looks at Tristan. Tristan looks at the balcony and nods slyly at Tiffany as Houghton bolts for the door.

15

Los Angeles

"I expect you to be on your best behavior when you meet Amber Walston—otherwise known as your sister. She's gonna eat you alive if you behave even the least bit intimidated."

Vera grabs Amir's hand and sighs. She seems defiant as she leans closer to him. She whispers in his ear and laughs.

"I'm not going to fold—that money-grubbing bitch is in for a rude awakening when we meet. I intend to destroy her."

Page **318**

Amir steps out of the elevator. He grabs Vera by the arm and pushes her up against the wall. He watches her reaction.

"I hope I made myself clear earlier."

Vera jerks free of his grip and seems annoyed.

"I'm not giving an inch."

As they turn the corner and begin walking into a lobby decorated by large potted plants a woman comes up to Amir and kisses him passionately. Vera seems upset and grimaces.

"How is my husband-to-be doing today?"

Amir turns to face Vera and laughs.

"Vera, I want you to meet Amber Walston."

Amir seems pleased as he sees Vera's reaction. He grabs her by the arm again and forces her to face her half-sister.

"I told you I had a girlfriend."

Vera tries to pull free of Amir's grip on her arm but his strength overwhelms her. He looks at Amber. She licks her lips and faces Vera. Amber takes a step toward Vera and laughs.

"Face it *bitch*—you got played."

Vera attempts to slap Amir but Amber stops her. She twists Vera's arm backwards and slaps her across the face.

16
Orchid Bay
Pioneer Trail Mall

"How much do you charge?"

Harlow Lorenzo turns to face Matthew O'Rourke as Justin Derringer stands. Seconds later a fist slams across Matthew's jaw as Harlow screams. People gather as Matthew falls to the floor. Justin stands over him in triumph as Lachlan and Kyle come running toward them. Matthew winces as he tries to stand.

"I want him arrested for assault."

Lachlan looks at Justin.

"He insulted my girl. Asked her how much she charges for her services. So I decked the fucker—got him good."

Matthew stands and faces Lachlan.

Page 319

"Do your job—arrest him. Arrest this vicious brute."

Lachlan looks at Kyle and then Justin. He turns to face Matthew again as people standing around begin to whisper.

"If I arrest Justin Derringer for hitting you I'll have to arrest you as well—for soliciting. Of course I'd have to report it and that means your license to practice law would come under scrutiny. Once that ball starts rolling there would be no way to stop it."

Matthew seems about to explode.

"That's blackmail. Harlow knows I was only kidding. I was playing on her name sounding like harlot. It was a joke."

Harlow faces Matthew. She lowers her voice.

"I was named after **Jean Harlow**. Of course I don't expect you to know who she was—on account of how dumb you are."

Matthew glances at the crowd and then Justin.

"You're going to pay for hitting me."

Lachlan grabs Matthew's arm.

"Making threats will get you several years in a nice prison up the coast. This ends now O'Rourke—or you and I will be having plenty of conversations about how much time you'll be spending bending over for some very close friends of yours up the coast."

Matthew glares at Justin and then storms off. Harlow and Justin face Lachlan. Lachlan seems worried and sighs.

"Expect trouble. He's not one to ever accept blame for anything he does. He and his brother are two peas in a pod."

They nod in agreement as Kyle looks at his cell phone and seems upset. He faces Lachlan and his brother seconds later.

17
Orchid Bay
Welsh Residence

"Where do we go from here?"

Maxwell looks at Lloyd Welsh and shrugs.

"It's up to you. I'm game if you are. I would like to get to know you—but it's your decision. You're in the driver's seat."

Lloyd looks out at the driveway.

Page **320**

"What should I call you?"

Maxwell glances at Caroline Welsh first and then Dayton Welsh. He faces Lloyd again and extends his hand and grins.

"Maxwell."

Lloyd glances at his parents and grins.

"I got no problem with that."

He faces Maxwell again.

"I've got some free time this summer."

Maxwell glances at Caroline and Dayton. He then faces Lloyd again as he nervously runs his fingers through his hair.

"Do you like camping?"

Lloyd appears unsure and sighs.

"I can learn."

Maxwell seems pleased and pulls out his cell phone.

"How would you like to meet your aunt? She lives in Maine—little town called Marble Hills—married—two kids."

Lloyd nods as Maxwell begins dialing.

18
Orchid Bay
Derringer Apartment

"I got here as soon as I could. There was a situation at the mall with Matthew O'Rourke. He and Justin got into it."

Tabitha sighs loudly.

"Is Justin OK?"

Kyle nods.

"He punched Matthew. O'Rourke made a comment about Harlow Lorenzo. Justin took offense and laid O'Rourke out."

He stifles a laugh.

"Lachlan Ball was with me when it happened. He set O'Rourke straight right away when that bastard tried to have Justin arrested. Lachlan told O'Rourke if he arrested Justin he would have to arrest him as well for soliciting. I thought O'Rourke was going to have a coronary. He's in a mood right now."

He notices Tabitha's behavior and sighs.

Page **321**

"I spoke to my grandmother earlier."

Tabitha notices a huge grin spread across Kyle's face. She takes a step forward and observes his reaction. He laughs.

"She asked so I let her. It was no big deal."

He watches as Tabitha takes another step forward.

"I've never seen my grandmother so happy. She said after you walked her to the front door of her home she asked you to come inside. You agreed and once inside she shut the door and told you she had something to ask. She told me she asked if she could touch your erection straining under your jeans. She made it clear you were always the gentleman throughout. She said she knew you were with me but it had been so long since she'd been near an attractive man and just wanted to touch your glorious erection. She said you were so sweet about it and let her slide her fingers across the full outline of your erect penis under the confines of your jeans. She made it clear it was her and not you that was the aggressor. She then said she pushed even further in asking to see your penis. She said you didn't hesitate."

Kyle runs his fingers through his hair.

"I had no choice at this point Tabby. I knew she meant no harm by it. She's seventy-two—it's been years since she's seen a man's penis—much less one from a young man of thirty-two."

Tabitha pulls Kyle toward her.

"You're full of secrets Kyle Derringer. What other naughty things have you done lately that I don't know about yet?"

Kyle laughs loudly as Tabitha seems annoyed.

"Should I be worried about my safety?"

Tabitha pulls him closer to her. He grins slyly.

"I did it. OK—I did it. Your grandmother got an up close look and liked it—said my penis was beautiful—spectacular."

Tabitha pinches Kyle playfully.

"What else happened?"

Kyle grins and stifles a laugh.

"She stroked it. OK—she stroked my penis for several seconds. Said it was incredible how hard I was—enjoyed it."

Tabitha seems upset. Kyle notices. He pulls her toward him and hugs her. They look at each other. Tabitha grimaces.

"Did something else happen?"

Kyle begins laughing and then stops—realizing how upset Tabitha appears to be. He reaches out to stroke her cheek.

"Nothing happened. She touched my penis and then thanked me for being so nice to an old lady. She told me to go home and make love to her granddaughter. Show her a good time—put a baby in her. She told me how wonderful it must be to be young and sexually active. She seemed envious of my youth and that I had my whole life ahead of me. Before I left she asked if I was offended and I told her no. I made it clear I would continue to go to dances with her and that nothing had changed."

Tabitha wipes a tear from her eye.

"I'm so sorry. It's just that you're so attractive. I don't want to stand in your way. I'll accept whatever choices you make."

Kyle looks at Tabitha curiously.

"What choices? What are you talking about?"

"I know what you gave up to be with me. I'm aware of your history with women. I know you have rights. You and I aren't married. You're a single guy. If you want to resume seeing other women I'm OK with it. I would even let you bring women to our apartment. I'd be more than happy to leave for a couple of hours so you could have some privacy. I just want you to be happy."

Kyle reacts and takes Tabitha's hand.

"First of all let's get something straight right now. I don't want anyone else. Oh and by the way I'm not a single guy. I'm in a relationship with you. We're married as far as I'm concerned. I haven't strayed even once since the first time we made love."

Tabitha seems about to cry.

"I just don't want you to feel trapped. I'm perfectly OK with you maintaining sexual relationships with other women."

She watches as he touches her cheek again.

"When you met me a year ago you told me you had been with over a thousand-plus women by your own estimates."

Kyle runs his fingers through his hair and sighs loudly.

"I was promiscuous. I admit it."

Tabitha tugs at Kyle's jeans.

"You told me when you were in college you spent a summer in Europe and slept with hundreds of women. Said you got two pregnant—stated you were not husband material."

Kyle wraps his arms around Tabitha.

"That was then—this is now."

He hugs her tightly.

"You changed everything for me. You were so sweet the night I took your virginity. You cared more about me than you did yourself. Made it clear you just wanted me to take what I wanted from you. Didn't want me to look back—not be concerned."

Kyle sighs loudly.

"I was very clear that night we made love. Left no doubt you were just a one-night stand deal for me—made no secret that I'd bedded all three of your sisters—had a threesome with two of them—scored with your cousin and aunt too. It's no secret I've been with most of the women in Orchid Bay—fucked my way up and down the coast. I don't regret anything I've done."

He reaches out to kiss her.

"What happened between us changed everything. I felt something. For the first time I felt something. I actually wanted to know you—care about you. I remember that night so clearly."

Tabitha looks at Kyle.

"When you pulled out of me I remember you looking at me and then your penis. I freaked out and said I was sorry. You looked at me and asked what I was talking about. I assumed I'd hurt you in some way and apologized repeatedly. You pulled me toward you and said I hadn't hurt you. Said what happened was incredible—told me you enjoyed making love to me. Then you looked at me and asked if I would want to continue seeing you. I was confused—thought you were done with me. You told me you would like to get to know me better—see if it could work between us. At first I thought you were playing me but you assured me you were dead serious. I said yes. Said I respected you—that you were an honorable man—that was a year ago come next month."

Page **324**

Kyle grins broadly and seems pleased.

"How about we go to the beach—have a walk along the shore. I think it's time you and I get serious. Especially since the talk about town is that we're expecting a child together."

Tabitha stifles a laugh and grins.

"I told Liana it wasn't true."

Kyle gestures knowingly and laughs.

"On my end I promise I won't whip out my penis again to give your grandmother a thrill. She's sweet but quite naughty."

Tabitha nods in agreement and leads Kyle toward the front door. They stop and kiss lightly for a few seconds.

19
Los Angeles

"I won't tolerate my bitch of a sister being your mistress. You and I are through—finished. You crossed the line."

Amber tries to push Amir away as his grip tightens around her wrist. He aggressively shoves her up against a closet.

"You have no choice. I've decided."

Amir looks down at his erection straining under his suit and grins. He watches as Amber notices and seems disgusted.

"I've put up with your other women—the slut in New York you got pregnant—that wretched whore in Miami that I found you in bed with six weeks ago—and the mother and daughter you had a threesome with in San Francisco last month—but my trashy sister? I'm *so* done with you Amir. I want you out of my life."

Amir looks at the files on his desk.

"I own you bitch. I have control of your estate in case you forgot. You have nothing—it's all mine—you signed everything over to me so your sister wouldn't get a dime. I own it all."

Amber becomes enraged and attacks Amir. He defends himself as she angrily slaps him across the face. She sighs.

"You said it was just a formality."

Amir laughs as he pushes Amber away.

"Exactly how dumb are you?"

Page **325**

Amir makes a lewd gesture with his finger as he grabs one of the files. He throws it at Amber and begins laughing. He watches as she glances at the file and turns to look at him.

"I'll kill you. I swear I will."

Amir grabs Amber and forces her down on top of his desk. He slaps her several times. She cries out amid his laughter.

"How dare you threaten me?"

She cries out as he forces himself between her legs. He hits her again and begins raping her as she calls out for help.

20
Marble Hills

"Tiffany said I would be protected here. No one would find me at your school. She said you'd make sure I was safe."

Gina leads Bridget to the library and closes the door behind her. She turns to face Bridget. She seems confused.

"This happened yesterday in San Francisco?"

Bridget nods. Gina sighs loudly.

"Are you sure she said her name was Tiffany?"

"She said her name was Tiffany Johnson."

Gina appears to realize that Bridget isn't aware that Tiffany is dead. She walks over to a nearby desk and picks up a yearbook. She flips it open and shows Bridget a photo.

"Is this Tiffany?"

Bridget looks at the photograph.

"Yes—yes—that's her."

She wipes sweat from her brow.

"She was with a really hot looking guy. Said his name was Jeremy. I assumed they were together. He was really brave."

Gina points to a photo of Jeremy Weissmann.

"Is this Jeremy?"

Bridget nods several times. Gina puts the yearbook back on top of the desk. She faces Bridget again and sighs loudly.

"Tiffany and Jeremy are dead."

Bridget reacts. She seems about to faint.

"No—they can't be dead. *They're real*. I spoke to them. They were as real as we are. I don't believe in ghosts."

Gina slowly walks over to where Bridget is standing.

"I've seen her. Others have to. I haven't seen Jeremy but other people have told me they've seen and talked to him."

Bridget looks at Gina and pulls away.

"I'm not crazy. *I saw them*. I saw them yesterday."

They hear footsteps and turn to see Tiffany walking toward them. Bridget reacts and faces Gina. Tiffany stops.

21
Orchid Bay
Orlonge Apartment

"Am I going to have to wear a tuxedo? Please tell me I'm not going to have to dress up like a penguin—*ugh*—no way."

Alison Orlonge wraps her arms around Lachlan.

"You're gonna dress up like a penguin and like it. What did you think you would be wearing—ripped jeans and no shirt?"

Lachlan laughs and faces Alison. He kisses her.

"Last time I checked you like me walking around with no shirt—clad only in a faded pair of old jeans—no underwear."

Alison slides her fingers between Lachlan's legs.

"I got no problem with my guy sporting the commando look at home. But to an art gallery opening—I think not."

Lachlan grins and kisses Alison again.

"What if I refuse?"

Alison points to a sofa and smirks slyly.

"Say hello to your new bed."

Lachlan reacts and seems visibly upset. They look at each other for a few seconds. She nods several times and grins.

TO BE CONTINUED

Page **327**

A Brief Look at the Thirteenth Episode

Revenge is a dish best served cold and for a few deserving people that's exactly what they get while others experience seeing those who deserve punishment get exactly what they deserve.

Episode 13
Tomorrow is Today

1
Orchid Bay
Orlonge Apartment

"You're gonna owe me plenty for this art show deal."

Alison Orlonge pulls Lachlan Ball forward and kisses him. She hugs him warmly. They look at each other. She smiles.

"What are your terms?"

Lachlan grins broadly.

"I haven't decided—right now I'll settle for you telling me I'm your world—that there won't ever be someone else."

Alison wags her finger at Lachlan.

"Sorry—there's already someone else."

Lachlan reacts. Alison points to a cat lying on the sofa several feet away. The cat immediately walks toward them.

"Colton."

Lachlan seems relieved and picks up the cat with a grin.

"He's the exception. How old is he anyway?"

Alison turns to look at a nearby table where a photo of her and Colton stand out among several others. She sighs.

Page **329**

"He's seven. He was a present to me from the mother of one of my exes. She found a stray cat with kittens and managed to find good homes for all of them. She kept the mother."

Lachlan strokes the cat and grins.

"I had a dog. He was my father's pride and joy. That little dog managed to survive the odds and lived to twenty."

Alison watches as the cat shoots her a look before leaving the room. She faces Lachlan again and seems bothered.

"Has Roland called?"

Lachlan shakes his head.

"He's probably still up the coast trying to avoid making a deal for info about Jason Shappe. As far as I'm concerned that case is closed. It was natural causes. Shappe is old news."

Alison looks at Lachlan oddly.

2

Marble Hills

"I thought you knew. Thought you saw me come through the mirror while Anton Levitov was attacking you. But yes—Gina is telling you the truth. I'm able to walk through mirrors."

Bridget faces Gina and then Tiffany again.

"How come you're not transparent?"

Tiffany laughs.

"That's only Hollywood. They've never gotten it right no matter how many times they think they have. I appear as I was remembered. I can be anywhere at any time. People can only see me if I allow them to. I'm not alone—there are plenty like me all around the world—been that way for thousands of years."

"I thought when someone dies they toward a light? How come you didn't go? What's on the other side of death?"

Tiffany shoots Gina a cautious look.

"I have unfinished work still to do. Upon my death I found out that everything I thought was real was a lie—and so I set out to right the wrong that occurred. What I set in motion is finally coming to a close—and justice will be dealt accordingly."

Page **330**

"What happened to Anton Levitov after I left? I remember him begging for mercy as Jeremy began laughing loudly."

Tiffany glances at Gina.

"Anton is where he should be."

Bridget reacts.

"Is he in jail?"

Tiffany grimaces.

"Anton will never hurt you again."

She turns to face Gina again.

"I want Bridget Whitney to stay with you. Go to school here and have a normal life. She has no one. She's all alone."

Gina nods. Bridget seems confused.

3
Orchid Bay
Greasy Spoon Diner

"The condom broke—get over it already."

Gary Hachter seems annoyed as he watches Laurel Larsen pointing her finger at him. He rolls his eyes and sighs loudly.

"What do you want from me? It broke."

Laurel jabs Gary and grimaces.

"What if I get pregnant?"

Gary leans back in his chair and sighs.

"Ever heard of an abortion clinic?"

He notices her anger and stifles a laugh. Suddenly there is a scuffle outside the diner. He and Laurel see two brothers punching each other out in a heated fight on the sidewalk.

"This will look great on YouTube."

Laurel watches as Gary begins filming the fight on his cell phone while a crowd gathers around as Marc Zayler throws his older brother against a metal chair. Lyle Zayler jumps up and grabs Marc by the neck. They fall to the street as people cheer.

"She played you brother—said she loved you but loved my dick instead. I fucked her and she liked it. Get over it already."

Marc angrily slams his fist against Lyle's jaw.

Page **331**

"You're dead to me. Do you hear me?"

Lyle slams his fist into Marc's chest.

"Go tell it to someone who cares little brother."

Lyle punches Marc again.

"Your girl wanted a real man in her bed—so I got between her legs. Made her beg like a dog—fucked her for hours."

From behind Lyle is pulled to his feet by a pair of strong arms. Lyle is about to take a swing but stops when he realizes it is Grant Volker. Marc stands and faces his older brother.

"We're done."

He walks off without looking at Grant. Lyle stifles a laugh and looks at the small crowd gathered. He seems pleased.

"I banged his girl. It happens."

Grant seems annoyed.

"You never learn—do you. Always going after women you have no business being friendly with. Marc isn't going to forget what you did. This is the fourth time you've fucked a girl he really liked. Of course there's that matter with Erica Gersh's sister."

Lyle makes a lewd gesture with his finger.

"Sorry dude—she was way out of your league."

He shoves his hands into the front pockets of his jeans.

"She and I had more in common than the two of you ever could. I did you a favor—saved you from being humiliated."

Grant seems bothered by the comment as Lyle laughs and walks away. Grant angrily clenches his fist and sighs loudly.

"I hate that guy—I really hate him."

He enters the diner and notices Gary and Laurel looking at him. Gary walks over to where he's standing and smirks.

"It must be terrible to be you—no game."

Grant reacts as Gary and Laurel walk past him.

4

Los Angeles

"You're not going to get away with this. I won't allow you to make a fool of me. I know *people*—not-so-nice *people*."

Page **332**

Amir Iskandar grabs Amber Walston by her hair and throws her to the floor. He jumps on top of her in a rage.

"I've won. You've lost. End of story. I won't tolerate you making idle threats against me. I call the shots—not you."

Amber tries to push Amir off her but it only enrages him and he slaps her. She manages to grab a vase nearby. She hits him with it. He topples over and she manages to make it the front door before he grabs her again. He hits her and laughs.

"I'm not done with you yet, *bitch*."

Amber raises her hand to slap Amir as the doorbell rings twice. Before Amir can react Amber opens the door. She seems shocked to see Vera Holliday standing in the doorway with a gun in her hand. She seems upset. She notices Amber's appearance and looks at the gun. As Amir comes toward them in a rage she raises the gun and shoots him. A bullet rips through his chest seconds later. He falls backwards and gasps. Vera and Amber look at each other. They seem unsure of what to do next.

5

San Francisco

"I want him found. That old man is hiding somewhere in this city. He knows his days are numbered—knows it's over."

Marlisa Vigaro stifles a laugh as she faces Carlos Vente and Hobson Crusoe. She looks at a monitor on the wall.

"It seems Trevor Boleyn is actually Tristan Montgomery Bell. Somehow that old coot managed to survive dying in the Caribbean like everyone thought. He took Houghton Fawcett for quite a ride. Left Fawcett with nothing—not even a nickel—kicked him out of his mansion—ordered him to vacate immediately."

Hobson leans back on the sofa.

"Should I guess how you want to orchestrate his demise? I got a few ideas—all of them includes pain—plenty of pain."

Marlisa walks over to Hobson.

"I was thinking of sealing him inside an empty crypt at Colma. My family is buried there—they won't mind a bit."

Page **333**

She begins laughing and gestures with her hand as Carlos stands up. He glances at Marlisa as she dances in front of him and Hobson. She reaches out to take his hand. She grins.

"I want him sealed inside the crypt alive."

Carlos and Hobson look at each other and nod.

6

Orchid Bay

Orlonge Apartment

"Did Sidney Larsen tell you how many pieces of your art would be for sale? Seems to me it should be something he would have brought up with you before agreeing to the showing."

Alison shrugs and walks over to Lachlan.

"I'm just glad he's giving me a chance to let people have a look at my paintings. He also owns several galleries in Santa Barbara of which he mentioned displaying my art there also."

Lachlan gestures with his hand.

"I guess when you make it big you'll also want a boyfriend that knows art—not some jerk who fancies himself a novelist."

Alison reacts to Lachlan's comment.

"I don't want anyone else."

She pulls Lachlan toward her and hugs him.

"Don't you know how much you mean to me Lachlan? I could never imagine my life without you in it. We mesh together perfectly in every way. I knew you were the one when we met. Definitely husband material—father to my children."

Lachlan seems about to tear up.

"I just don't want you to regret being with me."

Alison kisses Lachlan.

"I don't have regrets. I wake up every morning thankful you're lying next to me—that you're such a wonderful guy."

Lachlan stifles a grin.

"What about when we role play and I'm an escaped killer who kidnaps you—making vile threats against your life."

Alison laughs and kisses Lachlan again.

Page **334**

"Love role playing if you must know. It's always a thrill when you overpower me while pretending to be a killer or some other freak that won't take no for an answer. No matter how tough you try to come across—you're always still a boy scout."

Lachlan points his finger at her.

"I guess I'm not cut out to be a scumbag."

Alison runs her fingers through Lachlan's hair and laughs.

"I like you just the way you are."

Lachlan seems pleased.

7
Orchid Bay
Paradise Pointe Bluffs

"How do you like fatherhood?"

Maxwell Pendergraft seems stunned as he realizes Tiffany is sitting in the passenger seat of his car. He pulls to a stop.

"I like it fine. He's a good kid."

Tiffany stifles a laugh and gestures with her hand.

"I need you to call Scott Malone."

Maxwell seems confused.

"Why?"

Tiffany seems annoyed.

"Just do it."

Maxwell looks at his cell phone.

"He's probably at LAX—getting ready to board a flight back to New York. What's going on? What are you up to?"

Tiffany grabs Maxwell's arm.

"I know he's at the airport—call him already."

She glances at Orchid Bay in a distance and smirks.

"He's about to get the story of his career."

Maxwell looks at Tiffany and picks up his cell phone.

"Is this about what you've been keeping from me—is this about Houghton Fawcett? I heard about his son's death."

Tiffany seems annoyed.

"He's not the story."

Page **335**

She gives Maxwell a sharp look.

"Sandra King is going to have to add an additional chapter to her book when it comes out in paperback in a few months."

Maxwell reacts to the comment and sighs.

"What's that supposed to mean?"

He runs his fingers through his hair. He turns to face Tiffany again and realizes she's gone. Maxwell grimaces.

8

Orchid Bay
Welsh Residence

"How are you feeling after meeting your biological father earlier? He seemed pretty nice—seemed decent—respectable."

Lloyd Welsh turns around to face his father and sighs. He watches as Dayton Welsh comes toward him. Dayton seems nervous as he reaches out to hug Lloyd. They embrace.

"I hope he was everything you imagined. I know it's still quite a shock—finding out your whole life was a lie. I'm sorry."

Lloyd pulls away from Dayton.

"You have nothing to be sorry for—you didn't do anything wrong. Crap happens—I'm dealing with it best I can. But what happened doesn't change anything. You're still my dad."

They look at each other.

"I wouldn't trade a moment with you for anything. You took me hiking—took me to the circus—got me to exercise with you every morning before school—even on weekends. Those memories are some of the happiest times I had—it was all you."

Lloyd notices Dayton's reaction.

"And yeah—sometimes you were a pain-in-the-ass with all the rules you had about being safe when we hiked. But I wouldn't want it any other way. You were my dad then and you're my dad now. Nothing has changed. Nothing will change. End of story."

Dayton pulls Lloyd toward him again.

"When did you become an adult?"

Lloyd pretends to shadow box with Dayton.

Page **336**

"You figure it out."

They hug warmly. Dayton sighs loudly.

"I want you to know I loved being your father. Some of the times it was hard to face—I admit it—but I never once wished things had been different between us. The memories I have of you growing up will always make me smile. If I have any regrets about being your father—it would be the times I couldn't keep my promise to you because of my damn job getting in the way."

Lloyd glances at the driveway.

"No worries—I understand."

He gestures at his car.

"How about we go for a drive—up the coast a bit?"

Dayton follows Lloyd to a car parked nearby.

9
Los Angeles

"How are you handling impending fatherhood?"

Ashton Markway seems upset as he faces his sister. Donna Markway watches his reaction as she walks toward him.

"What are you gonna do?"

Ashton shrugs.

"I'm not sure. Right now I'm just trying to figure out how to tell the folks. There's no easy way around that disaster."

Ashton runs his fingers through his hair.

10
Orchid Bay
Bay Street Condo

"I don't owe you anything."

Janet Virella seems about to slam the door to her condo shut as Houghton Fawcett aggressively forces his way inside. He walks toward the balcony and turns around. He seems enraged.

"You're gonna help me get all my money back before the week is out. That wretched man isn't going to best me."

Janet seems bored and faces the front door.

"I thought I made myself clear the last time we spoke. You're dead to me old man. I owe you nothing. I want you out of my life for good. It's just the way things are gonna be."

Houghton clenches his fist.

"He took everything from me with the help of that damn creature—she helped him—damn her—damn her to hell."

Janet rolls her eyes mockingly.

"I told you before I didn't believe you and I don't believe you now. You need to see a shrink—one that deals with old people losing their minds over having imaginary friends."

Houghton seems about to explode.

"You sound like your brother. Loren didn't believe me either—until she came after him—pushed him to his death."

Janet yawns loudly.

"I thought Loren took his own life?"

Houghton clenches his fist and shakes it.

"She did it—it was her—she killed my Loren. Pushed him off a balcony and then made it look like he took a header."

Janet glances at the front door again.

"I don't care either way. I want you out of here this instant or else I'm going to call the police—say you threatened me."

Houghton comes toward Janet.

"I'm not going anywhere."

Janet shrugs.

"Suit yourself."

She picks up her cell phone. He watches her begin dialing and reacts. She stifles a smile as she watches his reaction.

"You miserable bitch—you're no better than Loren. He never showed respect—always thought he knew better."

He laughs loudly.

"He found out differently."

Without warning he grabs the phone from her hand and angrily throws it on the floor. He faces Janet and sighs loudly.

"I'm done playing nice. You're going to help me or else I'll have to teach you a lesson—one that Loren never learned."

Janet tries to push Houghton away as he strengthens his hold over her. He slaps her hard across the face and laughs.

11
Los Angeles

"I just want you to know I hate you."

Donna reacts as Justine Ross licks her lips and glances over to where Bradford Styverson is sitting with her brother.

"He's so frigging hot. I hope you're putting him to good use. A body like that should never go to waste. Normally a man that tall should never wear such tight pants—but it works for him. I've never seen a man fill out a pair of old jeans that well."

Donna grins and winks at Justine.

"He's got quite a body no doubt—but he's the nicest man I've ever known—loves just sitting with me watching movies."

She glances at Bradford and Parker Ross sitting on one of the benches nearby at the Glendale Galleria. She faces Justine.

"He's so incredibly gentle and tender in bed despite him being over six feet. I felt so safe the first time he entered me. I think he's the one—someone for me to happily grow old with."

Justine sticks her finger in her mouth.

"*Ugh*—stop bragging about his lovemaking abilities."

Donna jabs Justine and laughs.

"What about you? Is there anyone special in Boston?"

Justine glances at Bradford again and sighs.

"Does he have a brother?"

Donna stifles a smirk.

"He does—but he's taken."

Justine clenches her fist in mock anger.

"I bet Bradford looks phenomenal with absolutely no clothes covering that incredible body. His penis must be something to behold when fully erect. His ejaculations must feel like a volcano erupting—I bet you cried when he shot his load."

Donna wags her finger at Justine.

"He's an incredible lover."

Justine licks her lips again and winks.

"I think when you get back to your apartment you should strip him naked and spray him with whip cream from head to toe. Then spend the rest of the afternoon licking him clean."

Justine makes a lewd gesture with her finger.

"I did that with David Sherwood."

Donna seems shocked. She glances at Bradford again. He laughs loudly several times as he continues speaking with Parker while looking at her. Justine notices his laughter and sighs.

"I bet they're talking about sex. That's the only thing guys ever talk about—explicit sexual positions and blowjobs."

Donna glances at Bradford again.

12
Orchid Bay
Paradise Pointe Bluffs

"Uh-huh—yeah I know its last minute."

Maxwell watches as Scott Malone turns to look at the crowded airport terminal at LAX and sighs. He grimaces.

"What is this about?"

Maxwell seems annoyed and sighs.

"I'll explain it when you get here. Tell Sandra I'm sorry. I'll make it up to her. I'll go out with her editor's daughter."

Scott stifles a laugh.

"You just signed your own death certificate buddy—but it's your funeral. Sandra will make sure you keep your word."

Maxwell nods and hears a sound.

"I've got to go—I'll see you in an hour."

He shuts off his cell phone and turns to face Tiffany. She watches his reaction and seems to be enjoying seeing how confused he seems at what appears to be unfolding. He sighs.

"Are you gonna tell me what you're up to?"

Tiffany glances at Maxwell's cell phone.

"Stop arguing with me—call Jeremy Winterfield."

Maxwell reacts and faces Tiffany once more.

13
Boston

"Uh-huh—I'm already on it as we speak—liquidating Houghton Fawcett's entire ill-gotten empire will be my pleasure. I have to hand it to you—when you told me your plan I wasn't sure if you were crazy or a genius—but it's the right thing to do."

Jeremy Winterfield leans back in his chair.

"As you know I'm friends with Pierce Colby—and he's married to Gina Bentley. She runs the school you mentioned."

He watches the reaction of Tristan Montgomery Bell from his office in San Francisco. They have an awkward moment.

"Where is Houghton Fawcett at the moment?"

Jeremy notices one of the lines on his cell phone blinking. He faces Tristan again and sighs. He seems confused.

14
Orchid Bay
Zayler Ranch House

"Hello brother."

Lyle Zayler looks at his brother and laughs. Marc Zayler remains standing a few feet away without any emotion.

"I thought I was dead to you."

Marc reacts and turns away from his brother.

"Your words not mine."

Without warning he pulls out a small handgun and shoots Lyle point blank in the chest. He watches as Lyle's face contorts in pain. They stare at each other as a spray of blood spurts from the wound in Lyle's chest and splatters onto his faded jeans.

"I win and you lose."

Marc turns away as Lyle tries to stop the blood pouring from the wound as pain overcomes him and he topples over. He watches Marc walk down the cobblestone walk before he loses consciousness. Marc hums a tune as he continues walking.

Page 341

15
Los Angeles

"I'll call you when I get back to Boston. Got my eye on someone actually—not that he's ever noticed me—workaholic."

Donna shoots Justine a cautious look.

"I thought you said Jeremy Winterfield was too old for you? Said he had a daughter just a bit younger than you?"

Justine stifles a grin and licks her lips.

"He does. She and I are close friends actually."

She makes a lewd gesture with her finger.

"He's single—and I'm single. I think he just needs a push in the right direction. Make him see he needs me in his life."

Donna glances at Bradford.

"Let me know how it goes Justine. I know from my own experiences that having someone in your life makes living a bit more interesting—especially if he has a picture-perfect body."

Justine shakes her fist at Donna and smirks.

"I hate you. I seriously hate you."

They hug warmly and watch as Bradford and Parker come toward them. Bradford notices Justine's stare and grins.

16
Orchid Bay
Hampshire Street Cafe

"Vera Holliday just called me—she's been arrested."

Daniel Brandt runs his fingers through his hair.

"Her half-sister was arrested also."

Warren Fuertes seems uneasy and sighs.

"Are you gonna take her case?"

Daniel seems panicked.

"I'm not sure."

He runs his fingers through his hair again.

"Vera claims it was self-defense."

Daniel glances at several people walking past them and faces Warren again. He looks at his cell phone and grimaces.

"Her half-sister is her witness."

Warren shoots Daniel a cautious look.

<h1 style="text-align:center">17</h1>

<h2 style="text-align:center">Pacific Coast Highway</h2>

"I was eighteen—just a bit older than you are now. All of a sudden I was a teenage father—not a clue what to do."

Dayton stifles a laugh and faces Lloyd.

"My parents helped—allowed me to continue going to college while your mother and I figured things out. They let us use the guest house—once your mother and I finished college things were easier. I got a job as a coach for Orchid Bay Community College. I made so many mistakes—didn't know what I was doing half the time—your mother and I started having issues."

Lloyd reaches out to hug Dayton.

"You were an incredible dad."

They look at each other.

"You were always there for me."

Dayton reacts and looks away as tears form in his eyes. Lloyd pulls his father toward him. He hugs him and sighs.

"I only hope I'm half the father you were."

Dayton pulls away and faces Lloyd.

"I never thought I'd hear you say those words after how we got into it over my terrible behavior with your mother."

Lloyd gestures with his hand.

"Ye without blame cast the first stone."

He stares out at the bluffs in a distance and grimaces.

"Last year I got Veronica Valt pregnant. She lost the baby shortly after. Gary Hachter is the only one who knew."

Dayton seems stunned and sighs.

"I had no idea you were sexually active."

Lloyd makes a lewd gesture with his finger.

"She wasn't my first. I've been with dozens of girls."

Page 343

Dayton wrings his hands and seems upset.

"What about Susan Osborne?"

Lloyd looks at his cell phone.

"She's different. Got to me somehow—made me feel something. I think I'll stick with her for the time being."

He stifles a laugh.

"I may even marry her. Make you a grandpa."

Dayton makes a fist at Lloyd.

"Don't you dare—I'm only thirty-four."

Lloyd laughs and pulls Dayton toward him.

"I just want to be like you—a father who learns from his mistakes—always ready to laugh and admit he's still learning."

Lloyd gives Dayton a shove.

"You were always the coolest father in Orchid Bay. Some of my exes thought you were quite the deal. Said numerous times when they ran into you that they thought you were a hot dad with no equal—one actually asked if you were dating anyone at the moment. Said her mother's bed had been empty much too long—thought you could work your magic on her mother."

Dayton throws his head back and laughs.

"No one ever said anything to me."

Lloyd jabs Dayton in his chest.

"You can still rock a pair of tight Levi's at thirty-four and turn every woman's head whenever you walk down the street."

Dayton looks at his faded jeans and grins.

"Uh-huh—I've still got it."

He laughs as Lloyd gently pushes him again.

"Seriously though—I'm glad we can talk on this level—not the father and son crap that usually is the deal—but as friends. I know you're not a child anymore and more than anything else I'd like there to be no barriers between us—no misunderstandings."

Lloyd reaches out to hug his father again. He glances back at the car where two tennis rackets can be seen propped up against one of windows. He stifles a grin and points at Dayton.

"I can still smoke you on the courts."

Dayton wags his finger at Lloyd and snickers.

"In your dreams—I'll crush you like a bug."

Lloyd glances back at the car and laughs loudly.

"Care to wage a bet on that—loser must admit defeat and post it on their social media page—along with a photo."

Dayton clenches his fist.

"Get ready to be humiliated."

Lloyd glances at the tennis rackets again.

18
Orchid Bay
Downtown Police Station

"This is an outrage. You're taking the word of a drug dealer over my client? I'll destroy you—do you hear me?"

Roland O'Brien watches as Gary Cavannaugh stands and looks over to where Lachlan is sitting. They exchange glances.

"I've ordered Jason Shappe's body to be exhumed. If I find any trace of what Dirk Veriteke says he gave your client I think you know where this is headed. Sarina Wolper is facing a murder charge and a lengthy stay in prison. She knew the risks—knew if Dirk blabbed she would be fingered. He blabbed—game over."

Gary glances at the briefcase in his hand.

"My client is innocent."

He turns and leaves without saying another word. Lachlan seems irritated as Gary slams the front door shut. Roland sighs.

"Who saw that coming? Sarina Wolper always seemed a bit too sweet to resort to a tactic like murder. Shappe must have really applied the screws to her—left her with few options."

Lachlan runs his fingers through his hair. He sits down at his desk again and leans back on his chair. He sighs loudly.

"Cavannaugh has been poking Amanda Mills for the last month or so. That dude isn't much better than Jason Shappe."

Roland grimaces and faces Lachlan.

"Cavannaugh and I have history. He fucked my sister in the backseat of his car the night of her junior prom and dumped her the next day—took up with her best friend later that day."

Page **345**

Lachlan reacts to the revelation and leans forward.

"Wasn't Erica Gersh your sister's best friend?"

Roland nods and glances at the door. He notices Gary on the sidewalk talking to someone. He faces Lachlan again.

"He played her too. Moved on to her sister and then hooked up with Jayne Osborne—dropped her two days later."

Lachlan gestures with his hand.

"I guess I shouldn't be surprised. He's the only lawyer I know that wears jeans and a leather jacket instead of a suit."

Lachlan stifles a laugh and lowers his voice.

"How long do you think it'll be before he cuts Amanda loose and beds his next conquest? I give it about a week."

Roland wags his finger at Lachlan.

<h1 style="text-align:center">19</h1>

Los Angeles

"You've got my seal of approval. Donna can't do better than you. You're a really sweet guy and she's lucky to have you. I have it on good authority she's seriously hung up on you by the way. She's faced a lot of toads but finally she's met someone worth her time. It certainly doesn't hurt that you're eye candy."

Bradford seems embarrassed as Justine takes his hand in hers and faces him. She glances over at a nearby cafe where Donna is ordering coffee. She faces Bradford once more.

"You're incredibly hot—tall and muscular—a god with a perfect body if you must know. Your penis must be magical—a fantastic piece of male wonder. I'm envious of Donna."

Bradford laughs nervously.

"I'm just a guy."

Donna pulls Bradford toward her.

"Have lots of uninhibited sex with Donna—fuck her every day. Take her again and again. She wants you to take control."

Bradford runs his fingers through his hair.

"I really like your style—like that you don't have a filter."

Justine makes a lewd gesture with her finger.

<h1 style="text-align:center">Page 346</h1>

"I can only be myself. I tell it like it is."

She reaches out to hug him warmly. As they embrace she whispers in his ear. He seems shocked and nods several times.

20
San Francisco

"I thought your vendetta was against Loren Fawcett?"

Marlisa turns to face Hobson and grimaces.

"He's dead. Died before I could exact my revenge against him for what he did to me. But his father is alive—he made Loren what he became—punishing him for what his son did works for me regardless. Besides—watching the look on that old man's face as he's sealed inside a crypt will be a wonderful experience to behold by yours truly. My family bought a whole slew of crypts at Colma decades ago—bought several crypts with large vaults. A few of them are still empty. There's one room with two huge vaults in the center. Houghton Fawcett is going to occupy one of those vaults. I want him put in the vault alive. I want him to know he's going to die—die horribly. Once the concrete lid is placed on top there's no way he can push it aside. I had vents drilled into the vaults earlier today. I want to make sure he makes it through a few days. Long enough for him to know he's gonna die. I've had cameras installed as well. I want to hear him scream for help until his voice gives out. He deserves his fate—deserves everything."

Hobson runs his fingers through his hair.

"I have a request."

Marlisa shoots Hobson a curious look.

"What sort of a request?"

Hobson looks at his erection straining under his faded jeans and grins broadly. Marlisa notices and stifles a laugh.

"You want to fuck him—don't you?"

Hobson laughs.

"He insulted me—called me a fag. I think it fitting that before Fawcett is sealed alive inside your family's crypt I have a go at him—give him a bit of what I gave Igor Levitov."

Marlisa dances several times in front of Hobson.

"Your wish has been granted. Do whatever you feel appropriate with Houghton Fawcett—just don't kill him."

Hobson grins slyly.

"I wouldn't think of it."

Marlisa turns to face Carlos.

"What's the word on Tristan Montgomery Bell?"

Carlos looks at his cell phone and sighs.

"Bell liquidated all of the Fawcett family business holdings according to my sources—turned it over to a lawyer in Boston named Jeremy Winterfield. Bell kept nothing for himself—not a penny from what I was told. Winterfield got everything."

Marlisa reacts to the news.

"I've heard of Jeremy Winterfield. He takes pleasure in destroying the lives of corrupt businessmen worldwide."

She stifles a laugh.

"He and I would've been quite the couple. That man is not to be trifled with—his name strikes fear in anyone who thinks they're above the law. Winterfield just doesn't bring sleazy crooks to their knees—he destroys their lives and likes doing it."

She faces Hobson once more.

21
Boston

"Uh-huh—exactly. I'm headed your way tomorrow—got something that will add to the fairy tale. Send Gina my best."

Jeremy nods a few times and as the screen of his phone goes blank he faces Miles Shefford. He snaps his fingers.

"Ever been to Maine?"

Miles shakes his head seemingly confused as Jeremy puts his feet on top of his desk. He seems pleased and smiles. He glances at his cell phone and gestures wildly with his hand.

"I'm going to a quaint little town outside Portland tomorrow morning. I think you should come along. Live a little."

Miles looks at the folder in his hands.

Orchid Bay
Greasy Spoon Diner

"I thought we had something?"

Gary looks at Amanda Mills and seems bored.

"Past tense—I've moved on. Sorry."

Amanda seems stung by the slight and grimaces.

"But you said I was different?"

Gary laughs loudly.

"I lied."

Amanda stands up.

"Everyone warned me about you. Said you'd play me for a fool and dump me—said you had a low opinion of women."

Gary glances at the empty diner and grins.

"I never said we were serious."

He stands up.

"I just wanted to fuck you—end of story."

Without warning Amanda throws the cup of tea in her hand at Gary. He reacts as the tea splashes across his leather jacket and jeans. Tears immediately fall from her eyes in a rush.

"I liked you—thought you liked me."

Gary seems irritated.

"I liked fucking you. That's all."

He grabs her arm.

"I've moved on—deal with it already."

Amanda takes a step forward.

"Who is she? Who are you fucking now?"

Gary begins laughing.

23
San Francisco

"Uh-huh—it's almost over. We're looking for the old man now. I've got quite the ending planned. He's gonna pay dearly."

Page **349**

Marlisa licks her lips as she looks at Corey Danforth staring back at her from his apartment in Orchid Bay. He sighs.

"What happens afterwards?"

Marlisa winks slyly and gestures.

"You'll have justice."

Corey nods in agreement.

24
Orchid Bay
Downtown Police Station

"What's the word on Vina Phamler?"

Roland turns to face Lachlan.

"She goes before a judge next week. No doubt she'll play the Karen role really well—work the judge's sympathies."

Lachlan rolls his eyes.

"Patrick Clerke has a fight ahead of him."

Roland nods in agreement. He is about to stand when the front door opens and he sees Marc standing in the doorway holding a gun. He and Lachlan appear shocked. Marc sighs.

"Lyle is dead. I shot him."

Roland and Lachlan react as they watch Marc cautiously take a step forward and hold the gun out in front of him.

25
Los Angeles

"You and I have a problem."

Donna closes the door and faces Bradford.

"It seems you've caught Justine's eye."

Bradford grins broadly and laughs.

"Have I? I didn't notice."

Donna pulls Bradford toward her.

"I think you have. I think you know the effect you've had on her. I think you're aware she really likes you. You shamelessly allowed her to flirt with you—list all your winning attributes."

Page 350

Bradford laughs as Donna kisses him lightly.

"Guilty on all charges—it is what it is."

Donna kisses Bradford again.

"She's got it bad for you. Told me the only thing stopping her from bedding you is her friendship with me. Said she'd never hurt me by going after you—just wanted me to know how attractive you were. Kept asking about how big your penis is when fully erect—asked for dick pics—asked several times."

Bradford stifles a laugh.

"I've never taken dick pics and would never. That's not who I am—no dick picks—none for her and none for you. I could never do something like that for any reason—I like my privacy."

Donna licks her lips.

"What if I insist?"

Bradford pulls Donna toward him.

"The answer is still no."

He watches as Donna runs her fingers through his hair. She seems pleased and kisses him. They look at each other.

"I just wanted to see where you stood."

Bradford wags his finger at Donna.

"She asked me for dick pics too. Wouldn't take no for an answer. But I stood my ground and said no—left it at that."

Donna seems about to cry.

"How did I find someone as wonderful as you?"

Bradford points his finger at her.

"It's all Maxwell Pendergraft's fault."

Donna begins laughing.

"I agree."

Her eyes fall on his jeans.

"I think we need to come to an understanding."

Bradford notices where Donna's eyes are focused. He watches as she reaches out to touch the buckle on his belt.

"Is that so? Do tell."

He watches as she unbuckles his belt and winks at him. She grins as her fingers touch the buttons. Within seconds her hand slides into his underwear. He moans loudly and laughs.

Page 351

"I see where this is going."

Donna faces Bradford and licks her lips.

"Do you have a problem with it?"

Bradford laughs and shakes his head. He lets out another loud moan as Donna's fingers probes his penis. Less than four minutes later he's standing before Donna completely naked. His erect penis proudly sticks out in front of him as he watches Donna's fingers glide along the exposed head. He giggles as her finger continues touching the head. She reaches out to kiss his penis and seems to enjoy his reaction. Donna faces Bradford.

"I think it's time you fulfill Justine's demands."

Bradford laughs and looks at his penis again and then lifts Donna into his arms. He carries her toward the bedroom.

26

Orchid Bay

Hampshire Street

"I see you've thrown caution to the wind ignoring what people in this town think by openly dating your daughter."

A fist slams into the face of Matthew O'Rourke seconds later. He falls on the sidewalk as Sidney Larsen stands above him with a clenched fist. Violet Lorenzo seems in shock. She notices her father's anger as he glares at Matthew. Violet tries to pull her father away but he stands his ground—ready to strike again.

"Say one more word and I'll break your neck."

Matthew rubs his jaw and stands.

"You're gonna pay dearly for hitting me."

Sidney looks at his fist.

"I ought to end you right now."

He appears ready to deal another blow to Matthew as he sees Roland coming toward them—followed by Lachlan.

"I want him arrested for assault."

Roland suddenly stops and looks at Sidney.

"What happened?"

Sidney faces Violet.

Page **352**

"This disgusting creep made a lewd comment about Violet—suggesting I'm having a sexual relationship with my daughter—so I popped him. He deserved it—plain and simple."

Roland faces Matthew.

"I thought I made myself clear about you running your mouth about people in this town. Have you learned nothing?"

Matthew rubs his jaw again.

"I can say what I want."

Roland grimaces.

"Uh-huh—and Sidney can pop you if he feels you slighted his daughter. Two can play your game O'Rourke—not just you."

Matthew points at Roland.

"I'm pressing charges."

Roland smirks.

"Actually you can't. You caused what happened to you. But Sidney Larsen can press charges against you for causing him and his daughter distress. Say goodbye to your legal career."

Sidney looks at Matthew and grins.

27
Orchid Bay
Paradise Pointe Bluffs

"I'm here—spill your guts."

Scott seems annoyed as he faces Maxwell. They stare at each other for a few seconds. Scott takes a step forward.

"Well? I'm waiting."

Before Maxwell can reply, Scott sees Tiffany walking toward them. Maxwell reacts as the apparition approaches.

TO BE CONTINUED

A Brief Look at the Final Episode

A long-held secret is revealed resulting in a depraved individual getting what he deserves as past and present events merge.

Episode 14
Finale

1
Orchid Bay
Paradise Pointe Bluffs

"Tristan Montgomery Bell is alive?"

Scott Malone sighs loudly and faces Tiffany Johnson.

"He's dead. He drowned when his yacht sank."

He watches as Tiffany takes a step forward. He faces Maxwell Pendergraft and seems annoyed. He gestures.

"I was there—he's dead."

Maxwell seems uneasy as he looks at Tiffany.

"He was picked up by the coast guard. They thought he was one of the Dutch passengers they rescued several miles from where the yacht went down. He pretended to be Dutch."

Scott runs his fingers through his hair. He faces Maxwell again and seems even more irritated than before. He grimaces.

"Why are you listening to this girl tell you some whacked story about Bell. He's dead. No one could survive the sea with sharks everywhere. They had him for lunch is my guess."

Scott runs his fingers through his hair again.

"Who are you anyway?"
Maxwell and Tiffany look at each other. He sighs.
"I think you know."
Scott seems confused. He looks at her closely and seems to remember. He faces Maxwell yet again and sighs loudly.
"How do you know this girl?"
He grimaces and points his finger at Maxwell.
"Are you sexually involved with her?"
Tiffany and Maxwell look at each other.
"Does the name Jennifer Parker sound familiar?"
Scott looks at Maxwell curiously and shrugs.
"Roland Parker had a niece named Jennifer. She was certifiable—killed numerous people in a small town in Maine."
Maxwell lowers his voice.
"Do you remember the name of her first victim?"
Scott notices Tiffany and Maxwell sharing a glance.
"What's going on Pendergraft?"
Tiffany takes a step forward.
"*I* was Jennifer Parker's first victim."
Scott reacts.
"What?"
He faces Maxwell again and then Tiffany.
"I'm Tiffany Johnson."
Scott faces Maxwell.
"What the fuck is going on?"
Maxwell glances at Tiffany and then Scott.
"She's telling you the truth."
Scott wrings his hands.
"Impossible."
Maxwell takes a step forward.

2

San Francisco

"Apparently he's in a little town near Santa Barbara called Orchid Bay. He's laying low—licking his wounds is my guess."

Page **356**

Hobson Crusoe watches as Marlisa Vigaro comes toward him from a mini bar. She seems annoyed and sighs loudly.

"I want him back here by nightfall."

She faces Carlos Vente.

"The crypt is ready."

He turns to look at Hobson.

3
Orchid Bay
Pioneer Trail Mall

"He didn't hit him. Tell me you're joking."

Kayla Larsen seems upset as she nods a few times and ends her phone call with Liana. She faces Patrick Clerke.

"My father took a swing at Matthew O'Rourke earlier. I think he broke Matthew's jaw—or something close to it."

Patrick stifles a laugh.

"I've got no sympathy for O'Rourke."

He gestures with his hand.

"He's his own worst enemy."

Kayla wags her finger at him.

"Liana said my dad laid him out pretty well."

Patrick seems pleased.

"Remind me to thank your father."

Kayla pretends to slap Patrick.

4
Orchid Bay
Paradise Pointe Bluffs

"I can't believe you think she's legit—certainly you can't be this stupid. This isn't Tiffany Johnson—she's an imposter."

Scott notices Maxwell turning to look at Tiffany.

"I'm *so* out of here."

As he turns to look at his car Scott sees a man in his early thirties walking toward him dressed in old fashioned clothing.

Page **357**

"Do you know who I am Scott?"

Scott reacts to the question as the man stands less than two feet away. They look at each other for a few seconds.

"When you were little you read my book—wanted to go to South America. Wanted to see what I saw in the Amazon."

Maxwell watches as Scott stands motionless while Tiffany seems pleased with herself for some reason. Scott turns away.

"It can't be. You died before I was born."

The man glances at Maxwell.

"Who am I Scott?"

Scott seems uneasy.

"You're my great-great grandfather Edward Malone."

Scott runs his fingers through his hair and faces Maxwell.

"Can you see him?"

Maxwell nods.

"I can see him the same as you."

Edward Malone laughs.

"I was one of the first men to see things many said were impossible in 1912. I published an account of my experiences in the Amazon later that year. A second expedition was organized years later and off we went. But I wasn't so lucky that time."

Scott wipes sweat from his brow.

"They said you were killed."

Edward turns to look at Maxwell.

"I was eaten by a pterodactyl if you must know."

Scott grimaces.

"This just—it isn't possible."

Maxwell takes a step forward.

"I've known about Tiffany from the beginning. After Roland Parker's niece began her killing spree Tiffany began appearing to one of her classmates. No one believed her."

They share a glance.

"Everyone in Marble Hills thought Gina Bentley had gone off the deep end. I absolutely refused to believe she was being visited by her murdered classmate. Then everything changed."

Scott seems to remember something and sighs.

"Was that what you were alluding to when we were at that hotel in the Virgin Islands? You clammed up something fierce."

Maxwell laughs and faces Tiffany.

"Now you know."

Scott looks at Tiffany and then Edward.

"People need to know."

Tiffany suddenly grabs Scott's arm.

"You will say nothing."

Scott tries to pull free of Tiffany's grip.

"I'll do no such thing."

Maxwell wrings his hand.

"You don't have a choice Scott."

Scott watches as Tiffany releases her grip on his arm.

"I do. I'm telling."

Tiffany glances at Edward then Maxwell.

"If you do I'll erase your memory of what happened here today. You won't have any recollection of the last two hours."

Scott shoots Maxwell a sharp look.

"She can't do that—can she?"

Maxwell and Tiffany look at each other.

"How do you think I was able to locate Niels Anderssen so quickly? Tiffany told me where to find him. It was all her."

Scott seems conflicted and gestures.

"This is just too much to process—this just can't be real."

Edward reaches out to touch Scott's shoulder.

"Am I here? Am I real?"

Scott faces Edward and sighs.

"This is just a dream. I'm going to wake up at any moment and feel really foolish. No one would believe me if I told them."

Maxwell stifles a laugh.

"Now you know how I felt. I thought I was losing my mind when it first happened. But then I realized there were others like me who had seen what I had. It got easier as time went by."

Scott faces Maxwell again.

"Say I keep my mouth shut about what I saw. Where do I figure into this story? Why me? I need to know details."

Page 359

Tiffany glances at the bluffs and sighs.

"Do you want the short version or the long version?"

"What do you think?"

Scott faces Edward and lowers his voice.

"I'm a writer like you."

Edward laughs.

"I know."

They embrace.

5
Orchid Bay
Bay Street Condo

"You can't be serious."

Houghton Fawcett seems stunned as he looks at Janet Virella. She slowly takes a step forward. In her hand is a gun.

"Do I look like I'm kidding?"

Janet takes another step forward.

"I want you gone—out of my life."

"Is that any way to talk to your father?"

Janet waves the gun around.

"I have a father."

Houghton stifles a smirk.

"I wonder what would happen if he found out you're not really his daughter. Found out your mother is a frigging slut."

Janet reacts.

"Get out."

Janet comes toward Houghton as he runs toward the door. She watches as he stops and faces her. He snickers.

"I think it's time I pay Mark Virella a visit."

Janet looks at the gun in her hand.

"It'll be the last thing you do."

She angrily points to the door and watches as he opens the door and leaves. As the door closes she sighs loudly.

"If he tells I'll kill him. I swear I will."

She looks at the gun in her hand and smiles.

Page 360

6
San Francisco

"Uh-huh—my people are looking for him now. He's as good as dead. That bastard can't hide forever—tick tok."

Corey Danforth runs his fingers through his hair as Marlisa stifles a smile from her condo in San Francisco. He sighs.

"Are you gonna film his bon voyage?"

Marlisa gestures slyly and winks.

"What do you think Corey?"

She begins laughing.

7
Orchid Bay
Greasy Spoon Diner

"How do you deal with it?"

Maxwell looks at Scott as he bites into his burger.

"It takes some getting used to—took me several months if truth be known. Every time Tiffany showed up I felt like I was being watched—but as time went by it got easier to handle."

Scott runs his fingers through his hair.

"How come she picked you?"

Maxwell shrugs.

"I think I found her. I wasn't supposed to be there that day at Glass Owl. But once I showed up there was no turning back."

He looks at the burger in his hand.

"It's actually a bit cool to be able to communicate with someone from the other side. She's helped me solve cases that were unsolvable. Tells me things—warns me—advises."

Scott wipes sweat from his brow.

"What does she want?"

Maxwell takes another bite of his burger.

"That's why you're here. She insisted."

Scott appears nervous and looks at his cell phone.

"She asked for me specifically?"

Maxwell nods.

"She knows we're friends."

Scott seems uneasy.

"What else does she know?"

Maxwell laughs.

"Do you have to ask such a question after she brought your great-great grandfather to meet you? I've long stopped asking her what she knows—she knows everything—she knows all my most intimate secrets—made it clear numerous times."

Scott jabs Maxwell.

"Like what?"

Maxwell points at Scott.

"Nice try."

They look at each other for a second.

"She knew about Lloyd."

Scott reacts.

"Why didn't she tell you?"

Maxwell grimaces.

"She told me I wasn't ready to know. It was up to Lloyd not me. He had to make the decision. It had to be his choice."

He lowers his voice.

"She was right."

Scott glances at his cell phone again.

"At least now I know what happened to my great-great grandfather. No one ever knew. He never returned from South America—everyone just assumed he had died. The expedition simply disappeared. There were attempts to find them but even the natives had no clue. They just said they never came back."

Maxwell finishes his burger.

"You should republish his book about the expedition and include what you know. People would buy it. Rediscover it."

Scott points his finger at Maxwell.

"How should I explain how I found out?"

Maxwell begins laughing.

"You're the writer—figure it out."

Scott points his finger at Maxwell again.

"What about Niels Anderssen?"

Maxwell seems confused.

"What about him?"

Scott sighs.

"He's just a kid."

Maxwell seems uneasy.

"I don't know what his deal was. Tiffany told me where he was being held captive and I just drove to the other side of St. Thomas and rescued him. To this day she's never spoken about it. I just did as I was told. It was the same way in New Orleans."

He runs his fingers through his hair.

"Weird stuff happened there too. Remind me never to walk through an abandoned cemetery on a foggy night."

Scott laughs and gestures at Maxwell.

"How much does Niels know about Tiffany?"

Maxwell seems bothered by something.

"On the way back Niels told me he had seen a teenage girl on the beach. I told him he was mistaken but he insisted. He began sketching what he saw and when he showed it to me I almost had a heart attack. There was no doubt in my mind that he had seen Tiffany. Tiffany herself wasn't aware he had seen her and when I told her she confronted him. He's never told anyone what he saw—not even his parents. He's kept her secret for over a year now. I've spoken to him several times since that day and he told me that on one occasion Tiffany took him somewhere."

"What do you mean she took him somewhere?"

"Niels said he saw **Princess Diana** talking with **Princess Grace**. Said he also saw the **Wright Brothers** and **Pocahontas**. Said **Anne Frank** was there too—with **Abraham Lincoln** and **Bob the Cat**. Said he also spoke to his grandmother who had died the year before. Said it was like watching a movie—but it was real."

Scott reacts and leans forward.

"How did he know who they were? He's barely a teenager from what you told me—kids his age hate learning history."

Maxwell playfully jabs Scott again.

Page 363

"Do I see signs of envy? Could it be that Scott Malone wishes he had seen what a preteen child saw? Inquiring minds would like to know if one as arrogant as you is a tad upset."

"I'm not jealous. I just find it odd that a child is witnessing such things—and keeping it quiet. When was the last time a child was able to keep a secret like this for a year? Impossible."

"Tiffany told me she told Niels that if he ever told anyone he would be made fun of—ridiculed—told him he'd never live it down once it was posted on social media by his classmates."

Scott winces. Maxwell pokes him again.

"I think we all know how mean children can be. When you and I were kids it was bad enough—but today it's a nightmare."

Scott nods. He looks at his watch and grimaces.

8
Orchid Bay
Spring Street Motel

"Oh how the mighty have fallen."

Houghton spins around to see Tiffany standing with her hands on her hips. She takes a step forward and laughs.

"Get the fuck out of my face."

She watches as Houghton shakes his fist at her.

"Oh-oh—I see I've touched a nerve."

She begins laughing.

"This place could use an air freshener. Something smells really foul. Oops—my bad—you forgot to use deodorant today."

Houghton angrily spins around to face Tiffany. But she's gone. He slams his fist against the wall. He begins cursing.

9
Orchid Bay
Bay Street Condo

"What's this? I didn't order anything today. Are you sure this is the right address? Maybe it's for one of my neighbors?"

Page **364**

She watches as the delivery man looks at the paperwork in front of him and nods several times. He faces her again.

"It's for you. No doubt about it."

Janet looks at Gavin Shippe and licks her lips.

"Have anyone ever told you how fiery hot you look in those tight Lycra shorts. Quite a nice bulge you have."

Gavin reacts and shoots her a dirty look.

"I've got a girlfriend."

He wags his finger at her.

"FYI—I don't do old women—I'm sixteen."

Stung by the insult Janet slams the door in his face.

"How dare he talk to me like that? I'm only twenty-six."

Janet opens the folder and reacts in shock.

"*That bastard lied to me*. It was all a frigging lie."

She clenches her fist in rage.

10

Orchid Bay
Spring Street Motel

"What do you want?"

Scott and Maxwell look at each other as Houghton stands in the doorway with a defiant look on his face. Behind them Tiffany appears. One moment she's behind Scott and Maxwell and the next she stands next to Houghton. She smiles.

"They're with me."

Houghton glances at a gun on top of a coffee table nearby. Tiffany notices and laughs. She grabs Houghton by the arm and as he watches the gun bursts into flames. They look at each other for a few seconds as Scott closes the door and sighs.

"What's the deal with this creep?"

Houghton lunges at Scott in a rage but is held back by Tiffany's grip. As she strengthens her grip on his arm sparks of electricity courses through Houghton's body. He winces. Maxwell turns to look at Tiffany. He notices she seems really angry.

"I guess I should start at the beginning."

Page **365**

Houghton lets out a pained cry as Tiffany intensifies her grip on his arm. She forces him to face Scott and Maxwell.

"Upon my death I was made aware of certain things concerning my family. Imagine what a shock it was to find out my whole life had been a lie. The man I thought was my father wasn't actually. Don't get me wrong—he was my father in every way a man could be a father—but biologically he wasn't. My father was actually someone else. I'm fully aware that you're familiar with the sordid behavior that Howard Madison engaged in before he met his demise. Familiar with the fact he had a penchant for teenage girls—enjoyed raping them and then casting them aside like trash. I'm also aware you know what happened to his daughter when she found out what he had done to her best friend—which led to him murdering his own daughter to keep his disgusting behavior from becoming public. But what you didn't know was that dear Howard had a friend—a friend from his college years that shared his disturbing fantasies concerning young women. Want to guess who this freak show was? How about another hint? This pervert came upon my mother and her friend at a party in Boston that Howard was throwing for his twisted buddies. My mother was offered a job as a hostess and went with Howard to Boston unaware what he had planned."

Maxwell shares a glance with Scott as they then turn their gaze to Houghton. Tiffany shoots Houghton a cautious look.

"When it became apparent what was going to happen to all the girls at the party my mother and her friend tried to leave. As they made their way to the door Howard had them both restrained and took them to some bedrooms down the hall. Howard raped my mother's friend and his friend Houghton raped my mother. This went on for hours. When it was over my mother and her friend were taken back to Marble Hills by Howard and threatened if they ever spoke of it. My mother's friend was such a mess after what Howard did to her she took her own life two days later. My mother found out she was pregnant a few weeks later but kept it to herself. She was engaged to my father and went ahead with the wedding. My father never knew the truth."

Page 366

Scott and Maxwell face Houghton again.

"You frigging bastard. Tiffany Johnson *is* your daughter."

Tiffany tightens her grip even further on Houghton's arm as he seems indifferent to the revelation. She sighs loudly.

"As I stated, upon my death I found out my true identity and set out to right the wrong that was done to my mother."

Houghton turns away and seems bored.

"It began with a trip to the Caribbean. Realizing what my dear father had in mind for Tristan Montgomery Bell I decided to add complications to his schemes. His rage toward Bell was due to the fact he assumed Bell killed his son—when in reality it was his other son who took out his older brother. Once the tragedy began unfolding I plucked Bell from the sea and made a deal with him. I save his life and he in turn would help me even the score against my father. Immediately he began to buy shares of Houghton's company—a little here—a little there. Not enough to be noticed but enough to do damage later. But Houghton unfortunately had quite a long enemy list—mostly the Whitney brothers—who controlled a large portion of the East Coast crime syndicate. As Houghton went about eliminating his rivals his own people sloppily messed with people without covering their trail. One of these people was a woman who was violated by two of Houghton's goons and cast aside like trash. Unfortunately for them she decided to seek retribution—and evened the score."

Houghton reacts to the revelation.

"She will be severely punished for her actions."

Tiffany stifles a laugh.

"How much would you like to bet?"

Houghton curses under his breath as he struggles against Tiffany's grip on his arm. She faces Scott and lowers her voice.

"When you and Sandra King were on that miserable island one of the misguided young men attempted to kill you—imagine the look on his face when he became aware of my presence."

Scott seems confused and sighs loudly.

"You were there? It was you that made him freak out? I remember he kept looking at something—mumbled a lot."

Tiffany turns to face Maxwell and laughs.

"I told him I was the angel of death. Said I had come for him and his brother—said his grandfather wanted to see them."

She watches Scott's reaction.

"How are they connected to Houghton Fawcett?"

Tiffany glares at Houghton.

"Should I tell them? Or shall you?"

Houghton curses under his breath again.

"Houghton's grandfather was the second cousin of their grandfather. Both fled Russia when the Communist Revolution took place. Houghton's grandfather made contact with their grandfather decades after—they trafficked in white slavery."

Scott seems disgusted and grimaces.

"It just gets worse and worse."

Scott faces Maxwell as someone pounds on the front door. A woman's voice can be heard yelling. She seems angry.

11
Orchid Bay
Orlonge Apartment

"What's going to happen to Marc Zayler now?"

Alison Orlonge faces Lachlan Ball as she massages his shoulder. He shakes his head as he stretches out on the sofa.

"His lawyer is leaning toward temporary insanity."

Alison sits down next to Lachlan.

"Lyle was a piece of work no doubt. He treated everyone like trash. I heard he slept with Loretta Osborne and then her sister hours apart. Filmed their encounter and then put it on his social media site to spite them for saying he was lame in bed a few months earlier—claimed they had an STD in the video."

Lachlan runs his fingers through his hair.

"His son is troubled too."

Alison gently strokes Lachlan's arm and sighs loudly.

"Is he still in a juvenile facility in Solvang?"

Lachlan nods and seems upset. Alison notices.

"I hope Lyle's kid hasn't tainted your view on becoming a father someday. I know you want to experience fatherhood."

Lachlan laughs and gestures.

"No worries—I'm still keen on fatherhood."

Alison smiles slyly and slides her finger across Lachlan's swelling erection straining under his jeans. She licks her lips.

"How about you show me how much you want to become a father? Make an impact—make me see things your way."

Lachlan stands and points to the bedroom.

12
Orchid Bay
Spring Street Motel

"This bastard has been lying to me for two years. He's been pretending to be my biological father—threatening to tell my father the truth. Then less than an hour ago I got a knock on my door and wouldn't you know it—this bastard isn't my father. He lied to me in order to keep his fucking freak show loser son in check. What kind of moronic lunatic does this? Damn you."

Janet shakes the folder in her hand.

"All to prevent his vile spawn from getting comfortable with the fact he was going to inherit everything one day."

She clenches her fist.

"He told me his father pulled the same trick to keep him in line back in the day. I bet he iced his old man to get his loot."

Janet faces Scott and Maxwell.

"My so-called half-brother tried to rape me by the way."

Scott and Maxwell share a look as Houghton snarls.

"You're a frigging liar. He wouldn't touch you."

Janet throws the folder at Houghton.

"I say differently."

She faces Tiffany and grimaces.

"Who the hell are you?"

Houghton starts laughing and points.

"Should I tell her or you?"

Tiffany takes a step forward.

"I'm his daughter. He raped my mother when she was in high school. Lied about what he did. Like father like son."

Janet turns around to face Houghton. Suddenly he grabs Janet and shoves her. He bolts for the door seconds later. As Maxwell is about to run after Houghton, Tiffany stops him.

"Let him go. He won't get far. He's on borrowed time. He just doesn't know it. His endgame is about to begin shortly."

Scott seems confused and sighs loudly.

"Are you saying what I think you're saying?"

Tiffany nods and begins laughing.

13
Orchid Bay
Orlonge Apartment

"I'm serious about what I said a minute ago. I'm done looking. I've found myself the right man to grow old with."

Lachlan seems pleased as Alison runs her fingers through his hair. He lies back in bed with a satisfied look on his face.

"I guess what just happened between us a moment ago clinched the deal. I'm something special without a doubt."

Alison pretends to slap Lachlan.

"I see you've gotten quite spoiled."

Lachlan laughs loudly.

"I've been spoiled from day one."

Alison tousles his hair and kisses him again.

"You're everything to me. You know I would do anything for you Lachlan. I can't imagine my life without you in it."

Lachlan pulls Alison toward him.

"Is that what I think it is?"

Alison kisses Lachlan lightly on the lips.

"Would you say yes?"

Lachlan grins slyly.

"Loretta Osborne will be pissed. She asked me to be her husband this morning after we fucked in the confessional."

Page **370**

Alison playfully chokes Lachlan as she snakes her fingers around his neck. She pretends to be enraged and grimaces.

"Should I confront that nasty whore and tell her to keep her filthy hands off my man? Make it clear you're mine."

Lachlan stifles a laugh.

"So it's official?"

Alison passionately kisses Lachlan.

"I won't tolerate someone like Loretta Osborne trying to bed you. She's bedded almost every guy in California—*ugh*."

Lachlan gently takes Alison's hand and faces her.

"I guess I have no choice but to say yes."

Alison begins kissing Lachlan repeatedly as he pretends to fend her off. He sits up in bed and pretends to be upset.

"Is it too late to change my mind?"

Alison shakes her fist at Lachlan.

"You said yes—I won't allow you to back out."

She watches his reaction and smirks.

14
Orchid Bay
Greasy Spoon Diner

"I bet you didn't think this day would come."

Hobson laughs as he forcibly shoves Houghton into the back of a van. Houghton tries to resist but is quickly subdued and punched several times. Carlos smiles broadly as he closes the door and faces Houghton with a sneer. Hobson begins driving.

"Do you know who I am?"

Carlos laughs as he punches Houghton in the jaw.

"You're nobody—nobody at all—a loser."

Hobson turns around and grins as he continues driving toward Pacific Coast Highway. Houghton recognizes Hobson and seems panicked as he faces Carlos. Carlos points at him.

"I heard you threatened my man Hobson. That was a mistake on your part. He takes being threatened personally."

Hobson makes a lewd gesture with his finger.

15
San Francisco

"I'll be waiting when you arrive at Colma."

Marlisa seems pleased as she looks at Hobson on her cell phone as he drives along Pacific Coast Highway in a frenzied rush. Houghton can be clearly seen in the background struggling with Carlos. Several times he's punched hard in the jaw as he tries desperately to free himself. She seems pleased and faces the vast cemetery. A few yards away a massive mausoleum looms up among several trees. She begins walking toward the trees.

16
Pacific Coast Highway

"I think an interview with Tristan Montgomery Bell is going to be my next move. Sandra is going to freak out when I tell her what happened. She never even had a clue Bell survived."

Maxwell jabs Scott and laughs.

"Get in line. He and I have plenty to chat about—seems to me he has quite a story to tell about Houghton Fawcett."

He runs his fingers through his hair.

"The real question however is how you're going to tell *your* story without mentioning Tiffany. Damned if you do and damned if you don't. Inquiring minds would like to know."

Scott pretends to take a swing at Maxwell.

17
Orchid Bay
Downtown Police Station

"Where is Lachlan today?"

Roland O'Brien grins and leans back in his chair as he faces Julia Danforth. He gestures with his hands. She turns around.

"He'll be in later. He's probably with Alison."

Julia comes toward Roland and grins slyly.

"Does that mean we're alone?"

Roland glances toward the door leading to a hallway where several jail cells are located. Julia notices and grimaces.

"Is Vina Phamler still in jail?"

Roland stifles a laugh.

"Uh-huh—she's not going anywhere. She's a flight risk as far as I'm concerned. Miles O'Rourke is fit to be tied."

Julia seems confused.

"What about Daphne Mills and Kyler Vanwick?"

Roland runs his fingers through his hair.

"They were transferred to Los Angeles. Murder is serious business. I'm sure they're having the time of the lives."

Roland runs his fingers through his hair once again.

"I heard Kyler's been beaten up twice already."

He stands and faces Julia.

"How about we get a bite to eat?"

Julia nods and follows Roland to the door.

18

San Francisco

Houghton struggles against Hobson's grip as he's brought before Marlisa standing at the entrance to a mausoleum.

"I should have had you killed when you threatened me last month. I should have put an end to you—but Loren—he said you were no longer a threat—said you were damaged goods."

Marlisa slaps Houghton and laughs.

"It was me. I took out your entire family. Hired Carlos and Hobson—employed their people to rub out your entire brood."

She begins laughing as she dances a jig.

"They are part of a huge enterprise of a vigilante justice group that rights the wrongs in society. They have a zero fail track record for a reason. Your brood didn't stand a chance."

She slaps Houghton again.

"This was supposed to be Loren's fate."

She turns to face Carlos. She seems angry.

"But that bastard took the coward's way out. Suicide instead of facing what he did to yours truly. Damn him."

Houghton tries to get at Marlisa.

"He didn't kill himself. *She* killed him."

Marlisa spins around and faces Houghton.

"What are you babbling about?"

Houghton seems to be looking for someone as Hobson punches him in the chest and forces him toward the front entrance of the mausoleum. A few yards away among the trees Tiffany appears. She stands silently with a smile on her face.

19
Orchid Bay
Orlonge Apartment

"I'll see you later."

Alison hugs Lachlan warmly and kisses him.

"I'm thinking of a June wedding."

Lachlan laughs loudly.

"Do I get a say in this deal?"

Alison wags her finger at Lachlan.

"You got vetoed."

Lachlan pulls Alison toward him.

"What if I turn out to be deranged murderer?"

Alison gently strokes Lachlan's cheek.

"I'd still marry you regardless."

They begin laughing.

20

San Francisco

Houghton struggles as Hobson straddles him. Both are naked as Hobson begins raping Houghton. Houghton cries out but it only seems to excite Hobson even further. A few feet away Carlos and Marlisa watch with huge smiles on their faces.

Page **374**

"Wasn't it you that said you wouldn't let a man have his way with you? Didn't you say you'd kill me with your bare hands old man? Oh my—what shall I do? Whatever shall I do?"

Hobson begins laughing loudly as he continues thrusting as he sits astride Houghton's naked body. Houghton cries out to Marlisa as he begs for mercy. Marlisa ignores his pitiful cries.

One Day Later

21

Los Angeles

"Is this goodbye?"

Maxwell faces Tiffany as she watches him pack a suitcase in a hotel room overlooking Century City. She stifles a laugh.

"We'll see."

She glances at the mirror.

"I have one more thing to show you."

Maxwell seems confused.

"Is this about Lloyd?"

Tiffany takes a step forward.

"Better."

Seconds later Maxwell watches the mirror come alive. As he reacts in shock a sarcophagus is seen inside a sealed room within a mausoleum. Tiffany seems pleased as Maxwell realizes that someone is inside the sarcophagus calling for help. He turns to face her. She takes a step toward him and gestures proudly.

"I told you yesterday what awaited Houghton Fawcett was worse than anything justice could inflict. It seems he ran afoul a vigilante group that dealt him the ultimate punishment. He's on borrowed time—locked inside a mausoleum with no way out. He won't be found for decades—not that anyone cares."

Maxwell seems shocked as Tiffany smirks.

"My wretched father is about to join my murderous late half-brother in a place where there's no joy—only misery."

They look at each other.

Page **375**

22
New York City

Scott and Sandra King embrace as he enters through the front door of their apartment. He looks at her and grins.
"Tristan Montgomery Bell is alive."
Sandra reacts.

23
Marble Hills

Pierce Colby watches as Gina Bentley is handed a check from Tristan Montgomery Bell while Jeremy Winterfield grins broadly. Tiffany stands nearby with her arms folded across her chest. Eddie Kane can be seen standing by the door silently.

Two Days Later
___

24
St. Thomas
United States Virgin Islands

Armand Bell reacts in shock as he stares at his father standing at the front door of his home. They look at each other for a few seconds. They embrace warmly. Tristan notices Trevor Bell staring at them as he sits in front of a large television.

25
Orchid Bay
Downtown Police Station

"Has his family been contacted?"
Lachlan nods a few times. He sighs loudly as he faces Roland sitting at his desk. They exchange nervous looks.
"How many stab wounds to the body?"

Page **376**

He looks at his cell phone in dismay and faces Roland.

"Kyler Vanwick is dead. He was apparently stabbed by his cellmate over a doughnut. He was stabbed sixteen times before guards intervened. He died on the way to the hospital."

Roland runs his fingers through his hair.

26
Orchid Bay
Hampshire Street Cafe

Zarina Fuertes is seen talking to Liana Danforth and laughing as Kyle Derringer and Tabitha Bairstow seem to be embroiled in a heated conversation at one of the tables near the front door. At another table Kayla Larsen and Patrick Clerke tease each other as they munch on a salad. Two tables away Gary Hachter and Lloyd Welsh argue about something on Gary's phone as Susan Osborne ignores them. At a table facing the park across the street Jayne Osborne and Ethan Vanwick hold hands and seem focused only on themselves as others nearby react.

27
Marble Hills

Gina and Tiffany silently stand at the front door of a small house shaded by large trees while a woman stares at them blankly for several seconds. Tiffany nervously glances at Gina not sure what to do. Moments later the woman takes a step forward and lovingly embraces her daughter as Gina smiles broadly.

About the Series Creator

Gary Brin was born in 1965 and has lived in the United States Virgin Islands, Hawaii and California. He has edited numerous original literary works over the years—both new and revised. In 2019 he established Standish Press to bring forth interesting fictional and historical material usually ignored by mainstream publishers because of specific views or content. In addition to publishing books, he also created the Nancy Hanks Lincoln Public Library (named after the mother of Abraham Lincoln) in 2014 to make available hard-to-find books to a worldwide audience.

Production Notes

Written by Wesley Adams and Daphne McGee
Manuscript edited by Gary Brin
Cover photograph from www.pexels.com
Original cover design and book layout by Gary Brin
Cover layout by Victoria Valentine
Additional help provided by Carlton J. Young
Series created by Gary Brin

Character List

Natalie Abdul
John Alohu
Jennifer Alsten
Kevin Alsten
Niels Anderssen
Tabitha Bairstow
Lachlan Ball
Chase Banfield
Gwen Bartlett
Gaston Bauer
Shirley Beecroft
Kirk Berfield
Vivien Bernsay
Armand Bell
Silas Bell (Heath Griffith)
Travis Montgomery Bell
(Trevor Boleyn)
Trevor Bell
Gina Bentley
Tim Bergman
Boris Birney
Byron Blakely
Nancy Blyden
Carrie Booker
Ward Brady
Daniel Brandt
Harper Brynton
Gary Cavannaugh
Patrick Clerke
Pierce Colby
Lauren Corrington
Mark Corrington

Tammy Cotler
Hobson Crusoe
Corey Danforth
Julia Danforth
Liana Danforth
Jenna deWilde
Victoria de Hoya
Lana Dempsey
Justin Derringer
Kyle Derringer
Karen Eberhardt
Lars Eisenmann
Houghton Fawcett
Loren Fawcett
Ralph Fawcett
Warren Fuertes
Zarina Fuertes
Erica Gersh
Maddie Gormley
Randolph Gregory
Oliver Grimke
Gary Hachter
Juliet Haskelle
Cameron Hodge
Vera Holliday
Ellery Hopkins
Amir Iskandar
Tiffany Johnson
Eddie Kane
Victor Kanjek
Sandra King
Martin Knappson
Kevin Kulkovich
Jared Lansing
Kayla Larsen
Laurel Larsen
Shirley Larsen
Sidney Larsen

Eugene Ledyard
Anton Levitov
Igor Levitov
Sasha Levitov
Larisa Lopez
Aaron Lorenzo
Colby Lorenzo
Harlow Lorenzo
Sawyer Lorenzo
Violet Lorenzo
Sergei Lycov
Gregory Maarsen
Wesley Madison
Edward Malone
Scott Malone
Ashton Markway
Donna Markway
Clyde Matheson
Wynette McClendon
Carter McKeon
Adam Mills
Amanda Mills
Carolyn Mills
Dana Mills
Daphne Mills
Evan Molloy
Cujo Momoa
Simon Momoa
Jessica Monet
Patrika Monvez
Diana Munroe
Sabine Norton
Roland O'Brien
Matthew O'Rourke
Miles O'Rourke
Tracey Oakfield
Alison Orlonge
Sergei Orlov

Victor Orlov
Vladimir Orlov
Jayne Osborne
Marley Osborne
Susan Osborne
Ryan Pena
Maxwell Pendergraft
Alexander Pendleton
Carmen Pendleton
Kelvin Penney
Vina Phamler
Lizette Richardson
Justine Ross
Parker Ross
Margo Sampler
Carlton Shappe
Jason Shappe
Miles Shefford
David Sherwood
Gavin Shippe
Marianne Singleton
John Smythe
Curtis Solle
Simon Spencer
Denise Stone
Bradford Styverson
Harcourt Styverson
Steve Syverman
Veronica Thibault
Ethan Vanwick
Kyler Vanwick
Lance Veltrope
Carlos Vente
Dirk Veriteke
Marlisa Vigaro
Janet Virella
Grant Volker
Marilyn Waaysend

Amber Walston
Alden Washington
Jeremy Weissmann
Caroline Welsh
Dayton Welsh
Lloyd Welsh
Bridget Whitney
Todd Whitney
Laura Wiley
Andrea Winterfield
Jeremy Winterfield
Sarina Wolper
Lyle Zayler
Marc Zayler
Peter Zimmerman

Real People and Real Animals Mentioned

Loni Anderson
Mary Astor
Lauren Bacall
Kevin Bacon
Ingrid Bergman
Bob the Cat
Humphrey Bogart
Ted Bundy
James Cagney
Charlie Chaplin
Gary Cooper
Bette Davis
Walt Disney
Bobby Driscoll
Marc Eliot
Steven Fabian
Errol Flynn
Jane Fonda
Anne Frank

Judy Garland
Lillian Gish
D. W. Griffith
Nathan Hale
Jean Harlow
Robert Harron
James Houghton
Ron Howard
Howard Hughes
Grace Kelly
Vivien Leigh
Abraham Lincoln
Tom Llamas
Jayne Mansfield
Meghan Markle
Marilyn Monroe
Julianne Moore
Gregory Peck
Andrew Perez
Mary Pickford
Pocahontas
Prince Harry
Princess Diana
Princess Grace
Ronald Reagan
Wallace Reid
Kyra Sedgwick
Sam Spangler
Britney Spears
Meryl Streep
Gloria Swanson
Elizabeth Taylor
Shirley Temple
Olive Thomas
Greta Thunberg
Lana Turner
Rudolph Valentino
Jonathan Vigliotti

Ruth Warrick
Natalie Wood
Wright Brothers
Jane Wyman

**Serials Used as
Inspiration for the Soap
Opera Book Series**

Daytime

All My Children
Another World
As the World Turns
Capitol
Days of Our Lives
The Doctors
Edge of Night
General Hospital
Guiding Light
Love of Life
Loving
One Life to Live
Santa Barbara
Secret Storm
Search for Tomorrow
Young and the Restless

Prime Time

Bare Essence (1982-1983)
Berenger's (1984-1985)
The Colbys (1985-1987)
Dallas (1977-1991)
Dark Shadows (1990-1991)
(1991 Revival Version)
Deception (2012-2013)
(2013 NBC Version)

Dynasty (1980-1989)
Emerald Point NAS (1983-1984)
Falcon Crest (1981-1990)
Flamingo Road (1980-1982)
For Love and Honor (1983-1984)
Grand Hotel (2018-2019)
Knots Landing (1979-1993)
Pacific Palisades (1996-1997)
Paper Dolls (1984-1985)
Pasadena (2001-2002)
Peyton Place (1964-1969)
Savannah (1995-1997)
The Yellow Rose (1983-1984)

**Books and Films
Incorporated into the
Storylines of the Soap
Opera Book Series**

Salem's Lot
1975 Novel

Salem's Lot
1979 Movie

Most Dangerous Game
1924 Short Story

Treasure Island
1883 Novel

Lost World
1912 Novel

Grimm
NBC 2011-2017 Series

For free public domain books please visit
www.nancyhankslincolnpubliclibrary.org

Standish Press

www.ingramcontent.com/pod-product-compliance
Lightning Source LLC
Chambersburg PA
CBHW072006190726

48293CB00001B/172